William Harrison Ainsworth

James the Second

Or, The Revolution of 1688

SALZWASSER
VERLAG

William Harrison Ainsworth

James the Second

Or, The Revolution of 1688

Reprint of the original, first published in 1865.

1st Edition 2022 | ISBN: 978-3-75258-879-8

Verlag (Publisher): Salzwasser Verlag GmbH, Zeilweg 44, 60439 Frankfurt, Deutschland
Vertretungsberechtigt (Authorized to represent): E. Roepke, Zeilweg 44, 60439 Frankfurt, Deutschland
Druck (Print): Books on Demand GmbH, In de Tarpen 42, 22848 Norderstedt, Deutschland

JAMES THE SECOND;

OR,

THE REVOLUTION OF 1688.

An Historical Romance.

EDITED BY

W. HARRISON AINSWORTH, ESQ.

A NEW EDITION.

LONDON

1865.

JAMES THE SECOND;

OR,

THE REVOLUTION OF 1688.

INTRODUCTION.—THE ERRORS OF A REIGN.

THE Revolution of 1688 had its origin in the previous century. It was in the conflict of creeds which then arose, under the capricious auspices of Henry VIII. that its first seeds were sown. Essentially a religious revolution, its spirit was kindled at the martyr-fires of Mary; burnt brightly and steadily under the fostering government of her successor, and forty years later under the wayward rule of Charles I., was roused into fanaticism by the innovations of Laud—thus paving the way for the Great Rebellion.

Wearied by the struggles of the Civil War, overawed by the despotism of Cromwell, and subdued by the reaction of the Restoration, it yet retained, in secret, something of its original vigour, requiring only to be aroused to become formidable. The nation saw a bugbear in the very name of Rome. It had learned to submit with patience to the abuses of power, to behold with indifference the extinction of its liberties; but its hatred of Rome, though associated with scarcely a shadow of religious freedom, remained unshaken. Aware of this fact, Charles II. concealed his predilections for Popery, and it was reserved for his successor to arouse, by an open alliance with the Pope, the slumbering hostility of his subjects.

James II. ascended the throne, on the 6th of February, 1685, amidst the acclamations of the people. While he called forth those manifestations of attachment which are usually awarded to a new monarch, he possessed the advantage of succeeding a prince, whose profligacy and venality had rendered him odious; and, though opinion was divided respecting his own character, it was anticipated that his habits of business would work a favourable change in public affairs. It is true, the fact of his being an avowed Catholic excited a feeling of distrust in the public mind; but it was hoped that, as he was not wanting in prudence, he would refrain from molesting the Protestant establishment, if it were only to conciliate prejudice, and allay apprehension. On the other hand, the Nonconformists looked to him from emancipation from the arbitrary laws of his predecessor; and the Catholics, long deprived of all rights of citizenship, and subjected to the most cruel oppression, hailed with delight the accession of a sovereign, whose profession of their faith secured them his sympathy, and might ultimately achieve for them more decided advantages.

The jarring interests of the several powers of the continent rendered James an object of universal attention abroad. The ambitious projects and vast power of Louis XIV., who then governed France, had spread a feeling of terror through all the civilised nations of Europe. Supported by an inexhaustible revenue, immense armies, and a navy greater than that of all Europe combined, surrounded by able and renowned commanders, his ambition seemed to aim at universal dominion, and some new conquest was continually extending his rule and his resources. Spain, weakened by long and repeated wars, was incapable of defending her unwieldy empire, and indeed, was so miserably impoverished, that she was unable to pay even the salaries of her diplomatic residents at the various foreign courts. The house of Austria was almost helpless, having, by a long course of tyrannical policy, driven Hungary to revolt, and thus removed a formidable barrier against the power of Turkey, whose victorious armies had twice made their way to the very walls of Vienna. Venice, formerly so potent, was sinking into insignificance, and, in this last stage of her career, displayed scarcely a vestige of expiring greatness. The German States wavered between their hatred of the house of Austria and their jealousy of the designs of France; and, in all Europe, only the unconquerable spirit of William of Nassau, Prince of Orange, the Stadtholder of Holland, opposed an effectual resistance to the French armies.

Left to fight the cause of Europe unaided, the successes of this able prince speedily secured him the co-operation of Spain —of several of the states of Germany, and finally, of the Pope, Odeschalki, a sagacious and spirited pontiff, who had ascended the papal throne under the title of Innocent XI. Yet overmatched by the prodigious resources of France, this holy alliance looked for succour to James, whose connection with the Prince of Orange—first, as the brother of the prince's mother, and secondly, as the father of his wife, must naturally incline him to espouse his interests. Louis was equally anxious to obtain the support of James, or, at all events, to prevent him from taking part with his enemies, and with this view, sought to divert his attention from affairs abroad, by stimulating him to extend his prerogative at home. James was but too well disposed to listen to his counsel; and thus, when he might have become the arbiter of Europe, contented himself with assailing his own subjects, while his court became a focus of intrigue for all the conflicting interests of the continent.

The internal condition of England was, in many respects, not adverse to the design entertained by James, in this position of affairs, of extending the royal prerogative, assuming the power of a despotic monarch. The people were almost universally sunk in the grossest ignorance; the age was one of slow communication; the roads, if they might be called such, hardly passable from their natural obstructions, were also infested by robbers, rendering travelling as dangerous as it was difficult; there were no manufactures, no middle class of landed proprietors, and but little political organisation; and, to render the task of subjugation still more easy, a rigorous censorship had almost silenced the press.

The lieutenants and deputy-lieutenants of counties, remote from the seat of government, exercised, in their respective districts, an almost feudal sway; the justices, composed of the inferior gentry, and aping the conduct of their superiors, beeame so many petty tyrants, daily committing the most flagrant excesses; the police was inefficient, and often secretly in league with the offenders against justice; and the judges themselves had, by their notorious and barefaced corruption, lost the respect of the people.

The ministry embraced the ablest men of the age—Halifax, Rochester, Sunderland, and Jeffreys, supported by a standing army of twenty thousand men, flushed with recent victory, and believed to be devoted to the king, and by a large and well-manned fleet; and the suppression of the revolt of Argyle, and the overthrow of Monmouth, with the severities which followed the latter event, and which were familiarly stigmatised as "the Bloody Assizes," had combined to give it a degree of power and stability, such as had rarely been possessed by any preceding administration.

Nor did the parliament itself offer a great obstacle to the establishment of a despotic government. Owing to the large number of charters which had been cancelled, or suspended in the course of the previous reign, a great many of the corporate towns had been disfranchised; and those which retained their charters were so much under the influence of the court, or of its adherents, that they returned servile and inefficient members—

men of low station, even clerks and petty tradesmen, whose only hope of advancement lay in complying with the wishes of the king.

Even the church, careful only for herself, was willing to second the king's views, so long as he refrained from assailing the establishment; and her ministers everywhere preached up the doctrine of passive obedience, as if it were actually an article of national faith.

But absolute power, if the ostensible object, was not the only mark at which the king aimed. While professing an attachment to religious liberty, he sought to break down the domination, if not the supremacy, of the established church. Claiming a share of the public patronage for the members of his own persuasion, he even appointed Catholics to commissions in the army, and to dignities in the church. In these views he was seconded by the queen, Maria d'Este, the adopted daughter of Louis XIV., a woman of great beauty, and not wanting in understanding, but, like her consort, a bigoted Catholic. James was tenderly attached to his queen, and, since his accession to the throne, she had acquired such ascendancy over him, that she even prevailed on him to dismiss his favourite, the Countess of Dorchester. The queen was ably seconded by the Catholic clergy, and particularly by the king's confessor, Father Petre, a Jesuit, and by his chaplain the Père d'Orleans, whose zeal even outstripped her own, and who aspired to nothing less than the complete re-establishment of Popery.

Meanwhile, James's proceedings were jealously watched by one of the most influential of his subjects, the Earl of Nottingham, who had held office under Charles II., and who had distinguished himself by unwavering attachment to the established church. Nottingham was probably the only man of his time who could command the uniform confidence of his party. Diligent in his habits, possessed of considerable talent and untiring perseverance, his only drawback was a fastidious caution, which sometimes allowed the favourable moment for action to pass by; but, to compensate for this, he was rigidly honest, and strictness itself in his principles. These virtues, which the venality of other politicians rendered more particularly conspicuous, gained him the respect of his very enemies, and he speedily began to be looked upon as the chief hope of the Protestant cause, and the rallying-point of all its adherents.

Nottingham was ultimately joined by a nobleman only second to himself in popularity. As the king developed his hostility to the established church, he found himself opposed in his very cabinet; and George Saville, Marquis of Halifax, one of the ablest of his ministers, expressed himself so decidedly on the subject, that the king immediately dismissed him. No longer under any restraint, Halifax coalesced with Nottingham, and the church party gained a new advocate—

> Jotham, of piercing wit, and pregnant thought,
> Endued by nature, and by learning taught
> To move assemblies.—DRYDEN.*

The inconstancy, however, which Halifax had several times exhibited was not calculated to inspire confidence in his sincerity; and the popular party looked with suspicion on a man who, by consenting to remain in office, had lent a sanction to the execution of Algernon Sidney and of Lord William Russell. But his known abilities, his wit, and his resistless eloquence, added to his high position and immense wealth, rendered him a powerful auxiliary, and his secession from the cabinet imparted new strength to the opposition.

The cabinet, indeed, soon became the theatre of further dissension. One of its leaders, Lawrence Hyde, Earl of Rochester, younger son of the celebrated Earl of Clarendon, and the king's brother-in-law, found himself opposed by the queen, whom his relationship to the princesses Anne and Mary rendered jealous of his influence. Rochester was not distinguished by eminent ability, but he derived importance from his high connections; and in parliament, he had signalised himself as an able and fluent speaker. "His infirmities," says North, one of the most zealous of his partisans, "were passion, in which he would swear like a cutter, and the indulging himself in wine."

He had a formidable competitor for the chief direction of the government in the Earl of Sunderland—a pliant courtier, polished wit, and able politician—who, by his captivating manner, had acquired great interest with the king. Sunderland quickly perceived the queen's aversion to him, and, whenever an occasion occurred, sought to turn it to his advantage. Rochester, in despair, endeavoured to strengthen himself against them by recalling the discarded Countess of Dorchester; but this unworthy scheme only accelerated his downfall. He even offered to embrace Catholicism; and desired to hear from some of the Romish clergy, to be appointed by the king, the arguments which could be advanced in support of their religion; but when his request was complied with, he professed that the proof adduced only confirmed him in his original faith; and thus, by flattering the Protestant party, he craftily evaded the disgrace which otherwise would infallibly have attended his dismissal.

Besides the queen, Sunderland had an able supporter in the

* Absalom and Achitophel.

Lord Chief Justice Jeffreys, whose vigorous understanding enabled him to form a just estimate of his colleague's genius. On the suppression of Monmouth's rebellion, Jeffreys was sent on a special commission into the disaffected districts, with orders to administer to the inhabitants a terrible lesson; and he had acted so completely up to his instruction, that, as was before intimated, his proceedings were known as "the Bloody Assizes," while he himself received the designation of the "Butcher Jeffreys." The trial of Mrs. Gaunt, a poor old woman, and of Lady Lisle, who was nearly eighty years of age, for only affording shelter to two suspected persons, and both of whom he sentenced to death, are memorable instances of his cruelty. Throughout the circuit, indeed, he conducted himself more like a monster than a man. "Nothing," says a record of the time, "could be liker hell than these parts: caldrons hissing, carcases boiling, pitch and tar sparkling and glowing, bloody limbs boiling, and tearing, and mangling." "England," writes Oldmixon, an eye-witness, "is now an Aceldama. The country, for sixty miles, from Bristol to Exeter, had a new and terrible sort of sign-posts—gibbets, heads and quarters of its slaughtered inhabitants." The poor people, indeed, were further persecuted by the ferocious Colonel Kirke, whose atrocities are too frightful even for relation. Nevertheless, on his return to court, Jeffreys was received by the king with great favour, and, as a reward for his zeal, was promoted to the office of lord-chancellor. In this new station, he began to counsel moderate measures, and steadily supported the advice of Sunderland, who, though opposed by a cabal of Romish priests, urged continually upon the king the necessity of moderation. Strange to say, they were abetted in this policy by the pope's nuncio, and by a large majority of the English Catholics.

But, whatever might be the sentiments of his ministers, whatever might be the secret views even of the pontiff himself, James threw off the mask, and soon openly displayed his hostility to the established church. A Court of High Commission was instituted, which, under the king, was to decide on all cases of ecclesiastical jurisprudence, and by this court a decree was issued prohibiting controversial sermons. Dr. Sharpe, Dean of Norwich, a bold and popular divine, bade defiance to the decree; and Compton, Bishop of London, his diocesan, was ordered to suspend him. Compton was possessed of great resolution, and, indeed, had originally served as a soldier, but on afterwards entering the church, had become the preceptor of the Princess of Orange; and though he expressed the utmost deference towards the king, he refused to obey the court. As a punishment for this temerity, he was suspended from his episcopal office.

The Court of High Commission was but one of the schemes which the king directed against the church. Successful in this, he turned his attention to the parliament, and sought to obtain from it an abrogation of those statutes which disqualified Catholics from holding office. The parliament, servile in politics, was steadfast in religion, and refused to repeal the obnoxious laws. In this dilemma, the king resorted to the unconstitutional measure of calling each member separately into his closet, and there, with mingled threats and promises, urged their compliance with his wishes. Even this plan failed; and, after a brief and stormy session, the parliament was prorogued, never again to meet.

Such was the state of affairs when, to the surprise of the whole kingdom, it was suddenly announced that the queen was on the point of becoming a mother. Nothing could exceed the joy of the Catholic party—nothing could equal the mortification of the Protestants, at this unexpected intelligence, which, if the child should prove a prince, might exclude from the throne the Protestant princesses, and secure the succession to a Catholic. Overjoyed at the prospect, the Papists already anticipated the fulfilment of their wishes, and confidently asserted that the child of promise would be a son. Public thanksgivings were even offered up at the Catholic chapels in various parts of the country, distinctly indicating these expectations, and Aphra Behn, the well-known comic writer, actually addressed the yet unborn child as "Royal Boy!" Such extravagant confidence excited suspicion, and a rumour arose from some unknown source, that the reported condition of the queen was a "pious fraud," and that the expected heir would be surreptitious. This rumour spread like wildfire; every action of her majesty, whether of seasonable precaution or the reverse, was tortured into a confirmation of it; and the suspicion soon became an article of popular belief.

The presumptive heiresses to the crown, the Princesses Mary and Anne, whose interests were involved in the question, naturally shared in the public suspicion of their stepmother. But the person whom it chiefly exasperated was William of Orange, who, in right of his wife, the king's eldest daughter, had long entertained a hope of inheriting the throne. A temporary cessation of the hostilities in which he was engaged, in behalf of the United Provinces, enabled him to look more narrowly into English affairs, and he soon found that a large party in England shared in his views, and were but too willing to espouse his cause. Through the medium of Van Citters, the Dutch ambassador, he opened a correspondence with the malcontents, and entered fully into all their grievances. But though conducted with the greatest secrecy, yet being necessarily confided to many, his intrigues were not unknown to James; and it soon became expedient to employ a less ostensible agent, who might more easily elude attention. A ready instrument for the purpose was found in Colonel Henry Sidney, the younger brother of the ill-fated Algernon Sidney, whose political opinions had caused him to be proscribed, and, while he was warmly attached to the Protestant religion, he entertained a bitter animosity towards James, and burned to avenge himself for the death of his brother.

Thus did James II. plunge from security into peril, and abandon a position of honour, in which he was the arbiter of the destinies of Europe, for that of a miserable caballer. The sequel of his career will appear in the following story.

BOOK THE FIRST.

CHAPTER I.

CHARLES MOOR.—THE FRENCH AMBASSADOR.

ONE fine spring morning, towards the latter end of the seventeenth century, a young man of tall stature and highly prepossessing appearance, and attired in a suit of deep mourning, halted before a mansion in the vicinity of St. James's Square, at that time occupied by Monsieur Barillon, the French ambassador at the English court.

The portal of the mansion stood wide open, disclosing a large hall terminated by folding-doors, near the entrance of which, in a large leathern chair, shaped like a sentry-box and studded with gold-headed nails, sat the Suisse, a portly and majestic-looking personage, clothed in a sky-blue livery, superbly decorated with silver, and holding in his hand a long silver-headed cane. Opposite him a bust of Louis XIV. looked down from a niche in the wall, like the tutelary genius of the spot. A motley group of persons thronged the hall—travellers bound for Paris, applying for passports; Grub-street pamphleteers; hangers-on of the embassy; and, to complete the medley, some half-dozen of that equivocal class, of both sexes, whose general course of life, or immediate object, veiled in affected mystery, opened a large field for conjecture.

Pushing his way through the assemblage, the young man addressed himself to the Suisse.

"Is M. Barillon within?" he inquired; "and if so, will you tell him, that Mr. Charles Moor desires to speak with him."

"His excellency *is* within, sir," answered the Suisse, with a strong French accent, "and expects you, I know."

And as he spoke he pulled a cord behind him; a bell sounded in the inner part of the house; and the folding-doors were instantly thrown open by a couple of French valets, in the sumptuous uniform of the ambassador.

"Achille," cried the Suisse, "conduct this gentleman, Mr. Charles Moor, to his excellency. Be pleased to step this way, sir," he added, with a bow to the young man, pointing inwards with his cane.

Thus invited, Moor passed forward, not sorry to escape the fawning civilities of the crowd, whom the prompt attention he had received from the usually insolent household of the ambassador, impressed with a very high notion of his importance.

Achille led the way up a spacious staircase to an upper chamber, where a couple of secretaries were seated at a table covered with boxes of despatches and other correspondence. Both were busily engaged in writing, and merely glanced at the valet and Moor, the former of whom passed on, and opening an inner door, which was sheltered from observation by a large screen, ushered the young gentleman into the presence of the ambassador.

Monsieur Barillon was a slight, middle-sized man, with an agreeable expression of countenance, and a searching grey eye; but bearing the appearance rather of a man of pleasure than of business. Wrapped in a loose brocade dressing-gown, he was lounging back in his chair, and caressing a remarkably well-turned leg, clothed in a pink silk stocking.

He received his visitor very affably, and, inviting him to be seated, motioned the valet to withdraw.

"You have, I presume, come but lately from my Lord Nottingham, Mr. Moor," said Barillon, as soon as they were alone. "His lordship professes much interest in you."

"Not more, I believe, than he really feels," replied the young man. "But may I ask if your excellency's inquiries respecting my father's marriage, which have caused you so much trouble, are still unsuccessful?"

"I am really concerned, after having kept you so long in suspense, that I cannot give you better news," returned Barillon; "but the affair is so excessively intricate, that it seems almost impossible to unravel it."

"I must take leave to differ from your excellency," rejoined Moor; "I cannot consider the matter at all intricate. The facts are plain and straightforward, and if you will permit me, I will refresh your memory on the subject. My father, the late Lord Mauvesin, when a young man, irritated by the coldness and neglect of the king, retired from the court, quitted England, and took up his abode in Paris. There he became attached to a most lovely woman, the daughter of the Comte de Treville, and secretly married her. I am the offspring of that union, but, unfortunately, I knew little of a mother's love, for she died within two years of her marriage with Lord Mauvesin."

"Ahem!" said Barillon, with a slight cough.

"Allow me to proceed," pursued Moor, colouring. "My earliest recollection represents me as the inmate of a Yorkshire parsonage, the owner of which, from whom I take my present name, was both my guardian and preceptor. As I approached manhood, he sent me to Oxford, and there it was that I first learned that he was not my father, but merely an agent of the Earl of Nottingham, who, for some unexplained reason, took a deep interest in my welfare. I remained at college till within the last few months, when a letter from Lord Nottingham summoned me to London; and, on my arrival, I learnt from him, to my infinite surprise, that I was the son of the late Lord Mauvesin, who has just died at Berne, in Switzerland. I learnt also that my father had written to his lordship from Berne a few days previous to his decease, avowing his marriage with Louise de Treville, and acknowledging me to be his son. Most strangely and unaccountably, however, this letter has disappeared."

"All this I have heard before," observed Barillon, with a half-smile; "and I have listened to you thus long because I wished to hear your own version of the story. Does it not strike you that if Lord Nottingham really had received such an important letter as you describe, he would have taken somewhat more pains as to its custody?"

"Yo do not doubt his lordship's statement?" rejoined Moor, quickly.

"Far from it," answered Barillon, "but the world may not believe him so readily. They will naturally wonder why he did not immediately place the letter in the hands of his legal adviser, with instructions to him to institute proceedings for the assertion of your rights!"

"But you know how the circumstance occurred," said Moor. "His lordship had scarcely recovered from the surprise occasioned by the perusal of the document, when he was suddenly called out of the room; and, in the hurry of the moment, he incautiously left the letter in an open writing-case. On returning, he found it gone, nor could he in any way discover by whom it had been abstracted."

"A most unfortunate circumstance for you," said Barillon,

shrugging his shoulders. "The absence of proof of your origin, which this letter would have afforded, secures to your father's nephew, the present Lord Mauvesin, the title and estates of the family."

"I have hopes from your excellency," rejoined Moor. "Lord Nottingham confidently believes that you will be able to discover some evidences of my mother's marriage, and my own birth in Paris."

As he awaited a reply, he looked earnestly in the minister's countenance, but it completely baffled his investigation.

"Lord Nottingham is scarcely entitled to my good offices," said Barillon, at length; "he seizes every opportunity of opposing the interests of the king, my master, and of abetting the designs of his enemies; while your rival, the present Lord Mauvesin, on the contrary, has always been on the best terms with me. If Lord Nottingham is really desirous to secure my assistance, the proper course will be to solicit it in person, and not through you."

"Your excellency well knows," replied Moor, "that in the present position of parties, his lordship cannot communicate with you personally. I have only, therefore, to thank you for the audience you have afforded me, and to retire. If you have any further communication to make to me, I am to be heard of at the Burleigh Arms, in Cecil-street."

"You will deliver my message to his lordship?" said Barillon, as the young man arose.

"Assuredly," answered Moor; "but I am persuaded he will decline the invitation. Whatever, however, may be his lordship's decision, I must take leave to say for myself, that I would sooner bear for ever the present stigma on my birth, than seek to efface it by treason to my country."

Before he had finished speaking, the door behind him was suddenly thrown open, and Achille, somewhat to Barillon's confusion, introduced another visitor, announcing him as "the Earl of Sunderland."

Though taken by surprise, and somewhat abashed at the presence in which he found himself, Moor ventured a glance at the new comer, who, as Prime Minister of England, could not fail to interest him greatly. The Earl of Sunderland was about forty years of age; but time had fallen lightly on his head. His person was still good; and, in his lofty features, he yet retained much of the beauty he had inherited from his mother—the far-famed Sacharissa of Waller. He was attired in black velvet, edged with silver, and his dress exhibited his stately figure to great advantage. But it was not in nobility of person alone that nature had been bountiful to Sunderland. Descended from an ancient and illustrious house, his father had died in arms for the throne, at the battle of Newbury, lamenting, with his latest breath, the probable consequences to his country of the success of the king—circumstances which could not fail, on the one hand, to recommend his son to the ill-starred monarch's successors, while, on the other, it won him the sympathy of the people. Carefully educated by his mother, he studied the science of politics in the leading courts of Europe, at which, on the accession of Charles II., he was early employed in several diplomatic missions, and hence he acquired such a perfect acquaintance with foreign affairs, that he was justly esteemed the first diplomatist of his time. He was afterwards recommended by Sir William Temple to the Duchess of Portsmouth, who, notwithstanding that he had voted with the opposition on the Bill of Exclusion, secured him the protection of the then Duke of York, under whose auspices he entered the cabinet of Charles II. His graceful manners, insinuating address, and polished wit, still more refined by intercourse with foreign courts, were qualities so much in accordance with the tastes of the monarch, that he speedily gained an ascendancy in his councils; and, at his death, retained his influence over his successor. With a genius less brilliant than that of the Marquis of Halifax, he had yet succeeded in driving him from power; and, by his interest with the queen, had triumphed over the exalted connections and more active abilities of the Earl of Rochester; but while he brought about the downfall of these popular favourites, he contrived to maintain a degree of popularity himself, and, from the moderation of his behaviour, acquired the credit of all the wise measures of his administration, while the odium of every arbitrary transaction was thrown on his colleagues. He even enjoyed the confidence of a large section of the Catholics, together with that of the Spanish ambassador, and of the Papal nuncio, who, knowing that the tendencies of the other ministers were decidedly Gallican, conceived him to be their only security against an alliance with France; and, to complete the anomaly of his position, he cultivated the most friendly relations with Barillon, who, though scarcely satisfied of his sincerity, rarely failed to lend him support.

Sunderland regarded Moor curiously as the latter withdrew.

"There goes a flaming patriot, my lord," said Barillon to the prime minister, as they were left alone, "who thinks it treason even to speak to a Frenchman."

Sunderland smiled, "Some of us are not so scrupulous," he said. "Who is he?"

"A *protégé* of Nottingham's," returned Barillon, "and the pretender to the Mauvesin peerage."

"Oh! is that Charles Moor?" exclaimed Sunderland, with some appearance of interest. "He is very like my poor friend the late Lord Mauvesin, and whatever may be thought of the young man's pretensions, his features alone, with me, give ample evidence of his paternity."

"Every one admits, I believe, that he is Mauvesin's son," observed Barillon, "and it is equally clear that Mademoiselle de Treville was his mother; but there is no evidence of any marriage between the pair."

"So I have heard," rejoined Sunderland. "However, it says a great deal for the truth of his pretensions, that he has the support of such a man as Nottingham. But to business, for I am come to you on a matter of the utmost importance. It would be idle and impolitic in me to conceal from you my anxiety at the present posture of affairs. Since the accession of your new adherent, Father Petre, to the cabinet, I have found the difficulties by which I am surrounded almost insurmountable. The Jesuit's influence over the king almost negatives mine; and the over-zeal he has exhibited in the cause of his religion, has excited such jealousy among the people, that the government has lost all hold of their affections. To aggravate this dilemma, the church party is about to form a league with the dissenters, and, under the guidance of Nottingham, their united strength will be sufficient, not only to overthrow the ministry, but to endanger the stability of the throne."

"Surely you exaggerate the danger, my lord," said Barillon, with affected uneasiness.

"Not a whit, sir," replied Sunderland; "and as I feel my own inability to cope with the crisis, I have resolved to resign my seat in his majesty's councils."

"I should greatly regret such a step, which would be fraught with fearful consequences," replied Barillon, quickly; "but can we not devise some means of inducing you to remain a little longer in office?"

"Possibly you might," replied Sunderland: "as I have just said, the church party is preparing to league with the dissenters, and it is my policy to keep them asunder. To accomplish this, some concessions must either be made to Nottingham, or measures of general toleration must be adopted. The queen, who honours me with her undivided confidence, leans to the dissenters; and I myself incline to liberty of conscience. But I fear that Father Petre will oppose both schemes; and, in that case, my success must depend on the support of your excellency."

"Am I to understand that you desire Father Petre's dismissal?" asked the ambassador.

"I shall be content if his influence with the king is counteracted," replied Sunderland: "this your excellency can accomplish."

"You may count upon my best efforts to do so," said Barillon.

"In which case you are sure to succeed," replied Sunderland, rising, "and in return you may calculate upon my support when you require it. Remember, you induce me to remain in office."

"I am charmed to think so," replied Barillon. And after an interchange of compliments between them, coupled with earnest assurances of mutual confidence and regard, Sunderland withdrew, attended by Barillon as far as the summit of the staircase.

As the ambassador returned to his chamber, rubbing his hands gleefully, for he flattered himself he had duped the wily minister, he was somewhat surprised to find it occupied by a stout personage, with an ill-favoured visage, blotched and inflamed by strong potations. This man, whom the ambassador instantly recognised as Elkanah Snewin, a constable, and one of the most diligent of his secret agents, was armed with a hanger, and wore a brace of pistols in his girdle.

"Soh, sirrah!" he exclaimed, sharply, "how came you here?"

"Beg pardon, your excellency," said Elkanah, bowing obsequiously, "but Achilles warn't in the way, and so as I was in a hurry, I made bold to come up the private staircase. My business is werry important, werry important, your excellency."

"Well, let me hear it," said Barillon, impatiently.

"I must be brief, your excellency, brief," answered Elkanah; "for I harn't a moment to spare. I received information that Colonel Sidney, the secret agent of the Prince of Orange, has just come over from the Hague, and will be at the Burleigh Arms, in Cecil-street, at two o'clock, for the purpose of meetin' some young gen'l'man. Your excellency is aware that the colonel's an outlaw, and if I could only nab him, I should, no doubt, find on his person a lot of useful papers. But I'm rayther afraid of the job."

"How? afraid!" exclaimed Barillon.

"Vy, your excellency sees as how Lady Sunderland—" stammered Elkanah.

"Ah, true!" said Barillon, "Colonel Sidney is her uncle."

"Somethin' more than her uncle, your excellency," said Elkanah, with a coarse leer; "lovyer would be nearer the mark."

Barillon, though he looked up, paid no attention to the observation.

"Sidney must be secured," he said at length, "and I will protect you from the vengeance of Lady Sunderland."

"Then I'll be off at vonce, your excellency," returned Elkanah.

"Stay," exclaimed Barillon, "a thought strikes me. Did you not say that it was at an inn in Cecil-street that you were to find Colonel Sidney?"

"The Burleigh Arms, your excellency."

"Do you happen to know the pretender to the Mauvesin peerage—Mr. Charles Moor?"

"Know him!" answered Elkanah. "Oh, yes! I knows him well enough, and a promisin' young feller he is."

"He also is at the inn in Cecil-street," said Barillon; "probably, indeed, he is the very young gentleman who is to meet Colonel Sidney. If you find them together, arrest him likewise."

"Now I've got your authority, I don't care what I do," rejoined Elkanah. "So vishin' your excellency a good mornin', I'll set about the job."

And with a scrape of the foot he clapped his hat on his head, and bustled out of the room.

CHAPTER II.

COLONEL SIDNEY.

Plunged in deep and earnest thought, Moor made his way along Pall Mall. Objects presented themselves to view as he passed on, that if he had been less absorbed by painful reflection, might have excited his interest; but, as it was, he scarcely noticed the seminary priests and friars, who now appeared openly in the streets, giving London the aspect of a Catholic city. He did not slacken his pace till he reached Cecil-street, and proceeding to its further extremity, entered a large inn adjoining the river, a signboard over the door of which announced it to be "The Burleigh Arms, kept by Jeremiah Littlehales, Licensed Vintner."

Jeremiah himself was standing in the passage, on the lookout, it appeared, for Moor; and advancing towards him with an air of mystery, he whispered in his ear,

"He's here, sir, a-waitin' to see you, sir."

"He! who?" exclaimed Moor.

"Why, the Spanish captain, to be sure," replied Littlehales.

"Show me to him directly," said Moor, quickly.

"This way, sir," returned Littlehales, "this way!" And he added, as if from habit (for no one called him), "Comin', sir, comin'!"

He then led the way along a narrow side-passage, and throwing open a door, made way for Moor to pass through, which done, he carefully closed the door behind him.

Moor found in the room a middle-sized, slightly-built, but apparently very muscular man, with remarkably black piercing eyes, and an enormous beard and moustaches—so enormous, indeed, as almost to look as if they were intended for disguise. His costume had a sufficiently Spanish air to warrant the assertion of Mr. Littlehales, that its owner belonged to that service, and consisted of a black velvet jacket, buttoned up to the throat, with a cloak of the same colour and material, dangling from the left shoulder, a pointed Spanish hat, black nether garments, and boots. In this attire few would have recognised the celebrated beau Sidney, who, according to Grammont, had triumphed over the heart of the first Duchess of York.

"Welcome, my young friend," cried Sidney, advancing towards Moor; "you are punctual to your appointment."

"It is from you then that I am to receive a letter for Lord Nottingham, Colonel Sidney?" said Moor, returning the other's greeting. "I was not aware of it."

"Yes," replied Sidney, "and I will give the despatch to you at once."

So saying, he drew forth a sealed packet, and presented it to Moor.

"It is not for Lord Nottingham himself, then?" observed Moor, glancing at the superscription of Thomas Howard.

"May he not, for some good and lawful purpose, style himself plain Mister Howard, as well as I may call myself Captain Fernando Gonzales?" returned Sidney, with a smile. "But put up the letter; more than one man's head perhaps, may depend on its safe custody."

Thus admonished, Moor thrust the letter into his vest, while Sidney pressed him to be seated, and took a place beside him.

"Notwithstanding a preconcerted arrangement, I should have delivered this letter myself to the Earl of Nottingham," he said, "but I found that he is not staying at Kensington, but has gone to Burleigh, in Rutlandshire."

"And I am to convey the letter to him there?" said Moor.

"Without delay," replied Sidney. "I am sorry you will have

so long a ride, particularly as the roads are bad, and infested with highwaymen. But these are slight obstacles to a resolute young fellow like you. Now tell me what is going forward in the political world? They are all at sixes and sevens in the cabinet, I hear; while the court is broken up with religious dissensions."

"Rumours have now and then reached me, I confess, which show a general jealousy of his majesty's religious opinions," replied Moor; "but I have been so occupied by my own private affairs, that I have given but little heed to them."

"What of Lord Nottingham?" asked Sidney.

"Lord Nottingham, I know, is warmly attached to the church," replied Moor; "but in the few conversations I have held with him on the subject, he seems to dread less an attack on the church than the prospect of an alliance with France."

"And well may he dread it," observed Sidney: "such an alliance would be the ruin of this country."

"The present attitude of foreign powers, it cannot be denied, is alarming," said Moor, "and may well embarrass our politicians. On the one side we see the French king, who has just signalised his orthodoxy by a cruel persecution of the Huguenots, setting himself in array against the Catholic monarchs of Austria and Spain, and even the Pope; and while he supports the Romish faith with fire and sword, uniting with the Turk and infidel against the Pope himself. On the other hand, the Pope, the Emperor of Austria, and the King of Spain, who are naturally no less interested in the maintenance of their religion, are found in alliance with the heretic Prince of Orange, and waging war on Louis, while both parties seek the support of our own sovereign. The latter, though he receives with open arms the persecuted Protestants of France, assigns them a place of refuge, and raises a subscription for their relief, is suspected of collusion with Louis; and while he professes to seek only general liberty of conscience, is accused of meditating the destruction of the Protestant church."

"It is plain, my young friend, that you lean to the king's side," returned Sidney, who had listened to this speech with a smile; "but you speak so frankly, that I cannot but answer you in the same spirit. The king, as you may have heard, has lately imposed a Papist dean on Magdalen College; and because the fellows refused to elect him—no person professing the religion of Rome being eligible to the dignity—has deprived them of their charter. Indeed, he rashly claims a power of suspending the laws, by which, in defiance of the Test Act, he nominates Catholics to official stations; and to cover the indulgence he shows to members of his own persuasion, is supposed to be meditating measures of encouragement to the nonconformist. These proceedings, coupled with the fact that he is surrounded by priests, afford, I think, conclusive evidence of his bad faith."

"Do you object, then, to the removal of the disabilities of the Protestant Dissenters?" asked Moor. "Surely there is little ground for apprehension in such a measure!"

"Leaving out of the question its propriety, what is the motive that dictates it?" retorted Sidney. "Is it not undertaken for the purpose of disuniting the Protestant party, and winning over the Dissenters to attack the church?"

"Even though it should be so," smiled Moor, "which I am far from admitting, a little evil may sometimes give rise to great good."

"You must admit, however, that the simple circumstance of the king receiving an ambassador from the Pope in a public audience is unlawful," rejoined Sidney. "Besides, he has recently appointed his confessor, the Jesuit Father Petre, to a seat in the privy council."

"I grieve to hear it," answered Moor with a sigh; "worse news for our poor country."

"The worst remains to be told," said Sidney, lowering his voice to a whisper; "they say the expected heir, whom the priests have foretold will be a prince, will not be *the son of the queen.*"

"It is a false and shameful rumour," exclaimed Moor; "and he who first propagated it knew it to be such."

Scarcely were the words uttered, when the door of the room was suddenly thrown open, and Littlehales rushed in.

"Fly, colonel! fly!" he cried to Sidney, "Elkanah Snewin, the constable, with a couple of myrmidons at his heels, is a-coming down the street."

"But he may not be coming to look for me," said Sidney, carelessly.

"I'm sure he is, from his looks," replied Littlehales; "fly! fly!"

"Which way?" demanded Sidney, starting to his feet; "not by the street?"

"No, no! through the winder," said Littlehales, in great trepidation; "there's a boat below, make off in it."

Darting to the window and withdrawing the bolt, Sidney hastily threw the sash open and passed through. The chamber, it appeared, was built on girders, which, resting on a tier of piles, broke out from the main fabric and abutted on the river. At high water the stream came directly under it; and though the tide was now on the ebb, the water was still well up with the outer piles, close to one of which, about ten feet below, and fastened by a chain to the window-sill, was a small boat, which Sidney easily drew alongside. With the aid of Moor, who had followed him to the window, he then lowered himself to the boat, and alighting in it, instantly pushed off.

Moor and Littlehales had hardly closed the window, when the expected official made his appearance.

"What, all alone, young squire?" he said to Moor. "Vere's your comrade? vere is he,—eh?"

Moor turned away, without deigning him a reply.

"Order out my horse," he said to Littlehales, "and let me have my reckoning quickly."

"Directly, sir," answered Littlehales, glad to be released, "your reck'nin' immediately."

"Now then," interposed Snewin, majestically, "none o' this nonsense! D'ye think as how you can overreach Elkanah Snewin, one of his majesty's constables? It may be, young squire, you'll have to go forth afoot, instead of on your prad, with a pair of bracelets on your wrists, and pay your next reck'nin' to the gov'nor of Newgate. Who have you got in your house, Old Jerry, eh?"

"What sort o' customer do you want, Mr. Snewin?" asked Littlehales, with affected indifference, though he trembled all the time in his shoes.

"You knows vell enough who I wants," answered Snewin, "so no gammon, but tell us at once who you've got."

"To begin at the top, then," said Littlehales, "there's old Hyams, the Jew pedlar, in the back-attic, as thorough a rogue as you'd wish to meet. He's a spare, middle-sized man, with a beard like a billy-goat, and a nose and chin like a pair of nut-crackers."

"Vell, go on," said Snewin. "I don't want Mr. Hyams just yet."

"Front attic's a country parson," resumed Jeremiah, "a great scholar, who has come to London with a sermon on the Millennium, hopin' to make a livin' by it; but he's locked up for his reck'nin'. There's no mischief in him, though, I'm sure; but I can't say as much for the blue bed-room."

"Ah!" cried Elkanah. "Vot sort of a feller is he?"

"One o' your knowin' ones," answered Littlehales, with a significant wink. "He goes in and out like a cat, never looks you in the face, and yet eyes you all over. I don't know what to make of him."

"Come to the pint!" cried Snewin, emphatically. "What's he like? Is he short, rayther thin built, and a good-lookin' phiz?"

"That answers to his description—rayther," answered Littlehales.

"He'll do," returned Snewin. "Just show us his crib, and we'll make him move his legs a bit."

"His *is* legs!" grinned Littlehales, "the bandiest I ever see."

"Is he bandy?" cried Snewin.

"His legs is like a hoop," replied Littlehales. "But come and see 'em, and if ever you see bandier——"

"My man's legs ain't bandy," interrupted Snewin. "Who else have you got?"

"There's a young Staffordshire squire in the best bedroom," said Littlehales, "who has just come to his fortin', and so he's also come to London to see life. He's got on famously, for though he's only been here a week, he drinks all night, sleeps all day, and swears like a lord. He's the last except the tap, and I can tell you who's there in a minute. There's——"

"That's enough!" exclaimed Snewin. "I'll have a peep round myself, and if you've only been tryin' to get me into a line, you'll stand a chance o' runnin' your own neck into a noose."

Chuckling at this stroke of facetiousness, he turned to the door, and called in two of his myrmidons, whom he had left outside. One of these, who was armed like himself, he instructed to guard Moor and Littlehales, charging those persons not to leave the room, as they valued their lives, and with the other he proceeded to search the house. But whether it was that there was nothing to discover, or that the inquisition was unskilfully executed, Snewin's labours were fruitless, and, after half an hour's absence, he and his satellite returned to the room much as they had left it.

"I'm certain the colonel has been here," he cried to Littlehales, furiously. "What have you done with him?"

"What colonel, Mr. Snewin?" answered Littlehales, with an appearance of simplicity. "If you mean Colonel Carpenter, he hasn't been since last night, when the Six-bottle Club met in the blue parlour."

"Colonel Carpenter be d—d," cried Snewin, furiously; "the colonel I mean, as you werry well know, is Colonel Sidney, the Orangerian spy."

"Never heerd of him, Mr. Snewin—never, as I'm an honest man and a good publican!" exclaimed Littlehales.

"You're neither the vone nor the t'other," cried Snewin, "and a day will come when I shall have you hard and fast for abettin' a traitor and a spy; and meantime I've made some discoveries in your cellar, my old cove, which shall go to the ears of the officers of the excise. As to you, young squire, it's not the last time we shall meet, take my word for it."

And dealing a vindictive look at Moor, he withdrew with his myrmidons.

Moor only tarried to proffer a few words of comfort to the poor terrified landlord, who sank into a chair after the constable's threat, and having discharged his reckoning, he mounted his horse, and rode forth in the direction of Highgate.

CHAPTER III.

THE GOLDEN FARMER.

An hour's hard riding brought Moor to the skirts of Finchley Common, where there was a small roadside inn, at which he paused to refresh himself, and while he was thus engaged, another horseman came up, who drew the rein for a moment, as if with the intention of halting likewise, but immediately afterwards changed his mind and set forward again. He had not proceeded far, however, when Moor overtook him, and finding him to be the king's chemist, M. Saint Leu, a French emigrant, with whom he was slightly acquainted, he slackened his pace, and entered into conversation with him.

Saint Leu exhibited some unwillingness to talk at first, but he speedily shook off his reserve, and then became almost eloquent. Turning the conversation on philosophy and literature, he spoke of the discoveries of Newton, the scientific labours of Boyle, the poetry of Milton, Waller, Marvel, and Dryden, and even the political writings of L'Estrange, in a manner that proved him to be both well read and well informed. In this way they rode on together for some distance, until they came to a more secluded part of the road, where stood a gibbet, from which dangled, in rusty fetters, the mouldering carcase of a highwayman.

"There hangs Jem Whitney!" said Saint Leu, "called by his familiars the Dimber Tulip, one of the most daring of the knights of the road. The Tulip thought it beneath him to rob on a small scale, so his last adventure was for seven hundred pounds, which he succeeded in carrying off, but with what result you now behold."

"This solitary spot is just the place for such an achievement," remarked Moor, "and indeed the whole common is very lonely; but there are so many people about to-day, that one need scarcely fear being robbed. How comes it that the road is so thronged?"

"I will tell you," replied Saint Leu. "All these people are Dissenters, and they are proceeding to a meeting, held by various persuasions to celebrate the liberation from prison of Richard Baxter, the nonconformist divine. I myself am going to the meeting, which is to be held at the further end of the common, where Baxter and others will deliver addresses."

Before Moor could reply, they were suddenly confronted by a third horseman, who rode across the common—a square-built man, with wide funnel-topped boots drawn up above the knee, and wrapped in a loose riding-coat of dark green cloth, from the pockets of which peered the butt ends of a pair of large horse-pistols. His broad-leaved hat was pulled over his brow, and he was mounted on a strong-boned grey horse, which seemed capable of going through any amount of work.

Riding leisurely forward, the strange horseman eyed the two companions very closely, and, as he drew nearer, appeared to recognise St. Leu, and slightly nodded to him. He then looked more narrowly at Moor, and not appearing satisfied with the investigation, cast an inquiring glance at Saint Leu. The latter replied by a significant gesture, and the horseman immediately rode off across the common.

"We were talking of highwaymen just before that fellow rode up," said Saint Leu, "who do you think he is?"

"A highwayman, I suppose," replied Moor.

"A very notorious one," said Saint Leu; "he is the Golden Farmer."

"Indeed!" interrupted Moor, whose suspicions had been aroused by the other's evident intimacy with the horseman; "as I have a long ride before me I must increase my speed. I wish you a good day, Mr. Saint Leu."

"Good day, then, if you will have it so," replied Saint Leu; "but you may possibly regret parting with me."

He did not, however, press his company further: and Moor, urging his horse into a gallop, rode forward, and ere long passed a party of some twenty or thirty pedestrians, headed by a venerable-looking man, mounted on a mule, who, he concluded, were repairing to the Dissenters' meeting. The pace at which he was proceeding, however, soon made him lose sight of them, and presently afterwards not a soul was visible, either upon the highway or on the wide common around. At length the road swept round a deep dry gravel-pit, and immediately beyond this, the view was interrupted by a dense thicket. As he reached this point, he was startled by a sudden scream.

Spurring instantly forward, Moor rounded the corner of the

road, passed the edge of the thicket, and found that the screams proceeded from two ladies, whose chaise had been stopped by the highwayman he had seen a short time previously.

Intimidated, it appeared, by the threats of the robber, the younger of the two ladies was on the point of surrendering her purse and trinkets when Moor dashed up to her aid.

"Off, villain!" he shouted to the highwayman, at the same time drawing a pistol.

"Come, no poaching on my manors, mate," replied the other coolly, "the Golden Farmer brooks no interference—so go your way."

"You are mistaken in me, ruffian," replied Moor, "I am no highwayman; and if it were not for the presence of these ladies, I would convince you to the contrary by sending a bullet through your brain."

The Golden Farmer laughed loudly and contemptuously.

"I paid you the compliment of supposing you to be a highwayman, my blade, because I saw you with a friend," he rejoined; "but since you put up for a gentleman, I've no objection to treat you as such, only don't meddle with me when I'm busy. The road is open to you, and I've no time for further parley."

"Do not expose yourself on our account, sir, I entreat you," interposed the younger lady, whose great beauty had already attracted Moor's attention, and, speaking in a slightly foreign accent, "the gentleman shall be welcome to these trifles, if he will only allow us to proceed."

"You hear what the young lady says, my blade," said the Golden Farmer, laughing, "don't expose yourself, I beg of you," he added, mimicking her accent.

Highly incensed, Moor sprang forward, and seizing the highwayman by the throat, nearly dragged him from his saddle. But the other, though taken by surprise, quickly recovered himself, and being a man of immense personal strength, a desperate struggle ensued between them. The cries of the ladies were now renewed, the more so as they perceived Moor was likely to be worsted in the encounter, when the sound of a horse's hoofs were heard round the corner, and Saint Leu galloped up.

"Hold! hold!" he shouted. "Leave him alone, Freeman, or I withdraw my protection from you."

"Call off your bull-dog, then, or I'll throttle him," roared the Golden Farmer, furiously.

"Let him go," cried Saint Leu to Moor, "he will do you no injury."

"Never," replied Moor. But before he could make further

effort, he received a severe blow on the chest from the highwayman, which knocked him from his horse, and before he could regain his feet, the latter had ridden off, and was disappearing behind the thicket.

"I hope you are not hurt, Mr. Moor," said Saint Leu, dismounting to his assistance. "I told you you would regret parting with me; but I little thought when I said so, that you were hastening to the rescue of my niece."

"Is this your niece, sir?" cried Moor, regarding with surprise the lovely girl, whose countenance expressed the liveliest interest in his safety.

"This is Mademoiselle Sabine Saint Leu; and the other lady is her gouvernante, Madame Desjardins. They are both very much indebted to you."

"Indeed, we are," said Sabine. "You have suffered much on our account."

"My only regret is, that I did not arrive a few minutes earlier," replied Moor. "I might have saved you any annoyance from this highwayman."

"I fear I shall be obliged to hang the rascal after all," said Saint Leu, "though he has some redeeming points about him—but I must now ask you, Sabine, how it happens that I find you here. I suppose you wished to attend the Dissenters' meeting? Was it so?"

"Precisely so, uncle," replied Sabine, "I prevailed on Madame Desjardins to accompany me. We anticipated no danger."

"If we had, we certainly should not have come," said Madame Desjardins.

"Why, here's your driver under the horses' feet," said Saint Leu, observing the postilion lying on the ground, "I hope the rascal hasn't killed him."

"No, sir," said the driver, getting up, and rubbing his head; "but he gived me a blow on the head, as knocked me off the horse, and I thought it best to lie still till he went away."

"Well, you are not much worse for the accident," observed Saint Leu, laughing, "and now let us be moving, for I wish to join my friends."

Upon this the postilion got upon his horse, and the chaise was put in motion, while Moor, who was irresistibly attracted by Sabine, rode beside her. The slow pace at which they proceeded enabled him to keep near her, and he was as much interested by her conversation as he had been struck by her beauty. At length, Saint Leu, who had been a little in advance, came back and joined them.

"I am surprised, Mr. Saint Leu," observed Moor, "that you, a foreigner, should belong to any of our dissenting sects."

"Neither do I," rejoined Saint Leu. "I abhor sectarianism of every kind; and for the liberty of worshipping my Maker according to the dictates of my conscience, I have forsaken my kindred and my country, and abandoned most things that render life dear to me."

He had spoken this with some emotion, but presently resumed with his wonted calmness.

"Yet I have something in common with the English Dissenters. Like me, they seek liberty of conscience. Like me, they are the victims of persecution. And like me, they brave it. Thus we sympathise with each other, and I would rather worship with them in the open air, than in the proudest temple built by man's hands. But you are tainted with the prejudices of the University, Mr. Moor, and will deride my enthusiasm."

"I am sincerely attached to the established church," said the young man, "but I would willingly relieve the Dissenters from all disabilities. I would leave them free to follow their own form of worship, so long as they will do so consistently with public order."

"That is all they ask," said Saint Leu, "the meeting which takes place to-day embraces numbers of the most opposite persuasions; and as we are now close to the spot, you may yourself judge of the propriety of their proceedings. I recommend you not to neglect the opportunity."

Moor was well inclined to listen to the suggestion, and a half-entreating look from Sabine decided him.

CHAPTER IV

OF THE GREAT DISSENTERS' MEETING ON FINCHLEY COMMON; AND HOW IT WAS DISPERSED.

Saint Leu's assertion that the English Dissenters had much in common with the nonconformists of other countries, was not unfounded. Excepting only the short interval of the Commonwealth, they had for ages been subjected to the most rigorous persecution. An act passed in 1593, during the reign of Elizabeth, inflicted the punishment of imprisonment on such persons as refused to attend the worship of the established church, or who were present at that of the Dissenters; and if the offence were not atoned for, by the conformity of the delinquents within three months, the punishment was increased to transportation for life. Scarcely had Charles II. ascended the throne, after a solemn promise of liberty of conscience, when this inhuman law was declared by parliament to be still in force; and a new act exposed the Dissenters to yet greater barbarity. By this statute, attendance at a meeting of Dissenters, where more than five persons were present, was punishable, on the third offence, with transportation for seven years to the West Indies; and if the convicted persons should survive the period of their bondage, during which they were to serve as slaves of planters, in a climate where laborious employment could scarcely fail to be fatal to them, they incurred the punishment of death if they returned to England.

Such were the severe penalties which could be enforced, with little more than the form of trial, by a summary conviction before two magistrates on conscientious Dissenters; and the meanest civil officer was empowered to disperse their meetings, and apprehend the preachers. This oppressive statute was subsequently repealed, but in the year 1670 another act was passed, which even improved on its cruel provisions. The pettiest constable could now consign to a dark and unwholesome dungeon, crowded with the most abandoned criminals, those pious and often learned men whom the Dissenters had appointed as their ministers, and who were here frequently doomed, while recoiling from the coarse ribaldry of their profligate companions, to suffer in body the extremities of cold and hunger.

Many of the aged ministers, we are told by Ellwood, perished in prison even before they were brought to trial; and some estimate of the mortality among them may be formed from the declaration of William Penn, who boldly asserted at the time, that from the period of the Restoration, "more than five thousand persons had died in bonds for matters of mere conscience to God."

There was no appearance of any assemblage on Finchley Common; but as Saint Leu and his party turned off the road on the right, they passed through a wood, and all at once came in view of numerous groups scattered over a hollow beyond it. Under cover of the thicket were ranged a number of vehicles of various kinds, together with saddle-horses, and here the party alighted, and left the chaise and their steeds in the care of the postilion.

The scene around was highly picturesque. Some of the assemblage were seated on the grass partaking of a frugal meal; others were conversing earnestly together, in knots of three and four; others, again, were reading aloud from the Scriptures, while a fourth group, either from choice, or because they were unknown, stood aloof from the crowd. At another point might be observed the thriving and comfortable, though puritanicallooking citizen, with his demure dame, and buxom daughters, in whose bright eyes a little too much of the love of the world seemed to dwell, attended by a couple of sturdy apprentices. Beside them stood an old soldier of the Civil War, who had fought with Cromwell's Ironsides; while further on was a group of old wives from Barnet, Finchley, and Highgate, mingled with the wealthy farmer and the labourer from the field. Here and there the sober Quaker, already distinguished by his garb, conversed with the zealous Independent. In all were manifest that rigid decorum, which constituted the distinctive feature of every sect of the Dissenters.

As Saint Leu and his party walked down the gentle slope, which descended from the thicket, they came abreast of a hollow tree, in which sat an old man, attired with the greatest simplicity, and having a venerable and patriarchal appearance. A large Bible lay open upon his knee, and he read forth, in a loud voice, the following words:—

"*Awake, awake, put on thy strength, O arm of the Lord! awake as in the ancient days, in the generations of old. Art thou not it that hath cut Rahab, and wounded the dragon?*

"*Art thou not it which hath dried the sea, the waters of the great deep: that hath made the depths of the sea a way for the ransomed to pass over?*

"*Therefore the redeemed of the Lord shall return, and come with singing unto Zion; and everlasting joy shall be upon their head: and sorrow and lamentation shall flee away.*"

Saint Leu paused on seeing the old man, and whispered to Moor that it was George Fox.

The illustrious founder of the sect of Quakers was the son of a poor weaver. Apprenticed early in life to a grazier, it was, while employed in keeping sheep in the fields, that he acquired that love of solitude and contemplation, which ultimately became one of his characteristics. When only nineteen, George Fox persuaded himself that he had received a divine communication; and from this time he supposed that a voice was continually crying to him, "There is one, even Christ Jesus, that can speak to thy condition."

Abandoning both his relations and his employment, Fox now became a wanderer, rambling night and day about the country, fasting much and often sitting for a day together in the trunk of a tree, and walking in the fields by night, with no other companion than the Bible. After eight years of seclusion, he first preached the strange opinions he had embraced at Manchester, whence he disseminated them, with surprising rapidity, through the whole of England. Their peculiar character exposed him to the persecution of the magistracy, and he was repeatedly committed to prison, from which, on representing his case, he was several times released by Cromwell. On the restoration of Charles II., he went to America, where he remained two years, when, returning to England, he was shortly afterwards taken into custody, and confined in Worcester gaol, but, after a long imprisonment, he was once more set at liberty. He now repaired to the continent, and, bent on disseminating his principles, travelled through Holland and Germany, enduring incessant fatigue and perpetual persecution, but everywhere preaching his singular opinions with boldness and effect. From this mission he had recently returned.

As he finished reading the texts cited, Fox looked up, and observing Saint Leu, slowly arose from the tree, and saluted him. It appeared they were well acquainted with each other, having met before at Amsterdam. After they had exchanged a grave and cordial greeting, Fox referred to the condition of the persecuted Huguenots.

"We are thrown in evil days," Fox said, "but thou heardst the assurance of the prophet, and the wicked king shall not always triumph. Though the heathen rage against us, and the monarchs of the earth have united to oppress us, we can always look to heaven for comfort. Let us then submit with patience to the ills which the Lord does not prevent."

"It is our duty to resign ourselves to the will of heaven," replied Saint Leu, "but we should not be equally submissive to that of man. The edict of Nantes, which guaranteed toleration to the Huguenots, was a fundamental law of France, and Louis XIV. perjured himself when he revoked it. While I speak of peace, this tyrant's licentious soldiers live at free quarters in our homes. We are denied the protection of the magistrates. Our wives and daughters are left defenceless, and our own children are bribed to betray us. Our houses are destroyed or deserted; whole villages are devastated, and while driven abroad over the face of the earth must we tamely submit to the persecutor?"

"Yea, must we," replied Fox, meekly; "we must tarry the Lord's pleasure. Let us ever beseech Him to strengthen and comfort us; for we are as weak to endure as we are impotent to redress."

"Yet if Heaven put a sword in our hand, we should not throw it away, but rather smite with it," said Saint Leu, sarcastically.

"Not so," replied Fox; "Heaven gives us the weapon for defence, and not for aggression."

At this moment they were joined by a man of tall stature, and though of great age, having a vigorous deportment and muscular limbs. His full ruddy face glowed with health, and a reddish beard, tinged with grey, clothed his cheeks and chin. He carried in his hand a stout knotted staff, more for defence it would seem than support; while leaning on his arm was a fair slight girl, with beautiful features, and eyes of translucent blue, though it was soon apparent from their vacancy that those bright orbs were sightless. The new-comers were John Bunyan and his blind daughter Mary.

A word of the former. Born of poor, though honest parents, Bunyan had been brought up a tinker, and had passed his early life in riot and drunkenness. He was first awakened to a sense of his errors by a woman, herself of light character, but who was so shocked by his excessive impiety, that, to his great astonishment, she reproved him for it; and, at the same time, a voice seemed to say to him, "Wilt thou leave thy sins and go to heaven, or have thy sins and go to hell?" Completely abandoning his dissolute courses, on the outbreak of the Civil War, he served as a soldier of the Parliament, and was present in several engagements. He was thirty years of age before he adopted the profession of a preacher, when he was chosen minister of a Baptist congregation at Bedford. In 1660 he was convicted of holding an unlawful conventicle, and sentenced to perpetual banishment; but, in the mean time he was committed to gaol, and remained in confinement upwards of twelve years. It was during this period that he wrote most of his tracts, particularly the "Pilgrim's Progress," which has since been translated into every European language. Interest having been made for him with Dr. Barlow, Bishop of Lincoln, he was, through the interference of that prelate, ultimately liberated; and, since his enlargement, had passed his life in travelling from place to place, exhorting and condoling with his brethren, and the other dissenting communions, wherever he met with them.

"We were speaking of resistance to persecution," observed Saint Leu to Bunyan, "is it lawful or otherwise?"

"Assuredly it is lawful," replied Bunyan; "we may justly defend our freedom, whether of conscience or of body. Maccabæus was a godly man, but he went forth against the heathen; and David himself was a man of war."

"The dispensation of the New Testament is Peace," answered Fox, "and Peace shall prevail. Yea, a day shall come, when the simple Word, whether spoken or written, shall have more weight with princes and rulers than the sword hath now. We are not as the brutes, friend John, but have judgment and understanding; and men shall one day turn the sword into a ploughshare and dwell together in unity. Then shall come to pass the words of the prophet, 'the work of righteousness shall be Peace, and the effects of righteousness quietness and assurance for ever: and my people shall dwell in a peaceable habitation, and in sure dwellings and in quiet resting-places.' "

"Would that day were come, if it were the Lord's will!" exclaimed Bunyan; "for the cruel tyranny of our present government is almost insupportable. The episcopal clergy should be looking to their own safety instead of oppressing us, for the scarlet woman of Babylon will soon ensnare them."

"We meet in peril, but not in fear," observed Fox.

"The Lord protect us!" ejaculated Bunyan, "our hazard is greater than you may suppose, for a band of the Amalekites has been seen hovering about, and they probably have intelligence of our meeting."

"More likely you have been misinformed," remarked Saint Leu. "I have come straight from London, and have seen nothing of any armed force."

"The spoiler cometh secretly even as a fowler spreadeth his nets," replied Bunyan.

"The Lord's will be done," said Fox; "if it be so, I shall rejoice that I am accounted worthy to suffer."

Bunyan turned an anxious look on his daughter.

"I will never suffer them to lay hands upon her," he murmured.

Meanwhile, Moor's attention had been occupied by Sabine.

"You have witnessed such an assemblage as this before?" he said.

"Often in France," she replied; "but there we met at night—often at midnight—by stealth and in terror. Scouts were posted around to prevent surprise from the soldiers; and while we prayed, or sang, or listened to the preaching of our ministers, a warning would come suddenly that the foes were upon us, and then such scenes would ensue as my heart bleeds to remember."

"The spirit which animated the early Christians seems to be revived among you," observed Moor; "the hapless Huguenots brave the terrors of martyrdom."

"They at least endure the utmost rigour of persecution," replied Sabine. "In our own case we were obliged to seek safety in flight, and it was with the greatest difficulty that we gained the frontiers of France, and made our way into the Low Countries. How happy are your countrymen that they can meet for worship in the broad day!"

"You are not aware then that these meetings are unlawful," said Moor, with a melancholy shake of the head, "and may be forcibly dispersed."

"Oh, yes, I know it," replied Sabine; "but though the meetings are illegal, the law is lenient to them, and does not molest them. If we had apprehended danger, we should not have come

—but see! there is a stir among the crowd. The service is about to commence."

At this moment a man appeared on the slope, whose approach excited a general sensation, and who was saluted on all sides with a hum of welcome. Lofty in stature and slightly built, his face was pale and careworn, but marked with a touching expression of resignation. The name which rose upon the lips of the crowd was that of Richard Baxter.

Originally a minister of the established church, Baxter, in common with many others, offended by the innovations of Laud, went over to the Dissenters, and siding with the parliament during the Civil War, was appointed, after the battle of Naseby, chaplain of Colonel Whalley's regiment, with which he served till the close of the struggle. He was opposed to the execution of Charles I. and to the abolition of monarchy, and, at great personal hazard, openly deprecated those proceedings, and even remonstrated against them with Cromwell. At the Restoration he was appointed chaplain in ordinary to Charles II., and afterwards assisted at the ecclesiastical conference in the Savoy, where, in his capacity of commissioner, he drew up a reformed liturgy, pronounced by Dr. Johnson to be "one of the finest compositions of the ritual kind he had ever seen." He was then offered the bishopric of Hereford, but declined it, alleging as his reason his nonconformity with the church—the attempt to frame a liturgy acceptable to the Dissenters having completely failed. Retiring to Acton, he opened a meeting-house in that village, for which he was arrested by the county justices and committed to prison. He did not remain long in confinement, but ten years afterwards, having preached and published five controversial sermons, he was again arrested, and by the arbitrary exercise of a cruel statute, was heavily fined for each discourse. Finally, towards the close of 1685, being convicted of holding a conventicle, he was committed for two years to the King's Bench, and from this prison he had but recently been liberated at the period of this history.

Baxter reeeived the congratulations of the two preachers on his enlargement with a look of heartfelt gratitude, and a faint smile illumined his pallid features.

"Let us but tarry with patience and our deliverance is sure," observed Fox; "the apostle Peter held fast his faith, and in the mid-watch of night, the angel of the Lord visited his prison; his bonds fell from his limbs; the dungeon-doors flew open, and he walked forth free."

"The Scriptures abound with comforting examples," replied Baxter; "but though we have not to endure in these days the terrible persecution which beset the apostles, imprisonment is not the only evil we have to fear. Better remain for life in a dungeon, than by our words or actions bring scandal on the cause of our Master."

"Your own life, at least, has been blameless," remarked Bunyan; "resisting the temptations of prelacy, fasting often, giving alms in secret, and in all things practising holiness. Me they may reproach. My lips have blasphemed, and my hand has worked iniquity, but you have ever been faithful and without guile."

"Would it were so!" exclaimed Baxter. "But, sinner as I have been, and am, I may yet be thankful that I have escaped the greater offences,—though my enemies accuse me of committing robbery and murder."

"Robbery and murder!" exclaimed Fox. "Thou, Richard Baxter; thou!"

"Even I!" rejoined Baxter. "Such are the crimes laid to my charge. Dr. Boreman, of Trinity College, Cambridge, avouches, that during the civil war, I killed a man in cold blood, and plundered him afterwards."

"What!" exclaimed Bunyan, sternly; "does it not content these friends of prelacy that they hunt us from place to place through the land, load us with bonds, and banish us to remote and fatal climates, but would they also vex us with their evil report? Surely the day is come when we shall no longer bear with their iniquity, and when he who hath not a sword shall sell his garment and buy him one."

"It is written in the book of Acts," said Fox, solemnly, "that when Paul was shipwrecked, and a viper fastened on his hand, the heathen said among themselves, 'No doubt this man is a murderer, whom, though he hath escaped the sea, yet vengeance suffereth not to live. Yet Paul shook off the beast into the fire, and felt no harm.' Take this unto thyself, Richard Baxter. Like unto the apostle, thou shalt shake off this calumny, and thine enemies shall marvel that thou art not hurt thereby. But the Lord shall be with thee.—And now, brethren, let us pray!"

So saying, he passed slowly down the slope towards the crowd, in company with Baxter and Bunyan, and followed reverently by the others.

While the preachers were descending to the hollow, the assemblage below crowded together, and united their voices in a psalm.

Though all joined in the solemn strain, it was strange to observe what conflicting emotions it raised in the same bosoms. The stern piety of the grim Cromwellian was mingled with hatred of his oppressors, and a fanatical aversion to prelacy;

the moody citizen, less indifferent to the world's goods, or to the hazard of life or freedom, which would inevitably attend a struggle with the authorities, still with difficulty reconciled himself to the necessity of submission; his wife, daughter, or sister, trembled with anxiety, and mourned in secret their defenceless condition; while the stolid rustic seemed alive only to the danger of his situation, and glanced frequently and earnestly around, in continual dread of interruption.

Amidst the deep silence, which, on the close of the psalm prevailed among the multitude, the voice of Fox arose in simple and fervent prayer. Touchingly depicting the affliction of his brethren, though acknowledging that their sins would justify a far greater measure of Divine indignation, and urging the frailty of their fallen nature as a plea for God's mercy, he implored the Almighty to lead them to submit cheerfully to His will; to strengthen them to endure their trials with patience and fortitude; to clothe them in the armour of righteousness, and to fill their hearts with love for one another, and charity towards their enemies; and concluded by beseeching the Supreme Being, for the glory of His name, to keep their minds in the knowledge of His word, and, as he ever tempered the wind to the shorn lamb, not to put more on their shoulders than they were able to bear.

Having finished his prayer, Fox was succeeded by Baxter, who, in language equally simple, and in a voice of emphatic solemnity, offered up thanks for his recent deliverance, imploring the Deity to compassionate those, who, more worthy than he was, yet pined in bondage. He adverted to the reviving power of Popery, and to the intolerance of the established Church, and prayed that, if it were the Divine will, these evils might be overruled, and that the saving truths of the Gospel might be again preached to all men in their own tongues.

Thus far the expressions of the preachers had been of a soothing character, calculated to allay the irritable feelings of their auditors; but having concluded his prayer, Baxter gave way to Bunyan, who was of a warmer and more rugged nature. Mounted on a bench, which allowed his venerable figure to be seen by all, he raised his hands for a moment in inward prayer, and then in a loud, clear voice, proceeded to address the assemblage. He took this text from Isaiah:—"*The people shall dwell in Zion, at Jerusalem; thou shalt weep no more; he will be very gracious unto thee at the voice of thy cry; when he shall hear it, he will answer thee. And though the Lord give you the bread of adversity, and the water of affliction, yet shall not thy teachers be removed into a corner any more, and thine eyes shall see thy teachers.*"

He represented this passage as an assurance to his brethren, in their present misery, that the Arm which they trusted would be with them, and would soon most effectually work their deliverance. But the daughter of Babylon was again seated in the high places; and it behoved them to shut their eyes against the vanity of her beauty, to blind themselves to her scarlet robes and her jewelled crown, and to shun her snares and her soft speeches. Her mouth was comely to look upon, but an adder's poison was within her lips; she held out her hand to them, grasping the cup of her idolatry; yea, she beckoned to them with her hand, but it was red with the blood of saints. They were told in the book of Revelations, that "the woman was arrayed in purple and scarlet colour, and decked with gold and precious stones and pearls, having a golden cup in her hand, full of abominations." They were also told, that the woman "was drunken with the blood of the saints, and with the blood of the martyrs;" and would they, to escape persecution, partake of the cup she held out to them? The groans of the Lutherans in Poland, of the Huguenots in France, of the Vaudois in Savoy —the weeping and wailings of the saints through the world— warned them against her; and, in their own land, they saw her in league with their oppressors, laying hands on the chosen, and committing them to prison. The preacher was torn from his flock, the father from his children, the son from his parents: they were buried in dungeons, rank with the breath of crime, or carried away into captivity, like the ancient Israelites, to work in bonds for cruel taskmasters. But the day was approaching, when the scarlet woman would turn on their persecutors: then the latter would entreat them kindly, and would draw near to them, and would seek to be as one with them in that day. But they would not be as one with the prelatists—they would accept no aid from Egypt or Babylon; they would put their trust only in the mercy of their Maker. There would soon be a lighting down of the arm of the Lord; a cheerful noise of trumpets and of timbrels, announcing their tribulation to be at an end. Then their stone of adversity would be changed into bread of comfort; their water of affliction into a sweet spring; their teachers, released from bonds, would not be removed into a corner any more, and they should ever see them among them.

It was with fixed and almost breathless attention—with faces alternately flushing or growing pale, and with hearts swelling or subdued—that the crowd listened to this discourse. The rude eloquence of the speaker was admirably suited to the disposition of his auditors. They had, however, at that moment, but little time to brood over his discourse; for scarcely had he brought it to a close, when a horseman galloped down the hollow, in whom Moor instantly recognised the Golden Farmer.

"Fly!" exclaimed the highwayman; "the devil is abroad; Colonel Kirke is at hand: he and his 'Lambs' will be down upon you directly."

Without tarrying to witness the effect of his warning, the Golden Farmer again clapped spurs to his horse, rode up the acclivity, and disappeared.

The reported approach of the dragoons spread alarm among the crowd, and a few of the country-folk, of both sexes, exhibited a disposition to retreat; but the mass of the devotees, whom Bunyan's discourse had already inflamed against the authorities, remained steadfast, while murmurs of resentment broke from them.

"I would my sword were girded on my thigh, like the man Barak's," said Ephraim Ruddle, a superannuated Ironside, "I would make a stand against Moab, and he should fly like Sisera."

"'Twould be shameful in us to submit," said Gideon Tuck, an earthenware-maker, "but what can potters' vessels, like us, do against hands of iron?"

"We can do nothing but fly," said a pretty damsel, who was leaning on his arm; "so let us run off to the waggon, and hide ourselves."

"Don't be frightened, Miss Deborah," urged a sturdy young fellow near her; "the 'prentices made better men flee before them, when they forced King Charles to raise the siege of Gloucester."

"Yonder are the Philistines!" shouted old Martha Higgins, a stern enthusiast from Barnet. "I see 'em comin', like wolves to devour the flock. The hand of the Lord be upon 'em, and turn 'em back, like Senacherib, when he fled in the night from before the walls of Jerusalem, in the days of Hezekiah, king of Judah."

At this juncture, a strong detachment of troopers was seen to wheel round one end of the neighbouring thicket, while a second party made its appearance simultaneously from the other side. They approached the hollow at a brisk trot, with their swords drawn; and now the female portion of the crowd gave free utterance to their terror, increasing the confusion by their outcries.

An attentive observer of all that passed, though little anticipating such a termination to the proceedings, Moor looked round for Sabine, intending to offer her protection; but he found that, in the confusion, he had become separated both from her and Saint Leu. Before he could discover where they were, the first party of troopers poured down among the crowd, and amidst fearful cries, mingled with their own coarse jests and laughter, began the task of dispersion. While this was going on, their leader, Colonel Trelawney, dashed up to the three preachers.

As he advanced, his glance fell on Mary Bunyan, and, stooping in his saddle, he placed his arm round her waist.

"Why, my pretty lass, what are you doing here?" he cried; "you're far too good-looking for a conventicle: we will go to church together."

"Let her go, spawn of Tophet!" exclaimed Bunyan, raising his staff.

Fox seized his arm, and at the same moment, Moor, who was standing by, drew Mary away.

"Do not let him tempt thee," said Fox to Bunyan; "the Lord will requite him."

"Ah! is there a wrestling within thee to hold forth?" cried Trelawney, jeeringly. "Keep it in, Broadbrim, for verily thou wilt need all thy doctrine for thyself."

"The Lord will be with me in my need," rejoined Fox, calmly; "and do thou remember what befel to Hophni and Phinehas, and do no more wrong to thy brethren."

Trelawney was about to make an insulting reply, when the leader of the other party of dragoons came up.

The personal appearance of Colonel Kirke (for he it was) was in keeping with his well-known ferocious character. Tall and gaunt in figure, with sharp, stern features, lighted up by eyes that seemed injected with blood, and bronzed by the suns of Africa, his naturally savage appearance was heightened by a wide cicatrice on his left cheek, occasioned by a wound he had received in a conflict with the Moors at Tangier. In this formidable personage—hideous by nature as well as hideous by crime—few could trace any resemblance to his sister, the lively and beautiful Mary Kirke, the Warmestre of Grammont. The barbarous character of the warfare in which Kirke had been engaged while in garrison at Tangier, had aggravated the natural ferocity of his disposition, and he found a fiendish gratification in the most refined acts of cruelty. His atrocities in the West of England, on the suppression of Monmouth's rebellion, have already been mentioned. On one occasion he tied a miserable wretch by a rope to a horse's neck, promising him life on condition of his keeping pace with the horse, at full speed, for the distance of half a mile, and executed the wretched man in spite of his performance of the task. On another occasion, he ordered a number of his prisoners to be brought out and put to death, while he and his troopers drank the king's health; and observing his men tremble with fear, he directed the trumpets to sound, telling them, with a diabolical laugh, that they should have music to their dancing. A vile scoffer of religion, though professedly a member of the Church, he was once urged by James to embrace the Catholic faith, when he told the monarch that, during his sojourn in Africa, he had promised the Emperor of Morocco, if he ever changed his religion, he would become a Mahometan, and he could not break his word. Such were the terrible pleasantries in which this atrocious jester indulged.

As Kirke reined in his horse, he raised a finger to his hat, which, like the hats of all his men, was decorated with the figure of a white lamb (a badge he had assumed at Tangier), and which, in derision of his pretension to Christian virtue, had procured his regiment the nickname of "Colonel Kirke's Lambs."

"The lambs have come into the fold," he cried, "and seek the shepherd."

"I will leave you to deal with the shepherds, Kirke," laughed Trelawney, "for I see a flying doe yonder, whom I should like to capture."

With this he spurred his horse towards the further end of the thicket, where he had just espied Sabine.

"Aha!" he muttered to himself, as he cleared the ground,—"this is lucky! It is the very girl that Barillon pointed out to me. Her abduction can now be accomplished without exciting the slightest suspicion."

Kirke, meanwhile, remained stationary. Seeing which, Baxter advanced towards him, saying, "Thou hast asked for the shepherd. Behold an unworthy one in me."

"And another in me," said Bunyan.

"Friend, I am the man thou seekest," interposed Fox; "I will teach thy hands to throw away the sword of Belial, and to renounce thy carnal-mindedness and world-seeking."

"For which I shall tie thee to a cart's tail," rejoined Kirke. And he turned to another horseman in the garb of a civilian, who had accompanied him to the spot: "Secure these three ringleaders, master constable," he said, "and my troopers will disperse the mob."

The troopers, indeed, were already actively engaged in this service; but a few of the crowd now rallied round the preachers, and, by their looks and murmurs, seemed disposed to offer resistance.

"The Lord slew Holofernes by the hand of a woman," exlaimed Ephraim Ruddle; "He will make us strong against Moab."

"Peace, peace!" cried Fox.

"Take my daughter, Mr. Ellwood," said Bunyan to a tall thin man in the garb of a Quaker, "and the Father of the fatherless will requite you."

As the friend and amanuensis of Milton took charge of the poor blind girl, Moor turned to retire. Before he could clear the hollow, however, he attracted the notice of the constable, who was no other than Elkanah Snewin. Though he had not found Moor in conference with Colonel Sidney at the Burleigh Arms inn, as he expected, Snewin had not dismissed his suspicions on that point, and Moor's presence among the Dissenters confirmed him in the belief that he was engaged in some political intrigue. Actuated by this suspicion, he now darted forward and laid hands upon him.

"Not so fast, my blade!" he cried; "What are you doing here, eh?"

Moor made no reply, but, mustering all his strength, cast off the powerful hold of Snewin, and threw him down. In the struggle, however, Snewin tore open his coat, and the letter he had received from Colonel Sidney, dropped from his vest.

Snewin instantly seized the letter, and his eyes gleamed with triumph as he glanced at the seal. Scrambling to his feet, he again seized Moor by the collar.

"Charles Moor," he cried, "I arrest you of high treason! It is the private signet of the Prince of Orange, I know it well," he added to Kirke.

CHAPTER V.

SABINE.

Separated from her uncle and Madame Desjardins in the confusion and terror occasioned by the troopers' approach, Sabine had gained, she scarcely knew how, the summit of the slope, and then became aware that her companions were gone. Her first impulse prompted her again to rush into the hollow in quest of her uncle; but the scared fugitives who covered the slope, compelled her to turn back, and she fled towards the wood. At this moment, Trelawney dashed up the acclivity with the evident design of seizing her. Outstripping the other scattered fugitives—with a panting heart, trembling, and almost breathless, Sabine cleared the outer extremity of the thicket, closely pursued by Trelawney, whose progress, however, was suddenly arrested by half a dozen men armed with bludgeons, the stoutest of whom caught his horse by the bridle, while the others surrounded him, and threatened to dismount him. Taking advantage of the interruption, Sabine plunged into the heart of the thicket, until, unable to proceed further, she stood still, and half-sinking with terror, supported herself against a tree. Though the brushwood and timber were here so thick that no external object could be distinguished, she still heard the shouts of the dragoons, and the trampling of their horses' feet, mixed with the rumbling of carts and waggons, while every now and then an outcry proceeding from some terrified female made her heart beat more anxiously. This turmoil lasted upwards of an hour, after which all became still, and she began to think that the assemblage was dispersed, and the soldiers gone.

Evening was by this time advancing; but, absorbed by her fears, and scarcely venturing even to raise her head, Sabine hardly noticed the deeper gloom gradually falling around her. As the prevailing stillness, however, continued undisturbed, she was roused to the necessity of exertion, and resolved to make an effort to gain the road, where, if her uncle were really hovering about, as she hoped he might be, she would most likely fall in with him.

She was stepping forth with this view, when a rustling in the bushes, as if some one were pushing through them, held her still. Footsteps were distinctly heard at a little distance; and she became sensible that several persons were approaching. Were they friends or foes?—It was impossible to say. Should she fly or remain where she was, when the next moment she might be captured? She was torn by indecision; but her fears were confirmed by the voice of one of the searchers.

"Never mind, sergeant," said the speaker, in a low tone; "it seems useless to beat the bush further. Keep a strict watch round the thicket, and I and Cornet Lucas will go lower down, near the road."

"It shall be done, colonel," answered his companion.

"Post your men carefully," resumed the other; "recollect, if you take her, you will be well rewarded."

"Make yourself easy, colonel," replied the sergeant, "you shall have her before the night is over."

Sabine with difficulty repressed a cry, while the men moved off in opposite directions.

When all was quite still, she rose from her crouching position, and endeavoured to peer through the darkness; but could distinguish nothing except the vague outlines of the trees and bushes, while every gust of wind that swept past startled her, as if it proclaimed the approach of an enemy. Afraid to leave her covert, she did not dare to remain stationary, while her knowledge that the thicket was guarded added to her perplexity. Some time elapsed before she could decide how to act. She then mustered all her resolution, and, breaking through the bush, endeavoured to gain the open common.

The difficulty of achieving a passage was increased by the darkness; but at length she reached a spot of sward, clear of brushwood; and she was hurrying across it, when the sound of an approaching footstep brought her to a sudden halt.

Immediately before her she discerned the figure of a sentinel, moving along at a slow and measured pace, and pausing every moment to listen and look around. He was so close to her, that she almost feared he had detected her, but she was shielded from his view by an intervening tree; and, as he did not advance, she [hoped she might still elude discovery. The man turned to retrace his steps; and observing a gap in the bushes, Sabine made swiftly towards it, and gained the common.

By this time the moon had risen, though at the moment she was obscured by clouds, which rolled over the sky in dense masses. The turf of the common was heavy with dew; the wind sighed fitfully, and swept past in hoarse, mournful gusts.

Sabine hurried on for some little way without interruption, till skirting an extensive hollow, she was alarmed by the sound of voices, and, looking in the direction of the sound, perceived the outlines of three or four gipsies' tents with a fire in front of them, round which some wild-looking figures were grouped. Probably she might have passed these persons unnoticed, if a dog had not commenced barking, and ultimately started in pursuit of her. The gipsies instantly set up a cry, and followed the animal. Sabine continued her flight without looking behind her; but though terror lent wings to her feet, the foremost of her pursuers was speedily up with her. Before he could lay hands upon her, however, two horsemen galloped up, and one of them, who was no other than Colonel Trelawney, dealing a blow at the gipsy, seized Sabine, and drawing her to his saddle, wrapped his cloak around her so as to stifle her cries, and then, attended by his companion, rode off.

After proceeding at a rapid pace for some time, Trelawney alighted before a large straggling building, half-farm, half-inn, on the road side. Almost insensible, Sabine was borne into the house by her captor, while his companion took upon him to explain matters to the landlord, who was busy with other guests, but who, hearing their arrival, had hurried out to welcome them.

The principal room of the inn was of considerable size, and

but dimly lighted. While depositing Sabine on a bench, Trelawney perceived that another person was standing near the fireplace. It was a young man, rather under the middle height, but richly habited, and of a haughty bearing. His head seemed disproportionately large for his body, and his features, though handsome, had a strange sinister expression.

"Lord Mauvesin!" exclaimed Trelawney, in surprise. "What has brought your lordship here?"

"Accident," replied the other. "I might put a similar question to you, Colonel. But who is this girl?" he added, glancing at Sabine.

"A prize I've taken at the Dissenters' meeting," replied Trelawney, laughing. "She is much too pretty to be left with those canting dogs."

"She is remarkably beautiful," replied Mauvesin; "but will you not call for assistance? She has fainted."

"Oh, she'll soon come to, I'll warrant her," replied Trelawney. "What ho, hostess! Take charge of this young lady. She has had a hurried ride, and is rather the worse for it."

Thus summoned, a stout good-humoured woman made her appearance, and seeing the condition of Sabine, uttered a cry, and disappearing for a moment, returned with some restoratives, which she applied with great zeal and solicitude to the fair sufferer.

Leaving Sabine in the care of the latter, Trelawney walked towards the fire with Lord Mauvesin.

"Do you know who this girl is, Trelawney?" asked the latter in a low tone.

"I do," replied the other; "but I must not disclose her name."

"Why not?"

"Nay, the secret is another's, not mine," said Trelawney. "Thus much I will tell you. She is from France, and is about to be conveyed back to her native country."

"She shall not be so if I can prevent it," replied Mauvesin. "I am strongly attracted by her, Trelawney. Cannot I make it worth your while to yield her to me?"

"I would strike a bargain with you if I could, my lord," said Trelawney, laughing; "but I cannot. I am under an engagement to Barillon. The girl is destined to a convent. It's a sad pity—but it must be."

"I tell you it must *not* be, Trelawney," cried Mauvesin, hastily. "A thousand pounds, if you surrender her to me."

"Hum!" exclaimed Trelawney, "my word is pledged to Barillon."

"Pshaw, you can easily make excuses to him," cried the nobleman. "But who is this? Another arrival!"

The exclamation was occasioned by the sound of horses' feet outside; and both Mauvesin and Trelawney became silent, expecting the appearance of a new-comer. As this did not immediately occur, however, Mauvesin again spoke.

"Do you accept my offer?" he asked.

"I will consider of it, my lord," replied Trelawney.

At this juncture the door opened, and a square-built man, in the habit of a farmer, with great funnel-topped boots rising above his knees, and a green riding-coat wrapped about his athletic frame, entered the room. Walking forward to a small table near the fireplace, with a "give ye good e'en" to the gentlemen, he sat down and called for a can of ale and a pipe.

As the farmer entered, Mauvesin and Trelawney regarded him attentively for a moment, and seemed somewhat disconcerted at his intrusion.

"Come, I see you assent to my proposal, colonel," said Mauvesin in an under-tone to Trelawney, "and as an earnest of my sincerity, accept this pocket-book. It contains five hundred pounds. We must get off the girl at once, and I have hit on a good plan of doing it. She shall think I intend to aid her to escape. I will just say a word to her apart, and, meanwhile, do you examine the contents of the pocket-book."

As Trelawney, in obedience to these instructions, turned to the fire, Mauvesin advanced to Sabine. The farmer chancing to raise his head at the moment, saw Trelawney count the roll of notes, and then thrust them with a look of satisfaction into his vest.

"Are you going towards Highgate, sir?" the farmer inquired.

"Why do you ask, friend?" said Trelawney, sternly.

"Only because it's my road home," replied the other; "and I should be glad of your honour's company."

"You look too much like a highwayman yourself, fellow, to fear molestation," replied Trelawney. "But if you can tell me where to find the Golden Farmer, I'll go with you."

"You'd better leave him alone, sir," said the farmer; "but if you're bent upon it, I might put you in the way of finding him."

"Do so," replied Trelawney, "and I'll pay you for your trouble."

"You *shall* pay me well if I do," muttered the farmer, puffing away at his pipe.

Meanwhile Mauvesin had joined Sabine, who was now restored to sensibility. The hostess had just quitted her, so that she was left alone. She looked up as the young nobleman approached, and, raising his finger to his lips to enjoin silence, he cast a hasty glance behind him, as if to make sure that he was not observed by Trelawney, and then said in a hasty whisper——"I am aware of your situation, young lady, and will do my best to extricate you from it. Will you place yourself under my protection?"

"Most thankfully," replied Sabine, reassured by his manner.

"Then I will slip out, and procure a horse for you," returned Mauvesin, "after which I will contrive some means of getting you away."

The farmer looked round as he retired; but continued smoking his pipe tranquilly, while Trelawney gazed into the fire. Thus several minutes passed by, when a loud report of fire-arms was heard close to the windows.

Sabine uttered an exclamation of terror.

"Hallo!—what's that?" exclaimed the farmer, starting to his feet.

Trelawney rushed to the nearest window, while the farmer went quickly up to Sabine.

"That door will lead you to the yard," he said to her; "there is a gate on the other side. Gain the road, and you are safe. Fly—fly!" he cried, seeing her hesitate, "I'll keep the colonel at bay."

Trelawney heard the last words, and instantly divining what was passing, darted towards Sabine, who arose on his approach, and made towards the door indicated by the farmer, while the latter threw himself in the colonel's way.

"Let her go!" he exclaimd; "what has she done?"

"Out of my way, rascal, or I'll cut you down," cried Trelawney, furiously.

"No you won't," replied the farmer, drawing a pistol, and levelling it at the other's head. "You don't stir a step, colonel!"

"You shall repent this, villain," shouted Trelawney; "what ho, house! where the devil is Lord Mauvesin?"

"Gone to help the young lady to escape," laughed the farmer.

Sabine meanwhile pursued her flight unmolested. On gaining the yard, she encountered Lord Mauvesin, who was hastily crossing from a stable on the other side.

"I was just coming for you, young lady," he said, "when I was alarmed by those pistol-shots, and have vainly tried to ascertain by whom they were fired. They are now bringing out the horses. We will pass through this gate to the road, and in a few minutes you will be in safety."

Almost as he spoke, indeed, an ostler, with a lantern in his hand, brought up a couple of horses, one of which was furnished with a side-saddle. After a word of explanation, Sabine suffered Mauvesin to lift her to the saddle, and to lead her horse into the farm-yard. As they approached the outer gate, Mauvesin, unobserved by Sabine, directed the ostler to acquaint Trelawney of their departure; and then, mounting his horse, he and Sabine passed on to the road, and set forward together in the direction for London.

They had not, however, proceeded a hundred yards from the inn, when another horseman, who had been hovering about, rode up to them, and Sabine, to her great joy, found it was her uncle.

A few hasty exclamations passed between them, when Saint Leu, turning to his niece's companion, recognised Lord Mauvesin.

"I owe my safety to this gentleman, uncle," replied Sabine.

"I am but too happy to have rendered you a service," observed Mauvesin, recovering from his surprise and confusion. "If I can be of any further assistance, I will willingly accompany you to town."

Saint Leu gave a reluctant assent, and they proceeded on their way.

Meanwhile, the ostler whom Mauvesin had left at the gate of the inn, with a message for Trelawney, heard a hue and cry in the yard behind and saw the farmer approaching.

He was closely pursued by Trelawney and his companion, with several waggoners and stable-men; but the ostler, who might have intercepted him, made way for him to pass, and he gained the road. There he mounted a horse, which was tied to a tree at a little distance, and instantly galloped off.

The sound of his horse's hoofs could still be heard when his pursuers gained the road.

"He has escaped us for the present," cried Trelawney, "but I will have him some other time. Gallop off to the thicket, Cornet, and bring up the men. Meanwhile I'll look after Lord Mauvesin and the girl."

"The lady 's gone, sir," said the ostler, touching his hat. "The lord told me to let you know he'd see her safe home."

"Oh, that's all right," answered Trelawney.

Returning to the inn, he partook of some refreshment, and then mounting his horse, rode off towards Highgate.

He proceeded at a leisurely pace, but was soon out of sight of the inn, making his way along a lonely road overshadowed with trees. With his thoughts engrossed by recent occurrences, he had ridden along for some distance, scarcely taking note of his progress, when he was suddenly confronted by another horseman.

"Stand and deliver!" cried the latter, presenting a pistol at his head.

"Soh, you *are* a highwayman, then?" cried Trelawney, recognising the farmer; "I thought as much."

"I am the man you wished to meet—the Golden Farmer," rejoined the other.

"Then this shall end your career," cried Trelawney.

And snatching a pistol from his holster, he drew the trigger. Sparks blazed from the flint, but that was all. He drew a second pistol with the same result.

A loud laugh broke from the highwayman.

"Your pistols were discharged near the inn-window," he said: "a comrade did it for me to distract you. But come, colonel, hand out your pocket-book, or you'll find that my pistols *are* loaded."

"Take it," answered Trelawney, drawing forth his pocket-book, "and may the devil's luck go with it."

"It has come into my hands quite as honestly as it got into yours, colonel," replied the other. "Good night, and a pleasant ride to you."

And turning his horse's head, he galloped away.

CHAPTER VI.

A PRISON SCENE.

WITHIN a few hours after the meeting on Finchley Common, Moor and his fellow-prisoners, Fox, Baxter, and Bunyan, were the inmates of Newgate. Accident having led to their joint arrest, they were lodged for the time in the same dungeon, where they were packed together with a crowd of offenders, accused of almost every shade of crime.

The interior of the prisons, at this eventful period, teemed with such horrors, that, as a learned writer observes, "they surpassed the imaginations of more civilized times," and can only be estimated correctly from the stern facts of history. Subject to no regulation, and without any provision for affording sustenance to the prisoners, the places of confinement were at once the scenes of profusion and famine. It was publicly stated in parliament, towards the close of the reign of Charles II., that "needy persons committed to gaol many times perished before their trial." While some died of hunger, or actually perished from cold, others revelled in continual debauchery. It was not unusual to leave the mouldering bodies of those who died, in all the torments of despair, for days together, in the dark and loathsome dungeons of the survivors. The description given by George Fox of the treatment he experienced in a horrible pit at Launceston, called Doomsdale, excites a feeling amounting to awe. Ellwood, the amanuensis of Milton, when confined in Newgate for his religion, saw the quarters of men executed for treason lying for several days close to his cell, and the hangman and the more obdurate criminals playing at bowls with the heads. The gaolers exercised an almost unlimited power over the prisoners; and such was the deplorable state of the laws, that persons were often incarcerated for no other offence than being obnoxious to one of the magistracy. Thus disposed of, they were soon forgotten, and if they even succeeded in obtaining a trial, it was easy to accuse them of nonconformity, and then to prevail on a packed jury to find them guilty.

The dreadful mortality which took place in the prisons has already been referred to; but when the gaol-fever once broke out, bringing to the despairing captives the often welcome relief of death, the contagion was not confined to those fearful abodes, but spread far and wide over the land. When the prisoners were brought up for trial at the assizes, it came forth with them into the court, and fell like a pestilence on the judges, jurors, barristers, and audience. Even those acquitted at their trial, or who purchased their liberty by the payment of fines, were liberated with impaired constitutions, and never wholly recovered from the effect of their confinement.

The Dissenters suffered most severely from this atrocious system; and besides the great mortality it occasioned among them, we learn from a tract of William Penn's, called "Good Advice to the Church of England," that by the operation of the cruel laws enacted against them "fifteen thousand families were ruined." Among those who died was William Jenkins, a celebrated nonconformist preacher, whose son, on hearing of his death, distributed mourning-rings among his friends, on which was inscribed "William Jenkins, murdered in Newgate." Young Jenkins afterwards joined the army of Monmouth; and in spite of the repeated intercessions of Sunderland, attested by a letter in the State Paper Office, dated 12th September, 1685, was ordered by Jeffreys to be executed.

After passing a night in the midst of such horrors as those described, with all that was loathsome and hideous around him, Moor, who was stretched near the door of the dungeon, was aroused by the entrance of a turnkey bearing a torch, which threw a lurid light over the dark walls, glistening with moisture, and over the haggard faces of the prisoners, some of whom were stretched on the ground, while others were in the act of rising. The turnkey was followed by two assistants, carrying large tin mess-kettles and cans, in which was the gaol allowance for the prisoners' breakfasts.

"I suppose it's no use asking if you're all here?" inquired the turnkey, gruffly.

"You'd better call the roll," observed a discarded drummer, who was awaiting his trial for robbery.

"He'd be like Glendower in the play, then," said Tom Booth, a player, under confinement for debt. "You may call rolls or loaves here till you're hoarse, but none will come."

"Friend, thou art lost in the vanity of plays and mummings," remarked a Quaker. "Eschew these snares of Satan, and I will show thee living bread."

"Better keep your bread for yourself, Broadbrim," cried the turnkey, "for you're likely to have a short allowance to-day. What do you say, Doctor Oates?"

His concluding words were addressed to a very singular-looking man, who on his entry, had risen from a litter of straw to his feet. He was of low stature and very ill-shaped, and had so short a neck that his head seemed to grow out of his body. His mouth was in the centre of his face, and a circle described with a compass from his lips, would include in its diameter his nose, forehead, and chin.

By the pretended discovery of a Popish plot in 1678, Titus Oates had for a time diffused among the Catholics, and even the stricter members of the Church of England, a universal feeling of terror. The son of an Anabaptist preacher, during the civil war he had been chaplain to the notorious Colonel Pride, the hero of the stratagem known as "Pride's Purge;" but he had conformed to the Church of England at the Restoration, and taken holy orders. As a reward for the discovery of the plot, he was assigned a lodging in Whitehall, and a pension of 1200*l.* per annum; and, by the direction of the House of Commons, he walked about with guards, lest he should be murdered by the Papists. He was called the saviour of the nation; and whoever he pointed at was taken up and committed. Although his revelations, when examined before the council, teemed with the most glaring blunders, the panic he had excited was so general, that no one dared to call attention to their absurdity. He spoke of Don Juan as having declared he would kill the king; and being asked what kind of man Don Juan was, he said that he was a tall black man. Charles II., who presided at the examination, on hearing the answer, laughed in his face, for he was personally acquainted with Don Juan, who was a short man, with red hair. The audacity of Oates was unbounded; and, during the heat of the plot, he even had the effrontery to appear at the bar of the House of Commons, in his canonicals, crying out in his peculiar vernacular, "Aye, Taitus Oates, accause Catherine, Queen of England, of haigh traison." Charles was so indignant at this insult, that he immediately put him in confinement; but was compelled by the clamours of the populace to set him at liberty. The careless monarch seems to have completely shaken off his usual inertness on this occasion. "They think," he said, "I have a mind to a new wife, but, for all that, I will not see an innocent woman abused." But though the queen was spared, an immense number of persons were condemned on the impeachments of Oates, and executed as traitors. The last victim was the unfortunate Stafford, who was beheaded on the 29th of December, 1680, in spite of the most powerful interposition in his favour. Five years afterwards, James II. ascended the throne, and Titus Oates was convicted of perjury. Ejected from his lodging in Whitehall, and deprived of his pension, he was sentenced to be imprisoned for life in Newgate, whence he was to be taken five times a year to the pillory, and then whipped through the streets from Newgate to Tyburn.

The miscreant laughed heartily at the observation of the turnkey.

"If he hays gaut sau mauch brayd, he con gayve me hays raytion," he said, in his broad accents. "This lawdging of yaurs is a fayne playce, mayster gaoler, and gayves me a hooge appetite."

"Friend, thou art in error," observed Fox: "it is written that 'man shall not live by bread alone;' and, verily, friend Barclay can tell thee of the true bread, which is free from the leaven of the world, even as the shewbread of the temple."

"Turn from lying and evil-speaking," cried Bunyan, "and fight the fiend within you, as Christian fought with the fiend Apollyon, in the Valley of Humiliation. Then shall your burden become light, and you shall find even this Slough of Despond like a fair and pleasant mountain."

"Daw yau da-are to prate to me, yau ra-anting dogs?" roared Oates. "Daw yau know aye awm Dauctor Taytus Oates, the sawviour of this nawtion?"

"Perjurer and murderer!" shouted a high-churchman, who had been committed for sedition.

"Stand to your text, doctor," laughed the turnkey. "You shall fight it out before you have any breakfast. Ho! a ring for the doctor!"

"The doctor 's a very Achilles in war," cried a Grub-street writer, recently convicted for libel. "He's like the saints in 'Hudibras,' who

'Prove their doctrine orthodox,
By apostolic blows and knocks.'"

"Let him play out his part," said Booth; and throwing himself into a theatrical attitude, he added,

"'Lay on, Macduff!
And d—d be he who first cries 'Hold! enough'"

"A ring! a ring!" cried several voices.

Obedient to this summons, the prisoners were grouping round the two disputants, when a tall, thin man, with long black hair streaming over his face, darted into the midst of them. The light of the torch fell full on his piercing eyes and meagre features, displaying a countenance marked with the sternest lines of fanaticism.

"Curse on you!" he screamed. "The words out of my mouth shall devour you, and smite you with everlasting fire."

Moor regarded the speaker with amazement.

"Is this a madman?" he asked of Baxter, who was sitting next to him.

"Either a madman or a blasphemer," answered Baxter. "It is Ludowick Muggleton."

Muggleton had not even the melancholy excuse for his blasphemy which Baxter was half-inclined to concede to him. Originally a tailor, he joined, in 1657, a brother craftsman named Reeves, in the more profitable vocation of a religious imposter. Reeves declared that they were the two last witnesses mentioned in Revelations, and that whoever opposed them in the spiritual and heavenly mission they were intrusted with, would be destroyed by the "fire," or curses that would "proceed out of their mouths." Reeves was to act the part of Moses, and Muggleton was to be his "mouth." Reeves affirmed, in his "New Testament," that our Lord had addressed him in these words: "I have given thee understanding of my mind in the Scriptures above all men in the world. I have chosen thee, my last messenger, for a great work unto this bloody, unbelieving world; and I have given thee Ludowick Muggleton to be thy mouth."

On the death of Reeves, Muggleton pretended to have a double portion of the spirit resting on him, and became very active in diffusing his tenets, which, attracting the notice of the authorities, at last led to his prosecution. He was tried at the Old Bailey on the 17th of January, 1677, and making no defence, was convicted of having published several blasphemous pamphlets, and sentenced to be placed three times in the pillory, and imprisoned till he could procure sureties for his future good behaviour.

Muggleton's address elicited a burst of laughter from his auditors.

"Thou shouldst not curse at all, friend," remarked Fox. "Cease to do evil, learn to do well, and the Lord shall deliver thee out of the hands of Pharaoh, and out of the house of bondage. But I speak unto ye all, as Jeremiah spake unto the Hebrews: 'They hearkened not unto me, nor inclined their ear, but hardened their neck: they did worse than their fathers. Therefore thou shalt speak all these words unto them, but they will not hearken unto thee: thou shalt also call unto them, but they will not answer thee.' "

"I'll answer for one," cried the drummer, in a snuffling voice.

Another loud laugh broke from the audience. Before it subsided, the door of the dungeon was again opened, and Elkanah Snewin presented himself at it. He was somewhat better habited than usual, having encased his sturdy person in a coat of quilted orange-coloured cloth, and his lower limbs in a pair of buff boots ascending above the knee, while a hanger was girded to his side.

"Turn up Charles Moor," cried the constable, "I've got a warrant to take him before the Privy Council."

Moor was immediately called by the turnkey, and taking a hasty leave of Baxter, the young man was consigned to the custody of Snewin. The latter received him with a grin of triumph; and hurrying him into a coach at the prison-door, conveyed him to Whitehall.

CHAPTER VII.

THE QUEEN CONSORT.

Mary of Modena's charms had been long a favourite theme with the poets of the age. She was now in the meridian of her beauty; and fully merited the praises so lavishly bestowed upon her. Still her lovely countenance was

> Sicklied o'er with the pale hue of thought,

as, indeed, had too often been the case since her consort's accession to the throne. Her luxuriant hair was turned up from the forehead in a sort of pile, or high top-knot, but fell in ringlets over the temples, where its jetty hue contrasted admirably with the marble paleness of her complexion, while it was in keeping with her dark lustrous eyes, celebrated by Lord Lansdown in one of his poetical epistles as—

> Those charming eyes, which shine to reconcile
> To harmony and peace our stubborn isle.

Descended from the illustrious house of Este, Mary had, early n life, on the death of her father, Alphonso IV., Duke of Modena, been adopted by Louis XIV., who settled on her a marriage-portion of two hundred thousand pounds. When in her fifteenth year, she was married at Modena to James, then Duke of York—Henry Mordaunt, Earl of Peterborough, being proxy for the duke, and afterwards conducting her to England. As Mary was a Catholic, the marriage was very unpopular at the time; but her agreeable manners, the innocence and goodness of her nature, and her obliging and unassuming deportment, soon overcame the prejudices raised against her by her religion, and moved even the sectarian Marvel to exclaim—

> Poor princess! born beneath a sullen star,
> To find such welcome when you came from far!
> Better some jealous neighbour of your own
> Had called you to a sound though petty throne.*

Her graceful behaviour, however, could not conciliate the ill-will of her adversaries; and Burnet relates that, "so artfully did the young Italian behave herself, that she deceived even the oldest and most jealous persons, both in the court and country: only sometimes a satirical temper broke out too much, which was imputed to youth and wit, not enough practised in the world." Yet this young princess—so lovely, so inexperienced, and so friendless—brought almost a child into the giddy vortex of a profligate court, was, as the bishop admits, "universally esteemed and beloved," and while her husband was continually engaging in some low intrigue, devoted herself patiently to the fulfilment of her duties as a wife. When James was sent as a kind of exile into Scotland, in 1679, he himself testifies to her exemplary conduct; for, though pressed by Charles II. to remain at court, "she chose rather," James says, "even with the hazard of her life, to be a constant companion of the duke, her husband's, misfortunes and hardships, than to enjoy her ease in any part of the world without him."

Though her influence over her husband had daily increased, Mary did not interfere in public affairs till after her elevation to the throne; and since that event, though she had been more than ever surrounded by ghostly counsellors, and though her interest and inclination alike prompted her to leave no means untried to re-establish popery in England, she had almost uniformly raised her voice in favour of moderate measures. This line of conduct subjected her to frequent reproof from the priests, and especially from Father Petre, who, with the subtle craft of his order, worked so effectually on her deep feelings of religion, that he won her support for proceedings otherwise obnoxious to her.

In a chamber at Whitehall sat Mary near a small table of

* Advice to a Painter.

massive oak, richly carved and polished, with her favourite attendant, Anna Montecuculi, a beautiful but artful Italian, standing beside her. Anna was the daughter of the well-known imperial general, and having been brought up from infancy with the queen, possessed great influence over her. But at this moment Mary scarcely seemed aware of her proximity. She was leaning over an open missal emblazoned with the illuminations of the previous century; but her eye wandered from her book to the wall, where hung gems of Titian and Murillo, with some sacred pieces of Bassano, or rested a moment on a neighbouring oriel window, encircled with the carving of Gibbons, and where a devotional stool, a small shrine, and a crucifix might be discerned. A rich Turkey carpet covered the centre of the floor; a chess-board lay neglected on the table; several Indian screens and tall China jars were dispersed round the room; and on one side glittered an exquisite cabinet of filagree silver.

Mary had been sitting thus for some time, when the chamber-door was opened by a page.

"The Earl of Sunderland is in the ante-chamber," he said, with an obeisance, "and requests an audience of your majesty."

Mary hesitated. As she was about to speak, Anna came behind her chair, and Mary looked up.

"I must tell his lordship my decision," she said to Anna, in a low voice; "Father Petre cannot object to that. No, no, I must see him."

Anna bowed; but, though affecting resignation, she did not appear satisfied.

"Admit his lordship," said Mary to the page.

With another profound obeisance, the page withdrew, and immediately afterwards returned, ushering in Sunderland.

Mary received the minister very graciously, and motioning Anna to the further end of the room, invited him to be seated.

"My business will not engage your majesty long," said Sunderland. "I have well considered the scheme of toleration I proposed to you, and an event has just occurred, which will give its immediate promulgation great popularity. May I hope that your majesty's intention to support me is unchanged?"

"Would I could see my way clearly in it!" rejoined Mary, anxiously. "I desire, sincerely, to act for the best; but so much is said on both sides, that I am quite distracted."

"I almost ventured to hope that you had by this time secured the king's approbation to the measure," said Sunderland.

"I should have done so," said Mary; "but Father Petre represents the project as prejudicial. He affirms that it will give the appearance of weakness to our cause, while at the same time it will foster heresy."

"The holy father's zeal makes him unwilling to arrest persecution, even when administered by a rival priesthood," observed Sunderland, in a sarcastic tone. "This measure would create dissension among our adversaries, and, consequently, could not argue weakness in us: neither can it be thought to foster heresy, for the Papists will share the general indulgence."

"Ah!—how gladly would I purchase toleration for them," cried Mary.

"I have been at great pains to conciliate opinions on the subject," pursued Sunderland, "and, depending on your majesty's support, anticipated success. In that case you would have been the happy means of opening the doors of the dungeons, and would have carried joy into a thousand families. Such is the scheme you have been persuaded to abandon."

Mary was silent; but her pensive look, and restless gaze, now turned on Sunderland, now on vacancy, marked the trouble within.

"It is very sad to think that these people should be treated so harshly, my lord," she said at length; "I could almost weep when I reflect upon what they have to endure. But why do they persist in their heresy? They are as cruel to us in provoking persecution, as we are to them in inflicting it."

"Your majesty must consider that I also am a heretic," said Sunderland, "and, by a parity of reasoning, ought to be persecuted too."

Mary smiled; but her smile was sad and faint.

"I would you were *not* a heretic, my lord," she observed; "but, indeed, what you say makes me lament that I did not broach the subject to the king."

"It is not yet too late, madam," answered Sunderland. "The council has not met, and your assurance to his majesty that you have well considered the measure, and approve it, will be sufficient to win his assent. We may not have such a golden opportunity as this again."

"Alas! it is too late," exclaimed Mary, "the king is closeted with Father Petre."

She paused a moment; but presently resumed, just as Sunderland was rising—

"Stay, my lord. You can tell the king the scheme has my support; and, as Father Petre is under the impression that I oppose it, here is my signet-ring as a pledge to his majesty of your sincerity."

With a profound obeisance Sunderland took the ring, and

dropping on his knee, Mary extended him her hand, which he raised to his lips.

"Heaven guard your majesty," he said.

Anna, who could scarcely conceal the rage and disappointment with which Sunderland's success filled her, touched a bell; the page without opened the door, and with another courtly bow the earl passed into the ante-chamber. Thence he made his way through several intervening rooms and galleries, past a scattered line of pages, ushers, and marshals, towards the council-chamber, in the ante-room of which the thoughts he had been turning in his mind shaped themselves into the following words:—

"The ring will hardly effect it alone, but it is not my only resource. I shall perplex Nottingham, madden Halifax, and liberate from prison six thousand Dissenters. The letter, too, may yet answer a purpose."

Thus musing, he approached a door, which an usher who was in waiting, threw open for him, as he did an inner folding-door, covered with crimson cloth, admitting the earl to the council-chamber.

CHAPTER VIII.

THE PRIVY COUNCIL.

SEVERAL of the ministers had already assembled in the room when Sunderland made his appearance, each of whom he saluted with a bow or a word of recognition. The chamber was prepared for the approaching consultation. In the centre was a long table covered with a scarlet cloth, on which were placed at regular intervals, silver inkstands, pens, and portfolios. High-backed chairs were ranged around the table, and a chair of state, surmounted on the back by a crown, stood at its head. The walls were covered with tapestry, on which the royal arms were woven. Lords Middleton, Melfort, Dartmouth, and Godolphin, were standing together conversing in whispers; old Lord Bellasis was leaning against the back of a chair, arranging his spectacles with one hand, while the other grasped the last number of Sir Roger L'Estrange's new journal called the *Observator;* and Lord Preston was talking in a low voice to the Lord Chancellor Jeffreys.

As the atrocious severities of the latter have been recorded, it is doing him no more than justice, to give equal prominence to such particulars of his life, as represent him in a more amiable light. His nature, though cruel, was not destitute of redeeming qualities, and these were displayed on more than one occasion.

While as yet needy and unknown, attending the assizes at Kingston, in 1666, Jeffreys made clandestine advances to the daughter of a wealthy merchant, in which he was assisted by a friend, who was the young lady's governess. The affair was discovered, and the confidante turned out of doors. Hearing of her dismissal, Jeffreys went to see her, took pity on her situation, and married her. He always treated her with the greatest affection, and she lived to see him Lord Chief Justice of England. During the time he held this office, he signalised himself by a very remarkable action. The mayor and aldermen of Bristol had been accustomed to sentence the various delinquents brought before them, in their magisterial capacity, to transportation for life, and then to sell them, for their own profit, to the West Indian planters. Jeffreys, while engaged on the Western circuit, heard of this abuse, and repairing to Bristol, ordered the mayor to descend from the bench on which he was sitting, in his scarlet robes and fur, to the felons' dock, and there to plead as a common criminal. He then made him and the aldermen enter into heavy securities to answer any informations laid against them; and, by his threats and reproaches, so terrified the offenders, that the infamous traffic was discontinued. Nor was he always deaf to admonition himself. At a later period of life, when lord chancellor, he was once sent by the court to influence a contested election at Arundel, in Sussex, and was directed to spare no exertion to secure the return to parliament of the court candidate. In order to intimidate the electors, he placed himself on the hustings, by the side of the mayor, who was the returning officer, and who, though he well knew Jeffreys, pretended to be ignorant of his person and rank. In the course of the poll, one of the court party tendered a fictitious vote, and the mayor rejected it, which so irritated Jeffreys, that rising in a passion, he insisted that the vote should be recorded, adding, "I am the lord chancellor of this realm." The mayor regarding him with a look of contempt, replied, "Were you really the lord chancellor, you would know you have nothing to do here," and turning to the crier, he added, "Officer, turn this fellow out." The crier seized Jeffreys by the arm, and, in spite of his remonstrances, fulfilled the mayor's commands. In the evening, the mayor was surprised by a message from Jeffreys desiring the favour of his company at his inn, but doubtful of the chancellor's motives, he declined the invitation. Jeffreys then went to his house, and said to him, "Sir, I cannot help revering one who so well knows the law, and dares so nobly execute it, and, though I myself was somewhat degraded thereby you did but your duty. You, as I have learned, are independent, but you may have some relation who is not so well provided for. If you have, let me have the pleasure of presenting him with a considerable place in my gift, just now vacant." So handsome and ample an apology excited the admiration of the mayor, who, having a nephew in straitened circumstances, mentioned the matter to Jeffreys, and he immediately appointed the young man to the vacant situation.

Sunderland addressed himself to Lord Preston, the secretary of state.

"You received my letter, my lord, I suppose, respecting the prisoner taken by Colonel Kirke last night?" he said.

"Yes," answered Preston, "and, according to your instructions, I instantly issued an order to bring him before the council this morning, together with the constable who apprehended him. They are now in attendance in the guard-room."

"Lord Preston and I have been talking over the matter, my lord," observed Jeffreys; "it seems that Colonel Kirke in his report accuses this young man of being an emissary of the Prince of Orange."

"So I understand," answered Sunderland, with an incredulous smile; "and therefore I think it right to have the matter thoroughly investigated. It will pave the way for our declaration of indulgence to the Dissenters."

"Admirably," concurred Preston.

"You do not intend to propose the declaration to-day, eh, my lord?" asked Jeffreys.

"Indeed but I do," returned Sunderland, "and if you and Preston support me I will carry it. Have you brought with you the written opinion of the judges?"

"It is here," answered Jeffreys, pointing to his portfolio. "Have you secured her majesty and the *corps diplomatique?*"

As he awaited a reply, the folding-door was thrown open, and two personages entered the room, at whose appearance the whole of the ministers arose, and bowing to the foremost of them moved towards the table. The new comers were James II. and Father Petre.

James II. was now in his fifty-sixth year, but his form was unbent, and, indeed, formally erect. He was somewhat above the middle height; his person had a commanding appearance; and his limbs were muscular and well proportioned. His complexion was fair, and though marked with the small pox, his countenance was pleasing, bearing so strong a resemblance to that of his father, that if he had only worn the pointed beard of the latter, it might have almost passed for the same. In its mild and engaging expression, one would have looked in vain for some trace of that spirit which, since his accession to the crown, had so often urged him to misrule, alienating from his service some of the warmest of his friends and the most faithful of his subjects. But it was still admitted by all that he truly loved his country. No monarch, indeed, since the days of Alfred, ever had the honour and glory of England more sincerely at heart. Reclaimed from his vicious excesses, he devoted almost all his time to public affairs, daily transacting a prodigious amount of business, correcting the abuses of the various departments of the state, promoting the improvement of the marine, encouraging trade, and carefully husbanding the public money. Weak in judgment, he yet possessed sufficient capacity to work out successfully the most elaborate schemes of others: bigoted in religion, his piety was at least sincere. If his rule was stern and unrelenting, he was arbitrary on principle, mistaking violence for vigour; and, though a vindictive enemy, he was a warm and steadfast friend.

Father Petre wore the sombre dress of his order. He was a dark, austere-looking man, with large bushy eyebrows, and his shaven crown well became his cadaverous countenance.

Originally only confessor to James, Father Petre had lately been appointed dean of his private chapel, and was now in constant attendance on the royal person. He was daily rising in the king's favour, and acquiring a larger share of confidence; and he could thus canvas with James privately the designs of Sunderland, whom he regarded as a rival, and whom he seized every occasion to oppose. Crafty, subtle, and ambitious, and versed in all the learning, the art, and the sophistry of his order, Father Petre was yet miserably deficient in practical knowledge of the English people; and, by his undisguised hostility to the Established Church, had raised in array against him all their religious prejudices. While, however, he was even criminally rash in his efforts to subvert the church, and re-establish popery, he secretly leagued with the French ambassador against the pope, with whom, in common with the whole order of Jesuits, he was avowedly at variance. He had, indeed, personal reasons for enmity to Innocent XI.,—that spirited pontiff having refused, even at the earnest solicitation of James, to create him a titular bishop, alleging as his reason that Jesuits were prohibited from accepting a bishopric, and that he would sooner make a Jesuit a cardinal than a bishop. James then requested the pope to create his favourite a cardinal, but this also was refused; and to mark his regard for Petre, whom his interest could not advance in the church, James had appointed him a member of the privy council.

Bowing to the assemblage, James proceeded to the chair of

state, and then desiring the ministers to be seated, Sunderland, in obedience to a gesture from the king, opened the business of the day.

"It is my duty to request your majesty's first attention to what appears a mysterious affair," he said. "Yesterday there was a meeting of Dissenters on Finchley Common, which was dispersed by Colonel Kirke, who arrested the ringleaders, and with them, a young man, named Moor, a *protégé* of the earl of Nottingham, and whom the colonel's report alleges to be an agent of the Prince of Orange."

James uttered an exclamation of anger.

"I have ordered the delinquent to be held in attendance in the guard-room," pursued Sunderland, "as I thought it likely your majesty might wish to examine him."

"You did right," answered James, quickly. "We may possibly trace the treason from the *protégé* to the patron, and if so, I will make a terrible example of Nottingham. Let the prisoner be brought in."

The usher in waiting left the room, and presently returned, accompanied by Moor and Snewin.

Moor looked pale and anxious, though his concern arose less for himself than for his patron; but he assumed a more composed aspect as he met the glance of James, who eyed him inquisitively, and with an evident disposition to prejudge him. Snewin, duly impressed with the importance of his position, bowed to the ground before the monarch.

"So, sir," said James to Moor, "are you aware why you are brought here?"

"I believe I am accused of treason," replied the young man. "If so, the charge is false. Your majesty has not a more loyal subject than myself."

"A fair speech, sir, but words are no proof of loyalty," rejoined James. "You are said to be a secret emissary of the Prince of Orange."

"I am calumniated," returned Moor, firmly. "I have neither seen the Prince of Orange, nor held any communication with him."

"How, sir?" cried James; but checking himself, he added, in a lower tone, to Sunderland, "have I misunderstood you?"

"Not at all, your majesty," replied Sunderland, "but the constable may have made a mistake. State briefly, sir, why you apprehended this young man," he added to Snewin.

"Please your majesty," said the constable, "I heerd yesterday as 'ow Colonel Sidney was to be at an inn in Cecil-street, to meet a gen'l'man there, and I posted off directly to arrest him. The Colonel got off; but I found this young blade in the house, and

I warn't blind, so when I finds him afterwards with the psalm-singers on Finchley Common, I just lays my hand on him, when out drops a letter from his pocket, and, snatchin' it up, I finds it sealed with the Prince of Orange's signet."

"Produce that letter, quickly, sirrah!" cried James.

"I'll just present it to your majesty," answered Snewin, with a profound bow.

With this he thrust his hand into his coat, but he did not apparently find what he wanted, and after fumbling a while in the pocket, he drew forth his hand and dived both hands into the outer pockets of his coat, but with equal ill-success.

"Quick, the letter!" cried James.

"I ain't a-got it, your majesty," stammered Snewin.

"Ha!" exclaimed James. "Is it lost?"

"More likely stolen, your majesty," observed Father Petre, in a soft tone. "At what time did you meet Colonel Sidney, yesterday?" he inquired.

"Your reverence, I see, adopts the story of the constable,' replied Moor, evasively. "I am wholly innocent of the offence imputed to me."

"There is no evidence that the young man has been in communication with Sidney," observed Jeffreys to Petre. "His majesty wishes him, I believe, to explain how the letter the constable mentions came into his possession. What have you to say about this letter, sir?" he added, before Petre could speak.

"It was brought to me at my inn, in Cecil-street, my lord," answered Moor, "by a gentleman styling himself Captain Ferdinando Gonzalez, and who desired me to convey it to Lord Nottingham, at Burleigh. This is all I can tell your majesty about it."

"The explanation is satisfactory," said Sunderland to James. "Captain Gonzalez is a person of note, and has been mentioned favourably to me by the Spanish ambassador."

Father Petre was still dissatisfied, but the other members of the council concurred with Sunderland; and James, who was unsuspicious to a fault, confiding even in avowed malcontents, was easily persuaded into the same opinion.

"You have explained away the charge brought against you, young gentleman," he said to Moor, with an affability which no one could more gracefully assume, "and are now free to depart."

"I should be proud to enjoy an opportunity of proving to your majesty that I am incapable of disloyalty," said Moor. And bowing, he withdrew.

"Who is this young man?" asked James, when he had retired.

"The new aspirant to the Mauvesin peerage, sire—the famous

child of mystery!" replied Sunderland, with a smile. "I am quite interested in him myself, and must try and do something for him. But I have now to call your majesty's attention to this meeting on Finchley Common. If some steps are not taken to prevent it, it will lead to the union of the Dissenters and the Church party. They must be kept asunder, and I have framed a declaration of indulgence to the Dissenters, which will effect that object. It has the approbation of the Lord Chancellor, and of the judges, who have drawn up a written opinion in its favour. With your majesty's permission, I will read it to you."

James assented; and Sunderland, opening a portfolio, drew forth a document, which he proceeded to read aloud.

It was the memorable declaration of indulgence to the Dissenters. The preamble set forth that "We have thought fit, by virtue of our royal prerogative, to issue forth this our declaration of indulgence, making no doubt of the concurrence of our two houses of parliament, when we shall think it convenient for them to meet." It then asserted the inalienable right of all men to worship their Maker according to the dictates of their own conscience. The king claimed this right for those of his subjects who dissented from the communion of the Established Church. He suspended all acts which restrained the freedom of worship; he cancelled those which disqualified any of his subjects from holding public employments; he liberated from prison all persons confined for religious opinions, nearly seven thousand in number; and, as a crowning act of clemency, he authorised all sects of Dissenters to meet openly for worship wherever and whenever they pleased.

A scheme of toleration so noble and comprehensive was far in advance of the prejudices of the age, and Sunderland was prepared, when he had finished reading it, for the exclamations of dissent which broke from several of his colleagues.

"We shall have the Church in arms," cried the earl of Middleton.

"The Church preaches non-resistance," said Lord Preston, "and therefore will not resort to arms."

"Do not suppose it will practise what it preaches," observed Lord Dartmouth. "Poor Doctor Marley, the late Bishop of Winchester, sent for me on his death-bed to warn his majesty by me, almost with his last breath, that if an occasion arose, the Church would belie her preaching."

"I will never agree to this measure," said Lord Bellasis. "It is an infringement of the constitution."

"Then, you know the law better than I do, my lord," remarked Jeffreys, in the heated manner habitual to him. "But

I am unwilling to believe it, when I am supported in my opinion by the whole of the judicial bench."

"It would make England a hot-bed of heresy," said Father Petre in an under tone to James. "It will blast for ever your majesty's pious hope of converting the country, and mar all our past labours."

James looked grave and thoughtful. His natural good sense comprehended the aim of the measure, and inclined him to assent to it. On the other hand, his bigotry, aroused by the insinuations of Father Petre, was instinctively adverse to so bold and sweeping a toleration of the heretical Dissenters.

"I fear it would strengthen our adversaries, instead of weakening them," he said, at length; "and would have the evil effect of encouraging dissent."

"Persecution will encourage dissent, your majesty," observed Sunderland, "while toleration will render it insignificant. This measure has the approbation of Count d'Adda, and no one can suspect the pope's nuncio of partiality for the Dissenters."

"But we may doubt his capacity to form an opinion," said Father Petre, quickly. "I am sure M. Barillon would not approve of it; neither would Don Pedro Ronquillo, the Spanish ambassador."

"I am anxious that they should have an opportunity of expressing their sentiments upon it," replied Sunderland; "and as I imagined it might be agreeable to his majesty, I have requested them to be in attendance. Does your majesty wish to consult them?"

"Let them be summoned," returned James. "They will not, I imagine, give you their suffrages."

The usher in waiting was sent to require the attendance of the three ambassadors, who, pursuant to an arrangement with Sunderland, were closeted in a neighbouring room, impatiently awaiting the summons. The council were still discussing the merits of the minister's scheme, when they were introduced.

Count d'Adda was a tall and very stout man, whose tonsure and sober garments marked his priestly profession. Don Pedro Ronquillo was of the middle size, well-made, and having a handsome, though rather sharp countenance, and quick black eyes; he was attired very gorgeously, always supporting a magnificent appearance, although, as his salary as ambassador was greatly in arrear, and he had quite exhausted his credit, no one could ever conjecture whence he derived his resources. Barillon was the last of the party.

James received them with a gracious salutation.

"So you have become a favourer of heretics, count?" he said to the nuncio.

"Your majesty refers to Lord Sunderland's concessions to them," answered Count d'Adda. "I do not sanction them for their own sake, but for the good they may work to you."

"Which is unquestionable," observed Don Pedro Ronquillo; "and, therefore, I humbly recommend your majesty to yield to the advice of your minister."

"In Spain, sir, I believe, the king is guided by the counsel of his confessor," replied James, sharply.

"Yes sire," said Ronquillo, "and that is the reason why our affairs succeed so ill."

James coloured at the retort.

"You forget what is due to the ministers of your religion, sir, as well as to his majesty," observed Father Petre. "But M. Barillon, I know, will not raise his voice in favour of heresy."

"I may see objections to these concessions, as well as your reverence," answered Barillon; "but, on the whole, I think them advantageous to his majesty's service, and consequently recommend their adoption."

"The queen, at least, will oppose them," said Father Petre, sullenly; "and his majesty will respect her pious scruples."

"I will be guided in my decision by hers," said James, hoping by this means to get out of the dilemma in which he felt himself placed.

"Then, I am authorised to inform your majesty of the queen's unqualified approbation of the project," said Sunderland; "in proof of which she has sent you this token."

So saying, he tendered the signet-ring to James, who received it with surprise, and cast a look of disquietude at his confessor. The latter, though secretly disconcerted, was too much an adept in dissimulation not to conceal his annoyance.

"I cannot resist such able pleading," said James, after a moment's pause; "but I fear we shall not achieve our object. The fragment of the True Cross, found in Saint Edward the Confessor's coffin, fell from my hands this morning—an augury, no doubt, of ill. Our Blessed Lady grant, as my intentions are good, that the decision I have formed may be for the advantage of our holy church, and the weal of the realm. Give me the declaration."

The important document was placed before him, and, receiving the royal signature, became a law of the land.

CHAPTER IX.

THE ENTERTAINMENT AT WHITEHALL.

The magnificent reception rooms at Whitehall were thrown open for a grand concert and ball. The principal saloon, described by Evelyn, as "that glorious gallery," blazed with light, streaming from numerous chandeliers, and reflected by superb mirrors. Hung with the choicest paintings, the walls exhibited the fairy tracery of Gibbons in their panelled oak; the ceiling glowed with gorgeous frescoes by Verrio; and statues and busts, in bronze and marble, of rarest workmanship, were placed on pedestals around.

The saloon was thronged with court beauties, sparkling with jewels, and gallants, in their richest apparel. Near the centre, at a round table, was collected a noisy party, consisting of the Dukes of Berwick, Grafton, and Northumberland, together with Lord Waldegrave, engaged at basset. The lower end of the room was fitted up with an orchestra, and amongst the musicians were the celebrated harpsichordist, Baptist, and the amiable and gifted Purcell; while Pordage, Gosling, and Mrs. Parker, stood on a platform above, awaiting the royal command to commence the concert. In front of the orchestra were grouped many wits and poets of the day, numbering among them Dryden, Evelyn, Lansdowne, and St. Evremond; and not far from them stood the philosopher Boyle, conversing with Sir Christopher Wren.

Divided from the rest of the hall by a silken cord, the upper end of the saloon was set apart for the queen and her more favoured guests. On one side stood James, in close conference with Father Petre; and in the centre, on a fauteuil, placed on a dais, sat Mary chatting with Catherine of Braganza, the queen-dowager.

Daughter of the celebrated Duke of Braganza, who was placed on the throne of Portugal by a revolution, in 1641, when he assumed the title of Dom Juan IV., Catherine was brought up, according to the custom of her country, in a convent, where she early acquired that zealous attachment to the Church of Rome which she maintained till the close of life. When little beyond her twenty-first year, she became the wife of Charles II., who received with her, as a dowry, the fortress of Tangier in Africa, the island of Bombay in the East Indies, and money and merchandise to the amount of half a million. On her arrival England, Catherine, in the first instance, made a favoural impression on the inconstant monarch, and in a confident letter to Lord Clarendon, written on the day of his marriage, thus describes her :—"Her face is not so exact as to be callec beauty, though her eyes are excellent good, and not any thing her face that in the least degree can shock me. On the contra she has as much agreeableness in her looks altogether as e'er I sa and if I have any skill in physiognomy, which I think I ha she must be as good a woman as ever was born. In a word think myself very happy, and I am confident our humours w agree very well together." Unfortunately for both, this antici tion was not realised; but it is due to Catherine to say that t blame did not rest with her.

Catherine brought with her from Lisbon a bevy of Portugue attendants, described by Grammont as "six frights, who call themselves maids of honour, and a duenna—another monst who took the title of governess to those extraordinary beautie and like the French domestics of Henrietta Maria, these ladi soon caused such confusion in the court, that Charles was oblig to send the whole cargo back to Portugal. In the list of perso appointed to succeed them, he had the effrontery to include t name of his favourite, Lady Castlemaine. Catherine instant drew her pen across it, and when Charles insisted on its bei retained, she replied that she would "return to her own count rather than be forced to submit to such an indignity." Persi ing in his purpose, the king shortly afterwards caused Lady C tlemaine to be presented at court, and hearing her name ind tinctly, Catherine at first gave her a gracious reception, but t next moment, being informed she was Lady Castlemaine, t insulted queen started from her chair, alternately becomi pale as ashes and red with shame and anger, when the blo gushed from her nose, and she was carried from the room a fit.

Becoming enamoured of La Belle Stewart, Charles was desiro of obtaining a divorce, when Buckingham, to facilitate his vie offered to carry off the queen to the Plantations. Charl rejected the proposal with horror, saying, "It was a wick thing to make a poor lady so miserable, only because she was l wife;" and from that moment the project of a divorce w abandoned.

"The Duke of Northumberland seems indifferent to pub opinion," Catherine observed, as she glanced at the basset-tab "He is as noisy as his brother Grafton."

"Yet I almost fear he is really married to this unfortuna young woman," answered Mary.

"The handsome Northumberland wedded to a poulterer's daughter!" exclaimed Catherine. "Impossible!"

"No, not impossible. The affair has been so adroitly managed, that his majesty cannot ascertain the precise truth," rejoined Mary; "but it is believed that Grafton has carried off the young woman to Ghent, and placed her in a convent."

"Grafton is a dangerous enemy," observed Catherine. "You recollect his two desperate duels, when quite a youth, and as a man, his fiery temper is unchanged."

"He leads a wild life," replied Mary, "and is as reckless in speech as in conduct. This morning only, the king rebuked him for his profligacy, urging him to atone for his errors by embracing our holy religion, and he replied, that he could not change his religion, for, though he had no conscience himself, he belonged to a party who had."

"He inherits the insolence of his mother," returned Catherine, calling to mind the many insults she had received from the Duchess of Cleveland. "Never shall I forget the day when Charles proposed to me to accord a public reception to that abandoned woman. Had it not been for the consolation of Lord Mauvesin, who stood by me at the time, and supported me by his counsel, I believe my heart would have broken."

"Poor queen!" sighed Mary. "It must have been a severe trial to you."

"But, see! here is the Count de Lauzun," cried Catherine, glad to change the topic. "Who is the lovely creature with him?"

Mary turned quickly, with a look of interest, towards the persons indicated, and perceived the Count de Lauzun approaching, accompanied by a young lady of extraordinary personal attraction.

Antoine Nompar de Caumont, Count de Lauzun, is described by the Duke of Berwick as the model of a courtier—noble, munificent, and sumptuous in his mode of living; addicted to high play, but always playing like a gentleman. The duke adds: "His person was so diminutive, that it was impossible to conceive how he had ever been a favourite with the ladies." Bussy Rabutin, who probably had received some affront from him, says: "*Lauzun est un des plus petits hommes, pour l'esprit aussi bien que pour le corps, que Dieu ait jamais fait.*" Saint Simon speaks of him as a small, fair-haired man, well-made in person, and having a lofty and imposing countenance: sad, solitary, and stern in disposition; very noble in his actions; extremely brave, and sometimes dangerously daring; haughty, insolent, and imperious; full of resources, industry, and intrigue; a good friend and a willing enemy.

Lauzun was a member of the illustrious house of Grammo and early in life had become the favourite of Louis XIV., a the accepted lover of that monarch's cousin, the Princess Montpensier. Loaded with royal favours, he treated the king return with the greatest haughtiness; and when Louis co sented to his marriage with the Princess of Montpensier, insisted that it should be celebrated with the honours used the espousals of the royal family. In the meantime the princ married him privately, and bore him a daughter, whom it w supposed he had sent to England. Louis, on consulting wi the princes of the blood, refused to have the marriage sole nised in the manner desired, when Lauzun charged him with f feiting his word, and, plucking forth his sword, broke it, telli the king that he did not deserve to have it drawn in his servi Having heard him to an end, Louis threw his own cane out the window, adding that, "it would cause him bitter regret strike a gentleman." Lauzun was imprisoned in Pignerol, ar bent upon escaping, worked his way through the strong walls the castle, when he was discovered on the outside by a sentin and carried back to his dungeon. At length the Princess Montpensier bribed the Duke of Mayenne with the principali of Dombes, to obtain his release, though Madame de Montesp and Luvois, dreading his influence over the king, if he shou return to court, stipulated that he should be banished to Englar He was persuaded to accede to this condition, and, repairing London, soon became a favourite at the English court, where commenced what Madame de Sévigné wittily calls "*Le seco tome de Lauzun.*"

The Count de Lauzun and his lovely companion, who was exquisitely attired as she was beautiful and graceful in persc advanced towards the queen.

"I come as a suitor to your majesty," said Lauzun, with profound obeisance.

"You can ask nothing I will not readily grant," answer Mary, with a gracious smile.

"Permit me, then, to present to your majesty Mademoise Saint Leu," rejoined Lauzun, bringing forward Sabine, ' young lady in whom I take a deep interest."

"She is welcome, both on her own account and on you Count," said Mary.

So saying, she extended her hand to Sabine, who, bendi before her, raised it to her lips. After a few expressions encouragement, intended to dissipate the embarrassme which was naturally felt by the young lady in her novel sitı tion, Mary turned to Lauzun, while Catherine kindly address herself to Sabine.

"You say you feel interested in this young lady, Count," observed Mary, in a low tone.

"I do, gracious madam," replied Lauzun, "and on some other occasion, when fewer eyes are regarding us, and fewer ears are listening, I will tell you why I feel so interested."

"What you have already said is enough, Count," rejoined the queen. "If you desire it, I will place her near my own person."

"You will confer an everlasting favour upon me, madam," said Lauzun, placing his hand gratefully and devotedly upon his heart.

Meantime another presentation had taken place. It was that of Charles Moor, who was introduced to the king by the Earl of Sunderland, as his newly-appointed secretary. James could not forbear a smile on seeing the young man, but Father Petre regarded him with a frown.

At this moment, Catherine chanced to turn round, and remarking Moor, exclaimed involuntarily aloud, "How like Lord Mauvesin!"

"Did your majesty remark that exclamation?" observed Sunderland. "It is a confirmation of the young man's parentage."

"Ay, but not of his legitimacy," observed Father Petre.

Mauvesin was loitering near the royal circle, and, hearing his own name pronounced, fancied the queen dowager had addressed him.

"Did your majesty speak to me?" he asked.

"No, my lord," replied Catherine. "Is that young gentleman your brother?" she added.

"No, madam," he replied, in confusion; "he is no relation of mine."

"He would not disgrace you, for he has a high and noble air," said Catherine. "I pray you, sir," she added to the usher in attendance, "bid Lord Sunderland present his friend to me."

Mauvesin turned away, and at the same moment Moor was brought forward and presented to the queen dowager by Sunderland.

A gracious reception awaited him, and the pleasure he experienced in the kindness of Catherine was not lessened by the presence of Sabine.

As Mauvesin moved off with a heart full of bitterness, he felt himself touched on the arm, and turning, beheld Father Petre.

"I read what is passing in your breast, my lord," said the latter, in a low tone; "you have found a serpent in your path, and would crush it."

"I would," replied Mauvesin, with concentrated rage.

"It is easily done," said the Jesuit in a low tone, and with a significant smile.

"Show me how," said Mauvesin, "and claim from me aught you please in return."

"Step this way, then," said the Jesuit.

"They are plotting some villany against Charles Moor," said Saint Leu, who had stood unnoticed within ear-shot of them; "I'll follow and ascertain what it is."

And he plunged into the crowd after the confessor and the nobleman, who made their way towards an ante-chamber.

An eloquent interchange of glances took place between Moor and Sabine. They were not unnoticed by Lauzun, who, looking up at the young gentleman's presentation to the queen dowager, appeared by no means satisfied with what he beheld.

"I did not expect this young man here," he muttered. "I have a further request to prefer to your majesty," he added in a low tone to the queen.

"Name it," said Mary.

"It is that you will prevent all intercourse between Sabine and that young man," he rejoined, in the same low tone as before.

"If you wish it, assuredly, count," returned the queen; "but who is he?"

"A pretender, whom I do not wish to encourage," said Lauzun. "By heaven!" he added, quickly, "they are exchanging love passages. I must interpose."

But ere he could do so, the king approached, and motioning Lauzun, took him aside, to the infinite annoyance of the latter, who cast an imploring look at the queen. His situation, however, seemed so droll to Mary, that she could not help smiling at it.

"This must not go too far, however," she said, at length, "or Lauzun may justly blame me."

But moments are ages in the lives of lovers, and the few words that passed between Sabine and Moor, though light in themselves, and apparently unimportant, assisted as they were by the eloquence of the eyes, had sufficed to awaken a tender interest in either bosom which no interruption could check, and indeed only tended to increase.

As Mary looked round, the queen dowager took occasion to present Moor to her, and the amiable sovereign was so pleased with his singularly prepossessing air, that she could not help mentally exclaiming,

"Lauzun must do this young man an injustice. He is too modest to pretend to aught above him."

Sunderland, who stood by, and remarked the favourable impression produced by Moor, endeavoured to improve it.

"I am glad your majesty likes this young man," he said, in a low tone; "he has many determined enemies, and your majesty's countenance will do much for him."

"I thought he must have enemies, my lord," said the queen, in the same tone. "Doubts have been already thrown out against him."

"Do not credit them, madam," said Sunderland; "be assured he will one day establish his claims, and wrest back his title from the person who has robbed him of it."

"I hope so," returned the queen. "In the meantime, he has won my good opinion."

At this moment the king and Lauzun approached. The monarch was in a merry mood, and clapping his hands together, called loudly,—

"A dance! a dance!"

The music immediately struck up a lively air, and James, looking round, cried—

"Let those who are young enough join it instantly. I would make one myself, but my dancing days are over. My last attempt was with Lady Bellasis, whom I see yonder, and then it was a failure. If aught could tempt me, it would be yon lovely girl," he added, glancing at Sabine. "But come, the hay! the hay! Don't you hear those inspiring strains, young sir?" he cried to Moor, take a partner, quick. Why do you hesitate? I'm sure the lady will not say you nay."

And he laughingly pushed Moor towards Sabine, who had only been deterred by the glances of Lauzun from giving him her hand earlier, and the young couple joined the dancers.

"The handsomest pair in the room, on my life," said the king, laughing. And he turned to walk towards a party of ladies lower down the room.

"This is most provoking, gracious madam," said Lauzun to the queen.

"I am sorry you find it so, count," replied Mary, with a little malice, "but I could not help it."

"I am sorry I brought her here at all," cried the count.

"It was unwise to do so, if you feared she might excite too much admiration," replied the queen, smiling.

"I will go and see what occurs," said Lauzun, moving off.

But he could not catch a glimpse of the young pair in the mazy circles of the dance, and thinking they might not have joined it, he proceeded towards the ante-chamber whither Father Petre and Mauvesin had retired.

The central group in the saloon consisted of three ladies, who were engaged in animated conversation. One of them was Lady Bellasis, whose name was just mentioned by the king. She was the widow of Sir Henry Bellasis, who was killed, in 1667, in a drunken fracas with Tom Porter, a groom of the bed-chamber, and his own intimate friend. On the death of her husband, Lady Bellasis retired from court, but returned in about two years, when the Duke of York, then married to Ann Hyde, publicly made love to her. He even went so far as to place a document in her hands, in which he solemnly engaged to marry her on the death of his duchess; and, at the same time, endeavoured, though ineffectually, to persuade her to become a papist. The Duchess of York died soon afterwards, and the story of the duke's engagement with Lady Bellasis reaching the ears of Charles, the monarch summoned his enamoured brother to court, and after insisting that he should pursue it no further, said, "It is too much to have played the fool once. It is not to be done a second time, and at your age." Lady Bellasis also was so alarmed by the king's menaces, that she consented to give up the original contract, provided she was furnished with an attested copy of it; and, as a reward for this compliance, Charles created her a baroness. She was tall in stature, and gracefully formed, but her features were by no means beautiful.

Next to her was Mrs. Godfrey, better known as Arabella Churchill; who, deficient alike in personal and mental attraction, derived importance from her high connections. She was the early favourite of James; the sister of Lord Churchill, afterwards the celebrated Duke of Marlborough; and mother of the scarcely less celebrated Dukes of Berwick and Albemarle. Grammont describes her as "a tall creature, pale-faced, and nothing but skin and bone;" and explains, in his own diverting way, the mystery of James's attachment to her. It was equally a source of annoyance to the Duchess of York, and of ridicule to Charles II., who, in alluding to his brother's peculiar notions of feminine attraction, used to say of him, that "his favourites were imposed upon him as a penance by his priests." Arabella had since united herself to Colonel Godfrey; but was still regarded with favour by James, and even by his queen.

The third lady was the Countess of Sunderland, as remarkable for beauty, as her companions were for the want of it. "She was a lady," says Sir Egerton Brydges, "distinguished by her refined sense, subtle wit, admirable address, and every shining quality." "She is one," observes Evelyn, "who, for her distinguished esteem of me, from a long and worthy friendship, I must ever honour and celebrate." Kennet lauds her for her wit and address, while, on the other hand, the Princess Anne, represents her as familiar with intrigues, both of gallantry and politics.

She even denounces her as a dissembler and hypocrite. "I can't end my letter," she writes to her sister, the Princess of Orange, "without telling you that Lady Sunderland plays the hypocrite more than ever: for she goes to St. Martin's in the morning and afternoon, because there are not people enow to see her at Whitehall Chapel, and is half an hour before other people come, and half an hour after everybody is gone, at her private devotions." She was accused by some of her contemporaries of carrying on a love affair with Colonel Sydney. Speaking of her being discovered in communication with the Prince of Orange, Mackintosh says, "Sunderland vindicated himself from all share in it, by the impossibility of his trusting Sydney, a man whom he must hate, as the known lover of his wife. D'Avaux, on the other hand, treats the favour of Sydney with the lady as the source of his influence over her lord."

"It is certainly very imprudent of Lady Dorchester to come over from Ireland," said the Countess of Sunderland; "and I am sure the queen will be highly incensed with her; for she only consented to the continuance of her pension, on condition that she remained away."

"But his majesty has already prohibited her from appearing at court," observed Mrs. Godfrey. "I protest I dreaded her appearance here. She is the rudest creature living."

"His majesty need not have troubled himself," smiled Lady Bellasis; "for Lord Dorset forestalled him. Have you seen his lordship's ode?"

"I have heard of it," replied Lady Sunderland. "By all accounts, it is bitter enough."

"It is very just, as well as very severe," replied Lady Bellasis. "I only remember one verse, but you may judge from it of the rest:—

"'Tell me, Dorinda, why so gay?
Why such embroidery, fringe, and lace?
Can any dresses find a way
To stop the approaches of decay,
And mend a ruin'd face?'"

"Fie, Susan!" exclaimed a voice behind her. "Fie—fie!"

And turning, Lady Bellasis perceived the king, who had come upon them unawares.

James, however, was in high good humour, and laughed loudly at their confusion.

"You were always fond of scandal, Lady Bell," he said; "and, indeed, few of your sex are not. But make yourself easy about Dorinda. She will not trouble you with her presence."

"I am enchanted to hear it," said Lady Bellasis; "and I am

not sorry your majesty has become acquainted with my real sentiments."

"If I were to approach every knot of ladies in the room, I should find them talking scandal, and very likely about you," said James; "but here comes Barillon!" he exclaimed, noticing the ambassador. "I am glad to see your excellency," he added. "I want a word with you in private."

And placing his arm kindly on the ambassador's shoulder, he nodded to the ladies, and walked with him to the ante-chamber, towards which others had directed their steps.

As Father Petre and Mauvesin entered this room, they found it apparently unoccupied.

"I can well conceive your hatred to Charles Moor," said the Jesuit. "And it will not be lessened when I tell you that it can be proved, by unquestionable evidence, that your uncle, the late Lord Mauvesin, *was* married to his mother."

"You are mistaken, father!" cried Mauvesin. "No such evidence exists."

"It is you who are mistaken, my lord," said Father Petre. "I am not in the habit of making idle assertions. What think you of the priest who married them as a witness? You suppose him dead; but I tell you he lives, and can be produced."

"Indeed!" exclaimed Mauvesin.

"You fancied when you burnt the letter, written by your uncle on his death-bed to Lord Nottingham, that you had destroyed all proof," said Father Petre, with a bitter smile; "but it was not so."

"How do you know this?" cried Mauvesin, becoming white as ashes, and trembling violently.

"No matter. Let it suffice that I *do* know it, and that I also know how the letter was stolen, and by whom it was placed in your hands."

"You have said too much!" cried Mauvesin, fiercely. "This information must never pass your lips."

"It never shall pass them, if we come to a clear understanding, my lord," said the Jesuit, contemptuously; "but threats will not purchase my silence. I hate this Moor, and will enable you to crush him, but the service must be paid by implicit adherence to me. I must be served in all things unhesitatingly."

"Unhesitatingly?" echoed Mauvesin.

"To begin, then, you must convey this girl—this Mademoiselle Saint Leu, as she is called—secretly to France."

"To France, father?" cried Mauvesin.

"It must be," said the Jesuit, in a freezing tone. "If not, Moor shall take your place, and wed her."

"I am ready to obey you," replied Mauvesin.

"It is well!" said Father Petre. "Now, listen to me. You must carry her off this very night. A lugger, in the service of the French government, is lying off Gravesend; the master of which will obey your orders, when he knows you come from me. I will give you the necessary credentials."

"If I am discovered, I shall for ever lose the king's favour," said Mauvesin, doubtfully.

"If you have misgivings, I have done," rejoined the Jesuit, with a sneer; "but remember, if she remains here she will wed Moor—and then——"

"It shall be done, father—it shall be done!" interrupted Mauvesin, hastily. "I will set about it at once. Give me credentials to the captain of the lugger."

"Here they are," said Father Petre, placing papers in his hand.

At this moment a man's head appeared from behind a large Indian screen standing near the door.

"A pretty scheme I have discovered," muttered Saint Leu, for it was he. "I must take instant measures to defeat it." And he slipped unperceived out of the room.

"And now to reassure you," said Father Petre, seeing Mauvesin still hesitate, "I will make this abduction the means of your rival's disgrace."

A vindictive smile lighted up Mauvesin's features.

"Suspicion shall fall on him," pursued the Jesuit. "Leave the means to me."

"There seems some mystery about Sabine," said Mauvesin. "Can you not unravel it, father?"

"Not now," replied the Jesuit. "You will learn all at Paris. Suffice it that the French king feels a strong interest in her, and will give her a marriage portion."

"How is it that Lauzun has come forward as her protector?" asked Mauvesin.

"Time will explain," replied the priest. "But see, here comes the count. Lord Mauvesin was speaking in rapturous terms of the beauty of Mademoiselle Saint Leu," pursued Father Petre to Lauzun, as the latter entered the room. "His lordship cannot conceal his chagrin at the evident preference which the young lady exhibits for Mr. Moor."

"You have observed it, then, good father?" cried Lauzun, quickly.

"I take little note of such matters," said the Jesuit; "but my attention was strongly called to it. I should grieve if she were to become the prey of an adventurer."

"This must not be," cried Lauzun. "Where are they? I have looked round the ball-room for them in vain."

"This almost seems to confirm what you hinted just now, my lord," said the Jesuit, with a significant glance at Mauvesin.

"What did he hint?" cried Lauzun, fiercely.

"His lordship thought he heard Moor propose an elopement," said the wily priest; "but it could scarcely be."

"There is no saying," cried Lauzun, quickly. "Such things have been, and therefore may be again. But it must be prevented. I cannot find Saint Leu. Curse on this rascal Moor! I will insult him in the face of the whole court." And he hurried out of the room.

The Jesuit looked after him with a satisfied smile.

"What course am I to pursue, father?" asked Mauvesin.

"I will guide you," replied Father Petre. "Come with me."

They were passing forth, when the king and Barillon entered the room, and stopped them.

"A word with you, my lord," said the monarch to Mauvesin.

"Nay, do not interrupt him, your majesty," said the Jesuit; "he is going to prevent a rencontre between the Count de Lauzun and Mr. Moor."

"In heaven's name go, then," said the king. "What is the matter, father?" he added, to Petre, as Mauvesin quitted the room.

"Lauzun is annoyed at the young man's attentions to Mademoiselle Saint Leu," replied the Jesuit.

"Oh! is that all," exclaimed the king, with a smile. "Lauzun is hasty. Our own presence may be necessary to check any outbreak. We will return to the ball-room."

As they moved forward, Barillon lingered for a moment behind with Father Petre, and exchanged a few hasty words with him.

"You have observed what is going forward," said Petre. "Does it not bear out my report to you?"

"Fully," answered Barillon. "I am now convinced of Sunderland's treachery, and transfer my confidence to you."

"I have engaged Mauvesin to execute our scheme," said Petre, "and have so arranged it that suspicion must inevitably fall on Moor."

"It is well," observed Barillon, laughing.

On quitting the ante-chamber, Lauzun glanced again round the saloon, and perceived Moor standing apart in a recess. The young man was quite alone, and Lauzun stepped hastily up to him.

"May I ask where Mademoiselle Saint Leu is?" said the count, with freezing politeness.

"I must decline answering, sir," replied Moor, with equal coldness.

"Decline!" echoed Lauzun. "Know you to whom you speak?"

"To the Count de Lauzun," answered Moor, bowing stiffly.

"Then if you know thus much you will know also that I have a right to make the inquiry," rejoined Lauzun, haughtily.

"I recognise no such right," said Moor. "All I can say is that she has left the palace."

"Left the palace! without my permission!" cried Lauzun. "With whom has she left the palace?"

Moor merely bowed.

"I will have an answer—a direct answer, sir!" cried Lauzun, stamping his foot. "Where is she gone—and with whom?"

"You will learn nothing from me, count," replied Moor.

"You have some base design in view, sir," cried Lauzun, transported with fury.

"I know not by what warrant you dare to use such language to me, sir," rejoined Moor, "or why you presume to interest yourself so much about Mademoiselle Saint Leu!—but if your design be to fasten a quarrel upon me, you have succeeded. If you desire to continue this conversation where it can be more freely pursued," he added, touching the hilt of his sword significantly, "I am at your service."

"I meet only my equals," said Lauzun, scornfully. "I will not fight an adventurer."

"The insult is as cowardly as it is unjust," rejoined Moor; "but the man who will dare to insult his own sovereign will be little scrupulous towards others whom he conceives his inferiors in rank. I leave you, count."

"Stay, sir,—not so fast," cried Lauzun, grasping his arm. "I will forego my resolution. I *will* meet you. In five minutes I will be in the park. Let us quit the palace separately."

"Be it so," replied Moor, sternly.

And they walked away in opposite directions. Moor was followed at a distance by Mauvesin, who had partially overheard their conversation.

Meanwhile, the king entered the ball-room, and seeing nothing of Lauzun or Moor, proceeded towards the queen. Mary addressed some inquiries to him respecting Sabine, which James was unable to answer, and an attendant was sent to summon the young lady to their majesties. In a short time the attendant returned with intelligence that Mademoiselle Saint Leu was nowhere to be found.

"How very strange," exclaimed Mary, "I must make the Count de Lauzun acquainted with the circumstance immediately."

"The count has quitted the palace, gracious madam," replied the attendant, "more than five minutes ago."

"Indeed!" exclaimed the queen, "and alone?"

"Quite alone, your majesty."

"Where is Mr. Moor?" asked the king.

"He is gone too, your majesty," replied the attendant.

"Ha!" exclaimed the king, "this must be looked to."

And he turned to give some orders in a low tone to an usher, who bowed and quitted the presence.

The ball, meanwhile, proceeded gaily, notwithstanding that the royal circle seemed disturbed, especially as no tidings could be gained of the absentees. Soon after this Mauvesin approached Father Petre.

"Well," said the Jesuit, in a low tone, "you have succeeded —she is gone!"

"She is gone, father," replied the other, "but I have had no hand in it."

"How?" said the priest.

"I suspect this cursed Moor has got the better of us!" said Mauvesin. "She is not to be found."

"You should not have lost sight of her," said the Jesuit, sternly. "If the scheme fails you will rue it."

"Moor has already been punished," said Mauvesin.

"By whom?" asked the Jesuit.

"Here comes the avenger," rejoined Mauvesin.

As he spoke Lauzun approached the royal circle. A strange smile played upon his features.

"Ah, count, I am glad to see you," said Mary. "We all want to know what has become of Mademoiselle Saint Leu."

"She is perfectly safe," replied Lauzun.

"And what of Moor? where is he?" asked James.

"In a surgeon's hands," replied Lauzun, with a smile.

"Then a *duel* has taken place," cried James, gravely. "Ah! count, you are incurable. No wonder our brother Louis banished you. If you are not more discreet I shall be obliged to follow his example."

"Nay, your majesty," interposed Mary, "the count, perhaps, is not to blame. But I hope the young man is not much hurt?"

"He has received a mere flesh wound," said Lauzun, laughing. "He is a very fair swordsman."

"Well, it will do him no discredit to have exchanged a few passes with the first swordsman of his day," said James.

"Not a whit," replied Lauzun; "and I have quite changed my opinion of him. He is a brave, high-spirited youth, and no adventurer."

Father Petre and Mauvesin exchanged looks.

"I am glad to hear you say so much, count," said Sunderland. "That is precisely my opinion of him."

"And mine," added the queen dowager.

"Things have gone on untowardly thus far," whispered Father Petre to Mauvesin. "But we will have our revenge."

BOOK THE SECOND.

CHAPTER I.

THE BISHOPS.—THE LULL BEFORE THE STORM.

The publication of the new scheme of religious toleration had all the effect that Sunderland predicted. The Dissenters, whom it so completely emancipated, received it with transport; the Church party was ashamed to condemn it; and the great body of the nation hailed it with joy. The prison doors were everywhere thrown open; men who had long pined in dungeons, in momentary expectation of perpetual banishment—some even under sentence of death, for no other offence than a conscientious dissent from the Church, were restored to unconditional liberty. Of the Quaker communion alone, more than twelve hundred persons were released from the various gaols; and the members of every sect were allowed the free exercise of their particular form of worship.

Addresses of thanks were poured in upon the king by every denomination of Dissenters from every part of the kingdom; and even five prelates of the Church lent a sanction to the Declaration. Distinguished Catholics were no longer the objects of popular abhorrence. The papal nuncio was invited by the civic authorities to a public dinner; and, on his way to Guildhall, was received by the populace with shouts. These demonstrations were followed by a profound quiet. "Not a speck in the heavens," says Sir James Mackintosh, "seemed to the common eye to forbode a storm. Even the ordinary marks of national disapprobation, which prepare and announce a legal resistance to power, were wanting. The current of flattering addresses continued to flow towards the throne, uninterrupted by a single warning remonstrance, of a more independent spirit, or even of a more decent servility."

But, under this calm surface, the busy spirit of faction was engendering a storm. Burnet wrote from the Hague, where he was in exile, to warn the Dissenters against the specious designs of the king. Lord Halifax, in an able pamphlet, entitled "A Letter to a Dissenter," sought to bring them into a league with the Church. In concert with Lord Nottingham, he formed a coalition with the earls of Rochester, Clarendon, and Danby, and endeavoured, by another pamphlet, called "The Anatomy of an Equivalent," to arouse the Church from its false security. On the other hand, the Government was not inactive. James himself made the cruelty of the Church of England the common subject of his discourse. It was even in contemplation to summon another parliament, and, in the meantime, the Declaration of Indulgence was moulded into a bill, under the imposing title of "The Magna Charta of Conscience," for the purpose of being submitted to the legislature. Sunderland opposed this ill-judged design; and, though his opposition was successful, James began from that moment to lose confidence in him. "It was thought," says Mackintosh, "that he himself even saw that he could not stand long, even by the friendship of the queen, since the French ambassador began to trim between him and Petre, and the whole French party leant against him." His adversaries, indeed, daily entangled him in new difficulties; and, though he frustrated their machinations for a time, he lost strength in every encounter.

At length, Father Petre proposed to attach to the Declaration of Indulgence an order that it should be read in the churches, which, though not absolutely an unconstitutional measure, was calculated to increase the hostility of the Church, while it could be of no advantage to the government. Sunderland urged strenuously on James these prudent objections to the order, at the same time expressing his belief that the bishops would refuse to comply with it; but his objections were overruled by Father Petre, who declared his determination to force it on the bishops, in the insulting language used by Rabshekah, the Assyrian general, to the officers of King Hezekiah. Sunderland, though ably supported by Jeffreys, was defeated; the bishops were ordered to distribute the Declaration in their respective dioceses; and an early day was appointed for the clergy to read it in the churches.

This sudden blow took the bishops then in the metropolis by surprise. Allowed only thirteen days from the issue of the proclamation, before they were to carry it into effect—separated from their brethren—distrustful of each other—with the eyes of England and of Europe fixed upon them, they were called upon for an instantaneous and unanimous judgment on a matter of vital difficulty. Overwhelmed with consternation, they turned for counsel to their lay leaders, who, while the danger was yet distant, had so often and so loudly vindicated their cause. But their hopes of assistance from this source were doomed to disappointment. The Earl of Danby fled to Yorkshire; Rochester was not to be trusted; Clarendon, though zealous, was unequal to the emergency; the Marquis of Winchester feigned madness; Halifax hesitated; and, unwilling to incur alone the responsibility of advising them, Nottingham would only recommend them to assemble together, and decide for themselves.

Meanwhile, the day appointed for the reading of the Declaration approached, and the bishops remained irresolute.

CHAPTER II.

LAMBETH PALACE.

About nine o'clock, one night in May, three men landed from a boat at Lambeth Stairs. A drizzling rain was falling, and though several barges and wherries were moored close by or grounded higher up on the sand, not a waterman or lighterman was to be seen near them. The adjacent passage of Bishop's Walk looked dark and lonely, and some lights which gleamed from the windows of the ancient gateway, opening to the palace of the Archbishop of Canterbury, and the few straggling houses on the road, opposite the south side of the church, in no way relieved the gloomy character of the scene.

Each of the men was armed with pistols and a hanger, and one of them carried a dark lantern, which, as they reached the bank, he carefully shaded, in order to avoid observation.

The foremost of the party, who was no other than Snewin, crossed over the road towards the church. The church-yard wall did not then extend, at the extremity nearest the river, beyond the transept of the church, so that the approach to the principal door was unobstructed. The three men posted themselves close to the door, whence they commanded a view of the palace-gateway, which almost adjoined the church, being terminated, on its inner-side, by the burial-ground.

Scarcely were they ensconsed, when a carriage turned round the church-yard, and approached the gate. It contained two persons; one of whom was a very stout man, somewhat advanced in years, and clad in the habits of a dignitary of the church. The other was Colonel Sidney.

As the carriage halted at the gate, Sidney, who had been leaning forward a little, suddenly drew back.

The gate was now opened, and the carriage rolled under the archway. The coachman was driving on, when he was arrested by the check-string; and, drawing up, a footman sprang from behind the carriage with a flaming link, and hastened to the door. Some one within seemed to hold it back, but at last, jerking round the handle, the servant drew it open. There was a footway in front of the carriage, opening upon one of the side towers, in which was the porter's lodge; and favoured by the momentary confusion, Snewin and his satellites ran round the horses' heads and gained it. They were rather abashed, however, when the reverend owner of the carriage stepped forth, to find themselves in the presence of the Bishop of St. Asaph.

Though possessed of but little talent, and perhaps less virtue, Lloyd, Bishop of St. Asaph, had contrived to render himself exceedingly popular. He was distinguished for his uniform opposition to the court, and his zeal against popery. But he was also noted for his peculiar views respecting the prophecies, which he was in the habit of applying to passing events; and, according to Evelyn, he waited with anxious impatience for the advent of the Millennium, believing it might certainly be looked for within the next thirty years.

As the Bishop of St. Asaph alighted he turned round to the carriage again and shut the door himself, and then, to the amazement of his servants, who were looking for the appearance of his companion, ordered the carriage to be driven off.

"T' other gen'l'man an't got out, your lor'ship—has he?" cried Snewin, touching his hat.

"What other gentleman?" rejoined the bishop, "who are you, and whom do you seek?"

"I'm Elkanah Snewin, one of his majesty's constables," said Snewin authoritatively, "and am in search of Colonel Sidney."

As he spoke he sprang upon the carriage-step and looked in. The vehicle was empty.

"What does this mean?" demanded the bishop, with well-feigned surprise.

"Never you mind, my lord," answered Snewin; "I'll see the colonel some other time. Come along, mates."

His concluding words were addressed to his two myrmidons, who, without reply, followed him through the gateway.

The Bishop of St. Asaph passed on to a small court in front of the chapel. As he approached the hall of the palace, Sidney, who had taken refuge behind one of the buttresses, rejoined him.

"I have eluded them for the present, my lord," he said, with a smile. "Do not forget how you are to account to the archbishop for my coming with you, for his grace will have nothing to say to Henry Sidney. I have promised Van Citters that all shall be settled to-night. A barge is in waiting at the horse-ferry, and you must go at once to Whitehall."

"I will do my best," answered the bishop, hesitatingly.

They now entered the hall, where several servants were in attendance, one of whom conducted them to an upper chamber, where they were received by the archbishop and Tillotson.

Sancroft, archbishop of Canterbury, was a prelate as distinguished for learning as he was venerable for piety. All his life he had been conspicuous for probity of character, for modest and amiable manners, and for incorruptible virtue, avoiding rather than seeking preferment, which he had accepted only at the command of the king. At the breaking out of the civil war, he was a fellow of Emanuel College, Cambridge; but having refused to subscribe to the Presbyterian Covenant, he was ejected from his fellowship, and obliged to fly to the Continent. Here he became acquainted with the most illustrious of the loyal English exiles, who soon discovered his exalted worth, while they admired his eloquence and learning. He returned to England at the Restoration, and was appointed chaplain to Cosin, bishop of Durham, and was afterward selected master of his college, at Cambridge. He successively held the deaneries of York and St. Paul's, and the archdeaconry of Canterbury, and was in possession of the last named-dignity when Charles II., contrary to Sancroft's own inclination, advanced him to the primateship. He is described by Burnet as "a poor-spirited and fearful man, that acted a very mean part in all this great transaction." Yet he had for two years been banished from the court, and when the event she was mixed up with attained their climax, he descended from his archiepiscopal throne into privacy, rather than violate his consecration-oath.

John Tillotson, the companion of this venerable prelate, was many years his junior; and though he had not yet been elevated to the episcopal bench, was destined, at a future time, to succeed his friend in the See of Canterbury.

Tillotson had received his early education among the Puritans, but was afterwards sent to Christ's College, Cambridge, where he gradually shook off his original prejudices, and exhibited a leaning towards the Church. He continued among the Presbyterians, however, till 1661, when he submitted to the Act of Uniformity. His first office in the Church was the curacy of Cheshunt, in Hertfordshire; but he soon quitted the country, and fixing his abode in London, was appointed preacher to the society of Lincoln's-Inn. He afterwards became chaplain to

Charles II., and, in this station, distinguished himself by preaching against Popery, by advocating the doctrine of non-resistance, and by converting the Earl of Shrewsbury. On the 2nd of April, 1680, he preached a sermon before Charles on his famous topic of non-resistance, at which all parties professed to take offence. Dr. Hickes, in his account of it, says, that a witty lord, standing at the king's elbow when it was delivered, said, "Sir, do you hear Mr. Hobbs in the pulpit?" Dr. Calamy's statement is, that Charles having slept while the sermon was delivered, a nobleman of his household stepped up to him, and said, "It is a pity your majesty slept, for we have had the rarest piece of Hobbism that ever you heard in your life." Charles, starting up, exclaimed, "Odds fish! he shall print it, then!" And the sermon was printed accordingly. But its publication did not affect the preacher's popularity. Though the principle it advocated was universally obnoxious, he was still enrolled among the popular party, and, in conjunction with Burnet, he had ministered to the last moments of Lord William Russell, attending him to the place of execution, and there urging him to disavow the right of resistance.

On the present occasion, he looked pale, and his features were swollen and slightly distorted, for he had only recently recovered from a fit of apoplexy.

The archbishop extended his hand to St. Asaph, and at the same time glanced inquiringly at Sidney.

"Allow me to present Captain Clifford to your grace," said St. Asaph. "He has been labouring for us among the Non-conformists, who have intrusted him with a message to you."

The archbishop bowed, though somewhat coldly. Tillotson looked earnestly at Sidney.

"I think, my lord, we had better await the arrival of our friends," he said.

He turned the discourse on other topics, and, while they conversed, other visitors were ushered, in rapid succession, into the chamber. These were Trelawney, bishop of Bristol, and brother of Colonel Trelawney, already mentioned in this history; Kenn, bishop of Bath and Wells; the bishops of Ely, Chichester, and Gloucester, and Drs. Patrick, Grove, and Shirlock. At last, the usher introduced Drs. Tennyson and Stillingfleet.

Tennyson is described by Mackay, as "a plain, good, heavy man, very tall, and of a fair complexion;" while Swift says of him,* "he was the most good-for-nothing prelate I ever knew." He took his degree at Bene't's College, Cambridge, where his talents attracted such favourable notice, that he was appointed

* In a manuscript note upon the first edition of "Mackay's Memoirs of Public Characters," preserved in the British Museum.

preacher of the university, and when the Great Plague broke out, dispersing in every direction the affrighted collegians, he had the courage to remain, with only two scholars and a few servants, during the whole time it prevailed. In 1680 he was presented by Charles II. to the vicarage of St. Martin's-in-the-Fields, and while holding this living he engaged in a conference with Andrew Pulton, a Jesuit, on the respective merits of the Protestant and Catholic Churches. Though he failed to convince his opponent by argument, this conference won him considerable reputation. Since that event he had attended the unfortunate Duke of Monmouth at his especial request, during his last moments, and after a vain attempt to reconcile him to his duchess, accompanied him to the place of execution. He afterwards acquired a momentary notoriety by preaching a funeral sermon on Nell Gwynne, for which he was much censured by some, but applauded by others, and he certainly enjoyed as large a share of popular favour as any of his reverend contemporaries.

Edward Stillingfleet had also distinguished himself at Cambridge, and after obtaining a fellowship at St. John's College, was presented by Sir Roger Burgoyne to the Rectory of Sutton, in Bedfordshire. In 1665, the Earl of Southampton appointed him to the Rectory of St. Andrew's, Holborn, when he removed to London, and soon became distinguished both as a preacher and writer. In the course of a few years he published several important works, particularly the "Origines Britannicæ," or the antiquities of British Churches, a work of profound research, which brought him immediate celebrity. After this he was appointed chaplain to Charles II., and being once asked by that monarch why he always preached before him from a book, which was not his custom elsewhere, he replied, "The awe of so noble an audience, but chiefly the seeing before me so great and wise a prince, makes me afraid to trust myself." Charles was well pleased with the compliment, when Stillingfleet added, "Will your majesty give me leave to ask you a question too? Why do you read your speeches to parliament when you have none of these reasons?" "Why truly, doctor," replied the witty monarch, "I have asked the parliament so often for money, that I am ashamed to look them in the face."

As the new comers took their seats, the archbishop reminded the company, in a few words, of the occasion of their meeting.

"Let us begin our conference in true wisdom," he added. "We have put our trust in man, and our confidence in princes, and they have failed us. Let us now seek help from on high."

The proposition was immediately agreed to, and the whole assembly knelt down, when the archbishop, in an earnest and devout voice, implored the divine blessing on their deliberations. The prayer concluded, they arose and resumed their seats.

"I believe we are agreed not to obey his majesty's orders," the archbishop then said, "but we have not decided how to evade it. It is proper that I should state to you clearly the grounds of my own objections. I do not oppose the order because it concedes toleration to our dissenting brethren, and though some of you, I fear, will differ with me on this point, you all know that it is no new opinion of mine. I think the king's order affects the very existence of the Church, and therefore, I am bound to oppose it. This gentleman, Captain Clifford," pointing to Sidney, "who is known to the Bishop of St. Asaph, has been in communication with the Dissenters on the question, and can acquaint us with their sentiments."

"I have consulted some of their most eminent preachers, your grace," observed Sidney, "and among others, Baxter, Howe, and Kiffin. They consider the order to be directed, not against the Protestant Church only, but against all other sects, and they implore you to resist it."

"If we resist the king," said the archbishop, "we violate the principle laid down at Oxford, in 1683, which expressly says, that 'if lawful governors become tyrants, or govern otherwise than by the laws of God or man they ought to do, they do not forfeit the right they had unto their government.'"

"And, moreover, we should disobey the injunctions of the Gospel," urged Tillotson. "St. Paul says, 'Let every soul be subject unto the higher powers;' and he adds, 'whosoever, therefore, resisteth this power, resisteth the ordinance of God; and they that resist shall receive to themselves damnation.'"

The Bishop of Bristol denied the application of this text. He was a truckling prelate, who, while the king had aimed only at absolute power, and left the Church unmolested, had been one of the loudest advocates of the doctrine of non-resistance; and, on one occasion, during the Monmouth rebellion, had so far forgotten his priestly character, as to take the horses from his carriage, to assist in drawing the cannon of the royal army to the battle-field of Sedgemoor. But the king's hostility to the Church had wrought a change in his opinions.

"That passage was addressed exclusively to the Romans," he said. "The apostles were accused by the Pagans of a design to subvert the constituted authorities; and, in this injunction, St. Paul showed that his mission had not that object, but sought to diffuse only a knowledge of God."

"Furthermore," urged Tennyson, "Nero was absolute, and the Romans knew no law except his will. With us, the king is as much bound by the laws, as we ourselves are bound by them."

"Holt and Pemberton, whom I have consulted on the question, both agree, that the king's order, being founded on the dispensing power, is unlawful," remarked Stillingfleet.

"And your grace has the declaration of eighty of the metropolitan clergy, that they cannot, in conscience, obey the order," observed the Bishop of St. Asaph. "For my own part, I believe we are warned of this enemy in the book of Revelations; and, in our resistance to Rome, we shall accomplish the prophecy therein declared."

There was a momentary silence when the Bishop of Bath and Wells addressed the primate. Kenn was an amiable and pious prelate, at once loyal to the king, and devoted to the Church. His conduct, in reference to the Monmouth rebellion, presented a pleasing contrast to that of Trelawney. Horrified at the barbarity of the victors, he had hastened, on the suppression of the revolt, to the presence of James, and throwing himself at his feet, besought him, with tears, to deal more leniently with the rebels. His intercession was successful, and had never been forgotten by the people.

"We have had argument enough, your grace," said the good bishop; "for, as no fear of consequences can deter us from doing our duty, no argument can persuade us to rebellion. We may protest, but we cannot resist. Let us, therefore, draw up a humble petition to the throne, praying his majesty to recall his order, as we cannot conscientiously obey it."

"The proposition is worthy of you, my lord," observed St. Asaph, in obedience to a private suggestion from Sidney. "The sole objection to it is, that there is only one day for his majesty to consider our petition, so that, if we decide upon it, it must be carried to him to-night."

"To-night?" echoed several voices.

"Late as the hour is, it must be done," said the archbishop. "Are all agreed to the petition?"

The answer was unanimously in the affirmative.

"It must be conveyed to his majesty, then, in the most dutiful manner that circumstances will admit," said the archbishop. "As primate of the Church, I ought to undertake the sole responsibility of the transaction; but as you are aware, I am labouring under the royal displeasure, and cannot appear at court."

"I should be a poor substitute for your grace, and an unworthy representative of the Church," observed Kenn; "but if accounted worthy, I will gladly convey the petition."

"You must not incur the danger alone," answered the archbishop. "There are five other prelates present; and it will be more respectful for all to go."

"Your grace is right," remarked the Bishop of Gloucester. "We will stand or fall together."

The bishops of Bristol, Chichester, and Ely readily assented to the proposition. St. Asaph was silent for a moment, but he was prevailed on by Sidney, unobserved by the others, to signify his readiness to accompany them.

"I rejoice that you are agreed," the archbishop then said. "Though I cannot go with you, I will draw up the petition, and my handwriting will prove my connection with it."

"Nay, my lord," interposed Kenn, "let the blame rest with us alone. As our primate, you may be singled out for punishment, and suspended from your exalted office."

"Our lives are in the Lord's hands," answered the archbishop, solemnly. And in a lower tone he uttered the words which he afterwards caused to be inscribed on his tomb; "'The Lord giveth, and the Lord taketh away; blessed be the name of the Lord!'"

Amidst a profound silence, he then drew up the petition, which he afterwards read to the assembly.

The document set forth that "their averseness to read the king's declaration arose neither from want of the duty and obedience which the Church of England had always practised, nor from want of tenderness to Dissenters, to whom they were willing to come to such a temper as might be thought fit in parliament and convocation; but because it is founded on a dispensing power declared illegal in parliament; and that they could not, in prudence and conscience, make themselves so far parties to it as the publication of it in the church, at the time of divine service, would amount to;" and it concluded by "humbly and earnestly entreating his majesty not to insist on their distributing and reading the said declaration."

In this memorable document, the archbishop met the views of all his companions. It was sufficiently temperate to satisfy the timid—sufficiently decided to please even Sidney. Having seen it approved of by all, the latter had no further purpose to accomplish at the palace; and as he desired to withdraw privately, he arose, and took his leave.

In the hall below, one of the valets hastened to attend him.

"Is the front gateway the only outlet from the palace?" asked Sidney, slipping a guinea into his hand.

"There is a garden-door, sir, opening into Bishops' Walk," answered the man.

"That will suit me exactly," rejoined Sidney. "Be good enough to show me the way to it."

Taking a key from a hook against the wall, the valet conducted Sidney through a postern in the Lollard's Tower, to the garden, and stopping before a door in the wall, unlocked it. After a hasty glance down the Bishops' Walk, Sidney passed out.

Hurrying in the opposite direction to the palace, he soon reached the ferry, where he engaged a boat, and embarked for Whitehall-stairs.

CHAPTER III.

THE MANDATE FROM LOUIS THE FOURTEENTH.

On landing at Whitehall-stairs, Sidney pulled his hat over his brow, and drawing his heavy cloak around him, quickly mounted the stairs, which, owing to the lateness of the hour, were completely deserted, and encountering a sentinel, by whom he was challenged, but who allowed him to proceed on receiving a password, entered a small court-yard adjoining the palace.

Arrived there, he coughed slightly, and was instantly joined by another personage, muffled, like himself, in a large cloak.

"Is it you, Van Citters?" asked Sidney, in a low tone.

"Ay!—ay!" replied the Dutch ambassador, "what success?"

"Complete," cried Sidney. "The bishops are ours—they have signed the petition."

"Bravo!" exclaimed Van Citters, "the first step is taken."

"They will be here presently," pursued Sidney, "and you must see them enter the palace. I must be gone. This is dangerous ground for me."

With a hasty adieu to the ambassador he crossed the court, plunged through the arched gateway at the further end, where another sentinel was passing to and fro, and gaining Parliament-street, shaped his course towards Charing-cross.

"Scarcely was he gone when another person, who had remained concealed behind a projection in the wall during his brief interview with the ambassador, glided after him, and eluding the notice of Van Citters, followed him cautiously into the street.

The night was profoundly dark, and the dull lamps suspended over the streets by ropes, or the occasional links borne by the passengers or their attendants, only served to render the gloom more palpable, when Sidney, as he was hurrying forward, caught sight of a young man advancing towards him, and accompanied by a link-boy. The appearance of this young man immediately checked his progress.

"Well met, Mr. Moor," he cried, stepping up to him, and about to take his hand, when he observed that the other's right arm was in a sling.

"What! a duel, ha!"

"A slight hurt, colonel," replied Moor, "but I have still one hand left for my king's defence," he added, significantly.

"Which king?" asked Sidney, in a low tone.

"King James, to be sure," replied Moor, "I own no other sovereign."

"Your loyalty will not perhaps, prevent you from doing me a service," said Sidney.

"I can render you none incompatible with my duty, colonel," replied Moor; "and I am scarcely discharging it in allowing you to pass free."

"You would find it difficult to arrest me in your present disabled condition," rejoined Sidney, laughing; "but I know you have no such intention. Deliver my message or not, as you think proper, to Lord Sunderland, but if you are a true friend to him you will tell him that if he does not resign to-night, to-morrow he will endanger his head. And now adieu, Mr. Moor; we shall meet again."

And he was moving off, when a man who had halted behind him suddenly dashed forward, and snatching the torch from the link-boy, held it up to his face so as fully to disclose his features.

"I arrest you in the king's name for treason, Colonel Sidney," cried Lord Mauvesin—for it was he—"and I arrest you also, Charles Moor, for aiding and abetting a notorious spy and traitor.—What ho! the guard! the guard! Call the guard, quick!" he added to the link-boy.

And as he spoke he threw down the link and seized Sidney, who, however, broke from him, and darted down the street in the direction of Westminster Hall.

"If you attempt to move, traitor, I will stab you," exclaimed Mauvesin, placing the point of his weapon at Moor's breast.

"It is you who are the traitor, villain," cried Moor, darting suddenly backwards. And drawing his sword with his left hand, he attacked Mauvesin with such vigour and determination, that, notwithstanding the disadvantage under which he laboured, he would readily have held his adversary at his mercy, if it had not been for the arrival of a detachment of the guard, who, on hearing the clash of steel, hurried forward. Along with the officer of the guard, came the Count de Lauzun.

"You are hard pressed, and by a left-handed man," cried the latter, as he laughingly interposed. "What's the matter?"

"Arrest him," cried Mauvesin, scarcely able to speak from fury. "Do you not hear me?—arrest him, I say!"

"Yes, we hear you, my lord; but why should we arrest him more than yourself?" said the officer of the guard.

"He is a traitor—a conspirator!" cried Mauvesin. "I caught him in close conference with an avowed agent of the Prince of Orange. Let him deny it if he can."

"Is this so, Mr. Moor?" asked Lauzun, gravely.

"The meeting was purely accidental," replied Moor. "Colonel Sidney stopped me in the street."

"It is false, traitor," cried Mauvesin; "it was an appointment—I overheard your conversation. You were charged with a warning message to Lord Sunderland."

"If you overheard what was said, you would know that I refused to receive the message," replied Moor; "but it was a simple caution."

"His majesty shall judge of its import," cried Mauvesin; "but we waste time in parleying here. Place this man in arrest, sir," he added, to the officer of the guard.

"Will you give me your word, Mr. Moor," interposed Lauzun, "that you will not make any attempt to escape." And on receiving Moor's assurance to that effect, he added to the officer, "I will be responsible for his appearance before the king. You may withdraw your men."

"You will take note of all that has passed, sir," said Mauvesin to the officer. "The Count de Lauzun may have to render an explanation to his majesty for his own interference."

"Do not concern yourself about me, my lord," rejoined Lauzun, contemptuously. "I am always ready to render explanation to those who have a right to require it of me. Come, Mr. Moor, we must to the palace."

"I attend you, count," replied Moor.

"You will find us at the palace, my lord," said Lauzun.

"I shall not lose sight of you, depend upon it," replied Mauvesin, following them as they moved off.

"Permit me to thank you, count, for your generous espousal of my cause," said Moor, as they proceeded, "as well as for the handsome manner in which I am told you have lately spoken of me to his majesty."

"I have only done you justice," rejoined Lauzun, carelessly. "But you have a warm advocate with me."

"An advocate, count!" exclaimed Moor in surprise. "In whom?"

"In Mademoiselle Saint Leu—my ward," rejoined Lauzun. "She always speaks of you with grateful interest."

Moor's heightened colour could not be seen, but his voice betrayed his emotion."

"Mademoiselle Saint Leu attaches too much importance to my slight services," he said.

"Sabine is now a great favourite with her majesty," answered

Lauzun; "and you will no doubt see her at the palace this evening."

Moor made no reply, for his feelings kept him silent, and they presently afterwards reached the palace.

It was a reception night at Whitehall, and the saloon was crowded, as on a former occasion, with court beauties and gallants. The queen occupied her accustomed place, and was conversing with Father Petre.

"And so you tell me Lord Mauvesin is passionately attached to Mademoiselle Saint Leu, father?" she said.

"Passionately," replied the Jesuit; "and I hope your majesty will exert your influence to promote his suit."

"But I do not like interfering in matters of the heart," rejoined Mary, "and she appears to have no liking for him."

"The match will be highly advantageous to her," replied Father Petre; "and your majesty will permit me to say, that it is scarcely worth while to consult a silly girl's inclinations when her true interests are served. Lord Mauvesin," he added, in a meaning voice, "is devoted to us, and at a critical juncture like the present, we can ill afford to lose so powerful a supporter."

"We must not lose him," said Mary, quickly.

"You will bind him to us for ever, by lending him aid in this matter," returned Father Petre.

"Well, I will see what can be done," smiled Mary; "but hearts are not to be forced even by a queen."

"If your majesty deigns to interfere, I shall account the marriage as settled," said Father Petre; "the only danger I apprehend is that of delay."

"I will speak to Mademoiselle Saint Leu at once," said Mary; and calling an usher, she gave him some directions, and then added to Father Petre, "leave me for a moment, father, and when I have spoken with her you shall know the result."

Father Petre made a low obeisance, and withdrew as Sabine advanced with the usher.

"You have always professed great attachment to me, Sabine," said the queen kindly.

"Not more than I have ever felt, gracious madam," replied the other.

"I am sure not," said Mary; "and you will believe that I feel great interest in your welfare. However much I regret to lose you, I shall not allow my own inclinations to interfere with your happiness."

"Lose me!" cried Sabine: "I do not understand your majesty."

"Have you sufficient confidence in my affection for you to allow me to dispose of your hand in marriage?" asked the queen.

"I am so taken by surprise that I scarcely know how to answer, madam," replied Sabine, blushing deeply, and then growing pale.

"Then I will answer for you," said the queen. "You will."

"Oh no! madam, oh no!" cried Sabine, hastily: "that is, unless——"

"Unless I happen to make choice of somebody quite agreeable to you—a good reservation, truly."

"I did not say so," replied Sabine, again blushing deeply.

"But I infer it," cried Mary, playfully. "Well, the match is in every respect desirable. The suitor is amiable and handsome, and desperately in love."

"Oh! your majesty," cried Sabine, casting down her eyes.

"More than that, he is noble," pursued the queen.

"Noble!" echoed Sabine, starting, and turning pale; "I have mistaken your majesty."

"How can that be? I have mentioned no name," replied the queen.

"It is needless, madam," said Sabine.

"What, then, you guess that I mean Lord Mauvesin?" cried Mary.

"I fancied your majesty might refer to him," said Sabine, coldly.

"And will you not marry him?" asked the queen.

"Not for worlds," replied Sabine, with decision.

"You are very resolute, mademoiselle," said the queen, somewhat piqued; "may I ask if your affections are already engaged?"

"Your majesty will excuse my answering that question," returned Sabine.

"Well, we shall see what the Count de Lauzun has to say on the subject," cried Mary.

"The count will not, I am sure, attempt to influence my inclinations," said Sabine; "but if he did, his efforts would be unavailing."

"We shall see," said Mary.

And as Sabine withdrew, Father Petre advanced to the queen.

"I cannot give you much hope from the young lady, father," observed Mary, "she is very resolute in her refusal. Your only chance is with the Count de Lauzun."

"Your majesty's influence with the count is far greater than mine," said the Jesuit, with significance. "*He*, at least, will obey you."

"I do not know that, father," replied Mary, "but I will try."

"If you fail, I have a plan in reserve," said Father Petre; "and see, here comes the count, and accompanied by Charles Moor."

"Shall I tell you what I think, father," said the queen. "I am of opinion that Lord Mauvesin has a rival in young Moor."

"Your majesty is right," rejoined the Jesuit, "and I shall take care that the rivalry does not long exist."

"You must use fair means, father," said the queen, "or I have nothing to do with the proceedings."

"Of course, madam," replied the Jesuit, "in love all means are fair."

As he spoke, Lauzun and Moor advanced towards the king, who was standing at a little distance engaged in deep conversation with Sunderland and Barillon; and they had scarcely made the customary obeisances, when Mauvesin came up. Father Petre watched the group with great anxiety, and noted that as Mauvesin addressed the king, a heavy cloud gathered on the royal brow. James then turned quickly to Moor, and notwithstanding Lauzun's interference, it was evident, from his angry glances and gestures, that the weight of his displeasure was falling on the young man's head. At the close of the king's speech, Moor bowed profoundly and withdrew, and Father Petre, unable longer to restrain, walked up to Mauvesin, and inquired what had happened.

"Moor is dismissed the court," replied the young nobleman, joyfully. "I will tell you why presently. But how speed you with the queen."

"But indifferently," replied Father Petre. "Step this way."

At this moment Lauzun looked round for Sabine, and seeing her at a little distance, was about to lead her away, when he was checked by a gesture from the queen, who called him to her.

"I am glad you have brought Mademoiselle Saint Leu with you," said Mary, "for it was in reference to her that I summoned you. She has had an offer of marriage."

"Indeed," exclaimed Lauzun, in surprise, "from whom?"

"From Lord Mauvesin," said the queen.

"His lordship does her much honour," said Lauzun, "but I must decline his offer."

"Oh, thank you, thank you!" murmured Sabine, pressing his arm.

"I cannot take your refusal, count," said the queen.—"I am sure your majesty will advocate Lord Mauvesin's suit with Mademoiselle Saint Leu," she added, turning to James, who approached her with Barillon and Sunderland, followed by Father Petre and Mauvesin.

"Assuredly," replied the king. "The match would be highly agreeable to me—highly agreeable, count."

"But not me," remarked Lauzun, "I would rather give her to the true man than to the pretender—to Charles Moor, who should be styled Lord Mauvesin, than to him who usurps the title."

James coloured to the temples. Sabine, already pale, was overwhelmed with confusion. Mauvesin gnawed his lips, and trifled with the hilt of his sword.

"The Count de Lauzun talks as if he had the disposal of this young lady," said Father Petre, stepping forward, "but he has no such right."

"Who will dispute it?" cried Lauzun, sternly.

The Jesuit merely bowed, and Barillon advanced.

"I will," he cried, "I claim her on behalf of the King of France, my master."

And he drew forth a despatch, bearing a large red seal, which he opened and presented to James.

"Ha! from our brother Louis!" exclaimed the king.

And, as he read over the mandate, Lauzun turned to Mary.

"I have to thank your majesty for your gracious attention to my ward," he said; "but, after what has occurred, you will forgive me if I remove her from the palace."

"You will, of course, exercise your own discretion in the matter, count," said Mary, drily.

Lauzun was moving away with Sabine, when Barillon planted himself before him.

"Not so fast, count," said the ambassador; "you must deliver that young lady to me."

"How, sir!" cried Lauzun, furiously.

"It must be so, count," said James, raising his eyes from the despatch, "such are the orders of the King of France, and you must permit me to say that I will see them obeyed."

Father Petre, Mauvesin, and Barillon, exchanged glances of triumph, while Lauzun with difficulty repressed the burst of indignation which nearly overmastered him.

"As you please, sire," he said to the king, "but you will repent your acquiescence with this tyrannical mandate. M. de Barillon, I now deliver this young lady to your charge; and look well that you violate it in no respect, or you will rue it to the end of your life."

"I obey my sovereign's commands, and not your threats, count," replied Barillon.

He then took Sabine's hand from Lauzun, who bowed round, and withdrew.

"Be not alarmed, young lady," said Barillon. "I am commanded by the king to place my house at your disposal."

Sabine made no reply, but suffered herself to be led from the room. As they descended the great staircase, she thought she beheld Lauzun and Moor in close conference in the side-passage.

Soon after Sabine's departure, Sunderand approached James.

"You seem charged with some extraordinary intelligence, my lord," said the king, looking anxiously at him.

"I am so, my liege," replied Sunderland. "Six bishops have just arrived at the palace, who request an immediate audience of your majesty."

"Six bishops!" exclaimed James, bursting into fury, "six traitors. Let me see them—let me see them."

"The great work is beginning to have effect, sire," remarked Father Petre. "These sectarians have come to remonstrate with you."

"They shall learn, to their cost, that I am their master," cried James. "Bring them to the council-room at once," he added, to Sunderland.

As the minister withdrew to obey the royal mandate, he darted a glance at Mary, who replied by a gesture of equal significance.

CHAPTER IV.

THE COMMITTAL OF THE BISHOPS TO THE TOWER.

The night was somewhat advanced, when the six bishops, intrusted with the petition to the king, landed from a barge at Whitehall-stairs, and approached the entrance to the palace; but it was no unusual hour of audience with James, who, like his predecessor, was singularly easy of access. The prelates were watched, at a little distance, by the Dutch ambassador, who lingered near the spot till they entered the palace. On making known their errand, an usher led them to an ante-chamber, where they were left to themselves.

Half an hour had elapsed, and their patience was well-nigh exhausted, when the Earl of Sunderland entered the room, and informing them that he had it in command to conduct them to the council-room.

"We are very unwilling to intrude on the king at this hour, my lord," cried St. Asaph, whose resolution began to waver, "and will be satisfied with imploring his indulgence through you."

"You will plead your cause better yourself, my lord," answered the wily minister; "his majesty awaits you."

With this he led the way to the council-room.

James was seated at the table, together with Dartmouth, Jeffreys, and Father Petre. On the king's right stood Cartwright, bishop of Chester; a prelate as notorious for his servility, as he was degraded by his vices. In one of his drunken moments, he had gone so far as to declare publicly that Sunderland and Jeffreys were scoundrels, who would betray the king; and, having denied the speech by his sacred order, he was at last, by the king's command, reduced to beg pardon for it in tears. Denounced by some as a secret Papist, and by others accused of a want of all religious belief, a fear of the consequences, as well as his own predilections, now disposed him rather to side with his episcopal brethren, than to lend his support to their avowed enemies.

As Sunderland introduced the bishops, St. Asaph bent the knee before the royal chair, and the other prelates followed his example.

"The time has now arrived for accomplishing your pious intentions, my liege," urged Father Petre, apart. "Remember, it was your august father's indecision that brought him to the block."

"I implore your majesty to bear in mind what Lord Halifax told you this morning," said the Bishop of Chester, "that your father suffered for the Church, not the Church for him."

James became pale as death.

"I will hear them," he said, in an agitated voice. "What is the meaning of this, my lords?" he added to the bishops.

"We have come to submit a humble petition to your majesty," answered St. Asaph. "It is signed by the Archbishop of Canterbury, and by ourselves, in behalf of the clergy of our respective dioceses."

"Rise, my lords, I pray of you," returned James. "I shall be glad to find that you ask nothing inconsistent with your duty to me. Let me see the petition."

"Be firm," whispered Sunderland to St. Asaph, as he received the document from him.

James took the petition graciously, but his brow contracted as he perused it; and, at last, he flung it angrily from him.

"You have been silent till the last moment, in the hope of taking me by surprise," he cried; "but you will find yourselves mistaken. You have preached unconditional obedience, and I will make you practise it."

"Your majesty has spoken well," observed Father Petre, in a low tone. "Only act as vigorously, and I shall consider our religion already re-established."

"You are urging his majesty to his destruction," said Sunderland, warmly.

"How, my lord!" cried James; "do you dare—"

"Forgive me, my liege," interrupted Sunderland, "but when pernicious advice like this is given you, I am compelled to denounce it."

"I will hear no more," cried James, impetuously. "I am determined both to enforce the laws, and to uphold my prerogative." And, turning to the bishops, he added, "Your petition, my lords, disputes the dispensing power. Are you aware that you are raising the standard of rebellion?"

St. Asaph again threw himself on his knees.

"I beseech your majesty not to say aught so hard and unjust of us," he exclaimed; "rebellion is the furthest thing from our thoughts."

"We have adventured our lives for your majesty," said Trelawney, "and would spill the last drop of our blood in your defence."

"Your actions scarcely bear out your words," cried James, scornfully. "God has given me a dispensing power, and I will maintain it."

"I hope your majesty will allow the same freedom of opinion to us which you have accorded to the Dissenters," implored Kenn; "I will honour the king, but fear God."

"I tell you, Bishop," cried James, "there are seven thousand men, even in the Church of England, who have not bowed the knee to Baal. I will be obeyed."

"God's will be done!" ejaculated Kenn, devoutly.

"You would be martyrs—ha!" cried James, furiously.

"Their lordships had better withdraw for a short time, my liege," said Sunderland.

"Recollect Lord Halifax's words, my liege," murmured the Bishop of Chester.

"Peace!" thundered James, waving his hand.

The usher in waiting then advanced, and, as he passed, Sunderland, unperceived, slipped a paper into his hand. The bishops were then conducted to an adjacent chamber.

"Your majesty must not hesitate now," said Father Petre, quickly, "to the Tower with them—to the Tower."

"Be content, father, they shall go," rejoined the king.

A bitter smile illumined Father Petre's cadaverous countenance.

"I implore your majesty not to resolve too hastily on this measure," said Sunderland. "Dismiss them to-night, and inform them of your pleasure another time—a week—a month hence."

"It is not often I can agree with the Earl of Sunderland, my liege," added Lord Dartmouth, "but I now entreat you to yield to his suggestion. Let me again remind you of the last words of poor Doctor Morley."

"Doctor Morley was an obstinate schismatic," rejoined Father Petre. "I pray Heaven to guide your majesty's judgment, and keep you steadfast to your pious purpose."

"My determination is unalterable," replied James, "they shall go to the Tower if it cost me my crown."

"It is likely to cost him his crown and something more," muttered Dartmouth to the Bishop of Chester.

"The chancellor tells me, my liege, that the committal of the bishops is a violation of the law," urged Sunderland, who had been vainly endeavouring to persuade Jeffreys to interpose.

"Such is my opinion," faltered Jeffreys, appalled at the responsibility of his situation.

"Do not talk to me of the law," exclaimed James, "I am above the law."

"Your majesty may be above the law, but we are not," rejoined Sunderland.

"His lordship is afraid of offending his ally, the Prince of Orange," observed Father Petre, sneeringly.

"I am afraid of endangering the crown," rejoined Sunderland, sternly; "but here comes one who has ever been at his majesty's side in moments of danger."

As he spoke the folding-doors were thrown open, and the queen entered the room. Father Petre uttered an impatient exclamation.

Mary looked pale and alarmed, and supported herself on the arm of the Countess of Powis, who was herself much agitated. As she stepped forward all the council arose, and James hastened to meet her. Assisting her to a chair, he gently reproached her for invading his deliberations.

"I thought my advice might be acceptable to your majesty," answered Mary. "You may have wiser councillors than myself, but you have none more sincere. Lord Sunderland, your look alarms me. Has anything gone wrong?"

"Nothing but what I hope we can repair, gracious madam," he answered, "but we must have time, and I implore the king to suspend his judgment on the question before him for a short period, till he can calmly consider what measures should be taken."

"Well and loyally spoken," answered Mary: and, sinking her voice, she added to James, "your majesty must acknowledge that his lordship speaks the truth. I implore you to listen to him."

"The Church will bear in mind this ill-timed interference,

madam," said Father Petre. "Better you were in your chamber with your handmaidens than in men's councils."

"Bethink you of Lord Halifax's saying, my liege," whispered the Bishop of Chester, again repeating his formula.

No look or gesture from James evinced that the boding words reached his ear, but he remained for a few minutes buried in deep thought, at the end of which he roused himself and said to Sunderland, "My Lord, you will signify to the bishops that I defer giving them an answer to their petition until this day three weeks, when they will appear before me, together with the Archbishop of Canterbury. The audience is at an end."

"You have saved the king, madam," whispered Sunderland.

"And blasted the hopes of our church," rejoined Father Petre, who overheard him, "for which it will owe you little gratitude."

"I have obeyed the impulses of my heart and conscience, father," replied Mary, "and am therefore satisfied with what I have done."

As the royal pair withdrew, Sunderland proceeded to dismiss the bishops.

The fact of the bishops having petitioned the king for the repeal of the order to read the Declaration of Indulgence in the churches, together with the reception that James had accorded them, was the next day bruited abroad throughout the metropolis. The excitement occasioned by the intelligence was universal, and all parties looked forward with the utmost impatience to the next Sunday, when the Declaration was appointed to be read. With four exceptions, the whole of the metropolitan clergy disobeyed the order; and even in the private chapel of Whitehall, the declaration was read by a chorister. Sprat, bishop of Rochester, who would have honoured the episcopal bench by his talents, if he had not disgraced it by his vices, was obliged to read it himself in Westminster Abbey, and before he had finished the perusal, such a disturbance arose that he could scarcely hold the proclamation. Even the Nonconformists extolled the resistance of the bishops; and the venerable Baxter, from his pulpit at Acton, denounced the proclamation as an insult to the Protestant religion.

"The whole Church," wrote Count d'Adda in a letter to the pope, "espouses the cause of the bishops. There is no reasonable expectation of a division among the Anglicans, and our hopes from the Nonconformists are vanished."

It was not by the papal nuncio alone that this demonstration of public opinion was regarded with apprehension. It caused equal inquietude to the king, the queen, and the ministers. But encouraged by Father Petre, James still cherished the conviction that the resistance of the clergy would be overcome by violence; and he was unfortunately placed in that embarrassing situation in which it was equally dangerous to advance or recede. Sunderland, however, continued his endeavours to persuade him to a moderate course, in which he was ably seconded by Dartmouth, Jeffreys, and Preston, but the condition of the queen deprived him of her more powerful support, and his efforts to promote conciliation were effectually thwarted by the insidious counsels of Petre.

Meanwhile, the petitioning bishops were summoned to appear before the privy council on the 8th of June, to answer a charge of misdemeanour. Leaving for after-narration such incidents of this history as happened in the interim, we shall at once proceed to show how the prosecution of the prelates was conducted.

On the afternoon of the appointed day the whole of the privy council assembled at Whitehall. Dispersed in knots round the room, they awaited with anxiety the appearance of the king, but meanwhile conversed, with affected carelessness, on the various topics of the day. Sunderland alone took no pains to conceal his uneasiness, and as he passed from one group to another, he exacted from his friends a promise of unqualified support.

At length, James entered the council-room, attended by Father Petre. He looked grave and anxious, and his brow was clouded with an ominous frown. Motioning the councillors to their seats, he opened the proceedings with a few prefatory remarks, in which he reminded his auditors of the momentous character of the case they were about to investigate, and concluded by advising them not to mistake in their judgments weakness for moderation.

"In shunning that error, my liege," replied Sunderland, "we must be equally careful not to confound violence with vigour. Let their lordships be introduced."

The usher disappeared, but presently returned, followed by the Archbishop of Canterbury, and the six bishops.

"So your grace has come at last," cried James, sternly, as the primate advanced. "It is some time since we met. I am sorry I cannot give you better welcome."

"I have laboured under your majesty's displeasure too long," replied the archbishop. "Age and infirmities, too, have kept me a close prisoner at Lambeth, but I have prayed daily for your welfare."

"You should have prayed also for a humble heart," answered James, bitterly; "you would raise a revolt against me."

"God forbid we should ever give you cause to think so, my liege," exclaimed the archbishop. "It is our duty rather to set an example of obedience to our fellow-subjects."

"Do you acknowledge this insolent writing as yours?" demanded James, pointing to the petition.

"I am not obliged to answer your majesty," rejoined the archbishop.

"Not answer me!" exclaimed the king, passionately. "By my faith! but you will find that you are obliged."

"Not so, your majesty," interposed Jeffreys; "no man is obliged to criminate himself."

"Are you his grace's counsel?" asked Father Petre, insolently.

"Tush, priest," replied Jeffreys, dealing him one of his blackest looks.

"What I would not answer on compulsion I will declare voluntarily," said the archbishop; "the hand-writing *is* mine. My brother prelates also desire me to acknowledge that their signatures are appended by them."

"Enough," said James; "having pleaded guilty, it only remains to decide on your punishment."

"It must be such as to prevent the repetition of the offence," observed Father Petre.

"They will soon come to their senses if deprived of their sees," remarked Lord Berkeley.

"Publish a declaration, my liege," said Sunderland, "expressive of your just resentment at the hardihood of the bishops, but stating also that it is still your gracious intention to treat them with clemency."

Jeffreys, Preston, and Dartmouth expressed their concurrence in this proposition.

"I exhort your majesty not to consent to such a declaration," said Father Petre, solemnly: "it will be holding out encouragement to rebellion. There is only one way of dealing with these insolent prelates, and that is by a prosecution."

"It were best to commit them to the Tower," said the Earl of Middleton.

"I like your counsel well, my lord," replied James; "but as Lord Sunderland recommends clemency, I will so far yield to him, that they shall be set at liberty on putting in bail. The Lord Chancellor will inform them of my determination."

"My lords," said Jeffreys, addressing the prelates, who, during this brief debate, had been removed to the further end of the chamber, and who were now brought forward again, "his majesty is justly indignant at the petition you have presented to him, which he regards as a tissue of sedition, and he has ordered you to be prosecuted for the misdemeanour accordingly. But, in the meantime, in his clemency he will vouchsafe you his permission to be allowed to go at large on entering into recognisances to appear at your trial."

"My brother bishops will do as they like," said Trelawney, abruptly, "but for my own part, I will never enter into such an arrangement."

"Even if willing, which we are not, we could not so engage," said Kenn.

"As peers of the realm, we claim our privileges," said the archbishop.

"Make out the warrant for their committal to the Tower," said James to Jeffreys, "and let them be placed in custody at once."

The archbishop bowed submissively, and passed out of the room, accompanied by the bishops. They tarried within the ante-chamber for a short time, when they were joined by the high constable of Westminster, who informed them that he was empowered to take them into custody, and convey them to the Tower. They expressed their readiness to accompany him, and without further delay followed him out of the palace.

The approach to Whitehall-stairs across the outer-court was kept clear by a party of the guards, under command of Colonel Kirke, but on either side were collected numerous spectators, among whom might be distinguished the pious and amiable Evelyn, and his courtier friend, Pepys. The spectators uncovered as the prelates appeared; but though every eye regarded them with sympathy, no one gave utterance to any expression of feeling, and amidst a profound silence, the bishops bent their steps towards the stairs. Here one of the royal barges awaited them, and attended by the high constable, and a strong escort of the grenadier guards, they embarked for the Tower.

Favoured by the tide, the barge passed swiftly down the river; and shooting the centre arch of London Bridge, arrived at Traitor's-gate. The Lieutenant of the Tower had been apprised of their approach, and the great wooden gates beneath the archway were thrown open to admit the barge.

As they passed beneath the black and yawning archway, a gloom fell upon the spirits of the bishops, which all their fortitude failed to dissipate. The boldest felt daunted at the prospect presented, by the probable effect of their imprisonment, which, if adverse to themselves, must involve the triumph of arbitrary power, and the consequent subversion of the Church, or if favourable, must produce a great national convulsion. But, depressing as it was, this very apprehension, raising them above any personal fear, gave to the virtuous among them a dignity and elevation of deportment that excited admiration.

As they mounted the steps, they were received by Sir Edward Hales, the Lieutenant of the Tower, attended by a party of the guard, commanded by Colonel Trelawney.

Sir Edward Hales was the first Roman Catholic who had been nominated, under a dispensation from the king, to a public appointment. A friendly information was laid against him in the Court of King's Bench, by his own coachman, for the purpose of establishing the legality of the dispensing power, and the judges had then decided that the royal dispensation qualified him to hold office. A bigoted Papist, he was in any case disposed to treat the dignitaries of the Protestant church with incivility, but the fact of their having disputed the dispensing power, by which alone he was rendered capable of holding his public employments, made him regard his venerable prisoners with especial dislike.

"Welcome to the Tower, my lords," he said, with derisive politeness; "I trust I shall have the pleasure of a long visit from you."

"Show us to our lodging, sir," said the archbishop, passing on.

As he moved with the others towards the entrance of the Bloody Tower, Colonel Trelawney stepped on one side, and took off his hat. The soldiers instantly cast down their arms, and threw themselves on their knees. One of the officers burst into tears.

The archbishop paid no attention to these demonstrations of regard, but walked on with his gaze fixed on the ground, while the other prelates imitated his example, though Trelawney, in passing, exchanged a glance with his brother. Conducted by Hales, they crossed the Tower green, and when in view of the chapel, the archbishop perceived that the door was open, and expressed a wish to join in the evening service, at the moment in course of celebration. Hales yielded a reluctant assent, and the prelates entered the sacred edifice.

The officiating clergyman chanced to be reading the second lesson as they made their appearance; and, by a strange coincidence, at this moment delivered the apostle's exhortation to the Corinthians, to approve themselves "the ministers of God, in much patience, in afflictions, in necessities, in distresses, in stripes, in imprisonments." As he read forth the passage, the whole congregation stood up.

Exasperated and alarmed, Sir Edward Hales quitted the chapel, and summoned the garrison to arms. By this time the bishops came out of the chapel. Hales received them with his staff at the door; and conducted them in silence to the Beauchamp Tower, which had been hastily prepared for their reception.

CHAPTER V

THE EXCISE OFFICERS.

In the hostel of the Burleigh Arms, in Cecil-street, were two garrets, which were rarely appropriated to the reception of guests. They were approached by a narrow back-staircase, entirely separated from the rest of the house; a circumstance which added materially to their ordinary quiet and seclusion.

On the night of the committal of the bishops to the Tower, the front garret, which was of considerable size, and very sombre aspect, was occupied by three persons, two of whom have been already presented to the reader, as Mynherr Van Citters, the Dutch ambassador, and Colonel Sidney, the third was Admiral Herbert, afterwards Earl of Torrington—a man of loose and dissolute character, who had originally been a great favourite of James, but having refused to embrace Popery, as an atonement for the errors of his life, he was dismissed from the king's service, and naturally went over to that of the Prince of Orange.

"It is strange we have no tidings from Holland," remarked Herbert.

"I am in hourly expectation of despatches from the prince," said Van Citters; "and have ordered them to be sent here, if any arrive in my absence."

"King James is doing all he can to help us," observed Sidney, with a smile. "Our agents also are hard at work. Johnstone has gone to see Bishop Trelawney in the Tower; and Speke is stirring up the Dissenters and the city apprentices."

"I distrust that Speke," rejoined Van Citters. "He owes his freedom to the king, if not his life, and yet he betrays him. When he has us completely in his power, he will be equally treacherous to us."

"I am quite satisfied of his fidelity," said Sidney.

Van Citters shook his head, but made no remark, and at this moment the door opened, admitting the portly landlord. Littlehales was accompanied by a tall man, closely muffled in a cloak, who advanced to Van Citters, and presented him with a box of despatches.

"They have just arrived, your excellency," he said; "and the messenger tells me are of the last importance."

Upon this the man withdrew, in company with Littlehales. Van Citters took some despatches from the box, and cast his eyes hastily over them, while his companions watched him in silence, endeavouring to discover from his looks the nature of their contents.

After a considerable interval, their impatience having become almost intolerable, the phlegmatic ambassador thought fit to relieve it.

"The prince has at last determined upon an invasion," he said. "He is secretly making preparations for this purpose, but before he declares himself, he requires an invitation from the leading men of this country, assuring him of their concurrence and support."

"There will be little difficulty in obtaining it, I hope," replied Sidney. "I am sure of Devonshire and Danby; and Halifax has promised to join us, if we can secure Nottingham. I hope to accomplish the latter point through the agency of young Moor."

"You must remember that Nottingham is a Tory," remarked Herbert.

"Be careful how you put yourself in his power," cried Van Citters. "And can you trust Moor?"

"I would trust him with my life," said Sidney.

"The best way will be to let Nottingham see our strength," returned Herbert. "I think with you, that his regard for the Church will induce him to listen to us, but he is timid and wavering. If he were sensible of the progress we have made, he would be less reluctant."

"Herbert is right," said Sidney. "I must persuade Moor to invite him to a general meeting at Mrs. Potter's.—But here comes some intelligence."

As he spoke, a stout, burly man entered the room, and was instantly recognised by the confederates as George Johnstone, an active coadjutor. Johnstone was the cousin of the celebrated Dr. Burnet, and the most industrious of his correspondents. From his high connections, he possessed considerable means of obtaining information—his sister being the wife of General Drummond, who was one of the leading persecutors of the Scotch Presbyterians, and his niece was married to the son of the Earl of Melfort, one of the ministers.

As he returned the greeting of the confederates, he produced a packet of letters, and presented it to Sidney.

"These are from the bishops of St. Asaph and Bristol," he said. "I suppose you have heard how they were received at the Tower?"

"All the town has heard it by this time," laughed Sidney.

"Speke has gone to spread the intelligence among the apprentices. But excuse me a moment."

And he hastened to peruse the packet of letters.

While he was thus engaged, Van Citters turned again to his despatches, and Herbert conversed in an under-tone with Johnstone.

"The prelates are full of confidence," resumed Sidney, at length. "Dr. Trelawney has enclosed me a letter from the Bishop of London, in which his lordship expresses a wish to join us."

"Secure him, by all means!" cried Van Citters.

"Invite him to the meeting at Mrs. Potter's," said Herbert. "His presence will have a good effect on Nottingham."

"No doubt," answered Sidney, "and I will take care he is present."

Here the door again opened, admitting two persons, the foremost of whom was addressed by Sidney by the name of Speke.

Speke's countenance was harsh and forbidding, and might well excite doubt in a less suspicious nature than that of the Dutch ambassador. He had been prosecuted during the previous reign for an infamous libel, accusing James, then duke of York, of having murdered Lord Essex in the Tower, and had been punished by a fine of £5,000. Liberated through the intercession of James, whom he had so vilely slandered, he acknowledges, in his "Secret History of the Revolution," that the generous monarch not only forgave his offence, but afterwards took him into favour. At this very moment, indeed, he stood high in the king's confidence, though he professed to his enemies that he was plotting his destruction.

"I have brought a trusty friend to see you, gentlemen," he said, presenting his companion. "He is called Ephraim Ruddle, and is an old Cromwellian. He has been working for us among the Nonconformists."

"He has done our cause good service then," replied Sidney. "As the Nonconformists stand by the Church, now she is in danger, so will the Church stand by them hereafter."

"They shall be relieved from all disabilities," observed Van Citters. "Such distinctions should cease among the brethren."

"Yea, should they," concurred Ephraim, in a strong nasal twang.

"Do you call these canting dogs our brethren?" muttered Herbert, with a look of disgust, to the ambassador.

"It won't do to be over-scrupulous just now," whispered Van Citters. "Do you find the Dissenters much concerned about the bishops?" he added to Ephraim.

"The elect look on and marvel, and cry 'Watch! watch! for the day of deliverance is at hand,'" rejoined Ephraim, in the same snuffling tone as before.

"But will they help us to accomplish the deliverance?" asked Van Citters.

"They are waiting the cry of the watchman at the gate, when there will be a shout of 'To your tents, O, Israel!'" returned Ephraim.

"Be seated," said Van Citters, "and let us know precisely the amount of your strength."

While Ephraim, sitting bolt upright in a chair, and twirling round his thumbs, entered into the details required of him, Sidney conversed apart with Speke.

"From this fellow's account, I suppose you have succeeded with the Dissenters," he said, "eh?"

"We have—but not without difficulty," replied Speke. "They thought, at first, that the bishops were resisting the Declaration of Indulgence."

"I feared they would be influenced by that," rejoined Sidney, "but you did not allow them to retain such an impression?"

"No, but it required great skill and subtlety to remove it," returned Speke, with a smile. "I told them the bishops only desired to have the Declaration of Indulgence sanctioned by Parliament, so that the king should not be able to repeal it, as he intended, when he had thrown all the power into the hands of the Papists."

"And that turned them?" asked Sidney.

"It went a great way," answered Speke. "Coupled with a few stories about the Jesuits and Anti-Christ, it brought them quite round."

"And the apprentices—what of them?" asked Sidney.

"The cry of 'No Popery' was all the persuasion they required," replied Speke.

"Did you concert a demonstration?" inquired Sidney.

"I did, both with them and the Dissenters," returned Speke. "Large mobs will assemble round the Tower every day as long as the bishops are confined there; and a deputation of dissenting divines will wait upon their lordships to-morrow, with an address of condolence."

"So far, then, all promises fairly," rejoined Sidney. "Whom have we here?"

The door opened, and Littlehales entered, ushering in a lady, whom, in spite of a closely drawn veil, Sidney instantly knew to be Mrs. Dawson, one of the attendants of the queen. Mrs. Dawson was a distant relation of Dr. Burnet, and an intimate friend of Mrs. Baillie, of Jerviswood, a sister of Johnstone, by whom she had been won to the interest of Sidney.

All the party arose at her appearance.

"I thought you and Mr. Johnstone would have been alone, Colonel Sidney," said Mrs. Dawson, in accents of alarm, and speaking to him apart, "or, at most, that no one but Mr. Van Citters would have been with you. Is not that Mr. Speke?"

"It is," answered Sidney, "but you need fear nothing from him. He is a friend."

"Still I would not have him know me," faltered Mrs. Dawson. "But he cannot distinguish my features, and I will only stay to tell you that Lady Sunderland will meet Mrs. Venables to-night, if she can contrive to enter the palace."

"I will take care that Mrs. Venables receives her ladyship's message," replied Sidney. "Will you admt, my young friend, Charles Moor, to the picture gallery?"

"It will be running a great risk," said Mrs. Dawson, hesitatingly. "However, let him come. And now that my message is delivered I must be gone."

"Permit me to attend you to your chair, madam," said Johnstone, stepping forward.

And he preceded her out of the room.

Shortly afterwards Sidney was about to follow, when Littlehales rushed into the room.

"Stop, colonel," he cried, "the excise officers have just pounced upon us, and will meet you on the stairs. Gather round the table, and make b'lieve to be at ease, or you'll excite their suspicions."

"This is devilish unlucky," cried Sidney.

"What shall we do with the papers?" ejaculated Herbert.

"I'll dispose of 'em, your excellency," said Littlehales. "Give 'em to me."

"And what's to be done with me?" demanded Van Citters, uneasily. "If they happen to know me, they'll suspect you all."

"Your excellency can get out on the roof," replied Littlehales.

"Ay, the roof! quick—quick!" cried Sidney.

And grasping the ambassador's arm, he hurried him to a dormer window, and assisted him to pass to a ledge without, whence he could scramble upon the roof. Leaving him there, he shut the window, and joined his companions at the table.

Meanwhile, Littlehales had swept all the papers into his apron, and by the help of a small ring in the floor, raised a plank, which was contrived as a place of concealment, and having shot the papers into the opening, dropped the board into its place again.

"Well done, Jerry," cried Sidney. "But where have you bestowed your decanters? These fellows must not find us here without wine."

"Here they are, sir," replied Littlehales, producing bottles and glasses.

Voices were now heard on the stairs, calling on Littlehales to open the door, and threatening him with the vengeance of the law for his delay.

"Comin', sirs, comin'," shouted Littlehales, opening the door, and admitting an excise officer and three assistants.

"Soh, here's a reg'lar gambolin' party," cried the exciseman. "I knew we'd find you out, Mister Littlehales."

"Who are these people, landlord?" demanded Sidney, with affected surprise. "What does this mean?"

"Come, no nonsense," returned the exciseman. "Just hand out the cards and dice, or I'll call in the watch, and pack you all off to the round-us."

"They arn't gamblers, Mr. Girdlestone," observed Littlehales, with ill-concealed terror. "They're the Grecian club, as always meets in this here hattic."

"That man looks like a Greek, certainly," resumed the exciseman, glancing at Sidney. "Barlow," he added to one of his assistants, "it's the colonel; ain't it?"

"What colonel?" asked the assistant, stepping forward.

Sidney met their gaze with perfect composure.

"Why, Colonel Underwood," replied the exciseman. "He's werry like him."

"Werry like Colonel Underwood," rejoined Barlow.

"You do not know whom you are speaking of, you insolent rascals," cried Sidney. "Be gone, or your office shall not protect you from my resentment."

"Well, it's true we ain't caught you in the act," replied the exciseman, somewhat awed by Sidney's commanding manner. "But sound the walls, mates! There may be some sly cupboards about, where old Jerry stows his liquors."

With a jeering laugh, his assistants quickly produced a mallet and chisels, and proceeded to sound the walls. But their labours were fruitless, and, after a diligent investigation, they relinquished their object.

"Snewin shouldn't have told you he'd send us, Jerry," the exciseman then said. "But come, we'll part friends. We don't mind drinking your health."

"Much obliged to you, Mr. Girdlestone, sir," replied Littlehales, "but I've no liquor good enough for you at present."

And he led the way out of the room.

As soon as they were fairly gone, Sidney hastened to the

relief of Van Citters, whom he found seated on a gable end of the roof. The ambassador was delighted to hear of the departure of the officers, and gladly returned to the room, where he and Sidney exchanged a few words apart, after which, the latter summoned Littlehales, and directed him to fetch a sedan-chair. A quarter of an hour elapsed before Littlehales returned from his errand, and entering the passage, he was greatly surprised to find a tall and elegantly dressed lady standing near the door.

"Servant, madam," he exclaimed; "anything I can do for you?"

"Only show me to the door, Jerry," replied the lady, in very masculine tones.

"Why, zounds, colonel, it ain't you, surely," ejaculated Littlehales, wonder-stricken at the sudden metamorphosis.

"No, it's Mrs. Venables, you dolt," exclaimed the lady.

"Mrs. Wenerables," echoed Littlehales, "I'm sure you look quite like a fine young madam, and not wenerables by no means."

"Hold your tongue, and open the door," cried the lady, impatiently, "and tell the porters to take me to Whitehall."

"Why, bless us, you ain't agoin' there, and in that disguise?" cried Littlehales.

"Do as I bid you, and ask no more questions," cried the lady, dealing him a sounding box on the ear.

And stepping forward, she entered the chair, which instantly moved off in the direction intimated.

CHAPTER VI.

WHAT HAPPENED IN THE PICTURE GALLERY OF WHITEHALL.

Originally constructed for Prince Henry, eldest son of James the First, by Inigo Jones, and completed under the auspices of the prince's martyr brother, Charles the First, the Picture Gallery of Whitehall was erected, to use the words of Walpole, "about the middle of the palace, running across from the Thames towards the banqueting-house, and fronting westward to the privy-garden."

Seized by the Parliament during the civil war, on the 23rd of July, 1645, it was resolved by the House of Commons that "all such pictures and statues at Whitehall as were without any superstition, should be forthwith sold for the benefit of Ireland and the North; and all such pictures there as have the representation of the Second Person in the Trinity, or of the Virgin Mary, should be forthwith burnt." Walpole's "Anecdotes of Painting" contains many curious particulars of the sale and dispersion of the royal collection.

The gallery was, however, partially restored. On his elevation to the Protectorate, Cromwell exerted himself to preserve such pictures and statues as had not been sold or stolen, and repurchased many of those scattered abroad. The collection was subsequently enriched by other gems, and by the native genius of Lely and Kneller, and thus again came to rank among the first picture-galleries of Europe.

Ten o'clock had sounded, when the usher ordinarily stationed at the entrance of the gallery locked the door, and taking away the key, marched off. Scarcely had he disappeared when a young man stepped quickly forward from the opposite end of the corridor, where he had remained concealed, and tapping softly against the door, it was instantly unlocked on the other side, and opened for him. This service had been performed by Signora Riva, one of the queen's favourite attendants, who, as the young man passed through, smiled, and pointing down the gallery, again closed the door, but did not lock it, and remained near it, while he walked quickly on in the direction indicated.

Here and there a lamp was lighted, dimly revealing some wondrous production of a great master, but generally the gallery was buried in obscurity. Hurrying forward between ranges of statues, the young man speedily found himself beside a lady, who advanced to meet him. It was Sabine.

"You are very rash in coming here, Mr. Moor," she said, in an agitated tone. "Do you not know the risk you incur by the step."

"I know it perfectly, but I would have incurred double the risk to exchange a word with you," replied Moor. "My letter would have acquainted you with my determination."

"You were very imprudent to write," said Sabine;—"very imprudent, indeed."

"Do not chide me," said Moor; "but tell me somewhat about yourself. I know that M. Barillon has consented to your remaining with the queen, on her majesty's undertaking that the Count de Lauzun shall not interfere with you; but I wish to know whether you are to continue at the palace."

"Not long," replied Sabine. "I have had no communication either with my uncle or the Count de Lauzun, but I believe I am to return shortly to France."

"To France!" echoed Moor, in a tone of despair.

"Nor is it likely I shall ever come back to this country,"

rejoined Sabine, in tones of almost equal sadness. "I have consented to see you in this clandestine manner,—of which you must disapprove as much as I do myself,—to bid you an eternal farewell."

"Oh no, do not say so, Sabine," replied Moor, taking her hand, which she did not withdraw. "If you go to Paris, I will go there too."

"It would be useless," said Sabine. "Efforts, I know, will be made to compel me to conform to the Romish faith. Indeed, I have been told by her majesty that a life of wealth and dignity will open to me if I assent,—but that I will never do. The alternative is a life of seclusion, and I may probably be sent to Switzerland. But, be it as it may, we can never meet again."

"I will not seal my own doom by agreeing to the sentence," replied Moor.

"It must be," said Sabine, gravely and firmly. "You have heavy duties to discharge, and will soon forget me."

"Never!" exclaimed Moor.

"From what I see passing around me, and from what I hear, I am certain that great troubles will fall upon this court and kingdom," rejoined Sabine. "A mighty religious convulsion is at hand, and it will be much if you escape a civil war. Ours is the Protestant faith; but though the bigotry of the king will no doubt hurry him into extreme acts, do not, Mr. Moor, do not forget your allegiance to him."

"I will never aid his enemies," said Moor; "but I cannot submit to see the Protestant Church oppressed. The king is surrounded by dangerous and designing men. Father Petre is hurrying him to destruction. Oh! that you could tell the queen as much!"

"Were I to tell her, she would not believe me," replied Sabine. "The Jesuit's influence is almost as great with her as with the king."

Before Moor could reply, Signora Riva, who had remained stationed near the door during the whole of the interview, rushed forward, and cried—"The king is coming; he is already at the door."

"Can I not pass out at the other door?" demanded Moor.

"Impossible!" exclaimed Sabine. "An usher and several valets are placed there. You will be recognised and arrested."

"Step behind this book-case," cried Signora Riva. "You may be able to get out by-and-by. Quick, here comes the king, and with him Father Petre."

Acting upon the suggestion, Moor retreated behind a massive book-case, while James and Father Petre slowly walked down the gallery. They were engaged in deep conversation, and did not become aware of the ladies' presence, until they were close upon them."

"Ha! what are you doing here, young mistress?" exclaimed James to Sabine, on perceiving her.

"Her blushes and confusion show that she has come to meet her lover," said Father Petre, regarding her sharply.

"Her lover!" cried James. "What lover? Young Moor has been banished the palace, and if he ventures here in defiance of my injunctions he will peril his head."

"Oh! your majesty!" exclaimed Sabine, in great alarm.

"You have only one way of averting his majesty's displeasure, and that is by revealing whom you came to meet," said Father Petre.

"I will disclose myself," whispered Moor to La Riva, from behind the book-case.

"That won't mend the matter," replied the confidante, aside to him, "so keep still. I will tell your majesty the whole truth," she added, advancing.

"That's right," cried Father Petre.

"We came here to meet Mrs. Venables—that's all," said La Riva.

"Mrs. Venables!" cried the king. "And who, in the name of mystery, is she?"

"There *is* a mystery about her, your majesty," observed Father Petre. "A person of that name has been in the habit of paying nocturnal visits to the palace, and I am by no means satisfied with the accounts I have received of her."

"Then I will satisfy you at once, father," replied La Riva, pertly. "She is merely a lace merchant—a friend of Mrs. Potter's of the Indian House at the New Exchange."

"Oh! is that all?" cried the king. "Well, it turns out to be a very harmless appointment after all—a little contraband, but nothing more. But I must pray you to retire, ladies. I would be alone with Father Petre."

And waving his hand, Sabine and La Riva made profound obeisances and withdrew, not without casting anxious glances towards the book-case.

"We can now pursue our conference without interruption, father," observed the king. "As I have just told you, I am resolved that the supporters of the rebellious prelates shall share their humiliation, and when the Anglicans are disposed of, we will think of some punishment for the Dissenters."

"Recall the indulgence you have granted them," rejoined Father Petre, "and show this heretical people that there is but One Church, and that Church must be supreme. The re-establishment of the Catholic religion by your majesty, will not only hallow your earthly crown, but win you a glorious one in heaven."

"Our blessed Lady guide and prosper my efforts!" exclaimed James, bending reverentially.

"Amen!" exclaimed Father Petre. "Your majesty must so frame your measures that its restoration shall be permanent. In the midst of life we are in death, and as the law now stands, your presumptive heir is the heretical Princess of Orange. Her accession to the throne would expose the Church to greater persecution than ever."

"But I am in daily hopes that heaven will bless me with a son," observed James.

"Even if the royal infant should prove a daughter, the crown must be that daughter's," said the wily Jesuit.

"It cannot be, while the Princesses Mary and Anne are living," said James; "the order of succession cannot be disturbed."

"Heaven will forgive any means you may use to benefit the true religion," suggested the Jesuit.

James mused a moment—his gaze bent fixedly on the ground. Arousing himself, he grasped Father Petre's arm, and said hurriedly,

"I have something to tell you, father, which concerns my very life. You must receive it under the seal of confession."

But before he could proceed with his disclosure, Moor stepped from behind the book-case.

"Hold, my liege," he cried; "I have thus far been an involuntary auditor of your conference, but whatever risk I may incur, I will not suffer you to proceed further."

"Base spy and traitor!" cried Father Petre. "Are you prying upon his majesty's secret councils?"

"How did you gain admission to the palace, sir?" demanded James, sternly.

"Pardon me, my liege, if I decline answering you," replied Moor.

"You have disobeyed my orders, and must bear the punishment," replied James. "You are a prisoner. Remain where you are."

And without further notice of Moor, James withdrew with Father Petre into a recess, and resumed his conference in a low tone.

At this juncture, the door at the opposite end of the gallery was softly opened, and two ladies entered, who, after looking round, and seeing no one (for Moor was screened from view by an intervening pillar), seated themselves on a fauteuil.

"And so there really is a scheme in contemplation to alter the settlement of the crown, in a certain event, my dear Lady Sunderland?" asked one of these persons.

"There is, my dear Mrs. Venables," replied the other. "I overheard the king and Barillon talking of it; and from what transpired, I am quite certain, that if his majesty is disappointed in his hopes of a son, he will settle the crown of Ireland on the Earl of Tyrconnell, who, since his appointment as lord-lieutenant, has won over to his interest all the Catholic population, and will be supported by France."

"Is it possible the king can be so besotted?" cried Mrs. Venables. "This exceeds even my opinion of his folly. But look!—is there not some one behind yon pillar?"

"I will go and see," cried the countess in alarm. And she passed with noiseless footsteps along the darkened side of the gallery, while Mrs. Venables retreated into a recess, and drew the curtains before her.

Scarcely was this done, when the door was again opened by an usher, and the queen and Lord Sunderland entered.

"You see you were mistaken, my lord," observed Mary, glancing down the gallery. "The king is not here."

"He may be at the other end of the apartment, your majesty," replied Sunderland. "Pray be seated, and I will go in search of him."

Having conducted her to the fauteuil, just vacated by the two ladies, he stepped quickly forward.

After the lapse of a few seconds, all becoming silent, Mrs. Venables peeped from behind the curtain, and seeing the queen, mistook her in the obscurity for Lady Sunderland.

"I thought I heard the door open," she said, quitting her hiding-place, and moving quickly towards Mary; "but I suppose I was mistaken."

Though somewhat startled by this sudden apparition, the queen instantly recovered her composure, and curious to know what it meant, said, in a low tone, "You need not be alarmed."

"I was afraid it might be the king, or your husband, Lord Sunderland," pursued Mrs. Venables.

"She takes me for Lady Sunderland," muttered the queen. "I'll humour the jest. Suppose it had been his lordship, what would you have done, madam?" she added, in the same low tone as before.

"Nay, call me Sidney," cried the other. "To you, at least, dear countess, I am not Mrs. Venables."

"It's the traitor Sidney, in disguise," thought the queen. "Here's a pretty discovery. But I must try and ascertain the meaning of his secret visits to the palace. You have something else to say than to make love to me?" she added, aloud. "You want some intelligence which I alone can impart!"

"Have you anything more to tell me?" asked Sidney, eagerly.

"What can she have told him?" thought the queen, puzzled. "You want me to win over Sunderland, I suppose?" she added, at a venture.

"Oh, if there were any chance of that!" cried Sidney.

"You think him inflexible," said the queen.

"I am sure of it," replied Sidney. "He is devotedly attached to the queen."

"Indeed!" cried Mary, much gratified.

"I could give you a thousand proofs of it," pursued Sidney, "and I cannot wonder at it, for her majesty seems to inspire unbounded devotion among her attendants, and were it not that ——"

"You are already too far advanced, you would return to your allegiance?" said Mary, with a smile.

"No," rejoined Sidney, "but I was speaking of the queen. She has the same influence over young Moor that she has over your husband. By the bye, I may tell you that Moor has ventured into the palace to-night to meet Mademoiselle Saint Leu."

"Imprudent!" exclaimed the queen. "And has Sabine agreed to meet him?"

"She has," replied Sidney, with a smile.

"I should not have thought it," rejoined the queen, musingly.

"Ha!" exclaimed Sidney, starting up in a very unfeminine manner. "Who is this? we are discovered."

As he spoke Sunderland and the countess appeared. They had accidentally met lower down in the gallery, and were returning together. The light of a lamp fell upon the features of Lady Sunderland, and proclaimed to Sidney the mistake he had committed.

"The countess, yonder!" he exclaimed. "Who, then, are you, madam?"

"I am the queen," replied Mary, with dignity; "but be not alarmed. For Lady Sunderland's sake, I will not betray you. But beware how you enter the palace again."

At this moment Sunderland and the countess came up. The latter seemed very uneasy, but was somewhat relieved by the queen's manner.

"His majesty will be here anon, madam," said Sunderland. "He is coming down the gallery with Father Petre. You have found a companion since I left you."

"This is Mrs. Venables, a friend of the countess's," replied the queen.

"I was stupid enough to mistake her majesty for the

countess," said Sidney, vainly endeavouring to hide his confusion.

"If you make no greater mistake than that you will readily be forgiven," said the queen, graciously.

"Who is this lady?" asked Sunderland, aside, of the countess. "Her features seem familiar to me."

"Very likely," replied Lady Sunderland. "She is an old friend of mine."

"With your majesty's gracious permission I will take my leave," said Sidney, trying to sidle off.

"No, no," said the queen, somewhat maliciously, "since you are here, you shall stop and see the king."

"Your majesty has promised not to betray me," whispered Sidney.

"And I will keep my word," replied the queen in the same tone; "but you must be punished for your rashness. I command you to stay."

"I have nothing to do but to obey," replied Sidney, almost forgetting himself into a bow.

At this juncture the party was increased by the Count de Lauzun.

"What brings you here, count?" asked the queen, as he came up.

"I came in quest of your majesty," replied Lauzun. "I have made a discovery, which is of some importance to you."

"What is it?" inquired the queen.

"A traitor is concealed in the palace," cried Lauzun.

"Impossible!" exclaimed Sunderland.

"You will find that I speak the truth, my lord," replied Lauzun; "but he will not get out so easily as he got in. The sentinels have all been changed, the password has been altered, and every one will be subject to the strictest investigation before leaving the palace."

"An excellent precaution!" exclaimed Sunderland.

"What is to become of me?" said Sidney, in a whisper to the queen.

"You have a very singular-looking lady with you, madam," pursued Lauzun, gazing inquiringly at Sidney.

"Oh, she is well known to me," interposed Lady Sunderland.

"It is a man in disguise," muttered Lauzun. "A lover of her ladyship's, I'll be sworn."

"This lady has come to see me," said the queen.

"You, madam!" exclaimed Lauzun, in surprise.

"She must be subjected to no annoyance as she goes forth," pursued the queen; "I will answer for her."

"As your majesty pleases; but if I might——"

"Silence, count," interrupted the queen, authoratively. "Here comes the king. Not a word of this story of the concealed traitor to him. It would excite him too strongly. Take such precautions as you may deem necessary, but no more."

"I will, madam," replied Lauzun, significantly. "If you do not want your friend to betray himself," he added, in an under tone, "let him be cautious. Father Petre will detect him at a glance."

As he spoke, the king and the Jesuit advanced towards them, followed by Moor.

"Can that be Charles Moor?" exclaimed Lauzun.

"And a prisoner," cried Sunderland.

"A prisoner," echoed Lauzun. "The imprudent young man has ventured into the palace. Let me entreat your majesty to intercede for him," he added to the queen.

"On condition of your compliance with my wishes in another respect," replied Mary.

"Be it so," said Lauzun. "Let Moor be set at liberty, and I obey you in all things."

At this moment the king and Father Petre came up.

"Your majesty will have need to keep stricter guard over your attendants," said James. "This young man has found means to enter the palace, and to speak to one of them without your knowledge or permission."

"Not without my knowledge or permission," said the queen. "If any one is to blame it is myself. Mr. Moor had my authority to enter the palace."

"And Sabine had your permission to meet him, no doubt?" pursued the king.

"She had," replied the queen.

"Ha! this alters the case. I have been over hasty with the young man. I allowed him no time for explanation."

"It was well for Moor that he did not," said Lauzun, in a whisper to the queen, "for his statement would scarcely have tallied with your majesty's."

"What say you to this, count?" said James. "Are you content with what the queen has done?"

"Perfectly," replied Lauzun.

"Then I have no more to say," said James. "Mr. Moor," he added, to the young man, who had been an astonished auditor of all that had passed, "you are at liberty. You are much beholden to her majesty."

"I am, indeed," he replied, with a look of unbounded gratitude.

"There is some mystery here which I cannot unravel," mentally ejaculated Father Petre. "What lady is this with your majesty?" he added, regarding Sidney earnestly.

"It is Mrs. Venables," interposed Lady Sunderland.

"Mrs. Venables!" exclaimed Father Petre, seizing Sidney's hand, and trying to drag her to a lamp that he might examine her features more closely. "Let me look at her."

"This is very rude treatment of a lady, father," interposed Lauzun. "I must beg you to quit your hold."

"Is the lady a friend of yours, count, that you thus interfere?" asked Father Petre.

"She is," replied Lauzun. "I introduced her to the queen."

"You were aware then of her frequent nocturnal visits to the palace?" cried James.

"Nocturnal visits—has she paid frequent nocturnal visits to you, madam?" cried Lauzun, "I was not aware of that."

"I thought not," said Father Petre. "Perhaps you will now permit me to interrogate her further."

"On no account," said the queen. "Mrs. Venables, you can quit the palace under the escort of Mr. Charles Moor, and since the object of your visits is at end, I will bid you farewell."

"Is this to be so, my liege?" cried Father Petre.

"Humph; I suppose so," replied the king, good-humouredly.

"Your majesty is duped," cried the Jesuit, out of all patience.

"Possibly," replied the king; "but it is my foible to be duped by women."

Meantime, Sidney had taken advantage of the queen's permission to depart, and with a well-executed obeisance to the queen, passed out of the picture-gallery, attended by Moor, and secretly congratulating himself on his narrow escape.

CHAPTER VII.

THE TRIAL OF THE BISHOPS.

So intense was the popular excitement upon the committal of the bishops, that day after day multitudes derived a melancholy satisfaction from merely gazing on the gloomy towers of their prison, while many of the chief nobility repaired to them, tendering them homage and advice. Pemberton, Holt, and Pollexfen, three of the ablest lawyers of the day, were engaged as their counsel, together with Finch, and the afterwards celebrated John Somers. In short, the whole Protestant community united in a determination to espouse their cause.

On the 15th of June, the first day of term, the bishops were brought before the Court of King's Bench by writ of *habeas corpus.* Their progress to Westminster Hall presented throughout a sublime and triumphant spectacle. Multitudes lined the banks of the river, and as the barge passed by, uncovered themselves, fell on their knees, and greeted the reverend captives with prayers and tears. On landing at Westminster-stairs they were received by a dense mass of spectators, who knelt down as they approached, and craved their blessing. When they had passed, these crowds followed them slowly and respectfully. An eye-witness of the scene, Count d'Adda, describes it with warmth in a letter to the pope. "Of the immense concourse of people," he writes, "who received them on the bank of the river, the majority in their immediate neighbourhood were on their knees; the archbishop laid his hands on such of them as he could reach, exhorting them to continue steadfast in their faith. They cried aloud that all should kneel, while tears flowed from the eyes of many."

Twenty-nine peers received them at the door of the hall, and attended them to the bar. The judges on the bench were Wright, Powell, Allibone, and Halloway, all of whom, with the exception of Powell, were mere creatures of the king. Powis and Williams, the attorney and solicitor general, were charged with the prosecution.

The proceedings were opened by Powis, who accused the bishops of composing and publishing a seditious libel, under pretence of a humble petition to his majesty. The bishops pleaded "not guilty," and were enlarged on their own undertaking to appear at their trial, which was fixed for the 29th of June.

Thus far the king had triumphed. He had successfully vindicated his prerogative, and the more sagacious of his ministers advised him not to pursue the contest further. Sunderland urged him to show generosity towards them, and, strange to say, he was supported in this advice by the papal nuncio, and even by the pope himself; but Father Petre and Barillon confirmed the king in his original resolution, and he ordered the prosecution to proceed.

On the morning of the 29th of June the bishops again appeared in Westminster Hall. The court was thronged with the noblest of the realm; a dense crowd filled every part of Old Palace-yard; and the neighbouring streets were rendered impassable by the assembled multitudes.

The vast concourse awaited the commencement of the proceedings in profound silence. Every countenance was marked with sympathy for the bishops, every eye sought the dock where they stood; their pale but calm countenances harmonising well with the occasion, while the grave faces of the counsellors beneath the settled attentive looks of the jury, and the stern deportment of the judges, with the variety and magnificence of the official costumes, and the profound attention of the audience, formed altogether a spectacle at once solemn and imposing.

After a brief interval, the silence was broken by the attorney-general, who, in a low voice—which, however, was heard in every part of the hall—called the attention of the judges to the libellous character of the bishops' petition, and then summoned Blathwaite, the clerk of the privy council, to prove its presentation to the king.

Blathwaite stepped forward with reluctance, and quailed on finding himself the object of universal attention.

"By whom was this petition presented?" asked the attorney-general.

"By the Bishop of St. Asaph," replied Blathwaite, tremulously.

"At what time and place?" returned Judge Wright.

"I object to his answering, my Lord," cried Pemberton, on the part of the bishops; "he is telling us what he heard, not what he saw."

Loud hisses broke from the audience.

"Silence!" thundered Judge Wright, who imitated the violence of Jeffreys, without possessing his ability. "You are trying to raise a disturbance in the court, Mr. Counsellor. You shall not deprive the Crown of the advantage of this witness's evidence."

"If the defendants are to be convicted on hearsay, my lord, I will throw up my brief," replied Pemberton, firmly.

A hearty cheer, which could not be checked, rang through the court.

"My lord, I withdraw the witness," said Williams, in a low voice. "I will prove the presentation of the petition by the evidence of a person of the highest rank, no less than the Earl of Sunderland. Let his lordship be called."

The crier obeyed, amidst a profound silence. No one answered the summons; and he repeated it twice with a like result, when irrepressible acclamations broke from the excited audience.

"Messengers have been despatched for the Earl of Sunderland in every direction, my lord," Williams then said. "Meanwhile, I will call another witness, Mr. Secretary Pepys."

A stout, middle-sized man, with a frank and prepossessing countenance, though now overcast with anxiety, answered to the call. Pepys was warmly attached to James, who, from his first entrance into public life, had been his steadfast friend and protector; but, at the same time, he was thoroughly devoted to the Church.

"You are acquainted with the handwriting of the Archbishop of Canterbury?" said Williams.

Pepys answered in the affirmative, and Williams produced the petition.

"What say you to this, sir? Is it the handwriting of his grace?"

Pepys hesitated. As he continued silent, the audience gave utterance to a cheer, which was instantly checked.

"Why don't you answer, sir?" cried Judge Wright, furiously.

"I am sorry to say it *is* the archbishop's writing, my lord," faltered Pepys.

"Enough," exclaimed Judge Wright, "you have proved the handwriting. Mr. Attorney, I shall now sum up the proceedings."

"A moment, my lord," said Powis, "let the Earl of Sunderland be again called."

"Robert, Earl of Sunderland, come into court," shouted the crier.

There was a brief pause. The silence was profound, and scarcely a breath was drawn by the vast and anxious crowd. At this juncture, Sunderland appeared.

As he advanced, his faltering step, pale countenance, and downcast looks were noticed by all. Anxious to avoid implication in the proceedings against the bishops, which had been undertaken in opposition to his advice, Sunderland had purposely kept out of the way, when he received an urgent message from the queen, imploring him to support the prosecution. From the moment of his appearance the friends of the bishops abandoned all hope of an acquittal.

"You were a witness to the presentation of this petition, my lord?" said Judge Wright, undaunted by the minister's disorder.

"It was brought to me by six of the defendants, with a request that I would present it to his majesty," replied Sunderland.

"Did you comply with their request?"

"No," answered Sunderland, "but I introduced their lordships to the king, and they presented it themselves."

"Do the counsel for the defence desire to examine the witness?" asked Judge Wright.

Somers here arose. A feeling of disappointment spread among the audience when they became aware that the defence of the venerable prisoners rested with so young and obscure an advocate.

"I have no questions to put to the witness, my lord," said Somers. "I acknowledge that my clients were the authors and publishers of this petition."

Loud murmurs arose from the tumultuous audience. Even the bishops themselves looked disconcerted.

"You hear that!" cried Judge Wright, to the jury, "the

counsel for the defence admits that the Crown has proved its case."

"I make no such admission, my lord," cried Somers, in a voice of thunder, "I even deny the right of the Crown to institute this prosecution. I appeal for my clients from the tyranny of the government to the justice of the law."

Rarely had such bold words been uttered in Westminster Hall. The judges frowned, while the audience, so lately a prey to disappointment, brightened with hope, and greeted the speaker with applause.

Silence being restored, Somers continued his speech. Leaving quite out of the question the conduct of the bishops, he directed his arguments against that of the government, proving, by a masterly review of the laws, that the power claimed by James, of suspending Acts of Parliament, as in the instance of the Declaration of Indulgence, was at variance with the very spirit of the English constitution, which could exist only on the united authority of the king, the lords, and the commons, and concluded by an eloquent and impassioned appeal to the jury, beseeching them, as Englishmen, to assert and establish this righteous principle, by awarding the bishops a verdict of acquittal.

Loud and renewed plaudits rang through the hall as Somers sat down. The law-officers of the king in vain endeavoured to combat his reasoning; the judges themselves, in their respective charges to the jury, failed to refute his arguments; and the upright and impartial Powell even pronounced an opinion in their favour.

The jury having retired, the audience awaited the verdict in agonising suspense. Meanwhile, every one discussed the speeches of the counsel, in whispers, with his neighbour. The multitudes without were informed of the progress of the trial, and debated among themselves the probable result. From all rose a deep, unceasing hum, which rolled through the lofty court like muttered thunder.

At length it became known that the jury could not agree on a verdict, and the court was adjourned to the following day. When the judges arose, it was with the utmost difficulty that the officers could clear the court. The crowd without hourly increased, and though no longer expecting a verdict, completely blocked up the avenues to the hall. Throughout the whole night, large mobs paraded the streets, shouting, but committing no acts of violence, and the first dawn found Palace-yard thronged densely as before.

At ten o'clock the bishops entered the court. The judges having mounted the bench, a solemn stillness pervaded the vast assemblage. The usual preliminaries being gone through, the crier summoned the jury to appear.

The excitement of the audience now became intense. The bishops maintained their composure, but their judges looked agitated.

"Are you agreed on your verdict, gentlemen?" asked Judge Wright of the foreman, Sir Roger Langley.

"Unanimously, my lord," replied Sir Roger.

"I am glad of it," returned Williams. "How say you then, are the prisoners at the bar guilty or not guilty?"

"Not guilty, my lord," replied Sir Roger, amid the hushing silence of the assemblage.

"NOT GUILTY!" echoed a thousand voices within the hall: "Not guilty!" repeated ten thousand without; and then such a cheer arose, that the old and massive roof of Westminster Hall seemed to crack.

The huzzas of the multitude passed with electrical rapidity through the city, and were caught up and renewed in every direction, producing, as has been aptly described, "a very rebellion in noise." They reached the Temple in a few minutes, and in a short time resounded in the camp at Hounslow, where they were heard by James, who was holding a consultation with the principal officers, and who angrily asked the meaning of the clamour. Being told by a bystander that "it was nothing but the soldiers shouting for the acquittal of the bishops," he answered gravely, "Do you call that nothing?" Yet with these ominous acclamations ringing in his ears, he persisted in the obnoxious policy which they condemned, and, returning to town, his first act was to degrade and insult the bench of justice. Judge Powell was dismissed for his honesty and independence, and the gross partiality of Wright was rewarded with a baronetcy.

Meanwhile, the people received the jury with the loudest plaudits, hailing them with tears in their eyes as their deliverers. In the evening, bonfires were lighted throughout all the streets, spread through the city, and even under the windows of Whitehall, where the pope was burned in effigy, while the bystanders, amidst the ringing of bells, and with shouts of joy and triumph, drank confusion to the Papists. Count D'Adda, who had strenuously opposed the prosecution of the bishops, and had been moved to pity by the first display of popular feeling, now viewing these wild excesses with alarm, declared, in a letter to the pope, that the fires over the whole city, the drinking in every street, accompanied by cries to the health of the bishops, and confusion to the Catholics, with the play of fireworks, and the discharge of firearms, and the other demonstrations of furious gladness, mixed with impious outrage against religion, formed a scene of unspeakable horror, displaying, in all its rancour, the malignity of this heretical people against the Church." The rejoicings were kept up through the whole of the night; but, the following day being Sunday, the mob dispersed at the approach of morning, and the streets resumed their wonted tranquillity.

BOOK THE THIRD.

CHAPTER I.

THE CONSPIRACY.—THE MEETING AT MRS. POTTER'S.

THE latent animosity of the people to the Church of Rome was now fairly excited, and every suspicion which jealousy or zeal could fix on the Papists, from the king downwards, was received by all with greedy credulity. It was at this inauspicious moment that the queen gave birth to a son, and the rumour before referred to, that she was imposing a supposititious child on the nation, was so universally believed, that whoever ventured to regard it with doubt was openly denounced as a concealed Papist, and an enemy of his country.

On Saturday, the 9th of June, the queen suddenly removed with the court from Whitehall to St. James's. As the latter palace had been prepared very hastily for her reception, a warming-pan was used to air the royal couch, and on this trivial circumstance the partizans of the Protestant succession founded their story of a fictitious birth. Pasquinades on the subject were fixed to dead walls during the night; and Partridge, in his "Predictions," printed at the Hague, boldly asserted that a spurious child had been "topped on the lawful heirs, to cheat them out of their estate."

"The stories," says Ralph, "were neither over-decent, well-bred, nor charitable." They were, moreover, as absurd and contradictory as they were disgusting, and it would be idle to adduce the various and unanswerable arguments by which they are refuted. The prince was born on Trinity Sunday, the 10th of June, at eleven o'clock in the morning, in the presence of forty-two persons, eighteen of whom were members of the council and the remainder ladies of rank; and by the command of James, the depositions of these witnesses were taken down, and are still preserved in the council-office. Dr. Chamberlain, a noted Whig, who had been oppressed by the king, and who was suspected of being a secret adherent of the Prince of Orange, was engaged as the queen's medical attendant, and would have been the last person in the world to countenance the alleged imposture. Mrs. Dawson, another attendant on the queen, who was actually in the pay of Sidney, solemnly made oath that a child was born. Dryden commemorated the royal infant's birth in noble verse—

> Born in broad daylight, that the ungrateful rout
> May find no room for a remaining doubt;
> Truth, which itself is light, does darkness shun,
> And the true eaglet safely dares the sun.

But the false opinion sank deeper and deeper in the public mind, and acquired confirmation from the infatuated bigotry of James. When the popular excitement was at its height, the infant prince was baptized with extraordinary pomp and magnificence, according to the rites of the Romish church, the papal nuncio being his sponsor, as proxy for the pope; and this ill-timed proceeding served to provoke still further the growing discontent of the people.

At this critical juncture the leaders of the Protestant interest began to canvass more openly the propriety of calling for assistance from the Prince of Orange. Ever on the alert, Colonel Sidney gained early intelligence of their disaffection, and lost not a moment in moulding it to his designs.

One night in July, just as it was becoming dark, two horsemen rode out of the avenue of Nottingham House, Kensington (subsequently enlarged, and raised to the dignity of a palace), and shaped their course towards London. The taller of the two was Charles Moor, and his companion was the Earl of Nottingham, described by Mackey, a political opponent, as "a mighty champion of the Church, his habit and manner very formal—a tall, thin, very dark man, like a Spaniard or Jew." Nottingham wore a broad-leaved hat, and a capacious riding-cloak, both of which, in conjunction with the darkness, served to shield him from recognition.

"I go to this meeting with great reluctance," remarked Nottingham. "It is the first time I have been a party to a secret opposition. Legal resistance to power should ever court observation."

"True," rejoined Moor. "When we have concerted our plans, we will avow them; and I hope that their moderate and patriotic character and the support they will undoubtedly receive from the nation, will have the effect of changing the intentions of our rulers."

"If this be all that Sidney seeks I will be his hearty supporter," returned Nottingham. "But I confess I doubt him. He is seeking rather to form a conspiracy than to organise an opposition. But time presses. Let us on."

Urging their horses forward, they proceeded through Knightsbridge to Charing-cross, whence they passed up the Strand to the New Exchange.

This was a pile of some pretensions, surrounding a paved court, on the site formerly occupied by Salisbury House. A colonnade ran round the area, from the tiled roof of which swung the signs of the shops behind, principally occupied by sempstresses, milliners, and mercers. The structure had originally been erected by the Earl of Salisbury, in 1608, when it was opened with great pomp and ceremony by James I. and his queen, who gave it the name of "The New Bourse of Britain." It was afterwards partly rebuilt by the Earl of Pembroke and Montgomery; and lastly, some years later than the date of this history, the estate was purchased by four brothers, who pulled down the Exchange, and raised on its site the buildings now called, from the circumstance of its erection, the Adelphi.

Leaving their horses at a neighbouring inn, called the "Maypole," Moor and Nottingham proceeded on foot to the New Exchange, and, entering the area, bent their steps to a large old-fashioned house in its furthermost angle. This was Mrs. Potter's, who kept what was called an "Indian House," a mart unknown to more modern times, but of which some notion may be formed from a description in Lady Mary Montague's "Town Eclogue" of "The Toilette:"—

Straight then I'll dress, and take my wonted range,
Through Indian shops, to Motteux's or the 'Change;
Where the tall jar erects its stately pride,
With antic shapes in China's azure dyed:
There careless lies a rich brocade unroll'd,
Here shines a cabinet with burnish'd gold.
But then, alas! I must be forced to pay,
And bring no penn'orths—not a fan away.

Ribands, head-dresses, tea, and perfumes, with many other articles of luxury and the toilet, were also vended at these emporiums; and the lighter wares were frequently disposed of by means of raffles. They were, likewise, used as places of rendezvous by fashionable loungers; and Colley Cibber, in his comedy of "The Provoked Husband," takes Lady Townley on "a flying jaunt to an Indian House."

Knocking at a private door, Nottingham and Moor were instantly admitted, and conducted to an upper chamber, where they found Sidney awaiting them.

"Our friends are all assembled in the adjoining room," he said, "I will secure this door, and we will join them."

This done, he led them to an inner room, where they found a party of twelve persons, consisting of the Earls of Devonshire, Shrewsbury, and Danby; Lords Halifax, Mordaunt, and Lumley; Admirals Herbert and Russell; the Bishop of London; with Johnstone, Speke, and Van Citters.

Nottingham was warmly welcomed, and as soon as he and Moor were seated, Sidney commenced:

"We have met for a great and holy purpose, my lord," he said, addressing Nottingham; "the preservation of our religion, and the redemption of our country. But our rulers are vigilant, treacherous, and powerful, and it is necessary that you should pledge yourself to inviolable secrecy."

"I doubt if this be lawful," replied Nottingham.

"Your word of honour will suffice, my lord," said Herbert.

"Pledge yourself, my lord," suggested Halifax, in an undertone; "it will commit us only to secresy, not to action."

"Well, I pledge my word of honour to divulge nothing," said Nottingham, after a moment's reflection.

Moor next pledged himself to secrecy, after which, Herbert, who had been previously instructed by Sidney, spoke on the subject of their grievances. "These," he said, "involved two great principles—freedom of person, and freedom of conscience. The king now menaced both their civil and religious liberty. Avowedly a Papist, he had baptised his heir in the church of Rome, and assumed the power of an absolute monarch. Under these circumstances, it became necessary to compel him to call a parliament, in which efficient measures could be taken for the preservation of their liberty and religion."

The speaker commanded profound attention; and Moor, who had no suspicion that his words were put forward only to mask his designs, was delighted with his moderate and constitutional views.

"You see, it is as I told you, my lord," he whispered to Nottingham.

"I am glad of it," replied Nottingham, "I will cheerfully second your patriotic efforts, Admiral Herbert," he added.

"And I also, as far as the king is concerned," cried Lord Mordaunt. "As for his reputed heir, I do not acknowledge him."

"He is a base-born cheat," cried Lumley.

"The matter will be fully investigated," interposed Nottingham. "Let us now consider only how we are to obtain a parliament."

"You may as well consider how to raise an army," said Lord Halifax, with a sneer. "The king will never consent to call a parliament."

"We will force him to call one," cried Lord Devonshire, impatiently. "Do not you agree with me, Shrewsbury?"

The personage addressed, though apprised of the whole design of the conspirators, turned pale at the idea of resorting to force. Like James I., Shrewsbury was timorous, from the circumstances of his parentage—his father having been killed in a duel by the profligate Duke of Buckingham, while his mother, attired as a page, stood by, holding Buckingham's horse.

"Why not call in a mediator?" he said, "that seems the proper course."

"Whom do you refer to, my lord?" asked Nottingham, sternly.

"I will reply to your question by another," replied Shrewsbury. "Before I abjured the errors of Rome, the law required me to swear that I would always defend the crown in the Protestant succession. Is not this principle the very life of the constitution?"

"Why, yes," answered Nottingham.

"When the succession is diverted to Papists, then, who so fit to interfere as the next Protestant heir?" resumed Shrewsbury. "In short, I propose that we should call in the Prince of Orange."

"You mean, of course, only for the purpose of obtaining a free parliament?" suggested Sidney.

"Of course," answered Shrewsbury.

"I will never assent to such a proposition," cried Nottingham. "It means nothing more than rebellion."

"You must retract that expression, my lord," exclaimed Herbert, laying his hand on his sword.

"I have no inclination to quarrel," replied Nottingham calmly, "I would cheerfully support you in a constitutional resistance to the king, but the design you contemplate is of another character, and I not only decline to countenance it, but will do my utmost to frustrate it."

And he arose, and moved towards the door, when Lord Mordaunt planted himself before him, exclaiming,

"You do not quit us thus, my lord."

"Having gone thus far, you cannot now retract," observed Admiral Russell.

"I am with you, my lord," cried Moor to Nottingham, at the same time drawing his sword; "we can force our way out."

"Hold, gentlemen," interposed Sidney, "Lord Nottingham and Mr. Moor are free to depart. They have pledged themselves to secrecy."

"They shall be silenced more effectually," muttered Lord Mordaunt, stepping aside.

Finding the way open, Nottingham and Moor quitted the house together.

"I can now breathe, freely," said Nottingham, as they gained the area of the New Exchange. "This is indeed a formidable conspiracy."

"Hush! we are watched," replied Moor.

And he darted to a neighbouring alley, into which, as he spoke, the figure of a man was observed retreating.

The stranger had retired but a few paces when Moor came up with him.

"Mr. Saint Leu," exclaimed the young man, in surprise.

"What! Mr. Moor! have you joined the conspiracy then?" replied Saint Leu. "Nay, do not doubt me; I know the purpose of the meeting here, as you will believe when I tell you I am waiting for Colonel Sidney. But our encounter is fortunate. Meet me about this time to-morrow night, at Charing-cross, and I will put you in the way of an adventure."

"Of what nature?" asked Moor.

"You will learn then," replied Saint Leu. "Farewell."

And he ran down the alley, while Moor rejoined Nottingham, and they hastened together to the Maypole, where they had left their horses.

Impatient to proceed, Moor hurried to the stable himself, while Nottingham walked slowly on. After a short interval, as Moor did not come forth, Nottingham returned to the inn and inquired for him. To his surprise he found that Moor had disappeared.

"Where is he gone?" he demanded of the ostler.

The ostler was unable to inform him.

"Tell him to follow me," replied Nottingham.

And mounting his horse he rode off.

When Nottingham and Moor withdrew from the meeting, a profound silence ensued. This was broken at last by Halifax.

"There is no use in remaining here," he said, "we must think of what is to be done, and defer proceeding till we meet again."

So saying, he arose and quitted the room, muttering as he departed,—

"Nottingham will probably betray them. Shall I forestal him with the king? I will think of it."

Meanwhile, the other confederates continued to dwell on the defection of Nottingham.

"I was against trusting him," said Herbert. "I felt assured he would not join us."

"I should be the last to counsel flight, but we must remember that Nottingham holds our lives in his hands," observed Admiral Russell.

"He will not betray us," exclaimed Sidney.

"I will trust my life in no man's keeping," cried Lord Mordaunt; "Nottingham must be silenced."

"This must not be," cried Sidney. "I would sooner lose my head than consent to his assassination."

Lord Shrewsbury also expressed his abhorrence of the project.

"Well, take your own course, my lords," answered Mordaunt. "Before we meet again, you will have reason to regret your forbearance. I wish you good-night."

"Russell and I will attend you, my lord," cried Herbert.

And they followed Mordaunt from the house.

Arrived in the area without, Mordaunt said quickly—

"We must follow this fool Nottingham, and secure his silence with a bullet."

"Why not defer it for a day or two, and meanwhile keep a strict watch over him," returned Russell, hesitatingly.

"If done at all it must be done at once," said Herbert.

"We lose time," cried Mordaunt. "Our horses are at the Maypole; we can soon overtake him, and then our fate will be in our own hands."

"I am with you," replied Herbert.

"And I," said Russell, "though I hope by persuading him to join us to avoid the necessity of bloodshed."

Passing onward, they approached the Maypole, when they perceived Nottingham walking down the street.

"He is waiting for his horse," said Mordaunt. "But where is Moor?"

"In the stable, no doubt," replied Herbert. "We can easily secure him there."

So saying they entered the tavern, which derived its name from a neighbouring maypole, 134 feet high, erected, says a rare tract called "The City's Loyalty Displayed," "upon the cost of the parishioners, and with the gracious consent of his sacred majesty, with the illustrious prince the Duke of York," on the first May-day after the Restoration. The maypole was annually decorated with garlands and streamers on the first of May, when crowds of revellers of both sexes danced around it, to the good old music of the pipe and tabor. On ordinary occasions it was garnished with three lanterns, which, we learn from the afore-mentioned authority, "were to give light on dark nights," a purpose which they very imperfectly fulfilled.

Situated immediately opposite to the Maypole, and contiguous to the New Exchange, the tavern was a place of general resort, and its accommodations were proportionately extensive. In addition to numerous parlours, it possessed the advantages of a bowling-green and a racket-court, and in these varied attractions promised to favour Herbert's design.

While the three conspirators were conversing on the outside of the tavern, Moor was, as Herbert had conjectured, in the stable, urging the ostler to despatch. The horses were soon in readiness, and Moor was following them across the yard, when a voice called to him from behind. Turning round, he observed a man in a neighbouring gateway, who beckoned him to approach.

"What do you seek?" asked Moor.

"I have something important to say to you," answered the other in a feigned voice. "Follow me to the racket-court."

So saying he disappeared through the gateway.

Moor hesitated a moment, but eventually followed him across the bowling-green to the racket-court, the door of which stood open.

The racket-court was very dark, and Moor was looking round for the stranger, when the door behind him was shut, and secured on the other side, and he instantly became aware that he was entrapped, though by whom or for what purpose, he could not conjecture. After vainly endeavouring to force open the door, he sought to alarm the neighbourhood by outcries, but without effect. He then passed hastily round the court, in the hope of finding some other means of exit; but though he scanned the wall on every side, his search was fruitless, and he returned disappointed to the door.

No other resource presenting itself, he again shouted aloud, when he heard a hasty footstep approaching, and the next moment the door was flung open, and Saint Leu appeared at it.

"Thank Heaven, I have found you," cried Saint Leu. "You may yet be in time to save him."

"Save whom?" cried Moor, "Lord Nottingham?"

"Ay, I overheard three of them planning his assassination," rejoined Saint Leu. "They have followed him, intending to effect their purpose in a lonely part of the road near Knightsbridge."

Uttering a passionate exclamation, Moor hastened to the stable-yard, and vaulting upon his horse, galloped furiously down the street.

Meanwhile Nottingham had advanced some distance on the road to Kensington. He proceeded at a moderate pace, thinking that Moor might overtake him, and having no apprehension of danger.

Passing Knightsbridge, he had just reached a part of the road then entirely unbuilt upon, when he heard a trampling behind him, and, turning round he espied three horsemen approaching him at full gallop. But as he did not suppose they were in pursuit of him, he did not increase his speed, and they speedily came up with him.

"I am glad we have overtaken you," cried Lord Mordaunt.

"Ha!" cried Nottingham, reining up, "Herbert and Russell, too! What is the meaning of this?"

"Simply that your lordship has our secret," returned Mordaunt, presenting a pistol at his head. "Swear to join us, or you are a dead man."

"Do not compel us to be your executioners, Nottingham," said Russell.

"Say rather my assassins," replied Nottingham; "I have already told you I have never yet been a traitor, and the fear of death shall not make me one."

"Die then, fool," cried Mordaunt.

But ere he could pull the trigger the pistol was dashed from his hand by Moor, who had suddenly galloped up and seized Mordaunt by the throat.

"Stab him, Russell," vociferated Mordaunt.

"You must defend yourself," answered Russell, sullenly.

While this was passing another horseman rode up, who proved to be Sidney.

"I am in time, then, to prevent bloodshed," he cried; "Nottingham, I am glad to see you safe. You cannot more deeply injure our cause, or offend the prince, than by acting thus," he added to the others.

"Proceed, Lord Nottingham, I will escort you home."

Herbert and Mordaunt turned moodily away, but Russell addressed himself to Nottingham.

"I ask your pardon, my lord, for the share I have had in this transaction," he said, "I was in hopes of forcing you to join us; but I would not have suffered them to injure you."

Nottingham made no answer.

"I call Heaven to witness, that I seek only the preservation of the Church and the good of my country," pursued Russell, and turning his horse's head he hastened after his companions.

Accompanied by Sidney and Moor, Nottingham resumed his progress homeward. The distance was short, but occupied them sufficiently long to admit of explanation. As they came in sight of Nottingham House, Sidney took his leave and returned towards town.

CHAPTER II.

HOW THE EARL OF SUNDERLAND CONFORMED TO THE CATHOLIC FAITH.

"This constant opposition of Lord Sunderland is intolerable," observed Father Petre, as he and Barillon were closeted one evening with the king. "I wonder your majesty bears it so submissively. Never was it more necessary than in our case for a sovereign to remind his ministers of the somewhat trite maxim, that 'union is strength.'"

"If you all made it a rule to agree with me in opinion," rejoined James, drily, "you would rather be flatterers than counsellors. Your reverence recollects, perhaps, the instance of Canute and his courtiers."

"I am no flatterer, my liege," replied Father Petre, somewhat piqued; "and though I may sometimes venture to differ from you, I should think I very imperfectly discharged my duty by cavilling at all your projects, especially when, as in the present instance, there can be no question as to their necessity and propriety."

"Sunderland is too cautious by half," muttered Barillon.

"Some people say it would be well for me if there were a greater leaven of caution in my council," said James, sharply. "Many good Catholics warn me that I am moving too fast."

"Such is not the opinion of your majesty's most approved friend and brother, my august sovereign," returned Barillon. "He applauds your pious schemes, and urges you to prosecute them with unremitting vigour. But your majesty can scarcely expect that measures which have for their aim the welfare of the Catholic faith will have the support of a heretic."

"Sunderland will not favour our religion, certainly," said James, in a musing tone. "I cannot trust him on that point. Yet it is strange the countenance he receives from Catholics—even from the Pope himself."

"His holiness is more of a politician than a churchman," said Barillon. "But Sunderland will be found a traitor to all. Has not the countess been discovered in correspondence with the Prince of Orange?"

"The woman who would be faithless to her husband may well be faithless to her king," observed James, slightly shrugging his shoulders.

"Sunderland sits very easily under the imputation," pursued Barillon, with a sneer. "But a sense of your majesty's peril compels me to speak boldly. You must hear the undisguised and unpalatable truth. Hesitation and dissension in your councils will endanger your throne."

"Your excellency shall hear the truth from me in return," rejoined James. "I believe I shall lose my throne in the attempt, but even at that hazard I am determined to re-establish the religion of Rome."

"You will find the most formidable opponent of your design in your own cabinet, my liege," said Father Petre. "Your excellency will, perhaps, acquaint his majesty with what Lord Sunderland told you this morning," he added to Barillon.

"Speak out fearlessly," said James, as the ambassador pretended to hesitate.

"After inveighing warmly against the unjustifiable (as he termed it) prosecution of the bishops," said Barillon, "his lordship expressed his determination to resist in future every measure calculated to be detrimental to the Established Church of this country."

"Ha! did he so?" exclaimed James, with a sudden explosion of passion. "Then I will soon teach him another lesson. I will strip him of his honours and appointments. To-morrow shall witness his dismissal."

"Why not to-night?" suggested Father Petre. "He is now closeted with the queen, endeavouring to bring her over to his views. Will your majesty authorise me to inform him of your intentions?"

"I will do it myself," rejoined James, sternly. "I will spare him nothing of his merited punishment. Come with me, and witness his disgrace."

And rising, he hastily quitted the closet, followed by the Jesuit and Barillon.

About an hour previous to the interview above narrated, Sunderland had sought a private conference with the queen, in her cabinet.

"Your majesty will believe that I would not seek you at this hour if my business permitted delay," he said. "I find that my enemies in the council, aided by the French ambassador, are prevailing against me. You, madam, I am well aware, are pleased to entertain a favourable opinion of me, and on some points I should feel assured, also, of the countenance of the king. But there is one question on which I am opposed to him, and my opponents will undoubtedly avail themselves of it to effect my dismissal."

"I understand your allusion, my lord," replied Mary. "Alas!

since you oppose the re-establishment of the Catholic church, you deprive me of the power of assisting you."

"But suppose I should incontestably prove myself the friend of your religion, instead of its enemy," said Sunderland, "what would your majesty say then?"

"How can you prove it, my lord?" demanded Mary. "No heretic—forgive me for applying such a term to you—can be a real friend of our religion."

"Your majesty is now a mother," rejoined Sunderland. "Not only is the throne of your consort, but the birthright of your royal son, is risked by this contest, and I solemnly warn you that any attempt to subvert the Established Church of England will result in the downfall of your line. It is this conviction that induces me to oppose the king's wishes, although, I repeat, I am eager to support the Catholic religion. In proof of my sincerity, if you will order your chaplain to be in attendance to-morrow morning, he shall witness my conformity to the religion of Rome."

"Ah! that, indeed, would be proof of your sincerity, my lord," cried Mary, joyfully. "Who has been the happy instrument of your conversion?"

"Your majesty," replied Sunderland, with an air of deep conviction. "The arguments you have used have sunk deeply into my heart, and have satisfied me that the religion of Rome is the only true faith."

"Heaven keep you in that belief, my lord," cried Mary, extending her hand to him, which he pressed respectfully to his lips. "But why defer the execution of your pious project till to-morrow? The Père d'Orleans shall attend you instantly in my private chapel."

"I am as eager for my reconciliation with your Church as your majesty can be for it," returned Sunderland.

"Remain here, then, my lord, and I will summon you as soon as all is in readiness," rejoined Mary.

And quitting the room, she left the wily minister to reflect upon the extraordinary step he was about to take. In a short time a page entered, and informing him that the queen awaited him in the private chapel, he immediately repaired thither.

Attended by Father Petre and Barillon, James proceeded to the queen's apartments, and, on the way, crossed a side passage leading to the private chapel. To his surprise, he heard the voices of the choristers chanting high mass, and summoning an usher stationed at the door, he asked the meaning of this unusual service, and was informed that it was the ceremonial of the admission of a neophyte to the Church of Rome, but who the convert was the man could not say, except that he was a personage of exalted rank.

"You see, father, that our religion is making progress," said the king, with a gratified smile. "Who can the noble convert be?"

"I hope not a time-server and a hypocrite," cried Father Petre, a sudden suspicion of the truth crossing his mind.

As he spoke, the folding-doors were thrown open, disclosing the interior of the chapel, blazing with light, and fragrant with incense, while before the altar, which was decorated with the sacred utensils, knelt the convert. On one side of him stood the queen, and on the other, the Père d'Orleans, in his full robes, and in the act of pronouncing a solemn benediction. At this moment the organ burst forth into a full peal, and the neophyte arising to receive the priest's embrace, disclosed the features of Sunderland. The ceremony over, the group descended from the altar, and James, who was filled with astonishment, advanced to meet them.

"Can I trust the evidence of my senses, my lord?" he said to Sunderland. "Have you, indeed, renounced your errors, and conformed to the true religion?"

"He has, my liege," replied Mary. "And after this, you cannot doubt the zeal and sincerity of your minister."

"It were impossible," replied James. "I came here to upbraid him, and, perhaps, dismiss him, but I will load him with higher honours."

Father Petre and Barillon exchanged glances of anger and mortification, while James, passing his arm affectionately over Sunderland's shoulder, and taking the queen's hand in his own, led the way towards the private apartments.

CHAPTER III.

LADY PLACE.

Lady Place, near Hurley, in Berkshire, a large pile of red brick, boasting little architectural beauty, but embosomed in a grove of noble trees, was erected in the reign of Elizabeth, by Richard Lovelace, a soldier of fortune, on the ruins of an ancient monastery, some remains of which were preserved in the western wing, and in the vaults of the mansion. An avenue of fine elms led to the hall, which, though situated on a gentle eminence about a quarter of a mile distant from the Thames, and overlooking a wide range of country, was extremely secluded.

At the period of this history, Lady Place was the seat of Lord Lovelace, an active partisan of the Protestant interest, who had long been regarded with suspicion by James's government.

In a vast subterranean vault beneath the great hall, which, from its size, and the remarkable landscape frescoes (attributed even to Salvator Rosa) with which it was adorned, gave a singular character to the interior of the mansion, were one night assembled, the Earls of Shrewsbury, Devonshire, and Danby; and Lords Lumley and Lovelace; with Admiral Russell, Colonel Sidney, and the Bishop of London.

The vault was approached by more than one secret entrance, and a single lamp shed a feeble light around it, leaving the greater part in obscurity, though here and there a niche might be distinguished, which had once been occupied by a coffin—the chamber having been used as a place of sepulchre by the holy brotherhood who once inhabited the monastery of Hurley. The walls and arched and groined roof were blackened with age, and a damp, mouldy odour pervaded the atmosphere. In the centre was an oaken table, at which sat Sidney, holding in his hand a parchment, which he had just read aloud to the assemblage.

"Now, my lords," he concluded, "we must have no further hesitation. If you really desire the assistance of the Prince of Orange, you must sign this requisition to him."

"The tyrant must be deposed!" cried Lord Lovelace.

"Hush! hush!" exclaimed Shrewsbury, timidly glancing around to see that no one was hovering about in the gloom. "This invitation will endanger our heads."

"What is more, it leaves us entirely at the Prince of Orange's mercy," observed Danby. "I am not an advocate for deposing the king, and we ought to stipulate that the prince should have no power to interfere in our affairs, except under certain restrictions."

"By imposing conditions, my lord, you will prevent his coming over at all," said Sidney.

"Well, then," replied Shrewsbury, with an uneasy look, "why not confine ourselves to a mere verbal invitation? This will prevent confusion hereafter; and free us from the apprehension of premature discovery."

"This is child's play," cried Sidney. "I repeat, my lords, that the prince will not stir without a requisition from you. You must give him the guarantee of your hands and heads. As to restricting his authority, I am empowered to declare that his highness will be ruled in all things by a Parliament to be assembled on his arrival. But I am weary of so much vacillation; and I now declare, once for all, that if you do nót sign this parchment, I will withdraw from the confederacy, and leave you to fight for yourselves."

"Give me the pen," said the Bishop of London. "I will be the first to sign."

"We will follow your lordship!" cried Russell.

And without further remark, they successively affixed their signatures to the document. Last of all, Sidney added his name to the list, when, as he took up the parchment, with a smile of triumph, a stone crucifix, placed in a niche in the adjoining wall, fell to the earth, with a dull, heavy sound.

"What is that?" cried several of the confederates, looking round in alarm.

"A good omen!" rejoined Lovelace. "Behold! the symbol of Rome lies prostrate."

"We accept the augury as favourable," said the Bishop of London.

"The coincidence is most strange!" exclaimed Sidney, advancing towards the fallen crucifix, when, to his surprise, he perceived the figure of a man standing within the niche. This person had evidently dislodged the cross by his approach.

"A spy here!" cried Sidney, springing forward, and dragging forth the intruder.

Exclamations were uttered by the conspirators, and several of them drew their swords.

"You then are the author of the miracle which we supposed had operated in our favour," cried Sidney. "Kindle a torch, and let me examine his features."

And as the light was brought, he recognised Lord Mauvesin.

"Ha! is it you, my lord?" cried Sidney, sternly. "Do you know the peril in which you are placed?"

"You fancy I am in your power, Colonel Sidney, but you are mistaken—you are in mine," answered Mauvesin, coolly. "The house is surrounded by troopers, under command of Colonel Trelawney. Snewin, the constable, awaits me without, and if I do not rejoin him in half an hour he will call in the dragoons, and conduct them here. You will then have to account for my disappearance, as well as for the purpose of your meeting."

There was a pause, during which the confederates regarded each other in silent dismay.

"I have no wish to disturb your deliberations, provided we can come to terms," resumed Mauvesin. "What I have to say is for your ear alone, Colonel Sidney."

"Follow me then, my lord, and remember that any attempt

to escape will be followed by your instant destruction," replied Sidney, drawing his sword, and walking down the vault with him.

"I have obtained certain assurance that you favour the pretensions of Charles Moor," said Mauvesin, pausing as soon as they were out of ear-shot of the others. "Now I will suppose, for the sake of argument, that that young man's claims to the Mauvesin inheritance are better than mine. It follows, in the event of a change in the Government, that you might enable him to dispossess me."

"Shrewdly guessed, my lord," replied Sidney, dryly.

"Will you pledge yourself to support me if I do not give you up to Trelawney?" said Mauvesin.

"Hem!" cried Sidney. "Well, I fancy there is no alternative," he added, after a moment's hesitation. "If you fulfil your engagement, Moor shall shift for himself; but should you practise any treachery, I will take care that the evidence I have collected is placed in his hands, and you will find it will quickly establish his claims."

"Have no fear of me," replied Mauvesin; "the coast shall be clear in less than half an hour."

And he was turning towards the recess, when a door was suddenly thrown open, and Charles Moor entered the vault.

Mauvesin muttered an imprecation and drew back, while Sidney and the other conspirators looked surprised and alarmed. Some drew their swords, and Lord Lovelace advanced with the torch so as to fling the light full on the face of the intruder.

"Colonel Sidney," cried Moor, undisturbed by the tumult around him, "I have come to warn you that the house is surrounded by troopers. Fly this instant, or you are lost; but before you pass, you must give me up the document you hold in your hands."

"Never with life," cried Sidney, firmly. "But how is it, Mr. Moor, that you take part against the Protestant church?"

"I deny that I am taking part against it," replied Moor. "On the contrary, I am ready to hazard my life in its service. But I will not abet treason to my sovereign."

"King James has forfeited his allegiance, and it is treason to your country to uphold him," returned Sidney.

"We shall not serve our country by delivering it up to a foreign invader," rejoined Moor. "But I will not argue with you, Colonel Sidney. Once for all, I command you to yield up that document to me. If you refuse, I will call in the soldiery."

"You had better consider how you are to execute your

threat, young man," cried Lovelace, planting himself before him.

"You see that resistance will be vain, Mr. Moor," cried Sidney. "Since you have threatened to denounce us you must remain a prisoner."

"His death alone will effectually preserve your secret," cried Mauvesin.

"Right," rejoined Lovelace. "There is no help for it. He must die."

Other voices concurred in the decision.

"Blood will tarnish our cause, my lords," cried Sidney. "There is a cell at the other end of the vault, where the prisoner can be secured, and we can decide hereafter on what is to be done with him."

Mauvesin again expressed his dissatisfaction, but he was overruled by the others.

Moor was then removed to the other end of the vault, and thrust into a small cell contrived within the thickness of the wall, the door of which was instantly closed and barred without.

"Your time must have well nigh expired, my lord," said Sidney to Mauvesin. "Do not linger a moment longer, or Snewin may become alarmed, and defeat your schemes."

"Why not dispel my fears for ever, and at the same time secure your own safety?" said Mauvesin, in a low and significant tone, and glancing towards Moor's cell.

"I understand you, my lord," rejoined Sidney, sternly. "But know that I would hazard my own life as well as the success of the great enterprise I am engaged in, rather than countenance deliberate murder."

Mauvesin turned sullenly away, and entering the recess, disappeared through a secret passage leading to a chamber above, where he found Elkanah Snewin, and with this ally he hurried out to Colonel Trelawney, who had posted himself outside the garden with a party of troopers. Calling him forth, Mauvesin told him that he had been misinformed; that he and Snewin had thoroughly searched the house, and that no meeting of conspirators had taken place that night at Lady Place.

In ten minutes after this, Trelawney and his men were on their way to Henley-on-Thames, while Mauvesin lingered behind meditating some desperate scheme.

Shut up in the cell, Moor remained for a considerable time undisturbed; but after an interval of about an hour, when profound stillness reigned throughout the vault, he heard footsteps approaching, and presently afterwards, a wicket in the door was unlatched, and Sidney presented himself at it, with a light.

"I have just seen Mr. Saint Leu, and learned from him that he brought you here, Mr. Moor," said Sidney. "This alters my opinion of your conduct; for I was under the impression that you had been playing the spy. You have placed your life in jeopardy; and my object is, if possible, to preserve it. There is only one way in which I can ensure your safety."

"If that involves my concurrence in your designs, I must decline it, whatever hazard I may run," replied Moor.

"You mistake me," replied Sidney; "I do not ask you to sacrifice your principles; but I set out for Holland to-night, and if I leave you a prisoner here, I cannot be responsible for the consequences. Neither can I set you at liberty without compromising my confederates, and therefore it is necessary that you should accompany me. Will you go?"

"I am in no position to refuse you, colonel," answered Moor; "I will."

"Then, give me your word that you will not attempt escape," said Sidney.

Moor gave the required pledge, and setting down the lamp, Sidney unbarred the cell-door, and allowed him to come forth.

Without a word more, he led the way to an aperture in the wall, and creeping through it, entered a long, narrow passage in which they were scarcely able to stand upright, and traversing it, they arrived at length at another small opening, admitting them to a close damp vault, half filled with old mouldering coffins.

At the upper end, a ladder led to a trap-door above, and they were mounting it, when a gleam of light suddenly shot along the wall, and instantly disappeared.

They listened a moment, but all was still, and cautiously raising the trap-door, Sidney led the way into what proved to be a church.

"Wait here a moment," he said, as they gained the transept; "I will return with the key, and in a few minutes you will be in safety."

Moor watched him descend through the trap-door, the light gleaming dimly on the ghostly walls of the church, which had originally formed the chapel of the convent, founded by Geoffrey de Mandeville, in the reign of William the Conqueror. The next moment the sacred structure was buried in darkness, and Moor was meditating on his situation, when he was suddenly seized from behind, and ere he could offer resistance, his arms were secured with a stout cord, and a bandage was passed over his head, so as effectually to stifle his cries. He was then hurried along, despite his struggles to free himself, by two men, who dragged him out of the church, and forcing him to walk forward for nearly a quarter of a mile, brought him to the brink of the river, and then tumbling him into a boat, pushed off into the centre of the stream.

While they were thus occupied, Moor contrived to loosen the bandage from his mouth, and called lustily for help. Voices were heard answering from the road; and, muttering a terrible imprecation, one of the captors fell upon Moor, and endeavoured to stifle his outcries with his hands.

The moon was partially obscured, but a trace of light appeared, revealing the thickly-wooded shores, faced by tall reeds and flags, extending some distance into the water, but leaving the mid-stream in obscurity. As Mauvesin and his accomplice arrived here, they perceived a boat starting in pursuit of them; and, exchanging a hurried whisper, they quitted their oars, and seizing on Moor, threw him into the river.

For a moment the men gazed at the water in which, after a struggle, their victim had sunk, when reminded of the approaching boat, they caught up their oars, and made for the opposite shore. At this juncture a splashing was heard, and Moor, who had contrived to free his hands from the cords, reappeared on the surface.

His enemies would willingly have knocked him on the head, but no time was allowed them for further violence, as the other boat was swiftly approaching, so, pulling ashore, they disappeared. The next moment the other boat came up, and its inmates, who proved to be Sidney and Saint Leu, drew alongside Moor, and hauled him in.

Assisting him to a seat, they congratulated him on his escape, and instantly resumed their oars.

"You will soon be out of your enemy's reach," said Saint Leu; "our horses are waiting for us a little lower down."

"And we must not draw the rein till we reach London," cried Sidney; "the brig I have secured will weigh anchor as soon as we get on board."

Moor made no reply, and after proceeding about half-a-mile, they pulled ashore, and landed in front of a small public-house, close to the water's-edge, and which a neighbouring wood rendered extremely secluded. Here they found the horses they had expected, and after Moor had swallowed a glass of brandy to restore his circulation, they mounted instantly, and rode off in the direction of London.

It was broad daylight by the time they reached Westminster; and here, while Sidney engaged a wherry to convey them to their ship, Moor lingered to take leave of Saint Leu.

"You will tell Sabine that my last thought was of her,"

he said, mournfully; "if I ever return I will strive to find her out."

"She needs no assurance of your devotion, but I will deliver your message," replied Saint Leu: "would that you could cease to think of each other!"

Silently pressing his hand, Moor joined Sidney in the boat, and in less than an hour afterwards they had set sail for Holland.

CHAPTER IV.

NOTTINGHAM'S COUNSEL TO THE KING.

FOILED in his attempt to overthrow Sunderland, Father Petre waited with impatience for the next meeting of the council, in the hope that he might still be able to accomplish his object. On the day in question, the whole of the ministers assembled at Whitehall, and, proceeding to the council-chamber, were presently joined by the king.

Rumours of a conspiracy had reached the palace, and James looked agitated and alarmed.

"Is there any certain information of this alleged conspiracy?" he asked.

"I have little doubt that a conspiracy exists, my liege," replied Sunderland; "but we have failed in our endeavours to discover the traitors."

"Perhaps Lord Nottingham could give us some clue to them," observed Lord Berkeley.

"If a conspiracy exists, Lord Nottingham should be sent to the Tower," cried Father Petre. "Whoever the malcontents may be, depend upon it he is at the head of them."

"Lord Nottingham is one of those who proclaim their discontent," rejoined Sunderland, "and this is not the practice of conspirators. For my own part, I place more reliance on an adversary like him than on many smooth-spoken courtiers."

"I quite agree with you, my lord," remarked Jeffreys.

"It may be so," cried Melfort; "but, in a crisis like the present, the arrest of Nottingham would be only a proper precaution."

"What do you think of it, Sunderland?" inquired James, anxiously. "There is no denying that Nottingham is dangerous."

Before the earl could reply, an usher opened the door, and

announced that the French ambassador requested an immediate audience of the king.

On receiving the royal permission, Barillon appeared, his disordered looks proclaiming that he was charged with some extraordinary mission. Advancing to James, he drew forth an open despatch, and presented it to him.

"This document, my liege, will inform you of a design to subvert your throne," he said, in an agitated voice. "The Prince of Orange, supported by a powerful army and fleet, is on the point of invading England."

Turning deadly pale, James received the letter in silence without regarding the exclamations of surprise which escaped his ministers. A pause ensued, but it was at length broken by the king.

"This news is but too well authenticated," he said. "I must instantly take measures for my defence."

"The king, my master, will support you with sixty thousand men, and a fleet of forty sail," cried Barillon.

"These will enable you to overcome the invader, at the same time that they will overawe the disaffected among your subjects," said Father Petre.

Several of the ministers were about to support this opinion, when Sunderland interposed.

"I entreat your majesty to decline the offer, however well-intentioned, of the King of France," he said. "Your people are ever jealous of foreign interference, and are especially averse to a close alliance with France. Besides, we have no need of such supplies. Why look for aid abroad, when your own forces, both by sea and land, are superior to those of your adversary?"

"You cannot be in earnest, my lord," cried Father Petre, furiously. "No loyal subject of his majesty will advise him to refuse this generous offer of assistance."

"I will not refuse it," said James. "At such a juncture I must not trust to accident, when I am offered the means of insuring success."

"The measure will have precisely the opposite effect to what you suppose, my liege," returned Sunderland. "I repeat that the intervention of the King of France will be highly distasteful to your subjects, and by alienating their affections from you, will make them the willing instruments of the invader. Your own army and navy will be the first to regard it as an insult."

"Your lordship is right with regard to the navy," observed Lord Dartmouth, the Admiral of the Fleet. "If they heard the French were to join them, they would instantly go over to the enemy."

"You do my seamen injustice, my lord," cried James. "They

have fought and bled by my side, and will not desert me in the moment of danger. M. Barillon will inform my brother Louis that I accept his proffered assistance."

"Your majesty having made this decision," said Sunderland, "I have nothing left but to tender my resignation. I am ready to lay down my life in your service, but with my consent no foreign army shall ever set foot in England."

A profound silence followed this speech. Torn with indecision, James darted a rapid glance at the other ministers, as if to assure himself of their support; but every eye was fixed on Sunderland. The very enemies of the minister seemed to dread his secession, and in all the council, Father Petre alone looked forward to it with satisfaction.

"Now is the time to accomplish his disgrace," whispered the Jesuit to Barillon, who was standing at his side; "say but a word, and our object is effected."

To his surprise, the ambassador seemed to discountenance his views. Indeed, though his personal dislike of Sunderland remained unshaken, Barillon entertained the highest opinion of his ability, and, since his last conference with Father Petre, he had received instructions from France to lend his support to Sunderland. Turning a deaf ear therefore to the Jesuit's solicitation, he urged James, in a whisper, to come to an understanding with Sunderland.

"It must be so," replied James, in the same tone; and he added aloud to Sunderland, "important as I deem these proffered supplies, my lord, I consider the service you can render me still more important. You will, therefore, retain your office; and M. Barillon will inform his august master, that while I feel grateful for the offer of his assistance, I have no present need of it."

"I rejoice to obey your majesty's commands," replied Sunderland; "and you will, I am sure, find it more advantageous to rely implicitly on the affection of your subjects than any allies. Meanwhile, something should be done to encourage the well-disposed, and to conciliate the disaffected."

"It is by coercion, not conciliation, that we must meet the disaffected," cried Father Petre; "and as a first step in this course, I again recommend the immediate arrest of Lord Nottingham."

"You speak well, reverend father," answered James. "Let a warrant for that purpose be prepared, and I will sign it."

In obedience to a gesture from the king, the clerk of the council proceeded to draw up the warrant, and James was about to sign it, when the usher announced the Earl of Nottingham.

James was so surprised at the announcement, that the pen dropped from his hand.

Every eye was turned on the door as the Protestant leader appeared. Always grave, his face was now clouded with anxiety, which he did not seek to conceal. Advancing, he bent the knee before the king.

"This visit is unexpected, my lord," said James, coldly. "To what do I owe the unusual advantage of your presence?"

"In your majesty's prosperity I held aloof, inasmuch as I could not approve of the proceedings of your ministry," replied Nottingham; "but information has just reached me that your kingdom is about to be invaded, and you must not find me absent in the moment of danger."

A deep flush mantled the king's cheeks. Turning his eye quickly round the council-board with a look full of meaning, he arose, and gave Nottingham his hand.

"Welcome, my lord," he exclaimed, with gracious dignity; "no one can better advise me what to do in this emergency. Take your seat by my side, and afford me the benefit of your counsel."

With a low obeisance Nottingham arose, and seated himself at the table.

"I would submit to your majesty a proposition for conciliating the Church," he said; "I recommend that all Catholics holding other than military employments, shall be dismissed your service; that the dean and fellows of Magdalen College shall be reinstated in their dignities; that the ecclesiastical commission, which has become so obnoxious, shall be abolished; that a proclamation shall be issued, announcing your majesty's intention to submit the question of the dispensing power to the decision of the Parliament; and, finally, that the royal charter shall be restored to the city of London."

"I will never consent to these measures," cried Father Petre, furiously: "they undo all that we have done; and if his majesty assents to them, he will undermine his throne."

"They are essential to its preservation," said Nottingham.

James was silent, restrained alike by the searching looks of Nottingham, and by a distrust of his own capacity; but a warm debate ensuing among the council, a large majority expressed their approval of Nottingham's proposition, and recommended its adoption.

"You have not joined in the debate, my lord," said James to Sunderland. "What is your opinion of the proposed measures?"

"I am sure, my liege, that they will be highly acceptable to your people," replied the earl.

"Then I will not hesitate to adopt them," returned James;

"and now for our military preparations. You will each place your respective departments on the most effective footing. My Lord Preston, you will attend me to the camp; and you, my Lord Dartmouth, will instantly set out for the fleet."

And dismissing the council, he quitted the room, and shortly afterwards proceeded on horseback to the camp on Hounslow Heath.

BOOK THE FOURTH.

CHAPTER I.

THE INVASION.—THE PRINCE OF ORANGE.

In 1580, when the United Provinces were struggling with Spain for their independence, William, first Prince of Orange, was appointed Stadtholder of the republic, and captain-general of its armies. After forcing the Spanish troops to evacuate the States, William I. was assassinated at Delft, on the 10th of July, 1584; but the Stadtholdership was continued in his family till William II., his grandson, endeavoured to render himself absolute, when the house of Orange became unpopular, and on the death of William II., the office of Stadtholder was abolished. Soon after this occurrence, his widow, Mary Stuart, daughter of Charles I., gave birth to a son, William Henry, who was confided by the States to the care of John de Witt, the celebrated patriot, then Grand Pensionary of Holland; and, perceiving early indications of the great capacity of the prince, De Witt purposely neglected his education, in order to obscure as much as possible the talents and virtues he was supposed to inherit from his ancestors, and which the Pensionary believed might prove prejudicial to the liberties of his country.

Notwithstanding this disadvantage, the prince had scarcely attained his twenty-first year, when an occasion arose which proved him a worthy representative of his race. Engaged in an unequal contest with the united forces of France and England, the Dutch, reduced to the greatest straits, fixed their last hopes on the young Prince of Orange. At the head of an inefficient force, William took the field against the vast armies of France, and forced them to retire, with great loss, to Alfen, from which place he ultimately compelled them to retreat over the frontiers. Meanwhile, his adherents rose in the different cities, and demanded the repeal of the edict which had abolished the office of Stadtholder. Surprised and terrified, the republican party everywhere yielded, with the single exception of Cornelius de Witt, the brother of the Pensionary, who, notwithstanding the menaces of the mob and the entreaties of his friends, refused to assent to the measure. Enraged at his resolution, the Orange party accused him of having offered a low barber, named Ticklaer, a bribe of 30,000 guilders, to assassinate William; and though the only testimony adduced against him was that of the barber, the venerable patriot was consigned to the rack, where, while suffering the most excruciating torment, he infuriated his enemies by reciting, in a calm voice, a passage from Horace.

Though obliged to acknowledge that the evidence would not justify a conviction, the judges sentenced the unfortunate statesman to perpetual banishment; but nothing less than his blood would satisfy the populace; and as he appeared at the prison-door, attended by his brother, the Pensionary, on the morning after his trial, an immense multitude demanded that they should both be put to death. Perceiving that their destruction was resolved on, the brothers had just sunk into each other's arms, when they were knocked down by the mob, and trodden under foot; after which, their crushed and mutilated carcases were dragged in triumph through the streets, next suspended from the common gallows, and finally cut into a thousand pieces, some of which were boiled and eaten by their inhuman assassins.

Raised to the dignity of Stadtholder of Holland, William in a short time compelled France and England to conclude a peace with the States, and proceeding on a visit to the English court, afterwards espoused the Princess Mary, eldest daughter of James, then Duke of York. Scarcely had the marriage been solemnised, when he conceived the design of ascending the throne of England, by intriguing for the exclusion of his father-in-law.

Baffled in his attempts to supplant James in the succession to the crown, the Prince of Orange began to affect the utmost deference for his father-in-law, but, at the same time, secretly fomented those divisions which the arbitrary policy of James excited among his subjects. By these means he caused himself to be regarded as the champion of the Protestant interest, both by the Church and the Dissenters; and the birth of a Prince of Wales determined him to appear openly in that character, and endeavour to drive James from the throne.

Under pretence of resisting the ambitious designs of Louis XIV., he entered into an alliance with the Pope, the Emperor, and the King of Spain, together with several princes of the Germanic Confederation, by which the contracting parties severally bound themselves to assist each other with arms and money to the utmost of their power. The League of

Augsburg, as it was called, served him as an excuse for making the most extensive preparations, both by sea and land, in which he was zealously aided by the States of Holland, and the Dukes of Zell and Wolfenbuttel; and shortly after the birth of tho Prince of Wales, he had collected a force of 14,000 men, together with a squadron of men-of-war, and five hundred transports, with which he waited only for a favourable moment to sail against England.

Louis the Fourteenth having opened the campaign on the continent by investing Philipsburgh, in the territories of the Emperor, instead of attacking Maestricht, which would have carried the war into the Netherlands, the Prince of Orange found himself at liberty to prosecute his designs against Eugland, and, accordingly, he issued a manifesto animadverting on the policy which had been pursued by James, referring in terms of especial acrimony to the prosecution of the bishops, and stigmatising the Prince of Wales as a base-born pretender, adding that he was invited over to England by a large number of the nobility for the purpose of redressing these grievances. His forces embarked in the *Zuyder-Zee*, on the 17th of October, 1688; and three days afterwards, the whole armament being assembled, the prince weighed anchor from Helvoetsluys, having first arranged his fleet in three divisions; the van being under the command of Admiral Herbert, the ceutre led by himself, and the rear by the Dutch vice-admiral Evertizen.

Favoured by the wind, this formidable armament shaped its course for the English Channel, amidst the roar of cannon from the shore and the acclamations of the adventurers on board. But, as night drew on, a violent gale arose, which so scattered the fleet, that when the morning dawned not two ships were to be seen in company. Crowded together on the previous evening, the vessels, in the darkness, had dashed against each other; the cannon broke from their lashings and rolled over the decks, which, cumbered with baggage and ammunition, and thronged with soldiers, afforded no room for the operations of the seamen; and the immense fleet was almost at the mercy of the wind and waves.

A great portion of the artillery and baggage, and nearly one thousand horses, were thrown overboard; and within forty-eight hours after his embarkation, William returned to the harbour of Helvoetsluys, followed only by three ships of war and a few transports.

In order to gain time and lull James into false security, he caused the most exaggerated accounts of this disaster to be spread in England; but his unhappy father-in-law was too surely informed that he was repairiug his losses, and might be expected to re-embark with the first easterly wind. On receiving this intelligence, James caused an enormous weather-cock to be raised on the north end of the banqueting-house at Whitehall, where it may still be seen, so that he might always be informed of the direction of the wind; that which blew from the east being now dignified with the title of the Protestant wind, while the other points of the compass were denominated Popish. This circumstance is thus alluded to in the popular ballad of "Lillibullero:"—

Oh! but why does he stay behind?
By my soul 'tis a Protestant wind!

The propitious wind came at last! and having in the mean time gathered together his scattered fleet, repaired the damages it had sustained, and taken on board fresh supplies of ammunition, William, on the 1st of November, again sailed out of Helvoetsluys. The English fleet, under Lord Dartmouth, was stationed off Harwich, for the purpose of intercepting him, but the wind which favoured the Dutch was adverse to the English, and the invading force arrived unmolested in the Channel. The splendid spectacle of six hundred ships sailing past was watched with interest, in the more contracted parts of the Channel, by thousands of spectators on either shore, by whom the flag-ship of William was distinguished in the van, as well by its greater dimensions, as from the standard which flew on its mast. The wind continued favourable; and on the morning of the 5th of November, 1688, the magnificent armament passed Dartmouth, and anchored safely in Torbay.

CHAPTER II.

THE LANDING AT BRIXHOLME.

It was a fine clear November morning, and the sun shone brightly on the Dutch fleet now thronging the broad basin of Torbay. Many of the vessels had already taken up their ground and cast anchor, and a string of signals* was flying from the mast-head of the admiral's flag-ship, commanded by Herbert, by which others were directed to their station. Boats were out from some of the men-of-war, and towing them forward; the

* The method of communicating by signals had been invented some years previously by James, then Duke of York, by whom it had been introduced into the English navy, from which it had been borrowed by other naval powers.

crews, as their vessels passed each other, exchanging loud hurrahs; sailors were seen aloft furling the sails; cables were heaved up from the locker, preparatory to casting anchor, to the sound of the fife and drum; and the cheering vociferations of the seamen could be heard far and wide.

Scarcely had the ship containing the Prince of Orange come to an anchor, when an accommodation-rope was shipped in the gangway, and the prince's barge lowered alongside. The yards of the ship were manned, as a mark of honour; a guard in the barge presented arms, while its crew stood up before them, with their oars aloft, and the prince, attended by Colonel Sidney and Marshal Schomberg, then descended to the barge.

William was dressed in a military costume, studiously fashioned to conceal the defects of his person. He was of middle stature, slight, round-shouldered, and singularly awkward in his gait. He was sharp-visaged, stern-browed, and eagle-nosed; but his eyes were bright and keen, and lighted up an otherwise cold and impassive countenance.

His companion, Armand Frederic de Schomberg, Marshal of France, was the son of Menard de Schomberg, who was employed by the Elector Palatine Frederick V., to negociate a marriage with the Princess Elizabeth, and died while the future marshal was yet an infant. Educated under the guardianship of the elector, young Schomberg soon manifested an inclination for the profession of arms, and displayed all those qualities that render men illustrious. When only sixteen years of age he was present at the famous battle of Nordlingen, where the Swedes were defeated by the Imperialists, and afterwards served at the retreat of Mayence, under the orders of Rantzau, who, for his meritorious conduct, gave him a company in his own regiment, in which the young soldier acquired new distinction. Incurring the displeasure of the Emperor, Schomberg proceeded to Holland, and entered the service of Henry Frederick, Prince of Orange, who soon took him into favour, and Schomberg remained with him till the prince's death, in 1650, when he repaired to France, where the civil war was then raging, and served with distinction in Poitou and Champagne, and at the siege of Rhétel, where he commanded the infantry. Cardinal Mazarin, as a reward for his valour, appointed him lieutenant-general of the army of Flanders, in which capacity he considerably increased his reputation; but while prosecuting the siege of Valenciennes he had the misfortune to lose his son, who was killed under his eyes in the trenches. He commanded a wing of the French army at the battle of Dunes, and contributed mainly to the success of the day; which ended in the complete overthrow of the Spanish army under the Prince de Condé. On the conclusion of the war

Schomberg repaired to Portugal, then threatened with a Spanish invasion, and was intrusted by the regent with the command of four thousand men, with which small force he successfully encountered the Spaniards on several occasions, and finally gained the decisive victory of Villa Viciosa, which put an end to the war. Previous to his leaving Portugal, the regent created him a count, and returniug to France, he was shortly afterwards presented with the baton of marshal, and appointed to the command of the army in the Low Countries. Here he forced the Dutch to raise the siege of Maestricht, aud then of Charleroi, and was about to enter Germany when a truce was signed with the emperor, and his orders to advance were countermanded. On the revocation of the edict of Nantes in 1685, he requested permission to retire to Portugal; and after remaining in that country for a short time, he repaired to the court of the elector of Brandenburg, and was in the service of that prince when he was invited by the Prince of Orange to accompany him in his expedition to England. Madame de Sévigné, who was intimate with his wife, describes him as "oue of the most amiable husbands in the world, without counting that he is a hero," and speaks of his mental acquirements and natural intelligence in terms of high commendation.

As the prince and his companions alighted in the barge, the guard grounded arms, and the crew dropped and shipped their oars, and under a royal salute from the admiral's ship, which was answered from that of the *William*, the barge was pulled towards the shore.

William glanced proudly at his fleet, and then at the shores of the bay, which, opening between two capes, called Hope's Nose and Berry Head, formed a vast semilunar basin, about twelve miles in circumference. Great ramparts of rock hung round the sides, from which, however, here and there, wherever a patch of earth presented itself, tall trees sprang up; and the bottom of the bay arose in a verdant slope, crowned with luxuriant woods.

At this point a row of cottages, forming the village of Brixholme, straggled up from the bay; and groups of fishermen and smugglers watched from the beach the approach of the barge, while above were seen some stout farmers and yeomen from the country, in carts or on horseback, and a man stood on the tower of the village church, making signals to another below, who instantly mounted a stout horse, and galloped up an adjacent lane, to carry off the intelligence of the arrival of the fleet to the villages in the interior of the country.

As the barge gained the beach, William was the first to spring ashore. He was followed by Marshal Schomberg, bearing his standard, and Sidney; and they all appeared surprised that no person of importance was there to meet them.

"Heaven sanctify our enterprise!" exclaimed William. "I come to defend the religion and liberty of England!"

A loud cheer arose from the soldiers and seamen, but the country people were silent. William turned with a look of disappointment to Sidney.

"A poor assemblage and a sorry greeting," he said, somewhat bitterly. "Where is the enthusiasm you promised me? where are the crowds?"

"Both will come in due time, your highness," replied Sidney, and taking off his hat, he waved it in the air, crying, "God save the Prince of Orange! Heaven speed the champion of the Protestant Church!"

The soldiers and seamen again cheered loudly, but the spectators still kept aloof, and gazed at each other irresolutely.

"Hum!" muttered William, with a dissatisfied look. "It would have been more auspicious if we had landed yesterday, seeing that it was my birth-day."

"It is more auspicious for our cause, your highness, that we have landed to-day," replied Sidney. "It is the anniversary of the deliverance of England from the popish treason of Guy Fawkes. We are once more rescued from the devices and treacheries of Rome."

"Once begun, I will not slacken in the work," rejoined William. "No coolness in the people shall discourage me. The troops will be landed without delay, and we shall be ready to march forward to-morrow. But see, here comes Dr. Burnet."

"As he spoke, the ecclesiastic in question landed from a boat and approached them.

Born at Edinburgh, on the 18th of September, 1643, Gilbert Burnet was the son of an advocate, who, after being exiled for his loyalty during the civil war, was created a lord of the Session at the Restoration, by the title of Lord Cramond. Swift, indeed, asserts that he was merely a *laird*, but this is merely a stroke of his malicious pleasantry.

Early distinguished for learning, young Burnet took the degree of Master of Arts at Marischal College, Aberdeen, at the age of fourteen, and afterwards visited both the English universities, whence he proceeded to the continent, and passed some time in Rotterdam and Paris. Returning to Scotland, he was presented by Sir Robert Fletcher to the valuable benefice of Saltoun, the duties of which he discharged in the most exemplary manner. As an instance of his generosity, it is recorded by Chalmers, that on one occasion, one of his parishioners being threatened with an execution for debt, he applied to Burnet for relief, when the latter asked him how much would be required to set him up again in his trade, and the man naming the sum, Burnet ordered his servant to pay it him. The servant replied it was all they had in the house. "Well," pay it to this poor man," rejoined Burnet. "You do not know the pleasure there is in giving happiness."

Shortly after his presentation to Saltoun, Burnet was intrusted by the Duke of Hamilton with the papers of his father and uncle, from which he compiled the "Memoirs of the Dukes of Hamilton;" and about the same time he clandestinely paid his addresses to the duke's niece, Lady Margaret Kennedy, daughter of the Earl of Cassilis, but their correspondence being discovered, he was compelled to fly to England, and he prevailed on the lady to accompany him. On arriving in London, he went over to the party of the duke's adversary, the Earl of Lauderdale, and, under his auspices, commenced his "History of the Reformation," which, appearing just as the popish plot was in agitation, accorded so well with the prevailing views, that its author received the thanks of both houses of Parliament. Burnet was successively appointed preacher of the Rolls Chapel, Lecturer of St. Clement's, and chaplain in ordinary to Charles II.; and while holding these preferments, distinguished himself by converting Wilmot, Earl of Rochester, of whom he afterwards published a memoir, which, Dr. Johnson says, "the critic ought to read for its elegance, the philosopher for its arguments, and the saint for its piety." He is best known, however, for his "History of His Own Time," a work which, though remarkable in itself, presents its writer in anything but an amiable point of view.

On the accession of James II., having become obnoxious to the Catholics, Burnet retired to the continent, and after visiting Paris and Rome, finally settled at the Hague, whence he waged a paper war against James, in which he was strongly supported by the popular party in England.

"Dr. Burnet was a large stout man, with a bold and somewhat presumptuous expression of countenance.

"Bustling forward, Burnet hastened to make his devoirs to William, who smiled as he approached, and offered him his hand.

"God save your majesty!" exclaimed Burnet; "I am first to hail you King of England."

"You are always very zealous in my service, doctor," replied William; "but let me be Prince of Orange till I am made sovereign of this realm by Parliament."

"I shall salute your highness in such manner as you may command," replied Burnet; "but, believe me, you are now *de facto* King of England."

"And if your highness and the Princess Anne should unhappily have no heirs, the doctor has provided for the future succession to the crown," observed Sidney, sarcastically.

Burnet coloured, but the affected gravity of Sidney's deportment, and the look of attention assumed by the prince, reassured him.

"Yes, your highness," he cried, "I have fixed on the Princess Sophia of Hanover as the next in succession; but these points can be settled hereafter. May I ask where your highness intends to encamp?"

"Encamp! eh!" cried William. "What is your opinion of predestination, doctor?"

Unconscious of the rebuke conveyed in these words, Burnet replied at some length, arguing strongly in favour of the disputed doctrine; and William listened with seeming attention, though his thoughts were really occupied by his duties as a leader.

As this was passing, another person in full uniform landed, and advanced towards them. Saluting him as General Bentinck, William caught him familiarly by the arm and took him aside.

Bentinck was William's early favourite, and their attachment was mutual, and of the strongest kind. Descended from a family that had long resided at Overyssel, in the United Provinces, Bentinck was born in 1649, and at an early age was appointed page of honour to William, and shortly afterwards was made gentleman of the bed-chamber. Previously to his promotion, William having been attacked with the small-pox, the young page was so attentive, that, during sixteen days and nights, William never called once that he was not answered by Bentinck, as if he were awake the whole period. On the prince's return to convalescence, Bentinck requested permission to return home, and had scarcely arrived at his father's house when he was himself seized with the disease in its most virulent form; but he recovered soon enough to attend William to the field. Here his station was always by the side of his master; and after serving him zealously in several important missions, he had accompanied him in the same vessel on his expedition to England.

"Our men seem dispirited Bentinck," said William. "I am afraid the people who invited us here will not be very forward to assist us."

"They have not had time to join us yet," answered Bentinck. "We shall no doubt meet some of them to-morrow. The troops, too, will be in better condition in the morning. They have been cooped up for a week in the ships; but the march will soon raise their spirits, and I have no doubt they will behave gallantly."

"The enemy, it seems, intends to leave us to seek him, instead of seeking us," observed William; "but here come our horses; let us mount and reconnoitre the country."

While the foregoing conversation had taken place, indeed, several horses had been landed, and mounting, William galloped off, attended by Bentinck, Schomberg, and Sidney.

During their absence, the disembarkation of the troops was continued, and conducted with such despatch, that, in the course of the day, the whole army had landed.

As night approached, dense masses of cloud gathered overhead; the wind rose to a gale; and when it abated, the rain fell in torrents. From the violence of the storm, it was with difficulty that the soldiers could maintain the watch-fires. Here a party of some twenty were stretched in the open field, round a glimmering fire—some already asleep—others leaning back on their horses, and others vainly endeavouring to keep alive the fires, while some few still sat bravely up, smoking their pipes, and handing round the social canteen. Deep silence pervaded the vast assemblage. No snatch of song, or burst of laughter, indicated that the soldiers were making light of the discomfort of their situation, and excepting an occasional shout from the sentinels, announcing that all was well, not a sound was heard. In this way the first night was passed by the invading army.

CHAPTER III.

THE MARCH TO EXETER.

The next morning found William surrounded by his staff, while scouts were constantly arriving with intelligence, and the principal officers of the army were making their reports.

The prince looked dispirited. The army was without provisions, excepting such supplies as could be procured from the ships, and various foraging parties had been scouring the surrounding country with but indifferent success. Added to this, the commissaries had been unable to muster sufficient waggons for the transit of the baggage and ammunition, and, in many cases, had been obliged to resort to violence with the neighbouring farmers, in order to obtain the use of their teams. Owing to these circumstances, the morning was far advanced before the army could commence its march.

The spectacle it presented in its progress was anything but cheering. The colours were furled and cased; the horses of the cavalry regiments looked jaded, and hung their heads; the soldiers, drenched with rain, and shivering with cold and hunger, marched along in silence; and the women were crowded in the baggage-waggons under tarpaulin covers. The roads were in many places flooded, or covered ankle-deep with mud; soldiers were constantly falling out of the ranks, unable to continue the march; and occasionally a field-carriage, used for the transit of cannon, would become so jammed in the ruts, that a halt was obliged to be made till it could be extricated. The inhabitants of the towns and villages through which they passed received them coldly, holding altogether aloof, or regarding them with stupified wonder; although William caused his proclamation to be read aloud, representing himself as their deliverer, and inviting them to join his standard.

In this way William marched onward for two days, and it was not until the third morning that he came in sight of Exeter, though it was only twenty miles from Torbay. Arrived within a mile of the city, the army was ordered to halt, and an officer was despatched to summon forth the mayor and corporation, while William prepared to enter the city, on their appearance, in a triumphal procession, which should excite the admiration of the citizens.

A momentary gleam of sunshine promised to favour his design, and he hastened to take advantage of it. The procession was opened by two hundred English refugees, in their richest attire, and mounted on Flemish horses, splendidly accoutred. These were followed by as many negroes, from the Dutch plantations in America, whose appearance was rendered more striking by richly-embroidered caps, lined with white fur, and plumed with white feathers. Next walked two hundred Laplanders, armed with broadswords, and with the skins of wild beasts thrown over their armour. Then came fifty gentlemen, and as many pages, supporting the banner of the prince, borne by heralds, who were succeeded by fifty war-horses, fully accoutred, and each attended by two grooms. William himself rode next, on a milk-white charger, and clad in burnished armour, supported on each hand by a number of officers in sumptuous uniforms. These were followed by two hundred gentlemen, mounted on Flemish horses, and attended by their pages; while six troops of the prince's body-guard brought up the rear.

In this order the procession approached the city, when it was met by a scout, who informed William that the mayor refused to receive him, and had thrown his messenger into prison. Mortified and enraged, William ordered a squadron of the body-guard to precede him, and bring the mayor to terms, while the procession followed more leisurely, and did not arrive at Exeter till some time afterwards. In the interim, the force in advance had presented itself before the mayor, who, as he had no means of resistance, was compelled to throw open the gate, and the Dutch guard instantly took possession of the city.

As the procession drew near, William espied his colour flying from the summit of the gate, announcing that the city had surrendered. But the reduction of a defenceless place afforded him little ground for exultation, and he looked in vain for some manifestation of popular sympathy. In obedience to a proclamation from the mayor, the shops were all closed, and the procession passed up the deserted streets in silence. Halting in the market-place, William caused a proclamation to be read, in which he announced himself as the champion of the Protestant religion, and called on the citizens to arm in his cause; but, though many of the latter looked on from the windows of the neighbouring houses, his appeal had no effect, and not a single person joined his standard.

Scarcely able to conceal his disappointment, William now inquired for the bishop and dean; and finding that both had fled on his approach, he resolved to take up his quarters in the Deanery. Here he was soon joined by the chief of his officers; and, by their advice, determined to make a further trial of the temper of the inhabitants, before he ventured to resume his march.

Meanwhile, as the public tranquillity remained undisturbed, the citizens began to feel more secure; many of the shops were opened, and the majority of the inhabitants went about their usual avocations. This show of confidence inspired the adherents of William with new hopes. The prince's proclamation was printed, and dispersed over the country; a large bounty was offered for volunteers and recruits; the persuasions of Sidney were exerted to overawe the bold, and the oratory of Burnet to overcome the scruples of the timid.

The large choir of the cathedral was crowded to excess, as Burnet ascended to the pulpit. Rich and poor, old and young, of both sexes, thronged even the aisles, while every face bore the impress of expectation and curiosity. Amidst profound silence, Burnet read forth his text, in a deep, sonorous voice, from the 107th Psalm:—"Whoso is wise, and will observe these things, even they shall understand the loving-kindness of the Lord."

The preacher proceeded to show that this loving-kindness had been signally manifested towards the Prince of Orange, in his present glorious expedition, preserving him from the dangers of the sea, and the snares of the enemy, and bringing him, at last, safely to the land which he sought to emancipate. He then lauded the prince's virtues, prowess, and patriotism—spoke of his attachment to the Protestant religion, and his right of succession to the crown, now occupied by a popish tyrant, and destined to a popish pretender, and finally hailed him as the deliverer of the nation.

His discourse gave rise to an indescribable scene of confusion. Men, women, and children, were observed scrambling to the door, overwhelmed with dismay. The whole congregation became disordered; and, perceiving this, Burnet became more intemperate in his language, and concluded by reading the prince's proclamation.

There was now a general rush to the door; but, persisting in his purpose, Burnet read the proclamation to the end, when he called out, in a loud voice, "God save the Prince of Orange!" To his surprise, no one cried "Amen!" and, looking round, he found that the whole of the congregation had retreated, and that he and a few choristers were the only inmates of the cathedral.

Full of rage, Burnet flung out of the pulpit, and hurried off to communicate with his master. But the news of his failure had preceded him; and on arriving at the Deanery, he found William and his leading officers consulting on what was to be done.

"The reports from every quarter are unfavourable," said William; "I suspect I have been betrayed."

"Our friends are backward, your highness, but there is no ground for supposing them treacherous," observed Sidney. "If we were only joined by one person of note, the whole body would come over to us."

"Then they are restrained by cowardice," cried Marshal Schomberg, "and therefore little reliance can be placed upon them."

"I will at least show them that they are in my power," said William. "If I am not joined by some of them before to-morrow night, I will publish the invitation they sent me, with the whole of their names attached to it, and then leave them to the fate they deserve."

"Give them a few days longer, I entreat your highness," cried Sidney.

"Not an hour!" exclaimed William. "Indeed, I cannot if I would; for we have now come to such a pass, that if we remain here, we must either pillage or famish, and I have no inclination to do either. What say you, Bentinck?" he added.

"I cannot conceal from your highness that I think our best

course would be to re-embark," replied the favourite; "the troops themselves begin to murmur."

"We must strike a blow first, if only for the honour of our flag," cried Schomberg.

"Hear me a moment, your highness," cried Sidney; "I see Speke in the ante-chamber. He has been among the Nonconformists, and I have no doubt brings us such a report from them as will determine you to push forward."

And passing to the open door of the ante-chamber, he beckoned Speke to advance.

William regarded the treacherous emissary with a look of suspicion.

"Well, sir, what news do you bring?" he demanded, sternly.

"Such as I would rather not report, your highness," replied Speke. "I went to the meeting-houses this morning, but could only gain admission by forcing the door. The Dissenters will not render you any assistance."

"Well, Colonel Sidney, what think you now?" cried William.

Lowering his voice, Sidney conversed with him in an undertone for several minutes, when they walked together into an ante-room, where William called an orderly, and giving him some private instructions, the soldier disappeared, but shortly afterwards returned, ushering in Charles Moor.

The young man's demeanour was resolute, though respectful, and was in no way affected by the stern look of William.

"You have demanded your liberty," said William; "I have detained you in order to allow time for escape to those persons who might be implicated by your disclosures. This, no doubt, has made you more anxious to proceed."

"I do not deny it, your highness," answered Moor; "I am anxious to warn my sovereign that he is surrounded by traitors."

"Your warning will come too late," rejoined William, with seeming composure; "the persons you would denounce are already beyond the king's reach, and have taken effectual steps for placing him in my power."

"Yet some of them owe all they possess to King James's bounty," rejoined Moor; "how then can your highness repose confidence in such men?"

"His highness will not trouble you for your sentiments on this subject, Mr. Moor," said Sidney, drily; "the distinguished patriots to whom you allude, have sacrificed every private consideration on the altar of their country. It would be well for you if you did the same. Nothing now can save James."

"If he seeks to pursue this contest, I certainly cannot answer for his safety," observed William; "but I will be no party to the violent measures which will be directed against him. You are devoted to his service, Mr. Moor, and may be the instrument of his preservation. A fleet horse is ready saddled for you at the door. Hasten to London and warn your royal master that his only safety is in flight. He must leave England instantly."

"I will tell his majesty that this is your highness's advice," answered Moor; "but I am bound to add, that I shall urge him not to adopt it. If I can prevail upon him, he will never quit England."

"I find I am mistaken in you, sir," said William, coldly; "I thought you were anxious to preserve the king's life."

"I am anxious to preserve not only his life, but his throne," answered Moor.

"He has lost his throne, and you would endanger his head," observed Sidney. "I procured you the offer of this service, because I thought it would be gratifying to you to be the means of saving the fallen monarch's life, at the same time that it would raise you up a friend in his highness. You must see that James has no alternative but flight or death."

"Better he should meet death than dishonour," replied Moor. "I will never counsel him to fly."

"Be it so," replied Sidney, coldly. "Let Lord Mauvesin be introduced," he added, to an attendant, and presently afterwards the young nobleman appeared.

"You are aware of his highness's wishes, my lord," said Sidney to Mauvesin. "He intrusts the execution of them to you."

"What if I fail in persuading the king to fly?" said Mauvesin.

"He must then be taken off by force," cried William.

"How can that be done, when he will be surrounded by an army?" asked Mauvesin.

"Easily," said Sidney. "Here is a cipher, which will let you know the numbers of the officers on whom you may rely, and the key I gave you this morning will furnish you with their names."

"If I can really rely on their assistance, your enemy will not give you much trouble," said Mauvesin, with significance. "But how are they to know I am authorised to treat with them?"

"By this signet," said William, taking a ring from his finger, and giving it to him.

"Lose not a moment," said Sidney. "Take Snewin with you and begone."

"As I hazard my life in this business," said Mauvesin, in a low tone to William, "your highness will promise me, before I go, that you will protect me from the schemes of this pretender."

And he turned to where he supposed Moor stood, when, to his surprise, he found the young man gone.

Moor, indeed, had marched boldly into the ante-room, and, observing the orderly in attendance, directed him to conduct him to the horse that had been prepared for him by the prince's command. Having no suspicion, the soldier obeyed, and they found the horse in an outer court. Springing to the saddle, Moor instantly rode off.

Scarcely had he disappeared, when Sidney and Mauvesin rushed into the court, followed by William himself, who directed instant pursuit to be made after him. At the same time fresh horses were ordered out, and in a few minutes Mauvesin and Snewin galloped off in the direction taken by Moor.

CHAPTER IV.

THORNLEYDOWN INN.

On the afternoon of the day following that on which the incidents last related occurred, a rustic group was assembled in front of Thornleydown Inn, a well-known and much-frequented hostel in those days, and even at a much later period, on the great West of England road. The party consisted of a stout yeoman, seated on the shaft of his cart, discussing a pot of nappy ale; a young farmer, with a glass of the same wholesome beverage in one hand, and the bridle of his horse in the other; and three or four other persons, who were seated on a bench near the door, with a narrow deal table before them, garnished with a mountainous loaf, a fat Wiltshire cheese, some horn cups and cannikins, and a couple of large brown jugs foaming with the nappy ale before mentioned.

"Well, masters, as I was a-sayin'," observed a lantern-jawed man, who filled the offices of parish-clerk and schoolmaster in the neighbouring village, "I was at Salisbury this mornin', and the talk there was, as how the Prince of Orange had gone to Ireland. There was news from Portsmouth that he'd passed by there, and Lord Dartmouth was sailin' after him."

"I heerd say he were gone to Wales, Master Gosling," cried a blacksmith, with his bared arms folded over his brawny chest. "It'll make it good for trade, if he comes this way, for some of his osses must want shoin'"

"If he do come this way, it'll be very tryin' for us, as well as for our cattle," said the young farmer; "for I've been told they always seizes your teams, and gives you nothing but kicks or pike-thrusts for the use on 'un. I'd rather keep clear of such customers."

"Well, I don't know but it would do good, though, for them troopers be rare drouthy fellows," cried the host, Dick Froggatt.

"Ay, they'll drink your cellar dry, no doubt on't, Master Froggatt," observed the farmer; "but they'll pay th' reck'nin' i' th' same way as they pays for their osses."

"May be," replied the host, checking his laughter; "but it's my opinion the prince be n't far off. There were a man rode by about half an hour ago, as if he'd break un's neck, as seemed as if he was flyin' on before 'un. I rushed out; but, Lor' bless you! afore I could get to the door he were out o' sight."

"I wish I'd seen that flyin' rebel," remarked Nat Peppercorne, the beadle; "go as fast as he would, I'd have stopped un', and made him give some account of himself."

"I don't see how you could, Master Peppercorne," interposed the schoolmaster. "He was most likely carrying intelligence of the prince's landing to the king."

"Don't tell me, Master Gosling," retorted Peppercorne, in an authoritative tone. "Do you think a man as was servin' his majesty 'ud ride at that rate? No, no! I promise you, he was some spy of that rebellious Prince of Orange."

"The prince is no rebel," answered Gosling, who, from his connection with the Church, was somewhat jealous of the reputation of the Protestant champion. "He's a hero, every inch on 'un, and will drive all Papishers where they ought to go."

"I'll tell you what it is!" cried Peppercorne, much excited, "I won't stand by and hear the king abused! Mind, I don't care who it is, but if any one talks about this here Prince of Orange, I'll put 'un i' th' stocks!"

"Then you'll have to put the whole country i' th' stocks," said Gosling; "for everybody talks about 'un."

"And I hope everybody 'll turn out and thrash 'un!" cried the young farmer. "We don't want him here."

"Speak for yourself, young fellow," said Gosling, sharply. "I for one am no friend of the Papishers."

"But I'm for the king, and down wi' his enemies!" exclaimed the farmer, becoming warm.

"Right, Gregory!" cried Peppercorne. "The king shan't be slandered. I've given Master Gosling fair warnin', and if he don't put a bridle on his tongue, he'll rue it."

But notwithstanding this interdiction, Gosling pursued his

theme, and would probably have proceeded to greater lengths, if the whole party had not been disturbed by the arrival of two horsemen, who, alighting, and giving their horses in charge to the ostler, entered the inn, preceded by Dick Froggatt.

It soon became known to the group of idlers without that the visitors had been expected by the host, and that fresh horses were provided for their progress onward; and various were the conjectures which this intelligence excited. But the gossips could not arrive at any satisfactory conclusion on the subject, and, after a time, one or two went off, and the whole party soon dispersed.

At this juncture, another horseman rode up to the inn. He was mounted on a strong grey roadster, who, though he had evidently been ridden hard, was in such good condition, that he showed no symptoms of fatigue. The horseman's dress was that of an officer of dragoons, consisting of a scarlet coat, laced with gold, with short, loose sleeves, terminated by lace ruffles, white doe-skins, and wide funnel-topped boots, armed with gilt spurs. A laced cravat was hung loosely from his throat, and a three-cornered hat, trimmed with feathers, was set fiercely upon his head. Dismounting, he took a pair of large horse-pistols out of the holsters, and, clapping them under his left arm, committed his horse to the ostler, giving him a few injunctions in a low tone, and then marched towards the house, the point of his long sword trailing on the ground as he pursued his course.

At the door he was met by Froggatt, who saluted him as Captain Hawker, and after a word or two had passed in an under tone between them, the host led his guest to a closet at the back of the bar, and pointing to a little hole in the wainscot, motioned him to be silent, and withdrew.

Meanwhile, the two persons who had previously arrived, were sitting in an inner room, discussing some cold meat and a flask of wine.

"Your lordship aint told me yet what this great job is," said one of them, "and I never goes about a thing blindfold; so, if you wants my help, you must e'en tell me what's in she wind. You know," he added, with a familiar grin, "there's no secrets between you and me, Lord Mauvesin."

The nobleman bit his lip.

"The secret is not mine, Snewin," he said, petulantly.

"It's all one to me whose secret it is," cried Snewin; "you wants me to lend a hand in it, and I don't stir a peg further till I knows the whole consarn."

Mauvesin reflected for a moment, and then considering that no harm was likely to arise from the disclosure, he revealed the whole design, on which he was engaged by the Prince of Orange, to his companion.

"This 'll make our jint fortins, my lord," cried Snewin, when the other had finished his relation. "Here's your lordship's partikler good health," he added, pouring out a tumbler of wine, and swallowing it at a draught. "And now let's order the horses, and set forward at wonst."

Their departure, however, was checked by a loud altercation at the door.

"Don't tell me, landlord!" cried an authoritative voice without. "Horses in the name of the Prince of Orange. No refusal. Ha!"

"Well, captain, they're not mine, that's all," answered the submissive voice of Froggatt; "here's the two gen'l'men they belong to, and if they're willin' I'm agreeable."

"Agreeable or not I'll have 'em," cried the captain, throwing open the door, and disclosing his stalwart person to Mauvesin and Snewin. "Ha, gentlemen! your most obedient. Painful necessity. Public service. Prince of Orange. Seize your horses. Must have 'em. No refusal. Ha!"

"Stay, sir, this necessity may be obviated," said Lord Mauvesin, rising, and stepping up to him; "before I part with my horses, I should require some better proof of your authority than mere words. But," he added, in a whisper, "if it is true that you are engaged in the prince's service you must know that I am in the same interest."

"Humph! ha! Easily said," cried Hawker.

"And easily proved," answered Mauvesin; "but before I can believe your assertion, I shall require you to tell me where his highness is at this moment."

"Exeter—ha!" replied the captain, with a knowing wink.

"Right," replied Mauvesin, with some surprise, "and I now believe you have come from his highness, but let me recommend you to be more cautious how you proclaim your connection with him. As for me and my companion, this signet will show you that we are engaged in the prince's service, and therefore must not be molested."

As he spoke, he displayed the prince's signet, which the captain affected to examine minutely.

"Good," he then said, bowing, and taking off his hat. "Honour of addressing Lord Mauvesin, ha!"

"You have," said Mauvesin, regarding him suspiciously.

"Captain Hawker, my name. Orders to accompany you. Glad I've overtaken you. Thought I was right, but always prudent. Never commit myself. Horses at the door. Bill paid. Mount."

So saying, the captain wheeled about, and led the way to the door, where the three horses were in readiness. All was settled in a trice, and they galloped off.

CHAPTER V.

SALISBURY PLAIN.

As the three horsemen proceeded, the waste on either side of the road gradually widened, the trees disappeared, and at length they entered the vast expanse of Salisbury Plain. The day was just closing, and numerous flocks of sheep could be seen in the distance, passing over the downs, like fleecy clouds, repairing to their various pens, while the tinkling of their bells alone broke the silence. On one side the travellers could just discern the tall spire of Salisbury cathedral piercing the air, but the city itself was scarcely distinguishable, and the eye extended for miles over brown downs, broken here and there by copse and brushwood, and cast up into ranges of barrows, which, in the distance, looked like large mole-hills, but presenting no trace of human habitation.

After riding rapidly forward for some time, the horsemen came in sight of a man standing in the middle of the road, and bending over his horse, which had evidently fallen from exhaustion.

"Ha!" cried Mauvesin, joyfully, "that must be the traitor, Moor. Let us on. We have the prince's authority to put him to death."

With these words, he plunged spurs into his steed, and galloped forward, coming up with Moor almost as soon as the latter was aware of his approach. He was closely followed by the others, but before Snewin could lend his patron any assistance, Hawker struck him a violent blow on the head with the butt of a pistol, which knocked him from his horse, and then levelled the pistol at Mauvesin.

"Out with the paper and the ring," he cried. "Overheard all, you see. Played the eaves-dropper. Good joke, eh? No joke if you don't comply. Bullet through your brain. Ha!"

"Hold!" cried Mauvesin, drawing forth a folded paper and a ring. "This is the act of a highwayman."

"No time for parleying," cried the captain, snatching the things. "Mount," he added to Moor, pointing to Snewin's horse. "Fresh hack. Carry you to London. Here's ring and paper. Ring, private signet of the Prince of Orange. Paper contains names of his friends in the king's camp. Understand, eh? Clap spurs to your tit. Take them at once to the king. Want to know your friend? Recollect the Golden Farmer. Ha? No thanks. Meet again one of these days. Perhaps at Tyburn. Good bye!"

All this passed with such rapidity, that before Mauvesin could recover from his first surprise, Moor had galloped off. As he disappeared, the Golden Farmer commanded Mauvesin to deliver up his purse, and dismount; orders which he thought it prudent to obey; when the Golden Farmer seized the nobleman's steed by the bridle, and clapping spurs to his own horse, rode away with both animals, leaving Mauvesin with his senseless companion in the middle of the plain.

Gazing furiously after him, the nobleman shook his hand menacingly, and cried,

"He thinks he has foiled me, but he will find himself mistaken. The paper he has taken will not help him to much information; and should the Prince of Orange fail, I yet possess the means of purchasing safety. One piece of luck has come of it; I am rid of Snewin," he added, stirring the constable's body with his foot. "No, he yet lives! Curses on the fellow for his clumsiness. Would he had killed him outright."

Meanwhile, Moor pursued his way, covering nearly twenty miles of waste, when he arrived at the outskirts of Salisbury, and dashing through a long straggling street, quitted the city, and again reached the high road. Night came on apace—cloudy and dark, but still the rider did not slacken his pace, and his horse bravely obeyed his will.

Hours passed by. The long, dark, cold night grew later and later, and still he pressed on. Now he was traversing a lonely lane—now crossing a bleak moor—now galloping through a wood—now dashing through a village or a town which, shrouded in darkness and in sleep, was quiet as a churchyard. On he rode, never drawing the rein, never abating his pace, with no companion but his thoughts, and nothing to disturb them but the tramp of his horse or the fierce blasts of the wind.

The morning broke at last—cold, raw, and veiled in thick fog. The road was as much deserted as during the night—not a single passenger appeared, not a labourer was in the fields. Shivering with cold, and dripping with wet, Moor still urged on his jaded steed, his fatigue becoming more insupportable every moment. But as the morning advanced the fog cleared away; the sun shone brightly forth, and, shedding warmth and cheerfulness everywhere around, Moor felt enlivened by the genial influence.

In another hour, he came in sight of Hounslow Heath, covered with the royal camp. Long lines of tents, interspersed with pavilions of various proportions, adorned with gorgeous colours, and decorated with streamers, stretched out before him. In the midst stood the king's pavilion, surmounted by a banner emblazoned with the royal arms; and on every side were seen groups of soldiers—some in their fatigue dress, preparing for parade, others in full uniform, and others on guard.

Scarcely able to keep the saddle, Moor expected every moment that his horse would sink under him, but the noble animal still bore up, making an almost supernatural, though dying effort to reach the entrance to the camp. Arrived there not without difficulty and some hindrance from the outposts, Moor spurred on towards a group of officers, who had been watching his approach with the greatest interest, and as he drew nearer, the principal personage among them advanced to meet him, and at the same time, Moor, reining in his steed, the poor animal fell to the ground, and, after a slight struggle, died.

Extricating his feet from the stirrups, Moor staggered forward and took off his hat.

"God save your majesty," he cried, "the Prince of Orange has landed, and is now in Exeter!"

Exclamations broke from the officers, but James was silent, though he turned pale as death. Recovering, he took Moor by the arm, and led him into the pavilion, where he filled a flagon with wine, and presented it to him. Moor eagerly drained the cup.

"I need not now explain to your majesty how it is that I am the bearer of this news," he cried. "It is necessary that I should first put you on your guard. The Prince of Orange intends to induce you, either by craft or violence, to quit your kingdom."

"Ha! is that his aim?" cried James, sternly, his wrath overcoming his distress.

"The prince's troops are chiefly new levies," pursued Moor, "and wanting both in spirit and discipline. Indeed, he is much dispirited himself, no one of note having yet joined him."

"Are you sure of that?" cried James, eagerly.

"Your majesty may rely upon what I have advanced," answered Moor.

"Then by heaven I will march for Exeter at once, and cut him and his rebellious host to pieces," returned James, rising.

"But I must warn your majesty that some of your officers are traitors," pursued Moor. "The invader places his hopes of assistance in them."

And drawing forth the ring and paper, he acquainted the king with the design they referred to, and how they came into his possession.

"You have rendered me a signal service," said James, when he had concluded. "The traitor Mauvesin shall not go unpunished. This paper has come to me in good time. Ho! the guard! Some arrests must be made before I leave the camp."

Yet he still looked hesitatingly at the outside of the paper, as if he dreaded the disclosures within; but at last, breaking the seal, he tore it open. The writing within was in cipher.

"See," he said, falteringly, "their names are as inscrutable as themselves. I am surrounded by traitors, yet know not whom to seize. Would that you had brought Mauvesin a prisoner. He must possess the key to this cipher."

"It may be, my liege," replied Moor, "but were I in your majesty's place, I should not hesitate to march boldly against the enemy."

"You are a young counsellor, but you have proved yourself both brave and skilful, and I will follow your advice," answered James. "I will give orders to march without delay. And now take some rest—you need it much—and when you are sufficiently recruited you shall attend me to London."

"An hour's rest will suffice for me, my liege," replied Moor.

And quitting the presence, he was conducted by an orderly to an adjoining tent, where, desiring the man to call him in an hour, he threw himself upon a soldier's couch, and was instantly asleep.

CHAPTER VI.

THE FLIGHT OF SUNDERLAND.

Roused by the orderly at the appointed time, Moor repaired to the royal tent, in front of which he found the king on horseback, surrounded by a party of horse-guards, and giving directions to their commander, Colonel Kirke. With a smile of cordial welcome to the young man, James ordered a horse to be brought him, and directed him to keep by his side. Soon after this, the whole cavalcade set forward.

As they passed through the camp, Moor observed that many of the tents were already raised, preparatory to the march, and a strong force was engaged in striking the remainder, while numerous fatigue parties were seen packing the baggage waggons, and the residue of the regiments were assembling at different points at the call of the bugle. Aides-de-camp and orderlies were galloping to and fro, sutlers and soldiers' wives were bustling about, drums rolling, trumpets braying, and all things indicated the immediate departure of the army.

At the boundary of the camp, the guard turned out, and presented arms to the king; and passing to the high-road, James rode quickly on in the direction of London.

The journey was silent and gloomy. On entering St. James's Park, they found the Mall almost deserted, but numerous groups were collected in front of Whitehall, conversing anxiously on the rumours of the day. As the king came in sight, a low buzz arose from the crowd, but it instantly subsided, and on drawing near, the monarch was received in solemn silence.

Entering the palace, James bent his steps towards the queen's apartments, followed by Moor, and as they reached the chamber adjoining them, where an usher and several valets were in attendauce, Moor was about to halt, but James motioned him to follow. The usher threw open the folding-doors, while two of the valets flung back a curtain within, and following James to the interior, Moor found himself in an ante-chamber.

"You had better remain here," said James. "Her majesty may wish to make some inquiries of you respecting the invader."

He pointed to a neighbouring bay-window, and bending deferentially, Moor retired thither, while the king passed to the room beyond.

Moor had been but a few minutes in the embrasure of the window, when he heard a step approaching, and, looking up, perceived Sabine. He uttered a joyful exclamation, and eagerly caught her hand.

"I am, indeed, rejoiced to see you again, Mr. Moor," said Sabine. "I was afraid those desperate men, who my uncle told me had carried you off, might have detained you a captive, or have forced you to serve against the king. Indeed, I have had a thousand fears about you."

"I am happy in the interest you feel in me," returned Moor; "but your uncle could have told you that I had nothing to apprehend. I was under the protection of Colonel Sidney, and he would not suffer injury to be done me."

"More than a month elapsed, and we had no tidings of you," said Sabine.

"That was unavoidable," rejoined Moor. "On my arrival in Holland I was offered the alternative of my liberty on parole or a dungeon. I accepted the former offer, but with this condition attached to it that I was to hold no communication with any one in England."

At this moment voices were heard without, and bidding a

hasty adieu to Moor, Sabine retired by the further door. As she disappeared an usher passed across, accompanied by the Earl of Sunderland and the Archbishop of Canterbury, whom he conducted to the saloon beyond, where he ushered them into the presence of James.

Both the prelate and the minister wore a grave look.

"I heard of the landing of the Prince of Orange, my liege," said Sunderland; "and I thought it proper to send for the Archbishop of Canterbury in order that he might advise with your majesty in this crisis."

"You did well, my lord," answered James. And he added to the archbishop, "Your grace's prompt attendance is very acceptable to me."

"I hope it may also be serviceable to your majesty," said the venerable prelate, "and not only in respect to your temporal but your eternal welfare."

"How?" cried James, angrily.

"I have hitherto forborne, my liege, to approach you with any arguments against the errors of the creed of Rome and favourable to the doctrines of the church of England," replied the archbishop; "but at the present time I would rather incur your displeasure than neglect the opportunity of submitting my opinions to you. If you would avert the wrath of Heaven you must govern yourself according to its Word. The church for which your august father suffered martyrdom, which clasped you as an infant to her bosom, which brought you up in the true faith of the Redeemer, and which is the sure bulwark of your throne, now calls upon you through me to turn to her again. I beseech your majesty to hear the Truth. Bring with you, if you please, the most subtle propagandists of Rome. Armed with the sacred truths of the New Testament, I will, with the Divine blessing, overcome them. Oh! your majesty," he continued, falling at the king's feet, "on my knees I entreat you to return to us. Give peace to your people! Avert from us a bloody civil war. Above all, make your own peace with Heaven!"

"I know that your grace's advice is tendered kindly," said James, taking the archbishop by both hands, and raising him, "and that you are animated with the best wishes both for my temporal and eternal good. But my heart is fixed in the holy faith I profess, and at this critical moment I desire to avoid subjects of controversy. Let us rather throw aside our differences, and join in opposing the common enemy."

"I will gladly render whatever assistance I can to your majesty," replied the archbishop, "but my best efforts will assuredly fail if you do not sacrifice something to the religious feelings of your people."

"The cry of your subjects is that in embracing Popery you virtually abdicated your throne, my liege," observed Sunderland. "Such is, indeed, the law, but they were content that your majesty should follow your own persuasions, so long as your august family were educated in the tenets of the Protestant church."

"And what is your own opinion, my lord?" asked James, sharply. "New converts like you are generally very decided in their views."

"Much may be said on both sides," answered Suuderland, "but human judgment is fallible, and princes have invariably consulted the interests of their kingdom, as well as their own consciences, in these matters. Thus your majesty's maternal grandfather, Henry IV., of France, of illustrious memory, though he had fought many a battle for the Huguenots, judged it prudent, on coming to the throne, to conform to Popery. Likewise your majesty's royal brother, though a Catholic at heart, professed Protestantism, never avowing himself a Romanist till the moment of his death. Now, I do not pretend to advise your majesty in so tender a matter. But seeing that the Archbishop of Canterbury offers to dispute the question with the best advocates of our holy religion, and bearing in mind the danger that threatens you, and the prejudices of your people, I cannot deny that it would be for the advantage of your majesty's service if you returned to the church of England—provided, of course, that his grace could make it apparent that you ought to sacrifice some little points of belief to the national good."

"And if I could be persuaded to adopt this course," observed James, drily, "might I hope that your lordship would be induced to follow my example?"

"The conversion of your majesty would, doubtless, open the eyes of many," interposed the archbishop.

"It would indeed bring back many to the Church of England," cried Sunderland. "And really the difference between the two creeds is more nominal than real. Supposing, then, that your majesty became reconciled to the English communion, I cannot say that I should not look very closely into the matter. There is, it must be owned, a great deal to be said for the Church of England—a very great deal."

"You have yourselves furnished me with the strongest argument against my apostacy," said James, with ill-suppressed anger. "You acknowledge that my return to the Church of England would lead to the conversion of many others. Thus I should not only peril my own soul, but should be responsible for the perdition of those who followed my evil example. I would rather lose my crown than endanger my salvation. You have your answer. If I think fit to alter my determination, I will let you know."

And with a slight inclination of the person, he turned away, and retired.

Sunderland and the archbishop remained stationary for a few minutes in low and earnest conversation, when they passed towards the antechamber where the usher in waiting hastened to attend them.

Seated in the recess formed by the bay-window, Moor escaped notice. After a time evening drew nigh, and valets entered with lights, and as the young man could not retire without the royal commands, he began to look anxiously for the re-appearance of the king. As night advanced and James did not come, Moor was growing impatient, when Sabine hurriedly entered.

Glancing timidly around her, she stepped hastily towards Moor.

"I was afraid you had gone," she said. "I came to warn you, that your friend Lord Sunderland is in great peril. The king has been persuaded by Father Petre to sign a warrant for his arrest, and he is to be sent instantly to the Tower."

"Surely, you are mistaken!" cried Moor. "It is little more than an hour since Lord Sunderland passed through this room after what I presume to have been a friendly conference with his majesty."

"It is too true," replied Sabine, "the king has been closeted ever since with Father Petre. I accidentally overheard their discourse, and if events go unfavourably for the king, I fear that some violence will be perpetrated. If favourably, Lord Sunderland is to be tried for high treason, and beheaded."

"I will go to Spencer House, and warn his lordship of his danger!" cried Moor.

"Do, do!" said Sabine. "You have not a moment to lose."

Passing into the outer chamber, Moor broke through the crowd of attendants, and hastened from the palace.

He now found, as Sabine had told him, that he must use the utmost despatch, for a party of dragoons were already being drawn up in the palace-yard, and he had no doubt that they were to be employed in apprehending the earl. But, in order to avoid suspicion, he was obliged to proceed leisurely till he reached the street, when he crossed over into the park, and ran down the Mall, passing through the Stable-yard to Saint James's place.

At the end of this street, he halted before a stately stone mansion, and knocking loudly at the door, it was opened by a porter, who, on learning that his business was of the last importance, instantly called a valet, and directed him to lead him to the earl.

Sunderland was alone with the countess. There was something in Moor's look, as he entered, that excited the minister's suspicions, and waving the servant from the room, he hurried forward to meet him.

"What is the matter, Mr. Moor?" he inquired.

"His majesty has issued a warrant for your lordship's arrest," replied Moor. "You must fly this instant, or you will endanger your head."

The countess uttered an exclamation of terror. Sunderland was speechless.

"The dragoons will be here in a few minutes," pursued Moor. "You must make all haste to the coast, where you will no doubt find means of reaching the continent."

"Fly rather to the Prince of Orange," said the countess. "He will rejoice to receive you, though the master whom you have served so faithfully, even to the sacrifice of your religion, condemns you to the block."

"No, no; I will go to the continent," answered Sunderland. "By a fortunate chance, there is a vessel lying in the river, which sails to-morrow morning, and the master of which I have often employed as the bearer of despatches. I would go to the queen, but I cannot trust these men, and there is no time for delay."

As he spoke, there was a loud knocking at the outer door, which alarmed the whole household.

"We are undone!" cried the countess.

"Not so," cried Moor, throwing open a French window; "we can make our way across the park, while you, countess, can lead the dragoons to believe that his lordship is in the house."

Catching at the prospect of escape, Sunderland hurried to an inner room, and presently returned equipped in a cloak and hat; then taking a hasty leave of the countess, he followed Moor through the window on to a terrace, leading to a small garden. There was a gate at the end of it, opening into the Green Park, at that time forming one enclosure with the larger park of St. James's.

Without experiencing any hindrance, the fugitives reached Westminster-stairs, where Sunderland called a wherry, and engaged it to carry him on board ship. As he descended to the boat, he took Moor by the hand, and bade him adieu.

"I will return soon," he added; "and, mark my words, it will be as prime minister of England."

The prediction was fulfilled.

CHAPTER VII.

THE ROYAL NURSERY.

ADJOINING the private apartments of the queen, at Whitehall, was another suite of rooms appropriated to the infant Prince of Wales. The principal chamber was lofty and spacious, and panelled with polished oak. The windows were shaded by light verandahs, and guarded at the bottom by trellis-work, while crimson curtains depended from above, where the whole was crowned by an ostrich plume, the Prince of Wales's badge, elaborately carved and gilded. Couches and ottomans were dispersed round the room; and, in one corner, under a canopy of state, surmounted by the royal arms, with the ostrich plume as the crest, stood a cot, adorned with hangings of crimson and gold, with the prince's device worked in silver round the border, and carved again over the two supporters. The room contained also a chair of state and footstools, a rocking-chair, and a *prie-dieu;* and on a small sideboard stood a massive gold waiter, bearing two vessels of the same metal.

The unconscious object of all this pomp, a delicate-looking infant, was lying in the cot asleep. He was watched by a lady, who was seated close by, near the fire, plying her needle diligently. While she was thus engaged, a door leading to an inner room was softly opened, and a man stepped in. Perceiving him, the lady was about to utter a cry, when the man motioned her sternly to remain silent, and throwing back his cloak and hat, disclosed the features of Johnstone.

The lady instantly recognised him, but she still looked alarmed.

"How could you venture here?" she cried. "If you are discovered you will destroy both yourself and me."

"Do not be alarmed, Mrs. Dawson," said Johnstone, "I have bought over the usher stationed at the private staircase, and therefore incur but little risk; but, even were it otherwise, the object I have in view supersedes all personal considerations. I must see *him.*"

"The Prince of Wales!" exclaimed Mrs. Dawson, a sudden flush mounting to her face. "What do you want with him? I will not have him harmed."

"Do you take me for a murderer?" answered Johnstone. "I would not hurt him for the world."

"Come then," said Mrs. Dawson. "Tread softly."

Taking a taper from the table, she led him up to the cot; and drawing aside the drapery, disclosed the sleeping infant.

Johnstone gazed in the child's face in silence for several minutes, pausing on each feature in succession with a keen and searching look.

"There may be a resemblance," he said, at last, as if making an unwilling admission, "but it is very slight."

"You will not be convinced," replied Mrs. Dawson, "or you would long since have thrown these prejudices aside. The proofs of the child's birth leave no room for doubt."

"I will not argue the matter with you," answered Johnstone; "but whatever may be the proofs adduced, you know that the disbelief I express is universally entertained. If the child lives, this will lead to endless bloodshed. He will be miserable himself, and will bring misery on the whole kingdom. It is in your power to prevent this mischief. Let me take him away, and I solemnly pledge myself——"

"Hold!" said Mrs. Dawson, interrupting him. "I cannot consent to any such measure. I have assisted you in everything else, but I will not harm the child."

"I solemnly engage that he shall be reared tenderly," cried Johnstone. "Nay, you shall have charge of him yourself, and your reward shall be a fortune and a title."

"Not for worlds would I so wrong him," replied Mrs. Dawson, vehemently; "but hark! the queen is coming."

Without making a reply, Johnstone hastened to the inner door, and had hardly disappeared, when a folding-door opposite was thrown open by two valets, and the queen entered, accompanied by the Count de Lauzun, Barillon, Lord Melfort, and Count d'Adda. They were followed by Anna Montecuculi and La Riva.

As the royal mother advanced to the cot, Mrs. Dawson touched a silken bell-rope, and two nurses entered by a side-door, and remained in attendance.

Softly as the queen trod, the child seemed disturbed by her approach; and though he had slept calmly under the gaze of his enemy, he now stirred at the step of his mother, and turned uneasily in the bed, uttering a low cry. Throwing aside the drapery, the queen caught him in her arms. The child cast a frightened look from the attending nobles to the maids of honour, and from them to the nurses, and then, closing his eyes on the splendour that surrounded him, threw himself on his mother's bosom. Seating herself in the chair of state, Mary drew him closer to her, and the child was speedily reassured. Pride beamed in the mother's eye, and joy glowed on her cheek as he raised his tiny hands towards her, and greeted her with a smile.

But while the royal parent was bending proudly and fondly over her son, and while her ear was eagerly drinking in the commendations of the courtiers, the smile disappeared from the infant's face, and he uttered a scream. The next moment his complexion became livid, his features contorted, and his little frame writhed with convulsions.

As she beheld this sudden change, Mary became so agitated, that the child almost dropped from her arms. Yet she refused to give him to Mrs. Dawson, who had hurried to her assistance.

"It is nothing serious, gracious madam," cried Lauzun; "but I will go for Doctor Chamberlayne."

"Stay," said Count d'Adda. "Let me have some water. Do not be alarmed, your majesty. There is no need of a surgeon."

A silver vessel, containing water, was quickly presented to him, and, repeating a short Latin prayer, he dedicated the lymph to religious uses. Meanwhile, the child's convulsions became so violent, that Mary could not hold him; and at last she was obliged to accept the assistance of Mrs. Dawson. At this moment the Nuncio dipped his hand in the holy water, and sprinkled it on the child's face, at the same time repeating a Latin prayer. Then bending over him, he made the sign of the cross on his forehead.

Each of the bystanders looked curiously, as well as anxiously, for the effect of this proceeding. When the prelate first touched the infant, his convulsions became more violent; but all at once, as the sign of the cross was completed, they suddenly subsided, and as the priest spread his hands over him, the child became perfectly still.

"Thank Heaven!" exclaimed Mary, joyfully, "the fit is over: the hand of His minister has stayed it."

The courtiers looked at each other in silence. Meanwhile, the child laid back in the queen's arms, and soon dropped into a profound sleep.

No longer under any alarm, Mary consigned him to the care of Mrs. Dawson, who deposited him in the cot. Mary then looked tenderly at him, and withdrew, followed by the courtiers and her attendants.

Mrs. Dawson now dismissed the two under-nurses, and they retired by the side-door; and recollecting some instructions which she proposed to give them, Mrs. Dawson was about to call them back, but changing her mind, she followed them. She had been absent only a few minutes, when the folding-door was again thrown open, and the queen reappeared, though now unattended, and looked round in surprise for one of the nurses. At this juncture Mrs. Dawson returned to the room.

"You should not leave the prince alone," said Mary, severely. "How is he now?"

And without waiting for a reply, she approached the cot, and drew aside the drapery. The child was gone!

Too much agitated to speak, Mary turned with a look of horror to Mrs. Dawson, and pointed to the vacant bed. The poor nurse was hardly less alarmed than herself, and uttered a sharp cry, which quickly brought her two assistants to the room, and in a moment all was bustle and confusion.

As it was supposed at first that the child might have awakened and crawled out of his cot, the apartment was thoroughly searched, but without success, and, overwhelmed with grief, Mary hastened to communicate the evil tidings to James, while Mrs. Dawson, who, though she did not dare to mention it, conjectured the cause of the prince's disappearance, ran from room to room in distraction. The alarm soon spread through the whole palace, and almost as soon as Mary reached the king's closet, she was joined by the Count de Lauzun, who hastened to console her.

"If it be indeed a scheme of the Orange party," he cried, "they will be foiled. Not a soul can leave the palace without first coming to me. But having taken every precaution, let us now go and question the nurses narrowly."

"You are right, count," cried James, pressing his hand. "That is the most proper course."

And they passed together towards the royal nursery.

In the mean time Mrs. Dawson was running to and fro in the same wild and distracted way, and wringing her hands, when she felt her arm grasped from behind, and, turning, beheld Johnstone.

"I thought to have carried him off," said Johnstone, producing the infant prince; "but the usher has warned me that they have changed the password—take him."

Uttering an exclamation of delight, and seizing the sleeping child, Mrs. Dawson pressed him to her bosom and disappeared.

A few minutes afterwards the royal parents and Lauzun entered the nursery. As they stepped forward they perceived Mrs. Dawson standing in the middle of the chamber, the very image of despair.

"The prince is not yet found, then?" cried James, sternly.

Mrs. Dawson burst into tears.

"Strange," exclaimed Lauzun, advancing towards the cot. "There must have been some foul play. He could not be taken hence without the connivance of his nurses."

As he spoke, he looked at the vacant pillow of the prince, and turning back the coverlet perceived the child lying at the foot of the bed. Uttering a joyful exclamation, he held him up and displayed him to his parents.

The delight of the king and queen was equalled only by their surprise, in which Mrs. Dawson seemed to participate. But when his first transport was over, James could not repress a look of displeasure.

"There must have been great carelessness here," he said to Mrs. Dawson; "you see what confusion this false alarm has created in the palace."

"Nay, do not blame her," interposed Mary, "it was I who raised the alarm. I missed my boy from his pillow, and did not think that he might have turned over to the bottom of the bed. But he is safe, thank Heaven. And we may now safely leave him to Mrs. Dawson."

"You may, indeed, madam," answered Mrs. Dawson; "I will guard him as I would my life."

Mary, who had received the little prince from Lauzun, pressed her lips softly on his brow, and smilingly handed him to Mrs. Dawson. Attended by James and Lauzun, she then quitted the nursery.

CHAPTER VIII.

THE RESTORATION OF THE CITY CHARTER.

The intelligence of Sunderland's flight spread through the metropolis like wild-fire. It was looked upon as one of those events which often precede and announce a great national convulsion, and, as such, struck terror into the boldest breast. The public mind now hung in uncertainty between two pressing evils—dreading, on the one hand, the ruin of the popular cause which might follow the triumph of the king; and, on the other, shrinking from submission to a foreign invader.

At Whitehall the great actors in the scene began to be alarmed. On the following morning the king and his leading ministers assembled in the council-room, and deliberated long and gravely on the threatening posture of affairs. While they were thus engaged, the usher of the council entered, and approaching James, requested an audience for the Spanish ambassador. James ordered him to be admitted, and the next moment Don Pedro Ronquillo made his appearance, dressed with more than usual magnificence

"I have come to offer my best services to you, my liege," said Don Pedro. "My august master is the ally of the Prince of Orange, as well as of your majesty, and I should be proud to mediate between you."

"Mediate!" cried James, sternly.

"His majesty is in a condition to impose terms, not to ask them," said Father Petre; "but were it otherwise, he would make none with this unnatural invader."

"That may or may not be judicious, reverend sir," replied the ambassador, stiffly. "I have no object in view but his majesty's advantage."

"His majesty is fully sensible of your zeal," sneered the Jesuit.

"Yes," said James, angrily; "I have even heard that the invader has been aided in his enterprise by the King of Spain."

"In what way, sire? asked the ambassador.

"With money," answered James.

"Your pardon," cried Don Pedro, with a smile. "They who gave your majesty that information, could know but little of Spain. Good care is taken that no money shall go out of that country. In the name of his majesty, my master, I declare that he has no connection whatever with the expedition. Moreover, I renew my offer to mediate between you and the Prince of Orange, and I engage to make the prince enter into a convention with your majesty, on one condition."

Don Pedro drew a folded paper from his pocket, and presented it to the king.

"My condition is, that your majesty will deny the authenticity of this paper," he said, "or, if that is impossible, will rescind it."

Glancing at the paper, James turned as pale as a corpse, and handed it to Father Petre, who bit his lips and was silent. But instantly recovering, he turned furiously on the ambassador.

"This is a forgery," he exclaimed. "You know it is so."

"If his majesty will tell me so, I shall be satisfied," answered Don Pedro; "but I need not tell you, my liege, that if it were known that you had entered into a secret treaty with France, such as this paper discloses, the people would desert you in a body."

"It is not for his majesty's allies to object to such a treaty, when they can lend him no assistance themselves," observed the Earl of Melfort; "but I confess that you speak the truth as regards the king's subjects."

"Your excellency must not divulge this secret," said Jeffreys, in a low voice.

"Unfortunately, it is known to others," returned Don Pedro.

"The only resource is, as I have already said, for his majesty to recall it. Let me implore you to do so, my liege."

James was silent, but looked inquiringly from one counsellor to another, seemingly lost in indecision. At last he turned to the ambassador.

"I will see M. Barillon about it," he said. "Come to me this evening, and I will give you an answer."

Upon this the ambassador withdrew, and, without recurring to the subject of the secret treaty, the council resumed the debate which his visit had interrupted.

Their deliberations were continued for upwards of an hour. At length it was decided that the measures of conciliation adopted by Sunderland should be still pursued; and, in order to display more strongly the gracious intentions of the king, it was determined to send the Lord Chancellor to Guildhall, in a state procession, with the forfeited charter of the city, which James had promised to restore.

Arrangements were quickly made for carrying this design into execution; and, in a short time, Jeffreys, arrayed in his robes of office, and holding the charter in his hand, entered a state coach in the palace-yard, where a procession was drawn up, consisting of four mounted trumpeters, followed by two heralds, in their tabards, and a troop of the horse-guards, who were succeeded by the mace-bearer, carrying the mace, and another officer bearing the sword of justice, making way for Jeffreys, whose coach was followed by a number of mounted officers and another troop of guards. As the procession approached the palace-gate, it was met by a guard of honour, who presented arms, and with a stirring flourish, the trumpeters passed on into Parliament-street, where an immense crowd had collected. The mob received them in silence at first, but no sooner caught sight of Jeffreys, than they gave utterance to a deafening yell, which would have quailed the stoutest heart. Jeffreys turned pale with fear, and thinking to appease the people, bent forward to the window, and held up the charter. But, mistaking his movement for a menace, the mob redoubled their hootings; and the chancellor was so terrified, that he shrank into a corner of the coach to hide himself from view.

Meanwhile the procession made its way onward, and, passing up the Strand to Temple Bar, proceeded along Cheapside to Guildhall. A messenger had been despatched in advance to apprise the authorities of the chancellor's approach, and the lord mayor and aldermen had assembled at the hall, with the common council and the chief of the livery, all in their state robes, to receive him.

The area in front of the hall was thronged with the populace, who, like the crowd at the palace, uttered fearful vociferations on the appearance of Jeffreys, while many saluted him aloud as "the Butcher," amidst renewed yells and hootings. In this way the coach advanced to the great door of the hall, where Jeffreys alighted.

His fear gave way to rage, as he stepped forward, and proceeding up a small passage, entered the hall. Here he was met by Sir John Eyles, the lord mayor, with the sheriffs, aldermen, and common council.

"So, my lord mayor! your currish citizens show themselves very worthy of his majesty's favour—ha!" he cried, in a terrible tone. "I say, they are a parcel of arrant rebels, my lord mayor. The king sent me to you with your charter, and you insult me for my pains. Zounds! I have a mind to take it back to his majesty, and tell him what a pack of rebellious hounds you harbour here. I will make you pay dearly for this outrage."

"I hope, my lord, you will not set down these rude brawlers as the city of London," said the lord mayor, in a deprecating tone: "the citizens have a great reverence for your lordship."

"In proof whereof, we have all assembled here to meet you, my lord," faltered one of the alderman; "and we greatly regret the rudeness you have experienced."

"By my soul, you shall regret it in another sort," cried Jeffreys. "You shall all pay his majesty a good round fine for this insolence."

"We will cheerfully submit to his majesty's pleasure, if we can only exonerate ourselves before your lordship," answered the lord mayor. "You have always shown great love for the city. I hope you will overlook the offence."

"When the king forgives, I will not be severe," returned Jeffreys, somewhat mollified. "But take care for the future. Now to my message. His majesty is graciously pleased to restore you your charter, and, by his command, I give it into your hands, my lord mayor, trusting you will feel duly grateful for the royal favour."

"You shall not find us slack in showing our loyalty and gratitude, my lord," answered the lord mayor; "and as an evidence of our intentions, I beg that you will allow us to return with you to his majesty, in order that we may present him with a dutiful address on the occasion. Meanwhile his gracious message shall be made known in every part of the city."

Jeffreys agreed to this arrangement, and, at the request of the lord mayor, consented to partake of a collation which had been hastily prepared for him in the council-room, whither he was accompanied by the chief officers of the corporation, while the mob without were informed, by sound of trumpet, of the restoration of the charter, an announcement which called forth the loudest acclamations.

In the mean time the yells with which Jeffreys had been saluted on leaving Whitehall had resounded through the palace, and created the greatest alarm. Sharing the general panic, Mary hastened to her consort's closet, where she found him in conference with Barillon, and saw at once, from their troubled looks, that they were full of misgiving.

"Your majesty has heard these fearful shouts," said Mary; "do you think the people intend to attack the palace?"

"There is little fear of that," answered James; "it is too well guarded. But the mob are evidently ready for mischief, and therefore I have determined to set out instantly for the army, and bring the contest to an issue as soon as possible. Do not distress me by opposing my resolution. I have sent for the Princess Anne to take leave of her, and to charge her to obey you in my absence as she would myself; and I only await the chancellor's return from the city to set forth."

"Your majesty is the best judge of what you should do," faltered Mary, scarcely able to restrain her tears. "I can only offer you my advice and prayers. Put your confidence in God and your good cause, and may Heaven preserve you!"

With these words she turned away, and James was so touched that he had no power to call her back. He was silent for several minutes after she had retired, when he renewed his conference with Barillon, and they continued in anxious debate for some time. They were still deliberating, when the Spanish ambassador was announced, and by command of James was admitted.

"I have done myself the honour to attend your majesty before the time you appointed," he said, "as I received information that you were about to join the army. You will find it extremely advantageous to you to settle this matter before you set forth; and as Monsieur Barillon is here, perhaps you will be pleased to do so at once."

His excellency refers to the secret treaty with my brother Louis," said James to Barillon, in an uneasy tone. "The treaty will only be acted on in case of necessity. I give you my assurance, Don Pedro, that I will not call in the aid of France till the last moment."

"I wish I could prevail on your majesty to accept it this instant," said Barillon.

"I protest against his majesty entering into an alliance with France," returned Don Pedro. "Such a treaty places Europe at the French king's disposal, and converts England into a French province. Let me implore your majesty to withdraw from this compact. The appalling shouts which greeted one of your ministers a few hours ago, should warn you not to give further offence to your people."

As he ceased speaking, they heard a loud noise, followed by thundering acclamations. James was so excited, that he hurried to the window, which commanded a view of the street, and looked forth. The ambassadors followed, and could hardly believe their eyes, on seeing Jeffreys in his coach, drawn by the populace, while the lord mayor and corporation rode on either side, and the people pressed forward to cheer him, throwing up their hats, and rending the air with plaudits.

Uttering a joyful exclamation, James was turning to the ambassadors, when he was joined by Mary, whose face beamed with pleasure, while tears of joy gathered in her eyes.

"This is new life to me!" she exclaimed. "Ah! your majesty; the English people may have their prejudices, but they are naturally loyal. They may be won by gentleness, though they will not be overpowered by violence."

"You are right," answered James. "Let me but once drive this invader out of the country, and my people shall have no cause to complain of me."

At this juncture, the vice-chamberlain approached, and informed the monarch that the chancellor had returned, accompanied by the lord mayor and corporation, who desired permission to present his majesty with an address of thanks. James directed the officer to precede him from the room; and accompanied by Mary, and followed by the two ambassadors, he passed on to the public reception-room, where the chancellor and the civic authorities awaited him.

Leading Mary to a chair of state, placed on a fauteuil at the upper end of the saloon, James took his place by her side, and saluted the officers of the corporation, who made him a profound obeisance.

"Welcome to Whitehall, my lord mayor and gentlemen," James then said; "I have had much pleasure in restoring you your charter; and if I can do you any further service, you will only need to let me know it."

"Your majesty's gracious words fill us with joy," replied the lord mayor; "and we humbly beg that you will permit us to present you with an address of thanks, which the corporation have adopted unanimously."

James assenting, the chamberlain of the city stepped forward, and read forth au address from the lord mayor, aldermen, and common council, filled with the most fervent expressions of loyalty and devotion to the throne; setting forth their gratitude to the king for the restoration of their charter; and concluding with a declaration of their attachment to the king, queen, and prince of Wales.

James heard the address with evident pleasure; and, at its conclusion, thanked the corporation in the queen's name, as well as his own, adding, that though the throne was now in some danger, nothing could shake his confidence in his people, and that he was determined to lead his army in person to the field, where he had often hazarded his life in the service of the country.

His kind words, and the gracious urbanity of his manner, made a deep impression on the citizens; and they withdrew from the presence with renewed expressions of attachment.

All this had had a cheering effect on Mary, who was now in the highest spirits, and, after chatting a moment with Lauzun and Barillon, she turned, as the deputation retired, to congratulate James.

"It was, indeed, a most agreeable surprise," replied James; and he added to Don Pedro, "and not more surprising to me than to your excellency."

"Neither could it be more agreeable to you, my liege, than it is to me," replied Don Pedro, who, if he could have detached James from his connection with France, would really have been glad to see him victorious; "but do not let this distract your attention from what is passing. Withdraw from your alliance with the French king, and commission me to negotiate with the Prince of Orange."

"I will not offer any counsel to your majesty on the subject of your alliance with my master," observed Barillon; "but I urgently recommend you not to enter into terms with the Prince of Orange."

"Hear my answer," replied James. "I will neither withdraw from my alliance with my brother Louis, nor enter into terms with the invader. If he sends to treat with me, I will dismiss his first messenger honourably, but I will hang the second, and answer his master from the cannon's mouth. Now to horse." And turning to Mary, he said, "Has the Princess Anne arrived?"

Mary changed colour. "The princess has sent to ask your majesty to excuse her," she said, "she is confined to her chamber by illness."

"My darling Anne ill!" cried James, anxiously. "I wish I had known it before; we would have gone to visit her together; but it is too late now. I must make your majesty the bearer of my inquiries to her."

Mary was about to say, in reply, that the princess might

possibly not appreciate this mark of paternal affection, as there was strong ground for believing that her illness was feigned, in order to avoid receiving his parting injunctions; but she instantly checked herself, unwilling to cause a pang to a heart which was already so heavily charged with sorrow.

After speaking to her for a moment in an under-tone, James walked with her to an ante-chamber, where he remained with her alone for a few minutes, when he returned to the saloon, wearing a cheerful look, though Mary's eyes were dimmed with tears.

Leading the queen forward, James stepped up to the Count de Lauzun, and took him affectionately by the hand.

"I leave her majesty under your protection, count," he said. "I am going, I trust, to victory; but," and he lowered his voice, "if it prove otherwise, I rely on you to place the queen in safety."

"You have laid me under an eternal obligation, my liege," replied Lauzun, placing his hand on his heart. "I was about to accompany you to the field, but you have honoured me with a higher trust. My life shall answer for her majesty's safety."

The king pressed his hand. He then bowed low to Mary, though without raising his eyes to her face, and turned, with affected gaiety, to a young man on his right, who was conversing in low tones with one of the loveliest of the queen's attendants.

"Now, Mr. Moor," he said, with a faint smile, "you must bid adieu to your mistress, and ride to the field with me. I cannot stir without my aide-de-camp."

Passing down the grand staircase, and crossing the great hall, James halted at the door of the palace, and raised his hat to the court, the male portion of which answered with a cheer, while the ladies waved their handkerchiefs. A gallant cavalcade was drawn up in the palace-yard, consisting of the personal attendants of the king, and a troop of the horse-guards; and stepping forth, James mounted a led horse, and directed Moor to take his place by his side, which done, the whole party spurred forward.

The road in front of the palace was thronged with the populace; and, as James came in sight, deafening cheers arose, mingled with cries of "God bless your majesty!"

A flush of pleasure suffused the king's face, and he could not conceal his satisfaction.

"This is a happy day," he said to Moor, "and yet it is a Protestant wind. It blows hard, too; but see how proudly my banner braves it."

Moor glanced towards the summit of the banqueting-house, where the royal standard was indeed floating proudly, with its gorgeous blazonry glittering in the sun. But before he could reply to the king's remark, a sudden and violent gust caught the flag-staff, and, snapping it in twain, the standard fell prostrate on the roof.

CHAPTER IX.

FEVERSHAM AND CHURCHILL.

WHILE the events just related were taking place in London, the king's army had pursued its march, and ultimately encamped on Salisbury Plain.

The morning was somewhat advanced, as two officers issued from a pavilion near the centre of the camp; and, halting outside, looked anxiously up the road to London. The foremost was the Earl of Feversham, the commander-in-chief, and his companion was Lord Churchill, afterwards the great Duke of Marlborough.

Lewis de Duras, Earl of Feversham, was a native of France, and son of the Duke de Duras, and brother of the Duke de Lorge. His mother was a member of the noble house of Bouillon, and sister of the great Turenne. At the Restoration, he bore the French title of Marquis of Blancfort, and, accompanying Charles II. to England, he was naturalised, and appointed to the command of the third troop of horse-guards, from which he was afterwards promoted to the first. He behaved with great gallantry in the sea-fight with the Dutch, in 1665; and some years afterwards, was raised by Charles II. to the English peerage, under the title of Baron Duras of Holdenby; and, having married Mary, the eldest daughter of Sir George Sondes, of Lees Court, Kent, who had been created Earl of Feversham, the same title was conferred upon him on the death of his father-in-law. In 1679, he was made master of the horse to Queen Katherine, and was afterwards appointed her lord chamberlain; and, on the accession of James II., was admitted into the privy council, and despatched as commander-in-chief against the Duke of Monmouth, whom he completely defeated, and sent a prisoner to London.

Feversham was tall and well-shaped, with a frank and expressive countenance, and resembled his maternal uncle, Turenne.

Born at Aske, in Devonshire, on the 25th of June, 1650, Lord Churchill was the son of Sir Winston Churchill, of Newton Basset, in Wiltshire, who had joined the standard of Charles I during the civil war, and suffered severely for his loyalty. It was probably owing to this circumstance that the education of the future hero was entirely neglected. Lord Chesterfield speaks of him as "unusually illiterate;" and he said himself that his whole acquaintance with history was derived from Shakspeare's plays. A letter in the Clarendon and Rochester Correspondence furnishes a curious specimen of his orthography. It is dated "*Jully* 4th, 1685;" and begins thus:—"I have *recived* your lordship's kind letter, and *doe ashure* you that you *waire* very Just to me in the opinion you had of me, for nobody living can have *bene* more *obsarvant then* I have *bene* to my Lord *feavarsham* ever since I have *bene* with him, in *soe* much that he did tell me that he would *writt* to the king, to *lett* him know how diligent I was,—and I should be *glade* if you could know whether he has done me that Justice."

But to compensate for the deficiencies of education, nature had endowed young Churchill with extraordinary personal attractions; and having at an early age been appointed page to the first Duchess of York, and ensign in the guards, these attractions soon opened to him the way to preferment.

"The Graces," says Chesterfield,* "protected and promoted him; for while he was an ensign of the guards, the Duchess of Cleveland, then favourite mistress to King Charles II., struck by those very graces, gave him five thousand pounds, with which he immediately bought an annuity for his life, of five hundred pounds a year, of my grandfather Halifax, which was the foundation of his future fortune. His figure was beautiful, but his manner was irresistible, by either man or woman." It was said of him, indeed, that he refused more gracefully than other people could grant, and that those even to whom he denied favours, were so charmed by his flattering manner, that they retired from his presence without feeling disappointment. To these advantages he added a coolness and self-possession which no circumstances could disturb, and however he might be provoked, his countenance never lost the singular mildness of its expression. As a drawback to so much excellence, however, he had a disagreeable voice, which Pope ridiculed in an unpublished poem, making him,

"In accents of a whining ghost
—— lament the son he lost."

His ruling passion was avarice; and he is spoken of by Swift, in one of his letters to Stella, as being as "covetous as hell, and ambitious as the prince of it." Lord Bolingbroke unwillingly admits his avarice, but adds,—"he was so very great a man, that I forgot he had that vice."

* Letters to his Son. Letter 136.

Churchill's first military service was at Tangier, where he served as a volunteer, though holding a commission in the guards; and having distinguished himself for skill and courage, he was appointed captain in Monmouth's regiment of grenadiers, and in 1672, when the duke was despatched with six thousand men to assist Louis XIV against the Dutch, Churchill obtained permission to accompany him. He remained with the duke throughout the campaign, and behaved with such gallantry at the sieges of Maestricht and Nimeguen, that he was complimented on his conduct by the great Turenne, who mentioned him in very flattering terms to the French monarch, and always spoke of him as "the handsome Englishman." On his return to England, Churchill's services were rewarded with the colonelcy of Littleton's regiment, and he was appointed gentleman of the bedchamber to the Duke of York, and, shortly afterwards, his master of the horse. From this period he became James's inseparable companion, attending him on all the occasions of his being sent into exile, both to Scotland and Holland; and he was with him in the *Gloucester* frigate, in 1682, when that vessel was wrecked on the Yarmouth Sands. On this occasion, James gave a flattering proof of his attachment for the young soldier; for, though he was awakened in the middle of the night, yet, regardless of all the terrors of the scene, his first inquiry was for Churchill, and his first care to see him safely bestowed in the only boat that was seaworthy. On the 1st of December, 1682, he persuaded the king to raise his favourite to the peerage, by the title of Baron Eymouth, and soon afterwards procured him the colonelcy of the horse-guards. It was about this period that Churchill married the beautiful Sarah Jennings, sister of La Belle Jennings, of Grammont, and afterwards celebrated as the favourite of Queen Anne.

On his accession to the throne, James seized every opportunity of conferring new favours on Churchill. After sending him as ambassador to France, to notify his accession to Louis, he created him a viscount, appointed him lord of the bed-chamber, and high-steward of the borough of St. Alban's; and in the following month sent him as major-general, under the Earl of Feversham, against his former commander, the Duke of Monmouth; and by his vigilance on the night of the battle, Churchill was mainly instrumental in obtaining the victory.

"There is no sign of his majesty coming, you see," said the Earl of Feversham. "I will wait another hour; and if he is not here by that time, I shall march towards the enemy."

"I defer to your lordship's arrangements, but, I confess, I am still of opinion that we should await the enemy here," answered Churchill. "It is a strong position, and covers the approach to the metropolis, and if an action ensues, our men will be fresh and vigorous, while the enemy will be wearied with his march."

"All this is true," rejoined Feversham; "but there is, as your lordship knows, a great point in making the first attack. By advancing, we shall give the soldiers more confidence, and at the same time defeat any treachery which may be in contemplation. The rumours that have reached us call for every precaution."

"If there were any ground for believing them," replied Churchill; "but I would pledge myself for the loyalty of our officers. Prince George is equally satisfied of it; and *à propos*, here comes his royal highness."

Turning, Feversham perceived the prince, and he and Churchill advanced to salute him.

Prince George, youngest son of Frederick III., king of Denmark, was born at Copenhagen on the 21st of April, 1653, and had attained his thirtieth year when he became the husband of the Princess Anne. He had previously travelled through France, Germany, and Italy, and as a soldier, had gained great reputation for personal courage, having destinguished himself in a signal manner at the celebrated battle of Landen, where his brother, Charles V., was taken prisoner by the Swedes, when Prince George, perceiving his situation, rushed into the enemy's ranks, and rescued the monarch with his own hand. He arrived in England on the 16th of July, 1683, to solemnise his nuptials with the Princess Anne; and Evelyn, who saw him the day after his arrival, says, "He had the Danish countenance, blonde; of few words; spoke French but ill." Macky describes him as "very fat; loves news, his bottle, and his wife;" and it may be added, that the prince was not only partial to wine, but was also given to dram-drinking. His temper was mild and gentle in the extreme, but his capacity was small; and the kindness of his heart frequently made him the dupe of designing persons, when he thought he was acting with perfect rectitude.

"We were talking of these slanderous rumours, sir," said Churchill, as the prince came up; "and I was assuring Lord Feversham, that the enemy reported what they wished rather than what they believed."

"Just so," replied Prince George, drawing forth a massive gold snuff-box, and taking a heavy toll of its contents. "There is no reason to doubt any of the officers. But see! yonder comes his majesty at last."

A cloud of dust rising on the road at some distance, proclaimed the royal approach. Turning to the pavilion, Feversham called his aide-de-camp, and gave him some instructions, and in a moment more trumpets were heard in every direction, ringing forth the stirring summons of "Turn out the whole army—turn out the whole army!"

The whole army, horse and foot, accordingly turned out, and mustered on parade, where they were drawn up to receive the king. Scarcely was the manœuvre effected, when James entered the camp, accompanied by Moor and his personal attendants, and followed by a guard of honour. He was received by the artillery with a royal salute, while the band of the guards struck up the national anthem, and the whole army presented arms.

Riding on to the parade, James was met by Feversham and his staff; and he complimented the general on the fine appearance of the army. But though he felt cheered by the imposing aspect of the troops, the king still doubted the fidelity of the officers, and he informed Feversham of the intelligence he had received from Moor.

"I have heard a like rumour, my liege," replied Feversham; "but I believe it to be erroneous."

"I will speak to the principal officers on the subject," rejoined James; "let them be called."

Accordingly, the word was passed for all field officers to step to the front. As they ranged themselves in a line, James informed them in a few words of the report that had reached him, adding that he disbelieved it, and to show his entire confidence in them, he had come to place his crown and his cause in their keeping.

"Your majesty will have no reason to repent your confidence," cried Lord Churchill. "We are all devoted to you."

"I shall rejoice to fall in your service, my liege," cried Colonel Trelawney. "My life will be a poor return for the favours you have conferred on me."

"Your majesty has conferred a new favour on us in discrediting this slander," observed Colonel Kirke; "but if I catch any of these Orange pips, I'll sow them in a soil from which they shall never rise till the Day of Judgment."

Prince George of Denmark, the Dukes of Grafton and Ormond, and other leading officers expressed themselves in a similar manner, and the whole body solemnly pledged themselves to stand or fall with the king. James then dismissed them, and they returned to the ranks, while the monarch passed down the front of the line and inspected each regiment in succession. As he approached the centre of the line, Moor, who had absented himself for a few minutes, rode up, followed by a couple of horsemen.

"Two messengers to your majesty," cried the young man. "Lord Danby, who was reported to have joined the enemy, has sent to say that he has raised Yorkshire in your behalf, and another messenger brings word that the traitor Lovelace and seventy horsemen have been attacked and captured at Cirencester by the militia."

James uttered an exclamation of pleasure, and the news passing quickly along the line, the whole army burst into a simultaneous huzza. As the cheers subsided, Lord Feversham approached the king.

"Now, my liege, let us advance," he said, "and victory is assured us."

"Not to-day," answered James; "Churchill recommends our staying here, and I cannot decide in a moment. We will talk of it to-morrow." And turning to Moor, he added, "Now for Salisbury. We will fix our quarters to-night at the bishop's palace."

With this he led the way to the road, followed by Moor and his guards, and galloped off in the direction of the ancient city of the plain. At the same time Feversham dismissed the troops, and they retired to their tents, talking over the events of the morning.

CHAPTER X.

THE MEETING AT STONEHENGE.

The night was somewhat advanced before Moor was released from his attendance on the king; but late as it was, he determined to return to the camp, in order to satisfy himself, from his own observation, of the good disposition of the army. It was very dark, and the road was extremely lonely, all communication between the camp and city being prohibited after sunset; but at length the moon rising, Moor discovered that he had strayed from the direct route, and at the same time perceived at a little distance the gigantic outlines of Stonehenge.

Lofty barrows ran in lines round a level plain, called the *Cursus,* which tradition asserts was used as a race-course by the ancient Britons; and in the centre of the area was a circular ditch, enclosing a mound of earth about fifteen feet high, and within the mound rose the mysterious pile which many suppose to be of ante-diluvian origin.

Unable to resist the temptation to explore the wondrous relic of a forgotten faith, Moor dismounted, and tying his horse to a thorn, proceeded along a sort of causeway, supposed to have been the original avenue to the interior of the enclosure. This embraced a circumference of about 300 feet, the centre of which had originally been occupied by three distinct circles of upright stones, one circle within the other. These upright stones were about five feet apart: they were fourteen feet high, and nearly eight in thickness, and each supported an horizontal stone, running from one to the other. Within the third circle was an enormous flat stone, lying prostrate, supposed to be a Druidical altar.

Only the front part of the outer circle, forming a sort of crescent, was now perfect, but many of the stones of the other circles were standing, while the remainder lay around in disorder—some leaning against other stones, some partly sunk in the earth, and others lying flat on the ground.

As Moor surveyed the mystic pile, rendered more solemn and striking by the darkness, which was revealed rather than broken, by the partially obscured moon, he could not repress an indefinable feeling of superstitious awe, but the impression was quickly effaced by the approach of footsteps, and mechanically drawing back behind one of the huge stones, he saw, without being himself observed, two men enter the temple.

"We are late," said the foremost, "but they have not been here, or they would have waited till we came. They may miss the road in the darkness."

"There's some one coming now," answered his companion. "Stand back, a little, my lord."

As they drew into the shadow of one of the gigantic stones, two other men, muffled in long cloaks, made their appearance.

"Orange!" cried the foremost of the new comers.

"Nassau," answered a voice; and the two men who had first arrived stepped forward.

"Ha! Lord Mauvesin!" returned his challenger. "We have kept you waiting, I fear. I have brought Lord Churchill to see you."

"Colonel Trelawney tells me you are the commissioned agent of the Prince of Orange, my lord," said Churchill. "I am anxious to offer my best services to his highness."

Before Mauvesin could reply, other footsteps were heard, and the next moment Colonels Kirke and Colepepper, and the Dukes of Grafton and Ormonde, entered the temple. Giving the password of "Orange," and being answered with the countersign, they stepped forward.

"We are all here now, except Cornbury," said Mauvesin, "and I saw him in Salisbury this morning. My instructions can be told in a word; the prince wishes to get the tyrant out of the way."

"It is natural that he should do so, but it will not be of easy accomplishment," observed Kirke. "The common soldiers are faithful to a man, and the king will never be persuaded to abandon them."

"There is a shorter way of settling the business," said one of the speakers, significantly.

There was a pause. His auditors, as well as the speaker himself, owed almost everything to the king's bounty, and the dark suggestion filled most of them with horror.

"No, no," cried Churchill. "We will carry him off. I have sounded my regiment, and can depend on its fidelity, and I shall seize an early opportunity of taking the king to the outposts, whence he can easily be removed to the prince's camp."

This proposition was more agreeable to the confederates, and after a short debate, it was acceded to. They then conversed for some time on the position of the army, and it was decided at last that whatever happened, they should at least prevent the king from advancing further, as he would otherwise block up William in the peninsula formed by the Bristol and English Channels—a measure which would be fatal to his enterprise.

These schemes resolved on, the conspirators took their departure, and Moor was again the only inmate of Stonehenge.

After waiting for some time, and finding all quiet, he ventured from his hiding-place, and passed out. There was no one in sight, and hurrying on, he soon reached the spot where he had left his horse, which he instantly mounted, and spurring on to the road, shaped his course for Salisbury.

On his arrival at the city, he answered the challenge of the sentinel with the password, which procured him instant admission, and riding on he speedily reached the bishop's palace. The king had retired, and would not be disturbed, and he was, therefore, obliged to defer communicating with him till next day.

CHAPTER XI.

THE RIDE TO THE OUTPOSTS.

The morning had scarcely dawned when Moor was again in attendance at the king's bed-chamber, and after a brief interval, he was introduced by the gentleman in waiting to the royal presence. James was in bed, but motioning the attendant from the room, he commanded Moor to advance, and stepping forward, the latter acquainted him in a few words with what he had overheard at Stonehenge.

The monarch heard him to an end without interruption, though the most poignant distress was pictured in his looks. Several minutes elapsed before he could control his agitation.

"This cannot be," he said, at last, in hurried accents. "You must have dreamed it, Mr. Moor—dreamed it. I have regarded these men not as subjects, but as friends. I have fought with them, fasted with them, revelled with them. They have been my companions in adversity, my favourites in prosperity. *They* betray me! No! no! depend upon it you have been dreaming, Mr. Moor."

"Dreaming, my liege!" echoed Moor, in amazement. "I assure your majesty that the meeting took place precisely as I have described it."

"Then you must have been mistaken as to the men," said James. "You could not possibly see them."

"I acknowledge that I did not see their faces, my liege," began Moor.

"I knew it!" cried James, quickly. "Believe me, my young friend, the persons you have named would sooner die than desert me. But, since you are positive you were not dreaming, I will inquire about the meeting at Stonehenge. Treason must evidently be at work somewhere."

"Your majesty's confidence in these traitors fills me with alarm," cried Moor, passionately. "I implore you not to trust them, or you are lost. Confront me with them, and I will make good my words."

"I cannot," replied James, "for though I feel assured that you believe them to be the men you saw, I have no more doubt of their fidelity than of your own, and nothing short of actual proof should induce me to insult them with suspicion. I would as soon question the dutiful devotion of my own child, the Princess Anne.

Moor felt that he could not pursue the subject further, and taking leave of the king, he withdrew. But though he had failed to awaken James to a sense of his danger, he could not dismiss the matter from his own mind, and after long reflection he determined to repair to the camp, and communicate the whole affair to the Earl of Feversham.

During his absence, James arose, perused and answered his private letters, and partook of a light breakfast, when an attendant ushered in Lord Churchill and Colonel Trelawney.

The monarch changed colour as the two favourites entered, but disbelieving the charges brought against them, he received them with his usual kindness.

"We have come to tell your majesty the news," cried Churchill. "The invader has advanced to Axminster, and will probably push on further before night, so that we may expect him here in a few days; and, as I command the outposts, I should be glad if you would inspect them."

"I will do so instantly," answered James, rolling back a chart which lay on the table; "I suppose we have pushed our posts to the end of the plain. Where is Kirke stationed?"

"Here, my liege, at Warminster," replied Churchill, placing his finger on the map.

"It is about three hours' ride, your majesty," observed Trelawney, but an orderly has been sent forward to prepare for your reception."

"It is well," replied James, "let us to horse at once."

With this, he led the way to the palace-yard, where the two commanders had left a troop of the horse-guards, who received them with a general salute. A horse was soon provided for the king, and he was about to mount, when his foot slipped, and he would have fallen, if one of his attendants, who was close behind him, had not caught him by the arm and sustained him. The stumble seemed ominous, and James was half inclined to turn back, but growing ashamed of his hesitation, he mounted his horse, and the whole party rode off.

James did not address a word to the two favourites till they reached the plain, when the fresh, bracing air seemed to revive him, and he talked with them very earnestly on the posture of affairs, and the temper and condition of the army. As they proceeded, the road gradually became more and more lonely, but they could still discern both the city and the camp occasionally, though they were sometimes screened from view by enormous barrows, or by the natural irregularities of the ground. As they proceeded, Trelawney became restless, and frequently glanced anxiously around, but Churchill was calm and collected, and although the king had again become moody, left nothing untried to sustain his attention, at the same time keeping the whole party at a gallop. After they had been riding thus for some time, however, James suddenly reined his horse.

"We must halt a while," he said, "I feel ill."

"You alarm me, my liege," replied Churchill, "but you can procure no aid here. With your leave we will push on."

"We have but a few miles to go, your majesty," cried Trelawney, "and you will then have every attendance. We will get on as fast as possible."

As he waited a reply, the king placed a handkerchief to his face which was instantly dyed with blood. Trelawney and Churchill instantly sprang to the ground, and helped him to alight, when Churchill supported him in his arms.

James felt very faint, and all that Moor had told him respecting Churchill and Trelawney came forcibly to his mind, for the first time exciting his suspicions. As he saw himself completely in their power, he even dreaded that they might avail themselves of his insensibility to take his life. At this moment, he heard them exchange a hurried whisper; his sight began to fail, the figures of the soldiers seemed to whirl round and round, when all at once he caught the sound of a trumpet, followed by the tramp of horse. The excitement had a favourable effect. The bleeding ceased, and his senses were fast returning, when a troop of cavalry galloped up, headed by two officers, whose horses were covered with foam, and one of whom sprang at once to the ground, and hurried forward to the king. It was Charles Moor, and his companion was the Earl of Feversham.

James extended his hand to the former, who raised it to his lips.

"I am glad we have overtaken you, my liege," said Moor. "The general heard you had gone to the outposts, and he thought it better we should follow you."

James pressed his hand, but made no reply.

"I suppose your majesty will not think of going on now?" said the Earl of Feversham.

"What, if Lord Churchill and I go on to Warminster, my lord?" said Trelawney, anxiously—for the appearance of Moor and Feversham excited his suspicions. "The outposts ought to be inspected without delay."

"Of course, of course," said Feversham, sharply; "but we may want both you and his lordship elsewhere. Fall in with your men. I will give you your orders presently.

The two commanders replied with a salute, and turning to their horses, were quickly in the saddle. Though suffering from weakness, James determined to return to Salisbury on horseback, and accordingly, leaving the command to Feversham, he rode back slowly, closely attended on the right by Moor, and followed by the whole party. And in this order they reached the city.

CHAPTER XII.

EST-IL POSSIBLE?

WORN out in body and mind, and harasssed by a thousand anxieties, James was in great need of repose; but scarcely had he entered the episcopal palace, when a courier presented himself, bringing intelligence of an advantage having been gained by a small body of the royal troops over a superior force of the enemy, at Wincanton in Somersetshire; and it was detetmined to hold a council of war to consult on what was to be done. Messengers were accordingly despatched to the principal officers of the army, requiring their immediate attendance; and in the interim James held a private conference with the Earl of Feversham.

"I have ordered Lord Churchill and Colonel Trelawney to remain in attendance, my liege," said Feversham, "because Mr.

Moor has confided to me the communication he made to you, and I fear it is but too true. Under any circumstances, it will only be a proper precaution to place them under arrest. Supposing them guilty, depend upon it they are not the only disaffected officers, and the arrest of two such distinguished persons will strike terror into the others."

"I see all the advantage of it," answered James; "but if they are innocent—as I desire to believe them—I should never forgive myself for such a step. Let us, at least, wait till we discover some corroborative evidence of their guilt."

While they were thus talking, they were joined by Barillon, who had just arrived from London, and becoming acquainted with the subject of their conversation, he strongly supported the advice of Feversham. But the longer they argued, the more obstinately James adhered to his resolution, and, at last, they gave up the point in despair.

The gentleman-in-waiting now entered, announcing that the leading members of the council had arrived, and James passed into another chamber, accompanied by Feversham and Barillon. Here they found Prince George of Denmark, the Dukes of Grafton and Ormonde, and Lord Churchill, together with Colonels Trelawney, Berkeley, Lewson, and Maine. After looking round, the king inquired for his nephew, Lord Cornbury, the commandant of Salisbury; and was informed that the messenger despatched for his lordship had not yet returned. But while he was talking apart with Barillon, the messenger arrived, introducing the assistant-commandant, Major Nunn; and James again inquired the reason of the nobleman's non-attendance.

"I will relate the whole affair to your majesty," answered Nunn. "This morning, Lord Cornbury ordered out all the garrison, consisting of three regiments of cavalry, and marched us off towards Dorsetshire. I did not like his proceedings, and after riding some distance, I demanded to see his orders. He evaded me for the time, and during a short halt, found means to escape, with three or four common troopers, and they have gone over to the enemy."

James uttered an exclamation of amazement. "Could my own nephew be so false, when the common men were so true?" he added, mournfully.

"*Est-il possible!*" exclaimed Prince George of Denmark, with an expression of horror, which he exaggerated by taking an immense pinch of snuff.

The other members of the council uttered similar exclamations, but before they could pursue the subject further, a voice was heard in the ante-chamber, and presently the door was thrown open, and a venerable-looking man, whose countenance wore the impress of the deepest sorrow, made his appearance. It was the Earl of Clarendon, the deserter's father.

Casting a distracted look round the council, the earl hurried up to the king, and threw himself at his feet.

"Pardon! pardon, my gracious master!" he exclaimed, in mournful accents. "Do not punish the father for the offence of the child."

"Heaven forbid!" cried James, extending both his hands, and forcing him to rise. "From my heart I am sorry for you. May you derive that comfort from Heaven which is denied you on earth."

"Oh! my liege, your gracious words overpower me," replied Clarendon. "What does not our house owe you! You raised my father to the highest dignities; you gave your hand to my sister; you have showered down emoluments and honours on myself and my brother. Yet my son—my only son, is the first to desert you!"

As he spoke, he covered his face with his hands.

"Be comforted, my lord!" said James, embracing him. "You have lost your son, but I will be both a son and a brother to you. Go now, and repose yourself. We will talk of it hereafter—when this wound is healed."

A profound silence followed Clarendon's departure. At length the council began to consider how they were to act against the enemy. Maps were carefully surveyed, reports examined, and a variety of opinions expressed, but no positive course was decided on, when, after an interval of nearly an hour, a letter was handed to the king, which he opened and read. As he did so, a look of surprise spread over his face, but it was quickly succeeded by a flush of indignation, strangely mingled with disgust.

"You all heard what Lord Clarendon said about his son," he then cried. "He has now written to me to say that, all things considered, he thinks it better to follow his son's example, and, accordingly, he has himself deserted to the enemy."

"*Ah, mon Dieu! mon Dieu! Est-il possible!*" exclaimed, Prince George with another huge pinch of snuff.

"The father and son may well go together, my liege!" cried the Earl of Feversham, with a look of ineffable disgust. "They are not worth consideration."

"Right, my lord!" cried Churchill. "But I must pray your majesty to adjourn the council. I must positively inspect the outposts this evening, and it grows late."

"We must decide on our operations to-night," answered James; "but I will not detain you and Colonel Trelawney. I shall remember your advice—namely, that we had better remain in our present position. You are at liberty to go."

Churchill instantly arose, as did also Trelawney; and, taking leave of the king they withdrew.

The council had been debating some time, when the door was again opened, and Moor was ushered in. Stepping forward, the young man made some communication, in an undertone, to the king, which violently agitated him.

"This is indeed sad news," said James, at length, "but I am more affected by their ingratitude than their desertion. Your fears of treachery were but too well grounded, my lord," he added, to Feversham. Lord Churchill and Colonel Trelawney have deserted to the enemy."

"*Mon Dieu! mon Dieu! mon Dieu! Est-il possible!*" exclaimed Prince George, taking a pinch of snuff between each exclamation.

The other members of the council seemed to be equally astounded.

"The dastards should be pursued," cried the Duke of Grafton. "But perhaps it is better to let them go. They will fall into our hands anon."

"If they do, let them be tried by a drum-head court-martial, and executed on the spot," cried Ormonde.

"They are traitors of the blackest dye," said Colonel Berkeley. "But let me beseech your majesty not to doubt the loyalty of your other officers. For my own part I swear to conquer or die. I will neither give nor take quarter. Is not this invasion without parallel? In the midst of profound peace, when our poor country, so long torn by faction, was enjoying all the blessings of your majesty's benign rule, this unnatural Calvinist—this Dutch pest, plunges us into all the horrors of civil war. And does any one dare to speak of quarter? Whoever does so is your majesty's enemy, and I denounce him as a traitor."

"I cannot blame you, but I must insist that quarter be given," replied James. "My wishes will be expressed in the order of the day."

"If they command quarter to be given I will obey them, my liege, though reluctantly," returned Berkeley. "But these base and unnatural desertions have over-excited me, and I crave your permission to retire."

James readily excused him, and Berkeley withdrew, leaving the council in full debate. Thus they continued for some time, discussing the question before them with great warmth, but without any sign of coming to a decision, when a proposition was made which required reference to Berkeley, and a messenger was sent to recall him. The messenger was absent nearly an hour, but at length returned, bringing information that the colonel had deserted to the enemy.

"*A—h! a—h! a—h!—Est-il possible!*" exclaimed Prince

George, nearly stifling himself with an enormous pinch of snuff.

"It is scarcely credible?" cried the Duke of Ormonde. "To hear him talk, one would suppose him the most loyal man in the country. I shall now doubt every one."

"I always doubt great talkers," observed the Duke of Grafton. "I thought Berkeley a traitor, but he masked his treason with furious words. But these desertions are infectious, and some steps should be taken to reassure the men. With your majesty's leave I will ride off to the camp."

"And I will accompany you, if his majesty will permit me!" cried Ormonde. "It may have a good effect on the men."

"I do not fear for the men, if the officers are faithful," observed Feversham.

"Let them go," said James, unable to disguise his uneasiness.

The two dukes accordingly withdrew. A pause ensued, but it was quickly broken by Feversham, who assured James that he might place the most implicit trust in the common soldiers. The remaining officers corroborated this opinion, and while they were all conversing, a page entered, and presented Feversham with a letter, which, as it was marked official, he opened and read. It was from his brother, the Count de Roye, and informed him that the Dukes of Grafton and Ormonde had gone over to the Prince of Orange.

"*Mon Dieu! mon Dieu! est-il possible?*" cried Prince George, nearly emptying his snuff-box in his consternation.

The king seemed stupified.

"I think, my liege, we had better adjourn our deliberations till night," resumed Feversham. "In the mean time, I will call the officers together, and ascertain how they are disposed. We can then decide more easily what is to be done."

"If I may venture a suggestion, I would recommend all the officers to be sworn," said Colonel Maine. "I would not trust my own brother after these desertions."

"Oh! swear them by all means," said Colonel Lewson.

"Confer on this point as you ride along," replied James. "Take Moor with you, my lord, and he can bring me an account of your proceedings."

Bending deferentially, Feversham withdrew, accompanied by Lewson and Maine, who, as they retired, were heard expressing their determiation to stand or die with the king. An hour afterwards, Moor entered the room, bringing intelligence that the two colonels had deserted Feversham on the road, and fled to the enemy's camp.

A—h! a—h! Est-il possible!" exclaimed Prince George, clearing out his snuff-box, and shutting it in despair.

James was silent, and sank into a reverie, in which he remained for some time, but arousing himself at last, he looked up, and to his surprise, found he was alone. A strange suspicion flashed across his mind, and summoning an usher, he sent him in search of Moor. The young man speedily made his appearance, wearing a sad but resolute look.

"Where is the Prince of Denmark?" asked James.

"I have but this moment heard of his departure, my liege," replied Moor. "I grieve to say that he has deserted to the enemy."

"What, *Est-il possible* gone too!" cried James, with a bitter smile. "Well, well, I can spare him better than a good trooper. Why he has left his snuff-box behind him—empty too, pah!"

CHAPTER XIII.

THE RETREAT.

It was night. James was again seated at the council-board, and around him were assembled Feversham, Barillon, the Count de Roye, and Lords Dumbarton and Melfort, debating gravely, but earnestly, the important question of the future operations of the army.

"The enemy has now advanced too far to be blocked in the peninsula of the south-western counties," observed Feversham, and our present position is by no means strong. I therefore counsel a retreat."

"Then we must cross the Thames," said Dumbarton. "That will enable us to cover London."

"Why not march against the enemy, and strike a blow at once?" said James.

"It is now too late, my liege," said Feversham. "The enemy has the country open before him, and he will not venture a battle. Our safest course is, to place the Thames between us, and protect the capital."

"I have received certain information that the Prince of Orange will decline a battle," said Barillon.

"Then, we have no alternative but to retreat," rejoined James. "Send off messengers to call in the outposts, and when they return, we will retire in order beyond the Thames. In the meantime, let our intention be kept a profound secret."

So saying, he arose, and dismissing the council, withdrew to take some repose.

It was a dark night, and the camp was as still as a churchyard, except for the occasional voice of a sentinel, pronouncing "All's well." Suddenly a trumpet was heard sounding a retreat; in another part the rolling drum and shrill fife called the host to arms, and in a moment all was noise and confusion.

Soldiers were now seen scrambling from the tents, officers running about; others riding to and fro; troopers leading forth their horses; squadrons assembling; battalions forming in line; women rushing out half-dressed; pioneers striking the tents; the baggage-train attaching horses to the waggons; artillery-men, headed by their officers, dragging forth the cannon; while the clang of trumpets, the roll of drums, and the shrill whistle of the "ear-piercing fife," together with the shouts of the officers, the cries of women, and the voices of the soldiers answering to the muster-rolls resounding on every side.

In a short time, some of the infantry regiments were in motion. The remainder quickly followed, marching by various routes towards Maidenhead, Windsor, Egham, and Chertsey, where they were to be distributed, while the rear was covered by the cavalry.

Unable from weakness to mount on horseback, James pursued his way in one of the heavy carriages of the period, drawn by six horses. About a dozen dragoons accompanied the vehicle, which proceeded at a rapid pace, and soon left the army behind.

After an interval of about an hour, it was overtaken by a strong force of dragoons, the commander of which ordered the party in attendance to fall to the rear, and as they did so, he completely surrounded the carriage. He was then observed giving some directions to the postilions, and soon afterwards the carriage turned into a by-road, and drove along as before.

The commander of the new party now fell back a few paces, and was joined by two other horsemen, who, though muffled in their cloaks, appeared to be civilians.

"We have him now," he said. "In an hour we shall well place him in the prince's hands."

While this was passing, the officer in charge of the first party of dragoons had fallen back from his men, and turning round, rode off unperceived in the opposite direction. After riding some distance, he was encountered by a strong force of troopers coming along very leisurely, and spurring up to their commander, he exchanged a few words with him in a low tone. The commander then ordered a halt, and calling forward a sturdy yeoman who acted as guide, they held a brief and rapid discourse together, when he gave the word to resume their march at a quiet pace.

Meanwhile, the king's captors urged the postilions to make every exertion; but it was soon found that the unwieldy vehicle could not be moved along cross-roads with the same facility as on the highway. Their progress was slow, and it was feared that the constant jolting of the carriage would alarm the king and lead to a premature discovery. Nor was this apprehension groundless. At first, James bore the jolting of the vehicle in silence, but after a time, finding that it continued, he turned to Moor, the only other inmate of the coach, and expressed his surprise that the road should be so bad.

As he was about to look forth from the window, sounds of confusion were heard without, and before he could discover the occasion of them the carriage was suddenly stopped. The next moment the door was opened, and Snewin presented himself, while Mauvesin and the Duke of Grafton were seen behind. Snewin had a pistol in his hand, but before he could raise it Moor wrested it from his trembling grasp, for unscrupulous as he was, the ruffian was alarmed at his position, and in the scuffle it went off, and lodged its contents in the roof of the coach.

Meanwhile, Grafton and Mauvesin were both springing on Moor, when several shots were fired, and at the same time their force was attacked both in front and rear. The darkness increased the confusion, and in a moment the two contending parties were mingled together in strange disorder. Moor had thrown Snewin to the ground, but as he sprang back into the carriage in order to protect the king, the constable picked himself up and escaped, while Grafton and Mauvesin flew to their horses under a volley from the royal party, and as they turned, Moor saw one of them swerve in his saddle. But his companion kept him from falling, and calling his men around him, bore him off, pursued for some distance by the king's dragoons.

All this had passed with such rapidity, that James had scarcely recovered from the first surprise when he found himself in safety. At this moment the Count de Roye, who was the leader of his deliverers, appeared at the carriage-door.

"I congratulate your majesty on your escape," he said. "I shall not leave you till I see you in safety."

"Be it so, count," replied James. "Mr. Moor tells me the traitors have escaped. Did you know any of them?"

"No, my liege," replied the count. "Mr. Moor had the best opportunity of recognising them, for I saw one of them struggling with him."

"Yes, it was a ruffian named Snewin," cried Moor, "and his companions were Lords Mauvesin and Grafton. But where are our postilions? Ha! the knaves were no doubt in league with them, and have decamped. You must lend his majesty three of your troopers' horses, count."

The advice was acted upon, and in a short time the carriage was again on its way, and arrived in London without further interruption.

A messenger had been despatched in advance to announce the king's approach, and though it was scarcely daylight when the royal carriage reached Whitehall, the whole household was astir. Alighting, James entered the palace, followed by Moor, and passing up the grand staircase was met by Mary, who, informed of his approach, had hurried unattended to welcome him.

The meeting of the royal pair was affecting in the extreme. They said but little, but their looks spoke more plainly than words the anguish they endured. Passing into a neighbouring gallery they were met by the Count de Lauzun and Sabine, and James, taking Lauzun by the arm, walked slowly on with him, while Sabine lingered behind, and was joined by Moor.

"I am afraid all is lost for the king," she said, after they had exchanged a few words.

"Not if he would venture a battle," answered Moor. "In that case he would be the victor; for his army is superior to the enemy's, and the common men, and the greater part of the officers, are faithful."

"Why do you not tell him this?" returned Sabine. "He would surely listen to the counsel of one who has shown such devotion to him."

"You are mistaken," answered Moor. "To all the representations made him on the subject, his answer is that he cannot rely on the soldiers. Depend upon it, he will not risk a battle. But do not be alarmed. I trust there is no immediate danger."

Such was not the opinion of the king; and as he walked forward with Mary and Lauzun, he made them acquainted with his sentiments.

"My despatches have informed you of the desertions, and of the disaffected state of the army," he said. "There remains only one course for me to adopt, which is to place the queen and Prince of Wales in safety, and then either treat with the Prince of Orange, or strike one blow for it."

"Your majesty says well," replied Lauzun. "But I would strike the blow first, and treat afterwards."

"Whatever is done, I will not leave my husband!" cried Mary.

"It must be," said James. "I will show you the necessity of it. But where is Father Petre."

"He has gone," answered Mary, hesitatingly.

"Gone!" echoed James.

"He craved my permission to retire to France, and I could not refuse him," returned Mary. "He said that it would be for your majesty's advantage, and his life was certainly in danger here—the mob were so violent."

"It may be better that he is gone," said James. "But what is this you say about the violence of the mob? I thought the people were with us."

"Ha, my liege!" said Mary, mournfully; "the mob change

with every current. Your enemies have been among them, and have made them believe that if you win a victory, it is your inteution to have a general slaughter of the Protestants. This has infuriated them against you; and they would, no doubt, have attacked the palace, if Lord Craven had not come to our assistance, with a strong force of the guards."

"You amaze me!" cried James; "but does not this show you how expedient it is that you should leave the country? Let me see you and our son in safety, and I shall be able to act with more decision.

"I will remain and share your dangers," answered Mary; "were anything to happen to you, and I were absent, I should never know peace again."

"I am but too sensible of your affection," returned James, tenderly; "never could I prize it higher than now, when those whom I have most loved are the first to desert me. But I conjure you, by your love for me, and for our son, not to increase my embarrassment by remainiug here. It is now in my power to protect your flight, but such will not be the case long."

"Let me add my persuasions to those of his majesty, gracious madam," urged Lauzun; "should you or the Prince of Wales fall into the hands of the Prince of Orange, our cause is for ever lost."

"I will go, then," faltered Mary; "but on condition that your majesty promises to follow me within twenty-four hours. No other consideration shall induce me to leave you."

James mused a moment, evidently in deep perplexity.

"I promise you, then, that unless thiugs take a more favourable turn, I will follow you in that time," he said. "My brother Louis will afford us an asylum, and something tells me we shall soon be called back by our people. We must now make immediate arrangements for your journey. I will myself notify it to the Princess Anne, and she will accompany you."

"Alas, my dear liege!" exclaimed Mary, tears gathering in her eyes, "you must now suffer a new sorrow—the greatest a parent can know. The Princes Anne has clandestinely left the palace, in company with Lady Churchill, and gone over to the enemy."

The king heard her in silence, but a deadly paleness spread over his face, and he looked as if he would fall to the ground. He was supported, however, by the Count de Lauzun, and in a moment or two his emotion, though far from disappearing, became less violent.

"Have they taken away my child—my darling Anne?" he cried. "Has she, too, forsaken me? Oh, God! this is too much!" and he added the ejaculation of the Psalmist—"Oh! if my enemies had only cursed me, I could have borne it!"

There was something so touching in this burst of grief, that both Mary and Lauzun were too much affected to offer the king consolation, and they were all silent for several minutes. Suddenly, however, James seemed to arouse himself, and seized Mary by the hand.

"Come," he said, wildly; "let us be gone. We will leave this unnatural land, where subjects betray their king, and children desert their parents. I will go out, in my old age, on the wide world, and find another home."

"We will go together," said Mary, with eagerness; "only death shall part us."

"Stay, my liege, I implore you!" cried Lauzun. "Do not throw away the slightest chance of recovering your rights. Remain here at least the time proposed by her majesty, and make sure that everything is really lost; meanwhile, I will escort her majesty to a place of safety."

"Be it so, then!" cried James. "I have yet a son left, who is too young to be perfidious; were it not so, I could now lie down, and pray God that my sorrows and my life might end."

"I will not add to your distress, by opposing your wishes," said Mary, "sad as it is to leave you; but I will instantly prepare for flight."

With this she turned away, leaving the king still leaning on Lauzun's arm. There was a pause.

"You said, count, you would escort her majesty to France," said James, at length. "I need not say how glad I should be if you render me this service; but, if I remember right, when you first came to this country, you were forbidden, on pain of death, to return to your own."

"True, my liege, but my sovereign will not punish me for my devotion to your majesty," answered Lauzun; "but if I even thought otherwise, I should not hesitate to fulfil your wishes."

"Louis will not punish you," said James, quickly. "Should you incur his displeasure, I will excuse you to him; but promise me—swear to me, that you will not leave the queen till she is safe in France."

"I do swear, sire, by everything I hold sacred!" cried Lauzun, solemnly.

"I should not have asked your oath, count," answered James, pressing his hand. "The bare word of the Count de Lauzun is the best of bonds: but I am low and sorrowful; and when my own child deserts me, how can I look for faith in strangers! But enough. Nothing can make me doubt you."

"Your majesty shall never have cause to do so," said Lauzun: "but time presses. With your majesty's leave, we will prepare for the queen's departure."

James assented, and turning round, they joined Moor, who was still in waiting, and passed out of the gallery.

BOOK THE FIFTH.

CHAPTER I.

THE ROYAL FUGITIVES.—THE CAMP OF THE INVADER.

FLANKED on one side by a sweep of the river Ax, the camp of the Prince of Orange extended, on the other, over an area of about four miles, to the small town of Axminster, in Devonshire.

In the centre of the town, near the ancient minster, was a massive stone building, usually appropriated to the clergy, but now surrounded by sentries, and occupied by the Prince of Orange, who was seated with Sidney, Schomberg, and Bentinck, in one of the upper rooms.

They had been conferring together some time, when an aide-de-camp appeared, ushering in Lord Cornbury.

"Lord Cornbury!" echoed William, staring at the new comer in surprise.

"Yes, your highness," replied Cornbury, much abashed; "I have come to offer you my services. "You are, no doubt, surprised that I do so, but the private considerations that bind me to King James cannot divert me from my public duty. I owe this sacrifice to my country and my religion."

"You say well, my lord," returned William, coldly. "You will remain in the camp till further orders. When I have any commands for you, I will send for you."

Upon this, the nobleman withdrew, much mortified at his cold reception; and William and his counsellors resumed their conversation. Bentinck said little, but Sidney and Schomberg seemed shocked at the perfidy of Cornbury; and though their discourse referred to other subjects, William alluded to it repeatedly, exclaiming, at last, after a long pause,—

"Perfidious traitor! I should as soon have expected to see his father."

Scarcely had he uttered the words, when the aide-de-camp ushered in the Earl of Clarendon. Sidney and Schomberg exchanged glances: a cloud passed over William's face, but instantly disappeared, and Clarendon hurried forward, and threw himself at the prince's feet.

"Welcome to England, mighty sir!" he cried. "Our laws, our liberty, and our religion, are now preserved."

"Their preservation is not yet secured, my lord," answered William, with freezing stiffness; "it will depend on a total change of persons. You apprehend me? Ha!"

"Assuredly, *your majesty*," replied Clarendon.

As he spoke, he gazed in the prince's face, but there was nothing to indicate that William heeded the title by which he had been addressed.

"We will talk of this another time," said the prince; "meanwhile, you will be assigned a lodging in the camp."

Scarcely believing that he could be dismissed so abruptly, Clarendon was about to speak again, but William waved his hand, and turned with a smile to Schomberg. Burning with shame and mortification, the nobleman retired, and, as he quitted the room, heard William say, in an indignant tone,—

"What monstrous ingratitude! But we can despise the traitor, while we profit by his treason."

"It were well your highness disguised your sentiments a while," urged Bentinck, "or you may drive them back to the enemy."

"Not in this instance," answered William; "this worthy pair have crossed the rubicon, and cannot return. But what news from Speke?"

"This despatch is from London," replied Sidney, "and represents the city to be in a state of ferment, owing to the discovery of a popish manifesto, in which the king engages, in the event of being the victor, to have a general massacre of the Protestants."

"The manifesto is Speke's own handiwork," cried Schomberg, angrily.

"Speke is over-zealous no doubt!" said William; "but I can hardly believe he would go the length of forging a manifesto. You must be mistaken, Schomberg; but let me hear the despatch." Before the letter could be read, the aide-de-camp again made his appearance, ushering in Lord Churchill and Colonel Trelawney.

The surprise of William and his counsellors was so great, that at first they seemed undecided what to say; but the easy manners and perfect self-possession of Churchill soon dispelled their embarrassment.

"I have come to offer your highness my sword," said Churchill, laying the weapon at William's feet. "I cannot raise it against the defender of the religion and liberties of my country."

"Yet he is willing to draw it against his benefactor," whispered Schomberg to Sidney.

"I will find a place in my camp for you, my lord," said William, with strained courtesy. "Take up your sword, I pray of you. I am so unprepared for your offer, that you must forgive me if I take time to consider it."

"I shall await your highness's pleasure," answered Churchill, indifferently. "I have little fear that my sword will rust in the scabbard."

"This is the first lieutenant-general I ever knew who deserted his colours," said Schomberg, loud enough to be heard by Churchill.

Despite these mortifying rebuffs, Churchill's countenance retained its look of composure, and without noticing Schomberg's remark he withdrew, followed by Trelawney, whom the prince did not even notice.

When they had retired, Sidney expressed his regret that they had been received so coldly.

"If this course is persisted in, your highness will be deprived of your ablest supporters," he said.

"I do not call every one who comes over to my standard, a traitor," replied William, "but I *do* call those traitors who, owing everything to their king, are the first to desert him."

"Your highness is in the right," cried Schomberg; "and so much do I distrust these men that I would place a guard over them."

"A despatch, your highness," said an orderly, advancing.

"What is this?" cried William, breaking open the letter, and glancing hurridly over its contents. "It is from Lord Mauvesin," he added, after he had perused it, "and he asserts that the enemy is on the point of retreating."

"Let us advance, then, and decide his fate by a battle," cried Bentinck.

"We are not in a position to come to an engagement," said William; "but we will press close on his rear. Give the order to advance at once."

His commands were obeyed, and in a short time large bodies of infantry were seen mustering in the camp, while squadrons of cavalry poured in from the various cantonments, and quickly assembled on parade. After a hasty inspection, they were told off in marching order, and amidst martial music and the cheering vociferations of the soldiers, moved off in the direction of Salisbury Plain.

At this moment a dragoon spurred up to William, who was riding at the head of the army in company with Schomberg and Sidney, and presented him with a sealed packet.

"This brings information," cried William, after glancing at the contents of the packet, "that the king is about to send away the queen and the prince. This must be prevented. He himself may go, but they must be secured, or all our labour will be thrown away. Find a trusty fellow, Sidney, and let him ride forward with the utmost speed. If he wastes no time on the road, he will be in London as soon as the king." And turning to Schomberg, he added, "Marshal, send off a despatch to Admiral Herbert, and bid him scour the channel with the whole fleet, in case the fugitives should get out to sea."

Replying with a military salute, the two officers turned their horses, and galloped off towards the rear.

CHAPTER II.

SIEGE OF NEWGATE.

THE return of the king to Whitehall, and the more significant fact that his army was in full retreat, soon became known throughout the metropolis, and, at an early hour in the morning, immense multitudes gathered in the streets, and blocked up every avenue to the palace. The almost total absence of women and children gave this concourse a very formidable appearance. It seemed that some great collision was anticipated, and the comparatively small number of respectable persons who were mingled with the mob, more as observers than abettors, looked grave and anxious.

The great mass, however, were clamorous and violent, and their disposition could easily be inferred from various flaring banners, bearing such inflammatory inscriptions as "No Popery!" "Remember Bartholomew's Eve!" "Who assassinated Sir Edmondbury Godfrey?" "Who murdered the Earl of Essex?" "Down with the Priests, and the Pope!" which were displayed on every side.

Party watch-cries were bandied about incessantly, amidst terrific yells and hootings; the sentinels round the palace were urged to come forth and join the mob, and on their making no answer, were saluted with jeers and groans, while a large section of the multitude chorused forth the ballad of Lillibullero, amidst the acclamations of the remainder. In this manner the greater part of the day passed by, but as the afternoon wore on, the mob, whether from indifference, or fatigue, became more temperate, and though yells and outcries continued to be raised occasionally, they gradually became less frequent.

At this juncture a horseman, followed by a mounted attendant, approached from Parliament-street, and endeavoured to make his way towards Charing Cross. Scarcely had he penetrated the mob, however, when he was recognised, and loud cries of "A Nottingham! a Nottingham! God save your lordship!"

At first Lord Nottingham took no notice of these acclamations, but rode along in silence, wearing a stern, though melancholy look, and casting down his eyes, but after a time, as the cheers grew louder and louder, and the people pressed closer round him, waving their banners, flinging up their caps, and invoking blessings on his head, he turned his face to them, and it was instantly seen that he was in tears. Suddenly the vast assemblage became hushed; there was a profound silence for a moment, when a deafening shout arose of "God save you! Nottingham."

Nottingham waved his hand.

"Home! home! my good people!" he cried.

There was a confused murmur, but it soon subsided, and as Nottingham rode forward the mob followed him, to the great chagrin of the principal ringleaders. As they approached Charing Cross, two persons broke away from the mass, and gliding into Scotland-yard and round the Adelphi, passed up the Strand to Fleet-street, where they halted, and, after conferring together for a few moments, they separated, one of them proceeding towards Ludgate-hill, and the other diving into Whitefriars.

This locality was then inhabited by a dense and heterogeneous population, comprehending thieves of every degree, with a strong mixture of gamesters, smugglers, runaway debtors, and sharpers of all shades and grades, who here formed a community of themselves, following their various pursuits in security, and whenever invaded by the authorities, banding together in self-defence. They were governed by laws of their own, to which the strictest obedience was enforced by an officer chosen by themselves, bearing the title of Duke of Alsatia, but who had formerly borne the less sounding appellation of Kit Clench.

Hurrying down a long, narrow street, the person before noticed made his way to a low public-house, bearing the significant sign of "The Jolly Cutpurses," and without heeding certain suspicious-looking characters who were loitering about the door, entered, and stepping up to the bar, exchanged a few words in a low tone with a very showily-dressed damsel, who was in attendance within. This done, the girl admitted him to the interior, and pointing to a door behind her, through which voices were heard laughing and singing, the stranger opened it, and passing in, found himself in a small room, redolent with tobacco-smoke, and the fumes of spirituous compounds, in which were seated four persons; one of whom was asleep, while two others were playing at dice, and the fourth was engaged in discussing a can of ale and a pipe.

It was to this last—who, indeed, was no other than the redoubtable Kit Clench, the Duke of Alsatia—that the stranger addressed himself.

"You have offered me your aid," he said. "The sum you demand shall be yours, but you must set to work at once, or there will be a general massacre of the Protestants."

"That cock won't fight with me, Muster Speke," answered Clench, with a wink. "But that's neither here nor there. Tip us the cash, and I'll be as good as my word."

"It is here," replied Speke, producing a heavy purse filled with gold. "Do your work effectually, and I will double it."

"Humph!" returned Kit. "What's to be done?"

"Why, we must raise a little excitement, or the people will lose their courage," answered Speke. "First it will be better to break into Newgate, and then burn down the popish mass-houses."

"All shall be done and no questions axed," rejoined Kit. "You wait here a bit."

With this he turned to the two gamesters, who, from the moment that Speke produced the purse, had watched their conference with intense interest, but had been unable to overhear what passed, and motioned them from the room. The two ruffians muttered something to each other, and then dealing a suspicious glance at Speke, arose and went forth with their leader.

Left alone with the sleeping man, whom he hardly deigned to look at, Speke became thoughtful and gloomy, though from time to time he darted an uneasy look at the door. At length a loud clamour was heard without. This was followed by the blowing of a horn, when the clamour was renewed, and Speke became sensible that a large mob had assembled in the neighbourhood, and were being harangued by some one, who was listened to with great attention. Before he could make out more clearly what was passing, loud outcries arose, and at the same moment Kit burst into the room.

"Now, then, all Alsatia is out," he cried. "Where's it to be first, Newgate or the popish chapels?"

"Newgate, Newgate," answered Speke. "You'll get fresh forces there."

"Come along, then," returned Kit, "we'll lead the way."

With this he rushed out followed by Speke, and hurrying through the bar gained the street.

It was now quite dark, but pushing up the street they came in sight of a mob consisting of between two and three hundred persons, some of whom bore torches, which, as Speke drew near, enabled him to distinguish many a stalwart ruffian, with sturdy-looking lads and even women,—if such viragos deserved the name. Most of them were armed with bludgeons, but some carried hangers and pistols, and they were all waiting with impatience the signal to set forward. Being joined by Clench and Speke, a cry was instantly raised of "Newgate, Newgate," which was caught up on every side, and with a terrific yell the whole party rushed up the street in the direction of the prison.

At this juncture corresponding outcries were heard in Fleet-street, and presently afterwards Speke came up with another mob, composed, apparently, of more respectable persons, but no less excited than the others; and perceiving Ephraim Ruddle at their head, he called to him, on which Ephraim united his forces with those of Clench, and the allied mobs pushed forward to the Old Bailey amidst the most appalling yells.

Arrived before the prison, they summoned the governor to surrender by thundering at the door, and, receiving no answer, endeavoured to break in; but being of great strength, and very skilfully secured, the door resisted their efforts. At last a sledge-hammer was procured, and a furious attack made on the door, which seemed to be gradually yielding, when it was suddenly opened, and a strong force of turnkeys, armed with cutlasses and muskets, rushed out, and pouring a volley into the mob, drove them back some distance, and then retreating, closed the door again. A deafening yell arose from the mob as they disappeared in the prison, and they required but little encouragement from the ringleaders to renew the attack. As they were pushing forward, they received an accession of force in the shape of a large body of apprentices, headed by our old acquaintance Mark Stovin, and with renewed vociferations they made a tremendous rush on the door, which gave way, disclosing the garrison of turnkeys, who, dashing forth again, drove them back. But after retreating a few paces the mob rallied.

"Down with them, mates," cried Kit, urging on his men.

"Ay! down with the Romanists! down with the mass-mongers!" shouted Mark Stovin.

The apprentices answered with a shout, and a furious attack was then made on the turnkeys, who, after a desperate struggle, were driven into the prison, pressed closely by the besiegers, among whom Ephraim Ruddle and Mark Stovin were particularly prominent. The turnkeys made another stand in the hall, but, at length, seeing that further resistance would be useless, they poured a parting volley upon their assailants, and fled, making their escape over the roofs of the houses at the back of the prison.

As the smoke cleared away, and the mob discovered their success, they became almost frantic with joy; some rushed on, with savage yells, in pursuit of the turnkeys; others hastened to break open the dungeons, and free the prisoners; many danced wildly round the hall, laughing, singing, and shouting—trampling on the bodies of their dead comrades, and jeering at the wounded. Then the liberated prisoners began to flock in, some in rags, many in the last stage of want or disease, others inflamed by spirituous liquors, and eager to join in any outrage.

At length, it was proposed to set fire to the prison, and torches and links were brandished about amidst the most terrible outcries, but the masonry of the building was of the most solid description, and nothing inflammable presented itself, added to which torrents of rain now poured down, extinguishing many of their torches, and the attempt to raise a fire proved unsuccessful. While it was still in progress, a tall, burly man, having a broad-brimmed hat pulled over his brow, from which rain poured off in streams, made his way through the crowd to Speke, who was watching the proceedings from the upper end of the hall.

"I have been seeking you everywhere," he said. "The king is about to smuggle off the queen and the child, and the scheme will probably be tried to-night. Go at once to Whitehall, and block up the approaches. If they are taken coming forth they are to be carried to the prince."

"This is easily said, Johnstone," replied Speke, "but suppose they should cross the river? What is to be done then?

"Oh, I will look to that," replied Johnstone. "I am going to Lambeth myself, and have already made arrangements to intercept them, if they go that way. Do you look to the Horseferry and Whitehall. I will send a couple of trusty fellows to London Bridge."

So saying, he hurried away, leaving Speke to seek the ringleaders of the mob, which he did forthwith, and ordering them to abandon the prison, led them forth in the direction of Whitehall.

CHAPTER III.

HOW THE QUEEN LEFT WHITEHALL.

It was drawing towards midnight, but late as it was, a young lady of rarest beauty sat in a chamber of Whitehall attired for a journey. She was weeping; but alarmed by a knock at the door, she hastily dried her eyes, and rising, found two persons in the passage without, one of whom stepped up to her. "I have brought a friend to see you, Sabine," said Saint Leu (for it was he), handing forward his companion. "But remember, you have not many moments to spare."

With this he retired, and his companion, who was no other than Charles Moor, took Sabine by the hand, and led her into the room. They had much to say to each other, but it seemed, at first, that their hearts were too full to give utterance to their thoughts, or that they shrank from approaching the sad cause of their meeting.

"I have just learned that you are to accompany the queen to France," said Moor, at length; "in short, that you are now to be surrendered to the French king. As the hopes I entertained of recovering my birthright, owing to the misfortunes which have fallen on my royal master, are now at an end, I would not ask you to remain here, and share my humble fortunes, if I did not see that your return to France will bring you misery. Oh! pause, Sabine, before it is too late, and do not condemn us both to endless unhappiness."

"Would that the decision rested with me," answered Sabine, unable to restrain her tears. "But alas! were I to follow the dictates of my heart, and give you my hand, the Count de Lauzun, on his return to France, would expiate my offence by perpetual imprisonment."

"It is true," said a voice behind them, and Lauzun stepped forward. "You must give up all thought of ever meeting Sabine again. With the all-powerful Louvois for our enemy, we shall have enough to contend against; and even as it is, I shall probably pass from the Tuileries to the Bastille. Farewell, Sabine must accompany me to the apartments of the queen."

Sabine lingered for a moment to bid adieu to Moor, and then followed Lauzun to another chamber, where they found Saint Leu, and then all three proceeded in silence to the private apartments of the queen. Arrived there, they were admitted by the page of the back stairs to a cabinet, where they found James seated at a table writing despatches.

"All has been prepared as you advised, count," said the king. "A boat waits at the Horse-ferry to carry you over to Lambeth, where a coach is ready to take you to Gravesend. There you will find the yacht, which will be distinguished till daylight by a lantern aloft, and afterwards by a red and blue streamer in the stern. Lord and Lady Powis are already on board." "Enough, my liege, replied Lauzun. "My own preparations are completed; and the sooner her majesty and the prince are ready, the better."

"The queen only awaits my summons," said James.

Upon which he touched a small silver bell, and Mary almost immediately afterwards made her appearance, followed by Lady Strickland, bearing the infant Prince of Wales.

Mary was disguised in a long Italian pelisse, with a capacious hood, drawn over her head; and her features could be further concealed by a thickly-folded veil. "Count de Lauzun," said James, in a tremulous voice, "I confide my queen and my son to your care. You will convey them to France."

Lauzun placed his hand on his heart. "Heaven so deal with me, as I endeavour to fulfil your majesty's wishes," he cried.

Then bending the knee, he pressed the king's hand devotedly to his lips. Mary seemed to be quite unconscious of what was passing. Intense emotion kept her silent.

Turning to Lady Strickland, who, at his request, placed the royal babe in his arms, James bent a long fond look on his face. The child was asleep, and his afflicted parent refrained from kissing him; but a hot tear fell on the infant's face. James then committed the child to Sabine.

At this juncture Lauzun stepped on one side, and pushed back a panel in the wainscot disclosing a secret passage, into which Saint Leu stepped with a lantern.

There was a solemn pause. Arousing herself at length, Mary gave James her hand, and clasping it in both his own, the king pressed it passionately to his lips. Mary then hurried towards the passage, and on reaching it turned round, and glancing at the king with a gesture of wildest grief, disappeared. James stood perfectly still for a moment, gazing vacantly on the opening, but, by a great effort, he succeeded in mastering his emotion. "Remember!" he then cried, waving his hand to Lauzun, who, having seen Sabine enter the passage with the infant prince, stood awaiting his last injunctions. "Remember!"

"Have no fear, my liege," replied Lauzun, closing the panel.

The passage was so narrow that they were obliged to proceed separately, Saint Leu leading the way. After a while they came to a flight of steps, and descending them, reached a short passage terminated by a secret door which admitted them to the chapel. Passing through the sacred structure, the fugitives made their way to the stone gallery. Rain was falling in torrents; the roar of the wind was nearly as loud as thunder; and the darkness was so profound, that not an object below could be distinguished.

In another moment, they arrived at the flight of steps leading to the privy-garden. At the bottom of the steps was a coach, which, as it was thought hazardous to employ one of the royal carriages, had been hired for the occasion. The coachman was sheltering himself from the rain under a neighbouring tree, but hearing footsteps, he hastened forward, and opening the carriage-door, Mary and Sabine, with their precious charge were placed inside it, while Lauzun sprang upon the box beside the driver, and Saint Leu, pursuant to a previous arrangement, got up behind. Both were well armed. Moving quickly down a long drive, the vehicle approached a gate, opening into Parliament-street, and was instantly challenged by the sentinel. "Who goes there?"

"The Count de Lauzun."

"Advance, Count de Lauzun, and give the countersign."

The coachman drew up, and alighting from behind, Saint Leu hurried up to the sentinel, and gave the required password, at the same time drawing forth a key, with which he unlocked the gate, and then threw it open. The carriage then passed through the gates, and the queen quitted Whitehall—for ever!

CHAPTER IV

THE QUEEN'S FLIGHT TO FRANCE.

Driving rapidly on, the coach soon reached the stairs situated near the end of the Horseferry-road, and just below the House of Lords. There it drew up, and alighting, Lauzun went in search of the boat which he expected would be in waiting. The darkness prevented him from seeing far, but going up to the water's edge, and finding no boat within view, he shouted several times, without receiving any answer. This circumstance placed them in a serious dilemma. Was it owing to accident or treachery that the boat was gone? A number of wherries were lying around, but there were no oars in them, and even if there had been, Lauzun would have hesitated to embark the Queen and Prince of Wales in such a storm, without an experienced waterman to aid them. His resolution was quickly taken. Returning to the steps, he knocked at the door of a small habitation, which he perceived from the sign belonged to a waterman, and was quickly answered by the owner from a window. The man, in a surly tone demanded his business, and on learning it declared that it would be madness to venture out in such a gale, and refused to comply.

But the offer of gold induced him to alter his resolution, and he retired from the window, and after a brief interval presented himself at the door, accompanied by a sturdy lad.

While this was passing, Saint Leu, who had remained with the carriage, observed the coachman peering about in a manner that excited his suspicions, and coming behind him, he suddenly threw the light of the lantern on his face, when, to his surprise, he discovered that the seeming coachman was no other than Johnstone. Uttering a hasty exclamation, he seized the emissary by the throat, and presented a pistol at his breast; while Lauzun coming up, helped him to secure him.

Glad to escape with life, Johnstone offered no resistance, and they forced him to mount the box, and then tied his arms together, and fastened him to the seat with the reins, binding a handkerchief tightly over his mouth, so as effectually to prevent him from raising an outcry.

Meanwhile, Mary and Sabine had remained in the carriage, unable to account for the delay. A thousand apprehensions seized the queen, but though naturally timid, she did not heed her own peril, provided she could secure the safety of her son. She heard the struggle on the box, and voices in dispute, but could not distinguish what was said, and her alarm became almost insupportable. Taking the infant prince from Sabine she pressed him tenderly to her bosom, resolved not to part from him with life. At this moment the carriage-door was opened, and Lauzun presented himself.

"All is well, gracious madam," he whispered; "you must not be dismayed at the storm. We will all die to preserve you."

"I do not doubt it," answered Mary, though her eyes were raised to Heaven, as if her trust lay *there!*

The queen and Sabine now alighted, and in a few minutes

they all reached the boat, which instantly put off. Hardly had this occurred, when Johnstone contrived to free his mouth from the bandage and raise an outcry, which was quickly answered from an adjacent house, and after a brief interval he was joined by a waterman, who mounted the box, and released him from his bonds.

"Now, give me a pull over the river," said Johnstone, "and I will reward you handsomely. I have a party on the other side who will help me to capture these fugitives."

"I wouldn't venter over for my weight i' goold," replied the waterman. "Not by no manner of means."

"What is to be done?" muttered Johnstone, in perplexity; "but they will find I have set a trap for them; and we will get at them over London Bridge." So saying, he turned the carriage, and drove with all possible speed towards the city.

Meanwhile the fugitives pursued their way. After a perilous passage, during which the boat was more than once well nigh lost, they reached Lambeth Stairs. Quick as thought the elder boatman grappled the stanchion of the stairs with a boat-hook, and at the same moment his son jumped ashore, and fastened the boat to a ring in the steps. This done, Lauzun landed and received Mary from Saint Leu, who lifted her from the boat, and the count then assisted her to the summit of the stairs. Having bestowed her in safety, he returned for Sabine, whom he instantly conducted to the queen, while Saint Leu discharged the boatmen.

Advancing a few paces, Lauzun looked around for the coach which the king had promised should be in waiting, but it was nowhere to be seen. Thinking it possible that the persons in charge had sought shelter from the storm at a neighbouring inn, from the open door of which, notwithstanding the lateness of the hour, light still streamed, he determined to proceed thither in search of it. Previously to doing so, however, he escorted Mary and Sabine to the porch of the adjacent church, where they were partially sheltered from the rain, and waited there till they were joined by Saint Leu, when he bent his steps towards the inn, which fronted the western side of the churchyard. Avoiding the open door, he turned under a dark archway then leading to the inn-yard, but now the entrance to a dirty retreat, called Chapel-court, and shaped his course for the further end, where a flickering light seemed to mark out the stables. As he hurried forward he heard a footstep, and turning, saw a man advancing with a lantern. But though he suspected something wrong, the count thought it better to pursue his way, and arriving at the stable-door he lifted the latch and looked in.

In front of him were six stalls, each of which was occupied by a horse, fully harnessed; ostlers were engaged in the duties of the stable, while three postilions, enveloped in capacious overcoats, were smoking short pipes near the window. As the count entered, they all turned to regard him.

"Is the carriage of the Sieur de Caumont here?" cried Lauzun.

"Yes, my lord," answered one of the postilions, stepping forward, and touching his hat. "We were obliged to take shelter from the storm."

At this juncture, the person whom Lauzun had seen in the yard, and who was no other than Snewin, came up, and the count was satisfied, from the manner in which the constable regarded him, that he was a spy. But though he was greatly disturbed by the circumstance, he affected unconcern, and giving directions to the postilions to bring out the carriage instantly, he hastened out of the inn-yard.

Finding Saint Leu, he communicated his suspicions to him, and gave him some instructions, and then flew to the porch where Mary had returned with Sabine. In a few minutes the coach appeared, drawn by six horses, and drove up to the porch, while Snewin came running on with his lantern, bent on examining the count's companions. But as he turned the angle of the churchyard, Saint Leu, who was lying in wait, ran against him, and tripping him up, sent him floundering into the muddy kennel, and smashed his lantern. This done, Saint Leu sprang upon the footman's board behind the carriage, into which the queen, Sabine, and her precious charge, with Lauzun, had already got, and word being given by the latter, the postilions dashed off at a gallop.

The party proceeded in silence. Mary was engrossed by her own bitter reflections. Lauzun was calculating in his mind the chances of pursuit, and bending a vigilant ear to the road. Sabine was thinking of her private griefs, as well as those of her mistress.

They had passed the road leading to London Bridge, when suddenly the count started forward, and let down the carriage-window. The rain had ceased, and the tramp of a horse was indistinctly heard in the distance, approaching at a furious pace. Lauzun shouted to Saint Leu to urge on the postilions, but though they made every exertion, the sound of the pursuing horse came nearer and nearer, and at last a voice was heard shouting, which was instantly recognised by Saint Leu, and he ordered the postilions to halt. Surprised and alarmed, the count was about to spring out of the coach, in order to ascertain the occasion of the stoppage, when Charles Moor dashed up.

"His majesty has sent me on, count, with a message to the queen," Moor said. "We found that the boat which was to have met you at the ferry, owing to some mistake, did not set out till after the appointed time; and as we learned at the ferry that a party had gone across, his majesty became very anxious, and desired me to make certain of your safety. I crossed London Bridge—felled a coachman, and beat down a couple of ruffians who would have intercepted me, and have overtaken you."

"You have done bravely," cried the queen.

"His majesty has sent you this casket, gracious madam," continued the young man. "It contains the most valuable of your jewels, and a letter for the King of France, which your royal husband requests you will deliver into his own hands."

"I will," cried Mary. "But is his majesty safe? Is he well?"

"He is both safe and well, madam," answered Moor. "Now postilions, on for your lives!"

And waving his hand to Sabine, he rode back, while the coach resumed its progress, proceeding at the same rate as before.

It was daylight before they reached Gravesend. Though occupied chiefly by fishermen and smugglers, that place was already of some extent, and the appearance of a coach-and-six at so early an hour, excited a general sensation. Among others, a party of soldiers, who had deserted from Tilbury Fort, on the other side of the river, and were on their way to join the Prince of Orange, rushed forth from a low public-house as the coach drew near the water, and threw themselves right in the way, commanding the postilions to halt, in order, as they said, that they might see if there were any papists in the vehicle. At this moment, however, Saint Leu seized the most violent of the ruffians by the collar, thrust him backwards, while his companions, seeing that both he and Lauzun were well armed, thought it advisable to make off. The carriage then moved on without interruption, and soon reached the river, when Lauzun, alighting, perceived in the mid-stream the yacht, distinguished, as the king had intimated, by a red and blue streamer in the stern. He found, also, a boat lying below, manned by two persons in the dress of seamen, but whom he recognised as two Irish officers sent by the king to attend them.

One of the officers came forward, and Lauzun hastened to assist the queen to the boat. Mary alighted joyfully, though with a trembling step. Holding her child, who was carefully concealed by her cloak, fondly to her bosom, she proceeded to the boat, followed by Sabine. A crowd of persons of both sexes had collected at the water's-edge, who pressed forward to gaze at her; but she kept her eyes on the ground, and her look was composed though she was very pale. Lauzun lifted her into the boat and placed Sabine by her side, and then seated himself behind them, while Saint Leu and the two rowers took their places and pulled off.

The wind had lulled, and was now only a refreshing breeze. The sun was up, and for the hour and season, shone with unusual brightness. The water was calm and clear. On one side the eye commanded an extensive view of Kent, with the picturesque town of Gravesend, sloping up to the verdant base of Windmill Hill, which towered high above; and on the other the vast marshes of Essex, with the fort of Tilbury peeping over the water, the batteries bristling with cannon. Mary could not restrain her tears as she turned a wistful gaze on the two shores.

In a few moments the boat reached the yacht, and mounting to the deck the queen was received by Lord and Lady Powis, who instantly conducted her and Sabine to the state cabin. Lauzun and Saint Leu remained on deck, where the greatest bustle now prevailed, and in a few moments all the canvas was spread, and the yacht sailed with a fair wind for the coast of France.

CHAPTER V.

JAMES RESOLVES ON FLIGHT.

It was late in the day before the flight of Mary and the infant prince was known to the royal household; but scarcely had it transpired at Whitehall, when it became known to the public. The agents of the Prince of Orange did not neglect such a favourable occasion for promoting his interests. The most monstrous artifices were resorted to for the purpose of inflaming the public mind against the king, and he was accused of meditating a sweeping vengeance on the people. The reports were as contradictory as they were absurd. It was now asserted that he intended to set the city on fire, and reduce it to ashes. Then, that an army of Irish papists was approaching, who were to live at free quarters, and have unbounded licence of pillage. Then, that all Protestants, men, women, and children, were to be slaughtered. Every fresh "invention of the enemy" was greedily swallowed; and the consequence was, that order was at an end. The authorities either kept out of the way or joined the populace; the shops were all closed; business was at a stand-still; and, to complete the confusion, the city was in the hands of the mob. It was in this conjecture that the king issued summonses to the chief nobility, requiring them to attend a meeting of the privy council. Very few had joined the Prince of Orange, and in the afternoon, when the council met, many were in attendance. When the king entered, and took his seat at the council-board, his appearance excited general sympathy. His countenance bore the impress of settled grief; his figure, usually erect, was bowed; his gaze was unsettled; and his step unsteady. There was a pause. For a moment party-spirit disappeared. Loyal sorrow seized the spectators; but no one seemed inclined to give expression to his feelings. At length, silence was broken by the Earl of Nottingham.

"We have been called together, in this adverse condition of affairs, to offer our humble advice to your majesty," he said. "If I may venture an opinion, the first thing to be considered is, how to restore peace to the kingdom. I should be loath to propose any thing offensive, but I think the best way of effecting this object, is to open a negotiation with the Prince of Orange." "Tush!" cried Viscount Dundee, impatiently. "The best way, and, indeed, the only way, is to force the invader to a battle. Victory must be ours."—"But his majesty cannot rely on his troops," insinuated Halifax, who had privately signified his adhesion to the Prince of Orange.—"I cannot, I cannot," faltered James. "Otherwise I would lead you on at once."—"Your majesty is mistaken," said Dundee, warmly. "I have this moment come from the army, and will answer for its devotion to you."—I verily believe the fidelity of the troops is unshaken, my liege," observed the Count de Roye. "I say—fight by all means."—"Your assurances change my opinion," cried Nottingham. "I thought the army could not be relied on, or I would not recommend his majesty to be the first to negotiate. If the army is faithful, I say advance. And should we even be defeated, his majesty will be in as good a position as he is now."—"Not so," said Halifax. "Now we have at least the name of an army. And this will be an advantage in treating for peace."—"Unquestionably," cried Lord Godolphin, who was also a secret adherent of the Prince of Orange. "I humbly implore your majesty to give this point the gravest consideration. Let us first restore peace, and we can settle other things afterwards."—"There is no help for it," said James, who notwithstanding the assurances of his officers, still doubted the army. "But on what terms will peace be framed?"—"Since your majesty does me the honour to adopt my advice," said Halifax, "I have no doubt, if I have sufficient authority, that I shall be able to negotiate a treaty which will be satisfactory to you. I have had considerable experience in your majesty's counsels, and my position in this kingdom must give my representations weight with the Prince of Orange. Should you think well of it, you know enough of me, I trust, to be assured that I shall have regard only to your interest."—"I am well assured of it my lord," answered James. "And I hereby invest you with the authority you require. Lord Godolphin shall accompany you. You can go to the Prince of Orange as my joint-commissioners, but I reserve to myself the power of ratifying or annulling your negotiation. Lose no time in setting forth. To-morrow the council will meet again, and we shall expect to hear from you."—"If possible, we will communicate with you, my liege," replied Halifax, "for the enemy, I hear, has now advanced to Maidenhead."

James arose, bowed to the assembly, and passed with a faltering step out of the room. In the ante-chamber he found Moor, and motioning the young man to follow him, entered his cabinet. Throwing himself into a chair, he sank into a reverie, in which he soon forgot everything but his sorrows. For a time he sat perfectly still, but as he continued brooding over his situation, exclamations escaped him. At last he gave way to a passionate burst of grief, and in broken accents, exclaimed, "God help me! God help me! Even my own children have forsaken me!" Greatly touched, Moor threw himself at his feet, and besought him to shake off his despondency. The king regarded him in silence for a moment, and then taking him by the hand raised him up.

"I will tell you my determination," he said, glancing anxiously around. "I am betrayed on every side, and if I remain here, they will place me in the hands of my enemy. The prisons of kings are the stepping-stones to the scaffold. But I will not be taken alive. I have arranged with Sir Edward Hales to engage me a means of conveyance to France; and I am resolved to fly to-night. You must go to Sir Edward and concert with him what is to be done."—"I implore your majesty to abandon this scheme," cried Moor, again sinking on his knee before him. "I conjure you, by your love for your royal son, not to think of leaving the kingdom. If you do, you lose your crown for ever, and deprive him of his future rights."—"I know your devotion for me, but in this instance you are wrong!" cried James. "My mind is made up. Do not distress me by further opposition to my will. Arrange with Sir Edward to be here at midnight, and I will be ready to accompany you."—"Since your determination is fixed, my liege," sighed Moor, "I will do my utmost to forward your design."

With this he pressed the king's hand to his lips, and withdrew. James remained some time in gloomy meditation. Throughout the day, indeed, he had been moody and abstracted, and the tidings brought to him, every now and then, by his emissaries, increased his dejection. He became distrustful of every one, and even feared that an attempt might be made upon his life. The flight of the queen, and his own evident uneasiness, raised a suspicion among the household that he intended to follow her, and every one watched him. This led the unhappy monarch to believe that a scheme was on foot to betray him to the enemy, and in this frame of mind, he looked with impatience for the moment when he was to take his departure. In order to lull the suspicions of the household, he retired to bed at ten o'clock; and so exhausted was he by the fatigue he had lately sustained, that he speedily dropped asleep. After a time, he was aroused by footsteps, and starting up, in alarm (for he was still haunted by a fear of assassination), he found Moor and Sir Edward Hales by his bedside.

"I have prepared everything for your departure, my liege," said Sir Edward; "but as you have given me such short notice, we shall have to ride nearly fifty miles before we reach the vessel. Perhaps, therefore, you would prefer waiting till we can bring her round to Gravesend."—"By no means!" cried James, quickly. "I will accompany you at once."

With the assistance of Moor and Hales he was soon disguised in the plain travelling garb of an ordinary gentleman, and, when about to quit the room, he caught up a small velvet bag from the table, and gave it to Moor. They then turned to a secret passage, by which Moor and Hales had previously entered the chamber, and traversing it, finally arrived at the stone-gallery. It was profoundly dark, but a ruddy glare was seen in the sky, like the reflection of a great fire. At the same time, a sullen roar was heard, evidently proceeding from a tumultuous mob at a distance. Scarcely venturing to look round, James followed his companions to the garden. They had proceeded but a short distance down the walk, when they heard footsteps, and the officer of the night was seen approaching, attended by a file of the guard, with whom he was going the rounds. James and Hales were about to retreat, but before they could so, Moor interposed, and being at this moment challenged by the officer, they saw that it was too late to escape, and suffered their young companion to advance and give the password. Moor remained with the officer till he was joined by James and Hales, when he was moving forward, but the officer stopped them.

"I am not quite satisfied yet!" said the latter. "My orders are positive. No one is to be here after eleven o'clock, and it is now past twelve."—"But I have given you the countersign," replied Moor.—"True," answered the officer. "But that is not enough. You must come with me to the officer of the guard."—"Impossible!" cried Sir Edward Hales, foreseeing that discovery would ensue. "We are engaged on business of the king's."

At this moment a resource suggested itself to Moor.

"Our orders are to proceed with the utmost dispatch, in token of which we are entrusted with his majesty's signet," he said. And turning to James, he added, "Let the officer see the authority, sir."

Drawing the ring from his finger, James handed it in silence to the officer, who calling forward a man with a flambeau, examined it attentively, and then he gave it back to the king. Raising the light, he looked earnestly in the king's face, but James turned away his head, and it seemed that he escaped recognition. The officer, however, still hesitated. "I suppose I must let you pass," he said, at length. "But I should be better satisfied if you would go with me to the captain of the guard."—"You will detain us at your peril," cried Moor, moving forward.

James and Sir Edward followed, and the officer remained stationary for a moment, as if undecided what to do, and then he hastened to communicate with the captain of the guard. Meanwhile, the king and his companions reached the gate, and having given the countersign to the sentinel, the man suffered them to unlock the gate and pass out. The king cast a glance at the palace, and then, with a sigh, hurried on with his companions, thinking it would be long before he would again inhabit the halls of his ancestors. He was mistaken. Fate willed that he should return sooner than he expected.

CHAPTER VI.

HOW THE KING REACHED EMLEY-FERRY.

On arriving at Parliament-street, the fugitive monarch found a hackney-coach awaiting him, which he entered with his companions. Passing down Abingdon-street, and the Horseferry-road, the vehicle soon arrived at Millbank, where the party alighted, and descended a flight of steps to the river. Here two watermen were in attendance, who assisted them into a boat, and then, with an indifference which showed that they had no suspicion of the rank of their passengers, rowed off.

The boat shot out rapidly into the stream, the whole party maintaining a profound silence. As they reached the mid-current, James asked Moor in a whisper for the velvet bag he had given him, and receiving it, drew forth a large seal, and cast it into the river.

"What have you done, my liege?" asked Moor, in an anxious whisper.—"I have deprived the usurper of the great seal of England," replied James, in the same tone. "Without it no public act is complete."

With this he fixed his eyes on the darkling current, and sank into his former reverie. Shortly afterwards the boat reached Vauxhall-stairs, and landing, the king and his two companions made their way to the road, where a groom was in waiting with three powerful horses, which they mounted without delay. The party made good progress, and the king seemed to gain confidence. Spurring on, they soon reached St. George's Fields, and shaped their course along the Kent Road for Blackheath. Arrived there, they pushed on for Woolwich Common, and so on towards Woolpeck. Scarcely a word was spoken on the road. It was weary, weary night; but morning began at last to dawn. Then came broad daylight; smoke curled from the chimneys of roadside cottages; labourers began to appear in the fields; and, in a word, day, and all its bustling cares, had fairly opened. Pushing on, the fugitives crossed the Medway at Ailesford Bridge, and soon afterwards arrived at a small inn, about two miles from Feversham, where, as it was thought expedient to avoid the appearance of having travelled any distance, Sir Edward Hales, whose seat was a few miles off, near Canterbury, had ordered a relay of horses to be in attendance. Alighting, James and Sir Edward entered the inn, intending to procure some refreshment, while Moor remained on guard at the door. Though he was very ingeniously disguised, Sir Edward soon began to fear that he should be recognised by the host, who, however, took great pains, by his indifferent manner, to impress him with a contrary opinion. No sooner, however, was the crafty landlord released from attendance on his guests, than he hastened to an upper chamber, where a sturdy fellow in the garb of a sailor, but having the appearance of a smuggler, was lying on a truckle-bed asleep, and seizing him by the arm, aroused him.

"They've come, Ben Ames," he said.—"Who're come?" cried the other, scarcely awake.—"Why, them as the horses is waitin' for, to be sure," replied the landlord. "One on 'em's the papisher Sir Ed'ard Ales, and if I'm anythin' of a judge t'other's Father Petre."—"You don't say so?" cried the sailor, starting to his feet.—"Yes, but I do," returned the host. "But make haste, Ben, and get the crew together, and then make off to Emley-ferry. Depend on it they're goin' aboard o' that there 'oy."—"We'll see if they do," answered Ames, with a grin.

With this he slapped a small tarpaulin hat on his ugly head and hurried out of the room, leaving the host to follow at his leisure. After a brief interval James and Hales, learning from Moor that the horses were ready, came forth, and rode off to Feversham. The streets of the little town were by this time astir with the inhabitants, and, as is usual in country places, they were much stared at; but no one seemed to recognise them, and quitting the town they spurred along the high road to the ferry. They had not gone above a mile, when they were alarmed by a loud shout, and looking round perceived a large mob approaching, who were evidently bent on arresting them. But before this could be accomplished, they reached the ferry, and as a boat was awaiting them, they instantly embarked, leaving their horses with a servant of Sir Edward's, who mounted one of them and galloped off in the opposite direction. Pushing off, the boat made towards a clumsy-looking, one-masted vessel, lying in the middle of the river, and arrived alongside of her just as the mob reached the ferry. The captain and a boy, who, with the two men in the boat, constituted the crew, observing the approach of the mob, began to unfurl the mainsail, while James, with the adroitness of a sailor, clambered up the ship's side to the deck, followed by his two companions and the boatmen. The mob on shore now shouted to them to surrender, while several parties sprang into boats and put off for the hoy. The master had by this time spread the mainsail, but he had yet to raise the anchor, and it was clear that before he could effect that object the boats would be able to board him. Foreseeing what would happen, Moor caught up a hatchet from the deck, and at one blow severed the hempen cable. At the same moment James ordered the jib to be hoisted. A fresh breeze caught the sails, and the vessel bore away amidst a loud hurrah from the crew.

CHAPTER VII.

REVERSES.

THE boats pulled on in the wake of the hoy for some time but finding they lost way, they ultimately gave up the chase Their leader, however, had no intention of relinquishing the pursuit.

"This can't last long," he cried to his men. "The breeze is a-freshenin'. It'll soon blow a gale, and she's too light on her heels to stand it out. So they'll have to heave to afore they gets to the Nore."—"We'll be down upon 'em, then, in a jiffey," replied one of his comrades.—"Ay, ay, we'll be aboard on 'em, afore long," returned Ames. "I'll tell you how to manage it."

So saying he jumped ashore, and the others gathered round him, while he proceeded to disclose his design. Meanwhile the hoy made all sail down the river, a reach of which soon hid her from view. Favoured by wind and tide, she went along steadily for some time; but, as Ames had predicted, the breeze began to freshen, and it became necessary to take a reef in the mainsail. As the day wore on, the wind became more violent, and they were obliged to lower the topmast, and take in another reef. Still the bulgy vessel, having her hold almost empty, and being built to carry a heavy cargo, rolled about like a tub, now on one side, now on the other; and as evening drew on, the master declared that it would be dangerous to proceed without more ballast. Too much of a seaman not to be sensible that this opinion was correct, James, though he dreaded delay, consented to heave-to for the night at Sheerness, whither they arrived just as it became dusk. A new cable having been recved, the vessel came to an anchor, when the master went ashore, and made arrangements for receiving the necessary ballast at daybreak. Meanwhile, James and Sir Edward Hales kept close to the cabin, and as the night advanced, being overcome with fatigue, laid down in their clothes on the lockers, leaving Moor to keep watch. The master and the crew betook themselves to the steerage, and worn out with the exertions of the day, likewise threw themselves on the deck, and were soon asleep. It was midnight. All was still, and as he kept watch in the cabin, Moor suffered his thoughts to wander from the king to Sabine, cheering himself with the hope that he would soon see the latter again. Suddenly he heard a plashing in the water, and listening intently he thought he could distinguish a step on the deck. Should he awaken Sir Edward Hales, or would it not be better to ascertain first, if there was any ground for alarm? With a noiseless step he hastened out of the cabin, and crept up the hatchway to the deck. Arrived there, he was about to spring to his feet, when he was seized by three or four men, and though he made a desperate resistance, was bound hand and foot. But shouting at the top of his voice, he aroused the king and Sir Edward Hales, and made them sensible of their danger. Sir Edward sprang to the cabin door, but before he could shut it Ames leaped down the hatchway, and forced himself in.

"Now, Sir Edward, it's no use makin' a piece of work," said the ruffian. "Better be quiet about it."—"You know me!" answered Hales, perceiving that resistance would indeed be useless, for three or four men armed with hangers and pistols, had crowded into the hatch, and others were seen above. "What authority have you for this interference?"—"You'll be told all that when you gets back to Feversham," answered Ames, with a derisive laugh. "But who's your shipmate here? He's very like a priest. I'm blessed if it ain't that black-muzzled Father Petre himself."

Exclamations broke from his confederates in the hatchway; and others on the deck, hearing of the supposed capture, gave a cheer. "Hush!" said Sir Edward to Ames in a low tone. "Send your companions away, and I will have some talk with you."

Ames ordered the men in the hatch to go on deck, and then sullenly awaited Sir Edward's proposal.

"You will gain nothing by taking us on shore," said Sir Edward. "Name the price of our liberty, and I will pay it you."—"Did you ever catch a weasel asleep?" replied Ames, with a knowing wink. "Why, all you've got's mine, so I needn't name no price. But come, hand out the blunt, and I'll see what's to be done."

James produced a purse of gold. Ames eagerly snatched the purse, and finding it weightier than he expected, expressed his satisfaction by a low whistle. At the same time he received another purse from Sir Edward Hales.

"Well, I'll see if I can get you off now," he said. "Keep quiet a bit, and I'll come down again."

With this he went out of the cabin, and mounted to the deck. Some time elapsed, and as he did not return James became extremely uneasy. At last, Sir Edward Hales determined to go in search of him, and was issuing forth with that view, when he discovered that the hatch above was fastened down. They were prisoners. There was now considerable bustle overhead. Presently they found that the capstan was manned, and they heard [illegible] sh of feet upon deck, followed by the hauling of ropes, and cries of "hoy—hoy" from a dozen voices, and it became apparent that the ship was under sail. James now felt sure that his captor had no intention of liberating him. Could it be possible that he had any suspicion of his real rank? Be that as it might, he could not hope long to escape recognition, and there was no doubt that he would then be given up to the invader. The possibility of such an event filled him with horror. Still dwelling upon it, his mind became a prey to the most harrowing reflections. At one moment he thought of the fate of his father, and saw himself dragged before a packed tribunal and condemned to the block. Then he meditated on the secret murders perpetrated by usurpers, and shuddered at the terrible picture which his imagination conjured up, of the dreadful end of the second Richard, and the mysterious disappearance of Edward V Clasping his hands together, he fervently thanked Heaven that his queen and child were in safety. From these gloomy thoughts he sank into a deep reverie, in which he remained plunged for several hours, taking no notice of Sir Edward, and unconscious that the night was fast waning. At length day dawned, and shortly afterwards the vessel was brought to an anchor. Aroused by an increased stir on deck, James supposed that he would now learn something of his destination, but a considerable interval elapsed before any one appeared. At last the hatch was raised, and Ames presented himself.

"They won't let you go," he said to Sir Edward, whom he still mistook for the principal personage. "I gave 'em all the the money, but it wouldn't do. They says as how you must be took afore the mayor."

Both his auditors heard this intelligence with consternation, but before they could reply they were joined by Moor, who, on the intercession of Ames had been allowed to leave the deck.

"They have brought us back to Feversham," he whispered to James. "It is impossible to resist, and it will be better to appear resolute and unconcerned."

James made a gesture of assent, and they all followed Ames to the deck. Here they found about thirty fellows, half-fishermen, half-smugglers, who received them with jeers and laughter, but on a word from Ames, they became more orderly. A boat was alongside, manned with an armed force, and Ames, directing the three prisoners to jump into it, they obeyed, and their captor following, the boat instantly pulled for the shore. A great crowd had collected here, embracing a mixture of the townsfolk and country people, with many fishermen and their wives, who set up a shout as the boat drew nigh, calling for instant vengeance on the papists. As the boat touched the beach, the mob made a rush forward, intending to drag the prisoners out, but they were kept back by the crew: and thus protected,

James and his companions stepped ashore. But they were now assailed with a shower of oyster shells, and other missiles, mixed with mud, while the most virulent abuse was poured in their ears, and so violent did the rabble become, that they expected every moment to be torn in pieces.

Moor kept close to the king, ready to sacrifice his life in his defence. Strange to say, James was quite composed. His face was, indeed, pale as marble, but his look and step were resolute, and Moor thought he had never looked so much a king as at the present moment. At this juncture an old sailor, making his way through the crowd, caught a glimpse of the monarch, and, uttering a loud cry, he burst between two of his captors, and threw himself at his feet.

"It is, it is my gracious sovereign," he cried. "Oh! my liege, what can have brought you to such a pass as this?"

The effect of this incident was as surprising as it was instantaneous. A confused murmur arose from the mob, and then they all became hushed. The men who had captured the king fell respectfully back. James himself was so touched by the sailor's loyalty, that his eyes filled with tears. "Thank Heaven!" he exclaimed, after a pause, "I have one faithful subject left."

He had more than one. No sooner was he recognised, than the mob became ashamed of their violence; and when it was perceived that he was in tears, no words can describe the reaction that took place. Every one instantly uncovered; many burst into tears; others threw themselves on their knees, and implored his pardon; and not a few fervently commended him to the protection of Heaven.

"As for me, your majesty," cried Ames, who was much affected, "I hope you'll order me to be hung; but I'll take my bible oath, that if I'd know'd it was your majesty, I'd never have touch'd a penny of your money. Howsumdever, there it is all back again."

And drawing forth the purse, he laid it at the king's feet.

"No, no; keep it," replied James, "and divide it with your men here; and I hope you'll all drink my health."—"That we will, and success to your majesty," cried a dozen voices. And loud cheers arose.

James cast a wistful look at the hoy; but a moment's reflection assured him, that in his present situation, it would be extremely hazardous to show any intention of resuming his flight. Walking up the street, he came to a small inn, the landlord of which was standing at the door, together with the hostess, and their buxom daughter, and as the king was worn out with anxiety and fatigue, he entered the little hostelry, while the landlord remained as a sentinel at the door. But the latter was not called upon for any exercise of his authority; for, though the people remained in front of the house, no one attempted to enter. All seemed to respect the temporary asylum of the monarch. James at once retired to a bedchamber, and having had little repose during the whole of the two preceding nights, soon fell asleep. Sir Edward Hales stationed himself on a chair at the door, and, after repeated efforts to keep awake, became as unconscious as his master. It was noon before the king arose, when his first inquiry was for Moor, who was nowhere to be found. James became uneasy, and after a conference with Sir Edward Hales as to how they should proceed, it was determined that they should repair to Sir Edward's seat, Hale's-place, near Canterbury, and thence make their way to some other part of the coast, where they could procure a passage to France. Leaving James in his chamber, Sir Edward proceeded in search of the host, with the view of procuring some means of conveyance to their contemplated asylum, but he shortly afterwards returned, and informed the king that they were prisoners.

"Alas!" exclaimed James, "what small dependence can be placed on a mob!"—"The mob are not to blame in this instance, my liege," cried Sir Edward. "I believe they are not aware you are under restraint. But the mayor is a violent partisan of the invader, and he has surrounded the house with militia, and will not allow any one to go forth."

At this moment the door opened, and a burly, vulgar-looking man stepped in. He was pushing rudely forward, without showing any respect for the king's presenee, when a severe look from James arrested him.

"Very sorry, your majesty, but I can't let you go away," he said, surprised into a degree of deference. "But I've sent to tell the Prince of Orange you're here, and directly his highness's orders comes I'll bring 'em to you."—"How, sir," cried James, angrily, "do you dare to talk of the prince's orders to me? Do you forget that I am the king?"

Exasperated at the assumed superiority of the fallen monarch, whom he had expected to find all submission, the mayor's face became purple with rage.

"No, I don't recognise you, James Stuart, as king," he said. "At any rate, you're not going to order here. You'll be kept in custody till the prince sends directions about you—strict custody."—"Ha, dog! ha, traitor!" cried a fierce voice behind him.

And Moor seized him by the throat, and hurled him backwards. "Base-minded wretch!" he exclaimed, "I arrest you for high treason." And turning to the king, he added, "I have brought Lord Winchelsea, the lord-lieutenant of the county, to your majesty's assistance. His lordship is now below with a strong force of the yeomanry, who have taken possession of the town."

On hearing these words, the miserable mayor, terrified out of his senses, crept on his knees towards James, and abjectly implored pardon. James reprimanded him severely, but though

Sir Edward Hales recommended him to send the offender to prison, he inflicted no further punishment on him than dismissal from his office. At this juncture, the Earl of Winchelsea entered, and hurrying forward, was about to fall at the king's feet, but James caught him by both his hands, and embraced him.

"Your majesty is at liberty to go whither you please," said Winchelsea. "But," he added, lowering his voice, "I implore you not to leave the kingdom."—"For Heaven's sake, my liege, listen to his lordship's advice," entreated Moor. "Let us return to Whitehall."—"I dare not!" cried James, with a look of distraction. "I shall be torn in pieces by the mob."—"At least let me ride up to town, and ascertain the feelings of the people," urged Moor. "I will undertake to be back by to-morrow night."—"Go, then," said the king, "and inform the lord-mayor how I am situated. Farewell!"

Repressing his emotion, Moor hastened from the room, and found his horse at the inn-door. Making his way through a knot of militia officers, and a mixed throng of yeomanry and civilians, he galloped off in the direction of London.

CHAPTER VIII.

THE FATE OF MAUVESIN.

WILD HOUSE, the residence of the Spanish ambassador, was a spacious and stately mansion, a little removed from Drury-lane, whence it was approached by a great gateway and court. In an upper chamber of this mansion, on a bed of state, lay a wounded man, whose face, inflamed from fever, was rendered yet more unsightly by an expression of rage and disappointment.

"Fool!" he exclaimed, to a short, sullen-looking man, seated at the bedside; "how could you suffer them to escape you? You might have been sure it was the queen and her child."—"I'm no more to blame than Johnstone," answered Snewin—for he it was. "He had two better chances than I had—one at the Horse Ferry, and t'other at London Bridge: but he let 'em slip, and Moor too."—"Curses on you both for your clumsiness!" groaned Lord Mauvesin; "but for my wound, I should have been on the spot myself, and she would not have escaped *me*. Perdition seize the hand that fired the shot against me. My veins seem on fire, and racking pains shoot through every joint, if I move."—"Then why don't you keep quiet?" said Snewin, brutally.—"Ha! do you dare to caution me, villain?" cried Mauvesin, his eyes kindling with fury.—"Wot if I do?" returned Snewin, leaning forward in his chair, with an air of defiance. "Wot if I do?"—"You presume upon my helpless situation, you cowardly hound," cried Mauvesin, gnashing his teeth with impotent rage.—"I shan't have long to be feared of you," jeered Snewin; "not long."—"What do you mean, villain?" shrieked Mauvesin, starting up in the bed, but instantly falling back on his pillow. "I know what you would insinuate; but it's false! I can't—I won't die."—"Keep quiet, and it'll be better for you," said Snewin: "but, to make all square and right, you'd better settle your worldly accounts. You recollect the letter I stole for you from Lord Nottingham. That job wasn't half paid for, and if I was to tell, you'd lose all—that is, if you recover."—"That letter was burnt," said Mauvesin.—"No, it warn't," cried Snewin; "no, it warn't."

Mauvesin looked hard at him for a moment, and then burst into a hoarse laugh, but the excitement renewing the pain of his wound, his laughter gave way to execrations, and he became so furious, and shouted so loud, that the noise was heard in the adjoining room by his valet, who rushed in alarm into the chamber, just as Snewin, perceiving that he had become delirious, was about to summon assistance. With a half-suppressed smile of great significance, the constable quitted the room, leaving the sufferer in care of his valet. On his way out of the house, Snewin found the various chambers and passages crowded with packages and boxes, and on inquiry, learned from an incautious domestic, that they contained plate and other valuable property, belonging to certain wealthy Catholics, who, fearing that their houses might be attacked by the populace, had brought all their moveable treasure to Wild House, and confided it to the care of the ambassador. Snewin's eyes sparkled as he thought of the vast plunder which these stores would furnish. The city was in the hands of the mob, and as Don Pedro was a Catholic, and an infuriated rabble were not very likely to pay respect to his sacred character of ambassador, it would be easy to incite them to attack his house. Full of this scheme he hastened forth, and proceeded in search of Kit Clench. Night had now closed in. There were few persons in the street, and those few hurried along as if they were in momentary expectation of being stopped and plundered. Calling a link-boy, who was loitering near the mansion, Snewin made his way to Duke-street, and thence to Lincoln's-inn-fields. As he approached the latter locality, a loud clamour saluted his ear. A red reflection in the sky denoted an extensive conflagration; and presently he came in sight of a Catholic chapel enveloped in flames. An infuriated mob collected in front of the structure, shouted with frantic joy, as they watched the progress of the destroying element; and as Snewin drew nigh, two stuffed effigies, swinging from a gibbet, fixed on a long pole, and representing the Pope and Father Petre, were exhibited to the mob, and then, amidst demoniacal yells, cast into the flames. Scarcely had this been done, when the roof fell in with a tremendous crash, while the interior of the building presented one body of fire. Making his way with difficulty through the crowd, Snewin found Clench in the foremost rank, and when he had informed him of the treasures deposited in the house of the Spanish Ambassador, it required but little persuasion to win the Duke of Alsatia to his scheme. His intentions were promptly communicated to the various ringleaders, and in a few minutes the whole multitude were bending their steps up Drury-lane. A fearful shout warned the inmates of Wild House of their intention to attack it. Resolving not to yield without a blow, Don Pedro Ronquillo called his household together, and leaving the lower part of the house, which was well secured by doors and shutters, posted them on the upper floor, whence they could use their fire-arms with more effect. Scarcely had he completed this arrangement when a shower of stones and brickbats were poured on the house, demolishing every window, and, at the same time, a general rush was made at the door, during which several of the rioters were knocked down and trampled to death. In the midst of the horrid yells uttered by these sufferers, and the vociferations of those around them, Don Pedro presented himself at an upper window, intending to exhort the mob to retire; but he was no sooner discerned than a tremendous outcry arose, while missiles were hurled at him from every quarter, forcing him to make a hasty retreat through the window. But still unwilling to resort to violence, and hoping to intimidate the besiegers, the good-natured ambassador ordered his servants to use only blank cartridges, and a volley was accordingly fired, which was received by the mob with derision. Don Pedro then reluctantly changed his plan, and a shower of bullets was rained among the besiegers; but it soon became apparent that their vastly superior force must overcome all resistance. The gallant Spaniard, however, held out as long as possible, and only at the last moment he gave orders for a retreat, and his little corps made their escape by an outlet at the back of the house, leading to Covent Garden.*

The mob rushed in a body into the house. The costly furniture, the rich hangings of the windows, the rare paintings, the statues, bronzes, vases, porcelain, shells, and articles of *vertû*, of which the ambassador had an unrivalled collection, were torn down, trodden under foot, broken, and scattered about. Some rushed with wild outcries to the cellars, where, while they drained the produce of some of the choicest vintages of Spain, they suffered the rich wine to flow in streams over the ground. Others ransacked closets and cabinets, fighting for the contents; but the majority busied themselves with the boxes and packages in the various rooms, and which disappeared with surprising rapidity.

* Don Pedro Ronquillo was afterwards indemnified for his loss by a grant from Parliament.

Lying powerless in bed, Lord Mauvesin had been an astounded auditor of this extraordinary tumult. Unable at first to account for it, he rang for his valet, and then shouted till he was hoarse, but without receiving an answer. In the confusion, he was forgotten, and Don Pedro left the house without him. The appalling din which followed the capture of the mansion left him in no doubt as to what had happened, and he expected every moment to be visited by the mob. But his expectations were not realised. The clamour drew nearer and nearer; he even heard voices in the adjoining room; but no one penetrated further. Nearly half-an-hour passed, and his suspense was becoming intolerable, when he became sensible that the apartment was filling with smoke. A fearful suspicion flashed across his mind, and the next moment it was confirmed. A tremendous outcry was raised below; a sharp, crackling noise was heard; the mansion was on fire! Aghast at the idea, he made a desperate effort to rise. A bright red glare now shone through the window, rendering the chamber as light as day for an instant, when a volume of smoke rolled up, involving everything in darkness. The flames were heard raging in the room beneath; the atmosphere became suffocating; and gasping for breath, with his hair on end, and almost mad with terror, Mauvesin tottered forward to the door. Crossing the ante-chamber, he reached a corridor, running along the summit of the ground-staircase, from which he could look down into the hall. It was completely lined with fire. The roar of the flames was terrific. They encircled the staircase, burst through the windows, and glided along the ceiling. Affrighted and confused, Mauvesin turned again towards his chamber, determined to leap from the window. But his strength failed him. He caught at the banisters, already on fire; they gave way; and uttering a loud cry, Mauvesin fell headlong into the burning gulf below.

CHAPTER IX.

HOW JAMES WAS PREVAILED UPON TO RETURN.

While the fire was thus raging, the incendiaries, stimulated by liquor, and made bold by success, watched it from Drury Lane, rending the air with their outcries. But impatient for more pillage, they grew wearied, and were beginning to separate into small knots, when it was proposed to attack the house of the Lord Chancellor.

"Ay, ay, Jeffreys shall have *his* turn now!" cried Clench. "I owes him a grudge, for when he sentenced me to the pillory, where my ears were clipped off close to my head, he told me to take a good look at his face, and never forget him; and curse me, if I ever will."

With this, the ruffian was leading the way towards Duke Street, Westminster, where the chancellor resided, when he accidentally caught sight of a man, who, as it seemed, was trying to avoid him. "Now, then, who are you, eh, master?" growled Clench, roughly seizing the person, and throwing the light of a link on his face.

The man was habited as a coalheaver. His visage was begrimed with coal-dust; his eyebrows were shaved off; and a large black patch covered his left eye. But the disguise could not baffle Clench; and uttering a loud whoop, he announced the individual to be no other than the object of their quest, the Lord Chancellor Jeffreys himself. Wonderful was the clamour and tumult which this discovery excited. The chancellor stood speechless and motionless, but his terror proved his preservation. Seeing that so exalted a personage had not escaped retribution, Clench was reminded that a day of reckoning might come to himself, and he was suddenly seized with a determination to befriend the chancellor. But it was not easy to save him from the rabble. Such a rush had been made at him, that those immediately around were in danger of being squeezed to death, and for a moment or two it was with the greatest difficulty that they could even preserve themselves. But by a free use of their bludgeons they succeeded in driving back the press, and Clench then declared that to prevent bloodshed he was resolved to carry their prisoner to the lord mayor. This occasioned another rush at the chancellor, while the most terrible outcries arose, mingled with imprecations on Clench, but being surrounded by a select band of adherents, that personage was again victorious. He now seized the chancellor by the collar and dragged him on at a quick pace, while his men pressed close behind, brandishing their bludgeons, and keeping up a running fight with the rabble. In this way they reached the city, and hurried up Cheapside to Guildhall.

A strong body of constables and the city watch were drawn up in the front of the hall, but as Clench had despatched a messenger to forewarn them of his approach, they suffered him to pass through with the chancellor, attended by three or four of his companions, while the others, uniting with the constables and watchmen, pushed back the mob. A conflict would probably have ensued, but, at this juncture, a horseman made his appearance in the square, and, endeavouring to force his way through the multitude, their fury was diverted to him. Uttering a terrific yell, the nearest ruffians were on the point of tearing him from his horse, but Moor—for he it was—spurred the animal sharply, and its plunges soon cleared a space around him, while he shouted out—"A messenger! a messenger for the lord mayor!" The constables and guard caught the words, and rushed forward to his aid. Taken by surprise, the mob broke aside, opening a passage for Moor, and the constables instantly surrounding him, he forced his way forward, and in another moment sprung from his horse, and entered the hall. When the flight of the king became known, Sir John Eyles, the lord mayor, summoned the principal noblemen then in London to Guildhall, to form a committee of public safety; and with this view, the Earls of Nottingham, Ailesbury, Melfort, Arran, Dumbarton, Feversham, and Lichfield, with Lords Mulgrave, Dundee, and Preston, were now assembled in the council-room. The lord mayor was about to join them, when the city chamberlain called him into the great hall. At this moment the door was thrown open, and Clench entered, dragging in Jeffreys, while a knot of ruffians, armed with bludgeons, followed, displaying traces of the recent conflict in their broken heads and bleeding faces. Much alarmed, the lord mayor demanded the meaning of the interruption.

"I caught him in the street, and he'd have been torn into ten thousand morsels if I hadn't brought him here," cried Clench. "But mayhap you don't know him, my lord. It's the Lord Chancellor Jeffreys."—"The lord chancellor!" cried Sir John Eyles, with a look of dismay; "that strange object, the lord chancellor! Impossible!"—"'Tis he, indeed, my lord mayor," replied Jeffreys, in a woful tone.—"Take him into yon inner room," said the lord mayor, quickly. "I will join you on the instant, my lord, and provide means for your safety. You and your fellows shall be well rewarded," he added to Clench.

As the chancellor disappeared, Moor entered the hall; and having disclosed his mission to the lord mayor, the latter led him to the council-room, where his intelligence was received with transport, and the king's letter was read again and again, drawing tears from the chivalrous Dundee.

"His majesty must be invited to return," said Nottingham, at length. "Had he not left us, all would have been well."—"It is not yet too late," cried Dundee.—"Fortunately it is not," said Feversham. "I will place myself at the head of the guards, and bring him back."—"You must not incur this grave responsibility alone," said Ailesbury. "We will all sign a petition to his majesty, imploring him to return."

The proposition was received with applause, and Nottingham, as president, was instructed to draw up the document, which done, and approved by the assembly, it was signed by each nobleman.

"We must now take measures to disabuse the public mind, and restore order," said Nottingham.—"That will be easily done," said Ailesbury. "I have already sent emissaries among the Dissenters, who will refute the slanderous reports raised by his majesty's enemies; and when the truth is known, I am confident there will be a reaction."—"If not, a few dragoons will restore quiet," cried Dundee, whose affrays with the Scottish Covenanters had failed to convey a warning. —"There is no need of bloodshed," said Melfort. "The best way is to refute calumnious reports, and restore the public confidence in his majesty."—"That is the only course we can pursue," observed Nottingham. "The Archbishop of Canterbury shall issue an address on the subject. Meanwhile, Lord Feversham can proceed in quest of the king."—"With your lordships' permission I will precede Lord Feversham, and stay his majesty," cried Moor.

The council approving of his determination, a fresh horse was ordered for him, which was soon in readiness; and having in the interim refreshed himself with a draught of wine and some cold viands, Moor departed secretly from Guildhall, and riding round Basinghall-street to London Bridge, shaped his course towards Feversham. During his absence James had been labouring under the greatest anxiety. Sensible that those who had been the strenuous opponents of his policy were now in the ascendant, he had little hope that Moor's mission would be attended with satisfactory results. How could he look for favour from his adversaries, when he had been deserted and betrayed by the creatures of his bounty? And how humiliating would it be to return to a capital, where he had ruled with almost despotic power, a suppliant and a prisoner! In his mind's eye, he already saw himself in the hands of the insolent mob, and conjured up, in anticipation, a parallel to the scene described by the poet—

> "When rude, misgoverned hands, from window tops,
> Threw dust and rubbish on King Richard's head."

Revolving such gloomy thoughts throughout the night, without obtaining the least rest, he arose in the morning with the determination of making another attempt to escape. No less dejected than himself, Sir Edward Hales shared his fears, and agreeing to the project, lost no time in making the necessary preparations. After a brief interval, he returned to the king, and informed him that all was ready; and muffling himself in a cloak, James followed him to the inn-yard, whence they proceeded by a back-way to the road, unquestioned by the sentinel at the gate, who supposed them to be two of the royal attendants. Passing at the back of some fishermen's cottages, they came to a field, which they hastily crossed, and emerging on the high-road, found a servant in waiting with two horses, and mounting them, they were about to spur forward, when Moor galloped up, and recognising the king, drew the rein.

"I have brought your majesty good news," he cried, uncovering, and suppressing the surprise he felt at the unexpected encounter. Then, without waiting to be questioned, he briefly informed James of the result of his mission.—"I do not see that the news is so very satisfactory, Mr. Moor," cried Hales. "The council being composed of the Protestant leaders, I cannot recommend his majesty to put himself in their hands."—"No, no," cried James. "Their object is to give me up to the invader. Let us ride on. My only hope is in flight."—"Oh! do not say so, my liege," implored Moor. "The council consists of men noble and loyal-hearted—who opposed you, indeed, in prosperity, but who will be faithful to you in adversity. I entreat you to accede to their petition, and return to Whitehall."

James hesitated.

"You speak of the council as if they possessed supreme power," he said, at length; "but admitting their good intentions, how can they answer for the temper of the people? What impression have you formed from your own observations? Were the citizens anxious for my return?"—"I confess, my liege, that the false reports spread by your enemies have for a time alienated them from you," replied Moor. "Great disorders prevail, and the city is in the hands of the mob, but your return will help to set all things right."—"It will more likely end in his majesty's destruction," observed Hales. "The experiment is too hazardous."—"I think so," cried James, "and will, therefore, go on."

Seeing further remonstrance was useless, Moor was silent, and, spurring forward, James and his companions soon entered the small town of Sittingbourne, where, as they rode up the High-street, they perceived two dragoons approaching, forming the advanced-guard of a whole regiment, which came close behind. James saw at a glance that it would be impossible to escape recognition, and prepared to discover himself. At this moment, the Earl of Feversham, who rode at the head of the main body, espied Moor, and divining who were his companions, ordered a halt to be sounded. Then, riding on, hat in hand, at the head of his staff, he approached the king, and, throwing himself from his horse, as James reined up, fell on his knee before him.

"God save your majesty!" cried the earl, in a broken voice; "the lords of council, assembled at Guildhall, have intrusted me with a humble petition to you."—"I know its purport, my lord," answered James, "and will comply with the wishes of the council. I will return with you at once to London."

The word was instantly passed for a general salute. The soldiers presented arms; the trumpeters sounded a stirring flourish; and in a few minutes the whole cavalcade was moving towards London.

CHAPTER X.

THE WELCOME TO WHITEHALL.

THE measures adopted by the council for refuting the reports raised by the king's enemies, which had had such an effect on the populace, were attended with complete success. The mob went from one extreme to the other; and nothing was now heard but expressions of sympathy for the fallen monarch, while a strong feeling of national dislike was roused against his antagonist. Majesty in distress is a touching spectacle, and the failings of the king were lost in the misfortunes of the man.

The steps taken for the restoration of public tranquillity were ably seconded by the citizens. The great majority of the rioters having been pacified by the representations of the council, became as zealous in behalf of the king as they had previously been eager against him; while those whose only object was plunder, were intimidated by large bodies of special constables, armed with hangers and pistols, who patrolled the streets. But this display of force seemed unnecessary. Public confidence was restored; the shops were all opened; business went on as usual; and no trace remained of the recent disturbances. At this juncture a proclamation by the council announced the king's intended return, and the intelligence was received by all classes with the liveliest joy. Splendid preparations were made for the monarch's reception. Triumphal arches were erected in the principal streets; loyal and affectionate sentiments were inscribed on the houses; flags and tapestry were hung from the windows; the craft in the river were gaily decorated with streamers; the bells of the various churches rang forth merry peals; platforms, ornamented with welcoming mottoes, were erected at the best points of view; booths stood in the more roomy thoroughfares, where refreshments of every kind could be procured; and well-dressed crowds filled the streets. The great press was on London Bridge, and it was with difficulty that a strong force of the guards could keep a passage open in the centre of this narrow thoroughfare. The houses were as crowded as the road; the windows, the roofs, and the very chimney-tops, being occupied with spectators. On the other hand, the agents of the Prince of Orange had spared no pains to get up a demonstration in his favour; and a hired mob was posted on the city side of the bridge, under the orders of Snewin, who was instructed to raise a disturbance with this view. Meanwhile a grand procession passed into Southwark, to meet and welcome the king, whose approach was announced by acclamations, growing louder as he drew nearer. As he came under the gateway of the bridge, the royal standard was hoisted above it; and this being the preconcerted signal, the Tower guns instantly fired a royal salute. Five hundred gentlemen rode bare-headed in front, followed by the aldermen in their state robes on horseback, while two heralds, in tabards, and a band of trumpeters, also on horseback, made way for the state-coaches of the lord mayor and sheriffs, which were succeeded by a troop of horse-guards. Next came the members of the council, mounted and arrayed in court-dresses, preceding the royal carriage, drawn by eight white horses, each attended by a groom, and surrounded by the yeomen of the guard, with the Earl of Feversham and a guard of honour bringing up the rear. Enthusiastic was the joy of the spectators on the appearance of the king. A heart-stirring shout burst from the throng. Men waved flags from the windows of the houses; ladies showered down wreaths of laurel and flowers; children threw up their little caps; and a resistless torrent of enthusiasts rushed on with the carriage on either side, waving their hats and rending the air with their huzzas. In this way the procession reached the city-end of the bridge, when Snewin and his adherents, uttering cries of "No Popery!" and "Down with the tyrant!" rushed forward, and completely surrounded the royal carriage. A scene of indescribable confusion ensued. Brandishing their bludgeons and hangers, the Orange party drove back the populace, many of whom were trampled under foot, while others were wounded, and, in the pressure behind, some were crushed to death. The royal grooms were knocked down under the horses' feet; the horses themselves became unmanageable; and the screams of terrified females, and the yells and outcries of the men, constituted a din truly appalling. For a moment the king was confounded by this unexpected incident, but arousing himself, he started up as if with the intention of ordering a charge upon the assailants. Before he could do so, however, Moor, who had been seated beside him, caught his arm, and held him back. "Compose yourself, my liege, I entreat you," said the young man. "This is some scheme of the invader, and you will frustrate it by remaining still. See!"

As he spoke the Earl of Feversham and the guards surrounded the vehicle, driving the rioters before them, and the next moment the infuriated populace rushed resistlessly in pursuit, overtaking and capturing Snewin. A summary punishment awaited him. While he stood speechless in the throng, livid with fear, and with his eyes starting from their sockets, a stout cord was thrown round his neck, and amidst the fierce yells of the multitude, he was strung up on a neighbouring lamp-post. In his struggles a letter dropped from his vest, which was snatched up by one of the crowd, who instantly disappeared with it. While the wretched constable thus expiated his numerous offences the royal carriage moved on, and entered the city. Here the procession was joined by deputations from the various city companies, and pursued its way amidst the ringing of bells, the firing of cannon, and the deafening acclamations of the spectators. The king's spirits revived as he proceeded, and he declared himself confident of the affection of the people. At last the procession arrived at Whitehall, and passing into the great court-yard, the royal carriage halted at the grand entrance. Alighting, James was received by the lords of the council, with heads uncovered, who attended him to the doorway, whence Lord Mulgrave, the lord chamberlain, in his official costume, advanced to meet him. James extended his hand, and sinking on his knee, Mulgrave raised it to his lips.

"Welcome, my liege, to Whitehall," he said, adding, in a lower voice, "your throne is no longer in danger."

Raising him up, James embraced him, and stepped into the palace. As he did so the royal standard was unfurled, and a salute of a hundred guns was fired from the park.

CHAPTER XI.

THE PRINCE OF ORANGE AT WINDSOR CASTLE.

THE retreat of the royal army, and subsequent flight of the king and queen, withdrew all opposition to the progress of the Prince of Orange. But though apprised of these events, William was so disheartened by the coldness of the people, that he advanced very slowly, and ultimately halted at Windsor, where, fixing his abode in the castle, he impatiently awaited an invitation from the lord mayor and citizens to enter London.

It was evening. William was seated in a state chamber, with an ostentatious display of regal pomp—a circumstance the more remarkable as he had always been averse to such exhibitions. He was attended by his favourite councillors, Schomberg, Sidney, and Bentinck, together with Lords Halifax and Godolphin.

"The council at Guildhall are taking too much upon themselves," said William, angrily. "What authority have they for their proceedings?"—"None, except as members of the privy council, your highness," observed Godolphin; "but they have been convoked by the lord mayor."—"For what purpose?" demanded William. "Obviously not for the preservation of the public peace, for the disorders in the city have increased."—"By advancing and putting an end to them, your highness would render the city a signal service," urged Halifax.—"Let the citizens invite me, then," said William.—"I am of opinion that your highness should not wait for an invitation," cried Schomberg.—"You are wrong," said William, sharply. And turning to Halifax and Godolphin, he said, "I have told you my wishes, my lords. You will do well to see them accomplished."

With this, he made a slight inclination of his head, and Halifax and Godolphin withdrew.

"Halifax is at his plots again," muttered William.—"I believe he is sincere in this instance, but I will not answer for some of the others," observed Sidney. "And your highness must excuse me, but your treatment of them is not calculated to win their regard."—"The treatment is such as they merit," said Schomberg, with a scornful smile.—"I do not fear their defection," returned William, shrugging his shoulders. "They have compromised themselves, and cannot retreat. But who have we here?" The door was thrown open, and scarcely waiting for the page to announce him, Halifax hurried in. His countenance betrayed the greatest disorder.

"Bad news! bad news! your highness!" he cried. "The king has been discovered at Feversham, and seized by the mob, who prevented his embarkation."—"Ha!" cried William.—"The worst remains to be told," pursued Halifax. "On hearing of the king's detention, the lords of the council sent to implore his return; and he has entered the city in a triumphal procession, amidst the acclamations of the people. He is now at Whitehall." William and his councillors listened to this intelligence in silence, the phlegmatic Bentinck alone exhibiting no trace of surprise or annoyance. After a moment's pause, William motioned Halifax to follow him, and walked out of earshot of the others.

"Your council in this emergency," he said, fixing his eagle eyes on the nobleman. "Ha! you hesitate. I should have thought your lordship could never be at a loss for a scheme."—"I have none suited to the present occasion," replied Halifax, coldly.—"I look to you for the removal of this difficulty, and I would have you know it, my lord," cried William. "You must get the king away again."—"I will do my best," replied Halifax, "but I will not answer for success. I would recommend your highness to write to the king, directing him to quit London, and fix his residence at Hampton Court; and I will, if possible, persuade him to go to Rochester, but you must not blame me if I fail."—"But I shall blame you," cried William, sharply. "You know my wishes, and I trust you will lose no time in carrying them out."—Halifax turned away, muttering, "And it is for this thankless man I have betrayed my master."

As he proceeded down the outer corridor, he heard a hasty step behind him, and turning, perceived Churchill.

"You look disturbed, my lord," said the latter, coming up. "Surely you are not so much affected by the news from town; for, though unexpected, I should hardly think it can peril your dukedom."—"Dukedom!" echoed Halifax. "What mean you, my lord?"—"I heard his highness had rewarded your services with that dignity," smiled Churchill.—"Does your lordship find him so lavish of his favours?" sneered Halifax.—"I, oh! I cannot expect favour," answered Churchill; "but Lord Halifax, the most popular nobleman of England, born, as Dryden says, 'to move assemblies,' is ——"—"The same as the gallant Lord Churchill," interrupted Halifax; "the same as every one who is not a Dutchman—nobody."—"Ha! is that your feeling?" said Churchill, pressing his arm. "You are going to town, eh? I will meet you to-night, at twelve, with a few chosen friends, at our rendezvous near Charing-cross."—"Be it so," replied Halifax, hastily.

With this they parted; and Churchill was pursuing his way up the corridor, when espying Lord Clarendon ascending a neighbouring staircase, he hastened after him. Before he could reach the landing, however, Clarendon turned down a side passage, and was admitted by a page to an inner chamber. In this chamber was a young man of middle stature, wearing the uniform of a colonel of dragoons. He was pacing to and fro with a hurried and impatient step, but as Clarendon entered, he threw himself into a chair. They were both silent for a moment.

"Well, you see what your fine schemes have brought us to!" said Clarendon, at length. "From being the favourites of a king, we have become the dupes of a would-be usurper, and every one rejoices at our downfall."—"You are ready enough to find fault, now you see that nothing is to be gained by it," answered the other, sulkily; "but if the scheme were so deplorable, I wonder you fell into it so eagerly. I did not wish you to forsake the king. On the contrary, it would have been better for us both if you had remained true to him."—"How could I look him in the face, when my son had been the first to desert him?" demanded Clarendon.—"I was not aware you were so sensitive," answered Lord Cornbury, with a bitter smile. "I was foolish enough to think you took the same view of the matter as myself, and considering the king's cause irretrievable, sought to curry favour with his rival."

"Your language is like your conduct," returned Clarendon, turning white with shame and anger. "But a truce to this recrimination. I cannot remain at a court where I have fallen so low, to be pointed at and derided by every minion in the palace, and it is my intention to demand permission to retire. You must accompany me."—"I? Yes, when I have paid this Dutchman in his own coin," said Cornbury, fiercely. "Do you think he shall make a by-word of me? You laugh. But if he is supreme to-day, he shall be abject enough to-morrow. The hand that put him up can pluck him down." And he struck his clenched fist violently on the table.—"Ha! ha!" laughed Churchill, who had entered the room unobserved. Cornbury half drew his sword, and Clarendon uttered an exclamation of anger and alarm.

—"Calm yourselves, my lords," pursued Churchill, with perfect sangfroid. "I have accidentally become acquainted with your sentiments, but be assured your secret is safe with me. It is on this very subject that I have come to talk with you. Suppose we return to our allegiance, and assist the king to his own again. Give me your hands upon it, and I will undertake to do it."—"Command me in everything," cried Clarendon, eagerly. —"I will give you both my hand and my sword," cried Cornbury. "I would give my life to be revenged on this Dutch boor." "You shall have ample vengeance," said Churchill. "Join me, then, in an hour in the Home-park, and we will go off to the king together."

And taking his leave, he proceeded to his own apartments. As the time appointed for the meeting drew nigh, he hastily equipped himself, and was descending to the court, when he found the stairs occupied by a guard, one of whom stepped up to him. "I am sorry to intrude upon you, my lord," said the officer; "but the prince has commanded me to place this paper in your hands."—"Ha! an arrest!" cried Churchill.

CHAPTER XII.

MOOR RECEIVES DISHEARTENING INTELLIGENCE.

The feelings of James on re-entering Whitehall, after the perils he had incurred, were not such as might have been expected. His joy was saddened by the reflection that, in those around him, he could see only the constant opponents of his arbitrary policy, while the sycophants whom he had loaded with favour, and who had been so loud in their professions of loyalty, were ranged on the side of his antagonist. More bitter still was the thought that he must number his own children among his enemies. The public rejoicings for his return did not close with the day. At night the city was illuminated; bonfires blazed before Whitehall; and a grand display of fireworks took place in the Park. James himself, withdrawing from his courtiers, and attended only by Moor, was a spectator of the scene from a window of the banquetting house. While he was thus employed, Saint Leu was suddenly introduced.

"God preserve your majesty!" said the latter, falling on his knee before the king; "I have come to assure you of the safety of the queen." And he presented James with a sealed packet, which the monarch pressed to his heart, and then gratefully regarding the messenger, proceeded to the inner apartments.

"Where is Sabine?" cried Moor, as soon as the king was gone.—"Lost to you for ever," replied Saint Leu, mournfully. "But calm yourself, and listen to what I have to say. You are aware that it was the intention of King Louis to place her in a convent, if she refused to abjure the reformed religion. On our arrival in France this purpose was formally notified to her, and in order to mortify Lauzun, Louvois, who knew what was passing, allowed the king no rest till he took the first steps in the cruel scheme. But in the interim Queen Mary informed the monarch of her attachment to you, and spoke of you so highly, as one who had displayed the most heroic devotion to your sovereign, and who enjoyed her especial favour, that Louis declared he would consent to your espousing her, if it were not for the fatal doubt that rested on your birth."—"Fatal, indeed!" exclaimed Moor, bitterly.—"I hoped to remove this doubt," said Saint Leu. "But Louvois now became urgent for Sabine's conversion, and it was impossible to accomplish my purpose in the time; and in this dilemma Lauzun revealed the whole affair to Madame de Maintenon. By her advice it was arranged that Sabine should return with me to England, but if my hope of being able to make good your claims should not be realised, she was to return to France. I have only to add, that the hope I entertained has been completely overthrown."—"Yet you speak as if it had been well-grounded," cried Moor.—"I made certain of success," answered Saint Leu.—"But you say Sabine is in England. Where is she? oh! where is she?" cried Moor, distractedly.—"You cannot see her," replied Saint Leu. "I am bound by a solemn promise to take her back to France. And see, I am summoned by the king. Farewell—for ever!"

CHAPTER XIII.

HOW JAMES WAS AGAIN PREVAILED UPON TO FLY.

THE clock of Saint Martin's Church had just told the hour of midnight as a sedan-chair, borne by two men, hurried along Charing-Cross, towards the statue of Charles the First. At this point a man muffled in a cloak, who had previously been concealed behind the statue, walked up to it, and before the chairmen could interfere let down the sash of the door, when he ascertained that the only inmate was a lady. The latter exhibited no alarm at his intrusion, but pulled the check-string, and the chairmen slackened their pace, while the stranger walked on by the side of the chair.

"I have been anxiously expecting your ladyship," he said in a low tone. "The hour I appointed with Churchill is past, and he has not yet come. What is to be done?"—"Lord Halifax surely cannot be at a loss how to act in any emergency," replied the lady, in an equally low voice. "But if Churchill should be unable to come to-night he will certainly be here in the morning, and that may answer our purpose as well. Enough for us that it is in our power to seat the king more firmly on the throne than ever." There was a brief pause.

"May I ask you one question, Lady Oglethorpe?" said Halifax, at length. "When you speak of Churchill being unable to come to-night, have you any reason to suppose that his absence is involuntary?"—"I have heard that he has been arrested, but I do not believe it," replied Lady Oglethorpe, hesitatingly. "In any case, you will not forsake the king."—"Rely on my devotion to him," returned Halifax. "But you shall hear more to-morrow, and meanwhile I bid your ladyship farewell."

With this he turned away, and proceeded with a quick step towards Whitehall, musing over the information he had received.

"Yes," he thought, "her ladyship will indeed hear more to-morrow, but that will be no fault of mine. I would have saved him if I could, but I cannot run such a great risk alone, and these time-servers cannot be trusted. If Churchill has been arrested he has by this time betrayed all he knew, and my own safety depends entirely on my fulfilling the prince's wishes. I have now no alternative." Full of these reflections he approached the palace-gate, and, giving the pass-word to the sentinel, entered the court-yard, when he made his way towards two men who were standing behind a neighbouring projection.

"I have kept you waiting, my lords," he said, "but we will not delay any longer. You have the prince's written order, Lord Delamere, have you not?"—"It is here," answered a stern-looking man, producing a paper; "but I would not exult over a fallen enemy. Let Lord Shrewsbury take charge of it."—"That is not the prince's wish," observed Shrewsbury, hastily. "He mentioned you, and really I see no use in my going into the palace at all. It is a very perilous as well as disagreeable business, for the king is still all-powerful here."—"We need not hesitate on that account," sneered Halifax, "for Count de Solms is at hand with a strong force of the prince's guards, and in a few moments the palace will be invested by them."—"Let us seek the king at once, then," cried Lord Delamere. "We waste time in debating here."

Halifax made no reply, but led the way to the grand entrance of the palace. The king had retired to his chamber some time previously. Assured of the safety of the queen, and supposing himself re-established on the throne, his mind was comparatively easy, and, on seeking his pillow, he soon fell asleep; but his dreams harmonised little with his previous thoughts, and, after a while, he awoke with a start. In the alarm of the moment he fancied he heard a noise, and was raising himself to listen, when the curtains of the bed were drawn back, and the Earl of Mulgrave presented himself.—"Forgive me, my liege, for invading your repose!" cried the latter, sinking on his knees; "but, alas! the business I come upon admits of no delay. Three noble lords, from the Prince of Orange, demand an immediate audience with you."—"Ha! are they so peremptory?" cried James, with a frown. "It is usual to attend on me in the day-time, not to arouse me at the dead hour of the night. Who are these courtly visitors?"—"Your majesty's commissioner, Lord Halifax, is one," replied Mulgrave, "another is Lord Shrewsbury; but I did not recognise the third."—"Ascertain who he is before you admit him," said James.

The king's uneasiness increased when Mulgrave disappeared, and he awaited his return with intense anxiety. At length, the door opened, admitting Lord Halifax, who was followed hesitatingly by Shrewsbury, and by a man muffled in a cloak. Halifax stepped up to the bed-side.

"I crave your majesty's pardon for seeking an audience at this unseasonable hour," he said; "but I am charged with a message from the Prince of Orange, which will not admit of delay. His highness has directed me to deliver this packet to you."

"Give it me," said James, with affected firmness, as he took the proffered paper, at the same time darting a suspicious glance at the man in the cloak. "Will it please your majesty to read it?" rejoined Halifax. "It requires instant attention."—"But, what if I refuse it attention?" demanded James. "Methinks you might find more suitable employ than this, my lord. The iron barons of old would have scorned to enter their sovereign's chamber at such an hour, even to obtain a Magna Charta. Lord Shrewsbury, too! It is long since I have seen your face, my lord, but I have not forgotten it. And—and—but I do not know your companion." "Will it please your majesty to read the letter?" said the person alluded to, without disclosing himself.—"I should know that voice," muttered James.

He fixed his eyes steadfastly on the stranger for a moment, then turned an uneasy look on Shrewsbury and Halifax; and finally, with a half-suppressed sigh, proceeded to read the prince's letter.

"This is impossible!" he cried, after he had perused it. "The prince cannot think that I would leave London, when my affairs promise so well again. My Lord Halifax, I took you for my friend; this is not a friend's part."—"You are mistaken, my liege," said Halifax, with feigned emotion; "if I advise you to leave the capital, it is because I know your remaining here will only cause bloodshed, without doing you any service. Count Solms and the Dutch guards have surprised the sentries in the park, and in a few moments will have invested the palace, when you will be a prisoner. Besides," he added, lowering his voice, and speaking more significantly, "I am in fear for your life; see who is with me!"

Looking up, the king's eye fell on Lord Delamere, who had

now thrown off his cloak, and stood at the foot of the bed, regarding him intently. James turned deadly pale; but if he had observed the nobleman narrowly, he would have seen more of sympathy than enmity in his countenance.

"The prince is right," he cried. "I thank you for your counsel, my lord," he added, in a whisper, to Halifax. "But I cannot go to Hampton Court. I will not go there. Anywhere else—anywhere, if it be a good air, near the sea. Say, Rochester, my lord—I will go there."—"Your majesty is aware it does not rest with me," replied Halifax, in the same tone; "but I will speak apart with my colleagues a moment, and do you what service I can in the matter."

James thankfully acquiesced, and the wily nobleman turned aside, and exchanged a few words in an under tone with Shrewsbury and Delamere.

"Their lordships agree that your majesty shall fix your residence at Rochester," he then said; "but we cannot pledge ourselves that the prince will sanction this arrangement." And sinking his voice, he continued, "For this reason, I recommend you to leave London instantly—even this very moment; and I will myself see everything provided for your journey. I cannot answer for your safety here a single hour."

At this juncture a trumpet was heard in the court-yard, followed by drums beating to arms, and the next moment the chamber-door was thrown open by Moor.

"The Dutch guards are advancing on the palace, your majesty," he cried. "Thank Heaven, we can now strike a blow, and they will bitterly repent their temerity."—"You do not know what you say, sir," cried Shrewsbury, alarmed at the idea of a collision. "The Dutch force is 5,000 strong, and is supported by a train of artillery. You cannot think to cope with them?"—"If a collision takes place, I cannot answer for your majesty's life," whispered Halifax to the king.

James looked round for Delamere, and perceived, with a shudder, that he had gradually advanced to the head of the bed.

"I will have no fighting," he said to Moor. "Our force is too small, and I would not have blood shed in vain. Go to Lord Craven, and bid him give up the palace to the Dutch commander."

While the monarch was speaking, the nobleman referred to entered the chamber, and overheard what was said. He was an old man, but his appearance was still gallant, such as seemed to denote the hero of "the imminent deadly breach," whose youthful chivalry had won the heart and hand of the fair Queen of Bohemia.

"I entreat your majesty to recall that order," he said. "The guards have turned out, and are in the best spirits, and I have no doubt whatever that I can repulse the enemy."—"The match is too unequal, my lord," replied James, "and I would not endanger the lives of my soldiers, when there is so little chance of success. No! The decree of Heaven is against us, and we must submit."—"Then I have worn this sword long enough," answered Craven, as he drew the weapon forth, "and as I can never wield it for another prince, I beg to lay it at your majesty's feet."

James was silent a moment; he then extended his hand to Craven, who pressed it to his lips, and after looking wistfully in the king's face, walked slowly out of the chamber. A pause ensued, when James, somewhat re-assured by the presence of Moor, whom he motioned to remain at his side, broke the silence.

"You must now be satisfied that I am desirous to come to terms with the prince, my lords," he said, "and you may therefore retire. To-morrow I shall be ready to leave London."

Hesitating how to reply, Halifax glanced at Delamere, who made a gesture of assent. "To-morrow be it then, my liege," he said. "At eight o'clock in the morning a barge shall be in attendance at the privy-stairs to convey you to Rochester."

So saying, he led the way forth, and James and Moor were left alone.

CHAPTER XIV.

THE KING QUITS ENGLAND.—CONCLUSION.

THE morning was cold and gloomy, and the clouds hung low over Whitehall. The banner on the roof of the banqueting-house drooped heavily down, surcharged with moisture. It was the standard of the Prince of Orange. A crowd had gathered in front of the palace-gate, whose looks evinced the liveliest sympathy for the king, while they conversed together in knots, or stood in circles round some noisy newsmonger, or scowled in silence on a strong force of Dutch soldiers, who kept the gateway. At last there was a general stir among the multitude, and a small party of horsemen rode up and made their way to the gate, the people receiving them with a low hum of welcome, and uncovering as they passed. Riding into the court-yard, the new comers alighted and entered the palace, where they were received by a page, who, in obedience to their commands, was about to lead them to the king, when James was observed descending the grand staircase, leaning on the arm of Moor, and followed by Halifax, Shrewsbury, and Delamere. The fallen monarch was pale and dejected, and so feeble that he paused, every two or three steps, to rest. He looked sadly at his favourite attendants, who, hearing of his approaching departure, had gathered in the passage to bid him farewell, and could not restrain their tears as he drew nigh. The party who had just arrived sank on their knees as the king approached. It consisted of the Earls of Nottingham, Aylesbury, and Arran, and Lords Melfort and Dundee.

"We have just heard of your majesty's intention to quit the capital," cried Nottingham, "and as we consider such a course to be not only ruinous to you, but highly prejudicial to your people, we have come to implore you to abandon it. Credit us, sire, your affairs are in a very promising condition, and nothing but the step you contemplate can prevent a happy arrangement of them."—"This interruption is ill-timed, my lord," cried Delamere, sternly. "His majesty's determination is fixed, and if he should recede from it, the Prince of Orange has commanded that he be taken hence by force."—"What is that you say, my lord?" cried Dundee, drawing his sword. "By force!—can I have heard aright?"—"Do not quarrel on my account," interposed James. "My resolution is fixed to go to Rochester. But, by your leave a moment;" and he waved Halifax, Delamere, and Shrewsbury to one side.

He paused till the three noblemen had drawn back, and then stepped into the midst of his little knot of friends.

"You see I must go," he said, in a whisper; "they surprised me in the night, and made me a prisoner. But this is not all. I have been warned that it is intended to assassinate me."

His auditors regarded each other in horror.

"My liege, I would still advise you not to quit London," said Nottingham; "but if you are determined to do so, we will attend you to Rochester, and see you placed in safe hands. That done, we will take the best care we can of your interest here."

James made no reply. His attention had again begun to wander, and after looking vacantly at the afflicted nobles, he silently resumed his way. The whole company walked slowly after him—many of the humblest servants of the palace following in the rear, weeping aloud. It was like a funeral procession—the king leading the way, and seeming, indeed, the chief mourner. Many persons who held offices about the court, or who possessed interest there, and thus obtained access to the privy-garden, had collected at the stairs, but they drew back as James came up, and took off their hats. The monarch did not seem to notice them, for he walked on with his eyes fixed on the ground till he reached the steps, when he paused, and turning to the bystanders, raised his hat. The crowd could no longer suppress their emotion, and many burst into tears, while others fell on their knees and commended him to the protection of Heaven. James regarded them a moment with a vacant gaze, and then descended to the barge, where he was received by several Dutch officers and the crew with the customary honours. Moor stepped hastily after him, and was followed by the faithful noblemen, when the barge pushed off and rapidly descended the river. It was past noon before the king reached Rochester, where his appearance took the authorities by surprise; but a large and commodious house belonging to Sir Richard Head was instantly prepared for his reception, and after a short halt at the Town-hall he was escorted thither by the Dutch guard. His dejection increased as the day advanced, and his manner became more and more restless, while he seemed to regard all who approached him with distrust. He suffered the noblemen who had accompanied him from London to take leave without alluding to the occasion of their coming, and finally, after sitting for some time in gloomy meditation, withdrew to his bed-chamber. Moor, who had been unremitting in his attendance upon him, was now able to retire, but haunted by a fear that some violence might be attempted, he could not dispose himself to sleep, and he ultimately arose, and again sought the presence of James. He found him in his chamber in conference with Lord Dundee and the Bishop of Ely, who were imploring him to return to London. While they were thus engaged, they were unexpectedly joined by the Duke of Berwick.

"I am glad to find your majesty," said the latter. "I arrived in town this morning, after you had gone, and received a communication of such moment that I instantly galloped after you. I must ask the favour of a private audience."

Dundee and the bishop now took their leave, and withdrew, and Moor also was retiring, but James motioned him to remain.

"My liege, you have been made the instrument of your own ruin," said Berwick. "The traitor Halifax came to you this morning, as a friend, but he was a wolf in sheep's clothing. He has exposed you to the very peril from which he pretended to preserve you. The invader has entered London, at the head of his army, and has been received in silence by the multitude. It is thought that a rising will take place in your favour; and, though, at first, it was only deemed necessary to induce you to flee the country, it is now judged expedient to get rid of you for ever."

"We will take horse at once, and make for the coast," cried James, in alarm.

"That would ruin all," rejoined Berwick, "for I find the house is guarded with unusual strictness; but I will secure a French lugger, which is lying at Chatham, to carry us to France; and if your majesty will be in readiness, will contrive to get you off at midnight." James readily acceded to this arrangement, and after a few words more, Berwick withdrew, leaving the king and Moor to make their preparations.

James became very uneasy as the night drew on, and Moor shared his apprehensions. The latter, indeed, observed several suspicious-looking men prowling about the house, who represented themselves to belong to the guard, but he found, on inquiry, that they had come after them from London; and this circumstance increased his uneasiness.

Midnight came at last. Muffled in their cloaks, Moor and the king waited anxiously for the Duke of Berwick; but the heavy moments passed on, and the duke did not make his appearance. One—two o'clock struck, and still there was no sign of his coming. The delay filled them with a thousand fears. Had he failed in his design of hiring the French lugger? or had his purpose been discovered by the guard, and measures taken to frustrate it? Tortured with suspense, James wandered restlessly about the room, forgetting that his footsteps might alarm the guard, while Moor stood prepared to defend him with his life against any hostile attempt. At length they heard a slight noise in the passage, and the door was softly opened by Berwick.

"All is ready, my liege," said the duke. "Follow, and be silent."

So saying, he led the way forth, and passed down a back staircase to a small door, which he opened, and they descended a flight of steps into a yard. From this another door brought them to the road, and proceeding a short distance they came to the river. Here they found a boat manned by two seamen, and Moor was about to leap into it, with the view of handing in James, when the monarch held him back.

"I will not take you any further, my young friend," said James. "I am going to seek an asylum at a foreign court, where I shall not require your services, and were it otherwise, I would not carry you with me at a time when it is essential to your interests to remain in England."—"Alas! my liege, you mistake," replied Moor. "All that I love will in future be in France."—"Not so," returned James. "I have this evening received a packet from Barillon, enclosing the certificate of your mother's marriage with Lord Mauvesin, which secures you the succession to the title and estates. Take it," he added, presenting him with a packet, "and with it, the consent of King Louis to your union with Mademoiselle Saint Leu, whom you will find in London with Lady Oglethorpe. Farewell!"

With these words he extended his hand to the young man, who sank on his knee, and pressed it fervently to his lips. Before he could regain his feet, James stepped into the boat, which instantly put off, and conveyed him from England for ever.

CPSIA information can be obtained
at www.ICGtesting.com
Printed in the USA
LVHW101934050422
715402LV00003B/50